Prudence Fairworthy was a natural temptress.

Alluring and lovely, entrancing—and untouched. Lucas Fox found her virginal innocence strangely disturbing. The appeal of this young woman who was a virtual stranger to him was hard to explain. Since returning to Marlden Hall he had seriously begun to consider marriage, and whenever he tried to think of a suitable candidate it was Prudence Fairworthy's image that lingered the longest in his mind's eye. Proud, wilful and undisciplined she might be, he admitted to himself, but she was also too lovely for comfort.

Lucas did not pause to understand the reasons for what he was about to do. He wanted her, and that was reason enough. But, with a wisdom born of experience, he realised he would have to tread with caution.

Paying court to Prudence would be like paying court to a powder keg.

Helen Dickson was born and still lives in South Yorkshire, with her husband, on a busy arable farm where she combines writing with keeping a chaotic farmhouse. An incurable romantic, she writes for pleasure, owing much of her inspiration to the beauty of the surrounding countryside. She enjoys reading and music. History has always captivated her, and she likes travel and visiting ancient buildings.

Recent titles by the same author:

CARNIVAL OF LOVE
CONSPIRACY OF HEARTS

LORD FOX'S PLEASURE

Helen Dickson

MILLS & BOON®

First published in Great Britain 2001
Harlequin Mills & Boon Limited,
Eton House, 18-24 Paradise Road, Richmond, Surrey TW9 1SR

© Helen Dickson 2001

ISBN 0 263 17194 9

Set in Times Roman 10½ on 11 pt.
04-0601-93311

Printed and bound in Spain
by Litografía Rosés S.A., Barcelona

Chapter One

May—1660

'Prudence! Prudence! Oh—where is that girl?'

Arabella's voice travelled along the narrow passageway from the busy kitchen and out into the square courtyard, where a girl was tending flowering plants in clay tubs of various shapes and sizes, an absorbed, preoccupied expression on her face. In the corner a leafy elm towered upright, its outstretched boughs offering welcome shade as she worked at teasing out the weeds from between a bed of gaily coloured pansies.

'Prudence! Why don't you answer me when I call you?' Arabella said crossly, coming out of the house and descending a narrow flight of stone steps to the courtyard, knowing perfectly well that this was where she would find her sister. Honeysuckle climbing in profusion up the walls scented the air and flowers spilled from pots and tubs in a vibrant blaze of glory. Prudence's enduring love of gardening never failed to amaze Arabella, and she felt a momentary stab of pride. Her sister's knowledge of plants and creativity, and the way flowers seemed to bloom around her, was quite remarkable.

Lively and full of energies she found hard to repress,

Prudence had a sweet disposition and a soft heart, but she was also in possession of a stubborn, wilful streak and tended to ignore every rule of propriety. When her mind wasn't occupied with gardening matters, her conduct was often reprehensible, and she was the despair of Arabella and Aunt Julia. Arabella put it down to an absence of male influence in her sister's life, and wondered what their brother, Sir Thomas Fairworthy, would make of her now he had returned from political exile in France.

Hearing Arabella's voice and that she sounded testy— clearly not at all pleased that she'd had to come looking for her—the girl immediately stopped what she was doing. Putting down her small spade, she turned towards her sister, absently wiping her soiled fingers on her skirt. 'I am here, Arabella,' she called, crossing the yard, a smile on her pretty, heart-shaped face with its halo of rich chestnut curls, her large jewel-bright amethyst eyes fringed with long sooty lashes. 'What is it? What is wrong?'

'Wrong! Everything is wrong. Upon my soul, Prudence, just look at the state of you,' Arabella reproached in exasperation, plunking her hands in the small of her waist as her eyes passed over her sister's soiled skirt and blouse and the smudges of dirt on her cheeks. 'I've been shouting fit to wake the dead, wondering where you could be. You know how much we have to do for tonight's supper party— and here you are, tending plants. Your hands would be better employed helping Aunt Julia and Goodwife Gilbey in the kitchen preparing the food.'

Prudence combed her hair behind her ears with her fingers, looking up at her sister. 'Where did you think I would be?'

'With Molly Rowan. You know how much I dislike you spending so much time with that girl. She's too forward by far, and that young man who works for her father and follows you around making sheep's eyes at you all the time is no better. He's both surly and rude. It would not do to encourage him, Prudence. I do not want you to be influenced by either of them.'

Molly was the same age as Prudence and the daughter of a nurseryman. The two had become friends when Prudence had come to London a year ago and she had paid a visit to Molly's father's nursery to purchase some plants. The fact that Will Price was always around when she went either to visit Molly or to seek advice from her father couldn't be helped since he worked there.

'I hope I have more sense than to be influenced by anybody, Arabella. And I have never encouraged Will Price,' she said, which was true, since she didn't like the way he looked at her. In fact, she always went out of her way to avoid him. 'I don't like him in the way you imply—and you're right. He is rude and coarse. He is also conceited and has little imagination. He is also silly and always showing off—and he's not going to like the competition one bit when London is once again teeming with swaggering Cavaliers. His looks are reasonable, I suppose, and he thinks he's God's gift just because he has the body of Adonis.'

Arabella peered at her sister intently with narrowed eyes. 'And what do you know about that, pray?'

Prudence shrugged, coolly unconcerned. 'I've seen him with his shirt off when he's working, that's all.'

'As long as you don't go falling for him like an Aphrodite. That would never do. Prudence, you are quite incorrigible,' Arabella scolded. 'I wish I understood you— and that you wouldn't visit Mr Rowan's nursery quite so often. I shudder to think what Thomas is going to make of you and your wild ways.'

Prudence's eyes registered alarm on being reminded that after nine years they were to be reunited with their brother that very day. 'I don't mean to be like that, Arabella. You won't tell him, will you?'

'You know I never tittle-tattle—but I just might if you don't clean yourself up and behave yourself when he arrives.'

Arabella still looked testy, but Prudence knew she wouldn't make things difficult for her with Thomas. Arabella was almost five years her senior, and tired of trying to discipline her. She always treated her imprudent behaviour with anxious forbearance. Her tongue was often sharp, but she was genuinely fond of her young sister, and more often than not treated her with warm affection.

'Come. There's no time for prattling. You must have heard the noise of the cannon from the Tower announcing that the King has crossed London Bridge. I want you on the balcony before the procession reaches the Strand.'

Like the whole of London the Maitland household was gripped by the excitement of King Charles's restoration to his throne; in fact, no one could remain immune from the fever that gripped London at this time. Ever since a move had been made towards the Restoration, London had begun to wake as if from a deep sleep. Effigies of Charles Stuart adorned with flowers were carried through the streets, where people paraded in Cavalier garb trimmed with frills and bows, and places of entertainment, closed during the Commonwealth years, were re-opening daily.

As soon as the King's ship, the *Royal Charles*, along with the rest of the fleet, had arrived at Dover, where the King had been received with obeisance and honour by General Monck—commander-in-chief of all the forces in England and Scotland, the man who had played the most crucial part in his restoration—the thunder of guns and cannon had spread all the way from Dover to London.

The procession had passed through Kent, the acclamation of the people along the way extremely moving for the returning Royalists. Church bells were rung, bonfires lit the length and breadth of the Kingdom, and the ways strewn with flowers. Greeted at Blackheath by the army drawn up by General Monck—that very army that had rebelled against him in the past—the King proceeded on his way to his capital.

Prudence moved towards the house to do her sister's bidding. She had been nine years old when she had last seen her brother, and now he was just a dim shadow of her past. But she was excited and looking forward to his homecoming. In his last letter he had told them the joyous news that he had taken a wife, a young woman by the name of Verity Ludlow. Having lost both their parents, Verity and her sister Lucy were taken to The Hague by their uncle after the Battle of Worcester. Unfortunately Verity would not be returning to England with Thomas. Her uncle had been taken ill and was unable to travel, so Verity and Lucy had remained at The Hague to care for him.

There was also another face Prudence dearly wanted to see in the King's procession—that of Adam Lingard, a young man with the fairest hair and the bluest eyes this side of heaven. Adam was five years older than her own eighteen years. Even in childhood days she had been drawn to him and had adored him ever since in secret, but he had never seemed so attractive as when he had ridden off from their village of Marlden Green in Surrey like some romantic, dashing hero to join his father in exile across the water in France three years ago.

'Arabella, do I have to stay on the balcony? Can't I go down to the street and watch with Molly?'

'No,' Arabella replied firmly. 'How many times do I have to tell you that you must watch the procession from the balcony along with everyone else?'

'But it's too far away,' Prudence complained.

'Goodness me! Don't argue. You will do as I say. Despite your reprehensible behaviour you are supposed to be a lady, and it would be most unbecoming for you to be seen mingling with the crowd. Already people are filling the street in readiness for the procession. By the time it arrives, the Strand will be so crowded you will be in danger of being trampled underfoot,' Arabella snapped. Then, as if ashamed of her irritation, with a tired smile she said more gently, 'Forgive me, Prudence, but I'm in such a state with our brother coming home after so long—and with so much to do. And to make matters worse, cousin Mary and her husband, accompanied by their tiresome offspring, have just arrived.'

With her usual sensitivity, Prudence noticed the sudden darkening of her sister's mood and strove to lighten it, knowing how much she had been dreading Mary's arrival for days. 'Take heart, Arabella. Now Thomas is home, things can only get better and you won't have to endure Mary's unpleasant temper for much longer.'

'Alleluia to that,' Arabella sighed. As they entered the house, she turned her head and studied her sister. With thick curly hair the colour of ripe chestnuts, her small chin and pert nose, Prudence was lovely to look at. Her face was golden from spending much of her time outdoors, and her flashing, amethyst-coloured eyes were a truly remarkable feature. Small and slender, loving and warm, vanity was beyond her visual sphere of things, but already she was openly admired by all who saw her, and Arabella felt a rush of concern for her sister's future. It was time Thomas came home, she thought. Perhaps he would be able to take her in hand.

And maybe then Arabella would have more time to spend with her betrothed, Robert Armstrong, who was as eager as she was for their wedding to take place now the King had returned. On finishing his law studies at Lincoln's Inn and unable to live any longer under the harsh regime of the Protectorate, Robert had gone to join his brothers in exile three years ago. Eager to be reunited with Arabella, he had returned to England a month ahead of the royal party, and had travelled to Dover to bear witness when the King stepped on to English soil.

'I can't help feeling sad for Aunt Julia, Arabella. She must be feeling quite wretched, knowing Uncle James will not be coming home from France with our brother. When Thomas wrote telling her of how he'd fallen ill with the smallpox and did not recover, it affected her deeply. She's going to so much trouble to welcome Thomas home.'

Sadness clouded Arabella's blue eyes. 'It's no trouble for Aunt Julia. After all, he is the head of the family now— now that both Father and Uncle James are dead. You know how devoted she's always been to Thomas—more so, per- haps, since her own two sons were stillborn. Not even cousin Mary could compensate for their loss.'

Hearing children's voices and Mary's strident tones com- ing from within the house, Arabella glanced down at her sister. 'You'd best go to your chamber and change your clothes before Mary sees you, Prudence. You know how she disapproves of you reading your gardening books and tending plants, when in her opinion your time could be best employed learning the skills that will enable you to find a husband.'

Prudence wrinkled her nose, the mere thought of having to endure the company and criticisms of cousin Mary in- definitely filling her with distaste. 'Mary resents us both, Arabella, and sometimes I think she would disapprove of whatever I do. Still, I don't suppose either of us can com- plain. After all, it was good of Aunt Julia to take us in when Father died. Being her brother, it was a difficult time for her, as well—and her sadness doubled when it was fol- lowed so soon by the death of Uncle James. I'm glad we were here to console her in her grief. But I only hope that, now Thomas has returned to England, we can all go home.'

'So do I, Prudence. So do I—although I shudder to think what state the house will be in after all this time.'

Their house in Marlden Green had withstood the might of Cromwell's forces throughout the long years of the Civil War, but, refusing to declare for Parliament and being un- able to avoid the fines and sequestrations imposed on him by the Protectorate, their father had been unable to stave off poverty. When he had died a year ago, unable to support themselves, Aunt Julia had insisted that Arabella and Pru- dence close the house and come to live with her in London, until the time when Thomas returned from political exile in France.

'When we left it was in a sorry state of disrepair,' Arabella went on. 'The roof leaked and the garden will be so overgrown by now that I won't be at all surprised to find a tribe of savages living in it.'

Prudence's eyes brightened. 'Where the house is concerned I won't be of much use, but the garden is another matter entirely. Mr Rowan has given me lots of advice, and I've spent time sketching a reconstruction and planning what to plant and where.'

Prudence's enthusiasm brought a smile to Arabella's lips. 'I'm sure you have, but don't forget it will take money, Prudence, and as you know we are as impoverished now as we were after the Civil War. Thomas may not be able to afford a gardener until the house has been made habitable once more.'

'I've thought of that, which is why I've been collecting seedlings and taking cuttings from the gardens of Aunt Julia's friends and neighbours.'

'With their permission, I hope.'

'But of course. I've collected enough to plant a whole park.'

Prudence followed Arabella into the huge kitchen, where Aunt Julia and Goodwife Gilbey had been preparing that evening's gargantuan feast to celebrate the return of King Charles for the past week. At one time ladies of Lady Julia Maitland's station would not have involved themselves in this kind of menial work, but ladies did all manner of things they had not done before the Civil War. With the day-to-day realities and hardships of such bitter conflict had come the discovery that there was more to living than the turn of a phrase, a beautifully coiffured head and pretty clothes.

To Prudence, the smell in the kitchen was mouth-watering, the combined heat of the cooking range and the summer day intense as finishing touches were put to the many wonderful dishes to be served later. Every surface in the kitchen and the adjoining pantries was covered with elaborate pies, a fricassee of rabbits and chicken, dishes of lobster, carp and cheeses, and a banquet of sweetmeats. The last of the joints of meat and small birds were being roasted on spits in front of the fire, a red-faced, dreamy-eyed kitchen maid—wiping the sweat from her brow with her sleeve—constantly basting them with spiced and seasoned sauce, which dripped off the turning joints into a dish on the hearth to be reused.

Sneaking a delectable-looking mince tart, fresh out of the oven when Goodwife Gilbey's back was turned, Prudence was about to go to her room, when suddenly cousin Mary appeared in the doorway like a spectre of doom, obstructing her path of escape.

Mary lifted her brows and stared disapprovingly at her young cousin's attire, her cold grey eyes lingering overlong on a rip in her skirt, caused when it had become snagged on a rose bush. 'You haven't changed, Prudence. Still tending your pots I see. There are some young ladies who care about how they look. Go and tidy yourself before you join us on the balcony for the procession.'

Prudence accepted that ill-intentioned rebuke with cheerful indifference. 'It will take more than soap and water to make a lady out of me, I fear, Mary, but I will do my best. In fact, I'm going to my room right this minute to do just that,' she smiled, an extremely fetching dimple marking her cheek. Popping the hot mince tart into her mouth she walked away, licking her sugared fingers as she went, her chestnut curls bouncing impudently.

Mary watched her go with profound irritation. Turning to find Arabella watching her, she raised her eyes heavenward and gave one of her exasperated sighs. 'The sooner that girl is married and under the influence of a husband the better it will be for all of us,' she retorted acidly, turning haughtily and going to her children, who were already securing their places on the balcony.

Mary was thirty years old, though the plain clothes she wore and unflattering hairstyle made her look much older. In Prudence's opinion, she was as plain and devoid of warmth and vivacity as it was possible for a human being to be. In the middle of her fourth pregnancy, she had two boys and a girl to her draper husband Philip, who had a shop in the New Exchange in the Strand. They lived in a three-storied house in Bishopsgate, and Mary visited her mother with the children several times most weeks.

Before the Civil War, Sir James Maitland and his wife Lady Julia had cherished hopes that their daughter would make a grand match, but with friends and families on opposing sides, and later the young men who were left fleeing into exile, the choice of eligible young bachelors had been severely curtailed. There were few males with their own royalist beliefs left to marry—only enfeebled youths and old men. Desperate for a husband and fearing that she would go through life as a spinster, poor Mary had finally settled for an ageing, cadaverous-looking widower, Philip Tresswell.

Prudence climbed the stairs to her bedchamber, thinking of her meeting with Adam and wondering what he would think of her now she was grown to womanhood. Her bedchamber was at the back of Maitland House, snug and cosy under the eaves. Built outside the city walls—along with others of well-to-do citizens—it was a fine house, secured from the city's teeming humanity, pollution and noise by a high wall. The front overlooked the Strand, the windows at the back of the house offering a splendid view of the lively River Thames. Prudence spent a good deal of her time watching small boats and barges of grandees making their colourful way up and down the busy waterway.

After taking a sponge bath she put on a hyacinth-blue, low-necked, full-sleeved dress with a pointed bodice and full skirt, open down the front to show a snow-white underskirt. In her meagre wardrobe this was her finest dress—and would best set off her charms and make her irresistible to Adam, she hoped. It was the first time she had worn it, even though Arabella had made it for her a year ago. She had saved it for today, wanting to look her very best when Adam came home.

Sitting in front of her mirror she combed her hair until it fell about her shoulders in thick, glossy curls. When she had finished she stood up and twisted herself about to get a better view, assessing herself with someone else's eyes—Adam's eyes. She wasn't tall, but she was slender and pleasingly curved and not skinny. She would never be a great beauty, but her face was quite pretty, she supposed—at least Molly told her it was—and Will Price certainly seemed to think so. Involuntarily she shuddered with distaste when that objectionable young man intruded into her thoughts. Dismissing him at once, she bent forward to assess her eyes. They were a curious shade between violet and purple, her eyelids etched with faint mauve shadows.

She frowned when she looked at her hair, for this she considered a problem. The fashionable colour was dark—her own was an odd shade of chestnut with coppery lights, and in her opinion there was far too much of it and it curled all over the place. Some women found they had to purchase extra locks and ringlets to fill out their hairstyles, but she had no need of such artefacts.

When she was satisfied that nothing else could be done to improve her appearance, she left her chamber, meeting Aunt Julia on her way to the balcony on the second storey. Aunt Julia's round face was still red from the heat of the kitchen, her fading hair escaping its pins.

Julia was pleasantly surprised when she saw her niece and stood and watched as she did a little twirl to show off her dress, laughing gaily. This freshly scrubbed young woman with glowing cheeks and shining hair was in stark contrast to the young ruffian she had become used to seeing—dressed in her old skirt and blouse, stained with dirt and with scratches on her hands from pruning shrubs.

'Why, Prudence!' she said, obviously moved. 'You look lovely. And that colour blue is so becoming on you. Why, you'll stun every gentleman in the procession.'

Julia remembered when Arabella had purchased the material from Philip to make the dress for her sister, Prudence never having accomplished the skills of dressmaking. They had all been somewhat surprised when Prudence had declared that she wouldn't wear it until the day King Charles came back to England to reclaim his throne, and Julia had thought it such a shame at the time when it looked so fetching on her.

But on closer inspection she suddenly realised that during the time Prudence had been at Maitland House, she had a figure that had evolved well across the frontier from girl to woman, and that perhaps she should have taken to wearing it sooner, for despite the stiffened bodice it was already a bit snug at the waist, and the neckline lower than she remembered—or was it that her niece's bosom was fuller?

'I think you had best go and secure yourself a good vantage point on the balcony, Prudence. My three grandchildren did just that the moment they arrived. The shouting and cheering I hear tells me that the procession will be here at any minute. Word has reached us that it's moving slowly and is so long that it will be nightfall before we see the end of it. It may be some time before we see Thomas, and he will more than likely be riding close to Lord Fox and Adam Lingard. That young man saw active service with your brother in Europe, I believe.'

Already occupying a special place in Prudence's mind, it wasn't the mention of Adam that caused her to look curiously at her aunt, but Lord Fox. 'Lord Fox? You mean the same Lord Fox whose estate adjoins our own in Surrey?'

'The same. If you recall, my dear, Thomas often mentioned him in his letters.'

'I know very little of Lord Fox or his family, Aunt Julia—only that his uncle has occupied Marlden Hall in his absence. I was too young to take in everything that was happening when Thomas left. All I was concerned about was that by supporting the King at that terrible time, if he had not escaped to France he would have been hunted down and hanged.'

'You are right, Prudence. We must thank God that he got away and that things have turned out the way they have. After being absent for so long, no doubt all three gentlemen will be eager to return to Surrey to pick up the threads of their lives,' the older woman said. 'Especially Thomas, now he has a wife. Now—enough gossiping,' she said, shooing her niece away. 'Away with you to the balcony.'

Prudence did as she was told, looking forward to being reunited with her brother. During his absence she had awaited his letters eagerly. They had been frequent, telling them of his life in exile. Practical and talented and not content to spend his time in idleness and debauchery, which was the case of many of the King's entourage seeking succour in Paris, Thomas and the energetic Lord Fox had left the capital to serve in the French army, embarking on what would turn out to be several years of active military service.

The whole of Europe was in a tangled web of international politics at that time. France was unsettled due to a struggle for power between Louis XIV and the French nobles. With the French King eager to be on good terms with the new English Republic under Oliver Cromwell, the exiled King Charles, who was politically unwelcome in France, was told to leave the French Court—a step that was a necessary preparation for an English alliance. Eventually he was invited to the Spanish Netherlands. After crucial negotiations, which were on the surface successful, and with his eyes fixed on his restoration and believing Spain could help him achieve this, King Charles had formed a Spanish alliance.

In Bruges where King Charles had founded his own regiment of guards, Thomas had transferred his allegiance and enlisted in one regiment of English guards that was placed under the Earl of Rochester, and went into service under the Spanish flag. Adam Lingard had joined him.

Lord Fox, having parted company with Thomas long before that, had become something of a mystery figure. According to Thomas's letters, he had embarked on a tour of the East to seek adventure and wealth as a soldier of fortune, and was not seen or heard of again until King Charles was preparing to return to England. Lord Fox had arrived in the Spanish Netherlands accompanied by his personal servant, a native from the Dark Continent he had acquired on his travels.

Rumour had it that he had amassed great wealth. However, in his absence his estate had been confiscated. If he were impatient to return home, no doubt he would succeed in securing his estate sooner rather than later for a price. Having fought with the King at Worcester, Lord Fox would have claims on his gratitude and may already be assured of a promise of favour from His Majesty, who was not returning to England a wealthy man.

Before going to join the others on the balcony, Prudence went to the courtyard and picked a sprig of May blossom which she secured behind her ear. She then picked a small bunch of sweet-scented flowers she intended throwing to Adam when he passed by. Securing the colourful blooms with a thin band of blue ribbon she went back inside, disappointed when she reached the balcony to find that the crush of family and servants was so great she had difficulty in seeing anything at all.

Pushing against Goodwife Gilbey's ample form and careful not to crush her posy, Prudence looked down on to the royal route to Whitehall, her heart uplifted by the sight that met her eyes. The whole of London was poised in pulsating anticipation. Tapestries, banners and garlands of flowers hung from buildings, and a giant maypole—forbidden during the long and miserable years of the Protectorate—had been erected further along the Strand.

The music the people danced to with their partners as they wound the colourful ribbons round the pole had to compete with the many church bells being rung all over London, the thundering of guns and cannon and trumpets blowing. Mingled with shouts of inexpressible joy from the people lining the route, it all became a cacophony of sound, and the merry jingle of Morris dancers' bells and the thwack of their sticks as they pranced along performing their ancient steps, not seen or heard for many a long year, gladdened the heart.

And then, at last, the procession came into view amid cheers of jubilation—a procession glittering with gold and silver and silken pennants fluttering in the breeze. Holding her breath, Prudence was spellbound as heralds blowing long slender trumpets passed by, followed by soldiers, the Lord Mayor and Aldermen of the city in scarlet gowns and gold chains. Then came the darkly handsome King Charles II, his cloak heavy with gold lace. Today was his thirtieth birthday. He was flanked on either side by his two brothers, all three attired in silver doublets.

The populace pressed forward the better to see, and they were not disappointed, for a sea of colour passed before their eyes. The slowly passing cortège consisted of noblemen and gentlemen displaying a style of dress and colour such as England had not seen in many years. Doublets in cloth of silver and gold, rich velvets, wide-brimmed hats with curling, dancing, impudent plumes, footmen and lackeys in liveries of scarlet, purple and gold. The people responded like a starving mass. Why, they asked themselves, had they waited so long in calling their King home? For that day every man, woman and child in England was a Royalist.

The procession went on and on, moving at a snail's pace down the Strand, past Charing Cross and on to the sprawling palace of Whitehall. For what seemed an eternity, Prudence stood waiting for Adam to appear, all the time growing more and more irritated by Mary's three young children either standing on her toes or knocking against her legs. Looking down into the heaving mass of people lining the street her eyes suddenly alighted on Molly, recognising her by her long blonde hair that fell about her shoulders. Miraculously she had managed to secure a place in front of the rest. Impulsively Prudence turned and slipped unseen back into the house and out into the street.

Unfortunately she was unable to penetrate the heaving crowd. She tried shoving and squeezing her way through, but it was no use, and she was too small to see over the heads. Dismayed, she was about to return to the house, when a man on the fringe of the crowd chose that moment to look round. Observing her plight, he took her hand, his face forming a semblance of a smile, his eyes glinting in his tanned features.

'Allow me. It is treacherous for a young woman to try and push her way through this crowd. In the time it takes you to reach the front you will be trampled.'

He nodded to the man he was with—a burly fellow with a small beard and watery, bulbous eyes. In amazement Prudence watched as between them they parted the heaving bodies like Moses dividing the waters of the Red Sea, and she walked through the parting of the waves like the children of Israel passing into the wilderness of Shur.

She turned to the gentleman to express her gratitude. Although he was not strikingly tall he was above medium height and reasonably attractive. He had dark brown hair that fell to his shoulders, a tanned complexion and a thin brutal mouth. Meeting his eyes she saw they held no shyness whatsoever. They were piercing, pale blue and bold and nakedly appraising. His gaze was very steady, giving him a peculiar intent expression, and there was some element of cruelty in their depths and in his presence which commanded the attention. Prudence was unable to interpret what she saw. It was of a dark and sinister nature and beyond the realms of her understanding, but she was repulsed by it and shuddered beneath his stare, drawing back, feeling distinctly uneasy and wanting to get away from him.

'Thank you so much.'

He bowed. 'For a lady as lovely as you, it is an honour,

mademoiselle,' he said, smiling into her eyes in a way that made her feel even more uncomfortable.

When the crowd had swallowed up the gentleman and his companion, Prudence shivered as if a cold wind had just blown over her. He had addressed her as *mademoiselle* but his voice wasn't accented so she doubted he was French. Perhaps he was much travelled. Finding herself beside Molly, the man who had made it possible was forgotten as she became caught up with excitement of the occasion.

Molly welcomed her with a wide, cheeky grin. 'Hello, love,' she said. 'Glad to see you've come down from the balcony. It's much more fun down here among the crowd. Things are positively humming today. Come to look for your brother, have you?'

'Yes,' Prudence answered, not having told Molly of her secret fondness for Adam Lingard. 'I shouldn't think it will be long before he comes along.'

'Have you ever seen such a sight and so many gorgeous men? These bluebloods certainly know how to dress and are so exciting to look at,' Molly enthused, her eyes devouring each Cavalier who rode past, positively melting beneath the smiles they bestowed on her. 'There won't be a girl in London safe tonight.'

Prudence smiled at her friend. With her full mouth, pert nose and vivid green eyes, Molly was extremely pretty. She was taller than Prudence, and had a superb figure, admirably displayed in a yellow-and-white striped dress with a tight waist and low bodice. Molly positively exuded good humour and a jaunty self-confidence Prudence couldn't help but admire. Turning from her, she allowed her gaze to wander. That was the moment when something compelled her eyes to look at a Cavalier astride a tetchy, splendid black thoroughbred advancing slowly towards them, his dark-skinned, Oriental-garbed servant riding by his side.

The man's tall figure, powerful and perfect in symmetry, commanded everyone's eyes and admiration. He was dressed in sombre black, his doublet slashed with scarlet, and his black curls tumbling to his white lace collar beneath his plumed hat. Exuding an animal magnetism, his face was swarthy, lean and devilishly handsome, with a long aristocratic nose, wide forehead and well-chiselled lips. His chin was firm and strong and indented with a small cleft. On the whole it was an arresting face, the face of a knave, a scamp, but it was also an arrogant face, a face stamped with pride and centuries of good breeding.

'Who is that man?' Prudence breathed, mesmerised by him.

'Why, don't you know?' Molly said excitedly, who was unashamedly knowledgeable in most things concerning the opposite sex. 'It has to be Lord Fox. I thought you of all people would know that since he comes from your part of the world. Handsome, isn't he?'

'And he knows it,' Prudence remarked drily when she saw him flash a smile at the crowd, his teeth brilliant white in his dark, attractive features. 'But how do you know who he is?'

'It can't be anyone else—not with those looks. He's reputed to be as dark and as tall, if not taller, than King Charles himself; his skin is burned almost as brown as a Moor's from his time spent travelling far and wide—in the East and in Africa. He's a man of mystery, and I heard tell that he's learned all manner of things and strange practices. It's also said that he's managed to acquire great wealth from his travels.' Molly became dreamy eyed as she devoured the swarthy, handsome man on horseback. 'He looks like a bloomin' prince to me.'

Prudence listened in thrall as Molly went on to tell her of Lord Fox's exploits and the reputation he had acquired abroad. She was amazed to learn that behind his easy façade lay a man of great intellect, of tremendous courage, daring and fierce determination. There also lay a ruthlessness and dedication to duty that made his enemies fear him. He was branded 'The Fox', so named because of his craft and cunning and the bloodshed he left in his wake. To his enemies he appeared like some black and terrifying malevolent spectre on the field of battle, outwitting and defeating all those who dared oppose him. Some even believed him to be under the personal protection of the Devil.

Prudence doubted the authenticity of what Molly had been told, reminding herself that her friend was easily taken in. Nevertheless, she was unable to repress a shudder as she dragged her eyes away from that particular gentleman and glanced at the two following in his wake. She suddenly felt her heart skip a beat on vague recognition of her brother. His face was older and leaner than she remembered, but it was him. Her eyes shifted to the man riding beside him, and a gasp of delight escaped her lips when she recognised Adam's smiling face.

Impulsively and recklessly—her two greatest faults—she closed in on the riders until Adam was almost level, lifting her arm to throw her posy, but at that moment the crowd around her surged forward, forcing the posy out of her hand prematurely, and she watched in dismay as it went soaring through the air, before coming to rest on Lord Fox's horse in front of him.

Chapter Two

Focusing his eyes on the posy, Lord Fox's lips parted in a lazy white smile. Withdrawing one of his gloves, he picked it up and held it to his nose. A ring of gold-and-ruby splendour flashed when it caught the sun. Turning his head and seeing so many smiling faces, he searched them all until his eyes alighted on Prudence, his instinct telling him that she was the one who had thrown the posy. He swept off his wide-brimmed plumed hat to her, revealing a shock of collar-length jet black curling hair, which shone beneath the sun's rays.

Replacing his hat, he stared at her long and unashamedly hard, his eyes boldly impudent, interest flickering in their depths. Treating those around her with another smile, this one even more dazzling than the one before, becoming caught up in the heat of the moment and with laughter rumbling in his chest and a roguish gleam in his eyes—the kind of gleam that must have charmed every female along the royal route from Dover to London—he suddenly reached down and plucked Prudence off the ground as if she weighed nothing at all, settling her in front of him, facing him, on his horse, his iron-thewed arms encircling her and holding her close.

Looking down at the delectable bundle of nubile flesh, her glorious hair in wild confusion, he allowed his gaze to linger on the entrancing perfection of her flawless skin, tanned to the colour of pale honey. Meeting her startled eyes and noting that they were the glorious colour of two huge saturated purple pansies beneath the heavy sweep of her sooty black lashes, Lucas thought she had the face of an angel.

'Dear Lord!' he breathed, completely enchanted. 'I truly think I must have died and gone to heaven—and, if that be the case, then I must tell St Peter to lock the gates and keep me in.'

Prudence should have anticipated his next move but, so taken aback by what he was doing, and unaccustomed to men of Lord Fox's calibre, she was totally unprepared and left with no time to protest when he lowered his head and captured her lips with his own.

His kiss was slow and deliberate, his lips warm and skilled. Placing his hand behind her neck, he splayed his fingers through her soft hair, holding her head firm. Lucas knew that she was frozen with pure surprise. Her lips were like ice for the first few seconds, then slowly they warmed under his, warmed and softened, parting a little so that her breath sighed through. Feeling her yield, he tightened his arms to support her. She was like a flower, fragrant and sweet.

Never having been kissed before, Prudence didn't know what to expect or how to respond, but as his mouth boldly courted hers, his tongue savouring and parting her lips to probe and explore, she became lost in a sea of sensation. In that moment she felt the hardness of his body under the velvet doublet. She breathed in the essence of him, the scent of him, hardly able to grasp what he was doing.

When he finally withdrew his lips from hers, she stared into his eyes—gypsy's eyes, green and brown and flecked with gold, eyes that made her think of brandy, ripe golden corn at harvest time—and the dark glow in their depths was as mysterious and deep as a rushing mountain stream. Her senses swirled and she felt a tremulous frisson of excite-

ment, of danger, as primeval as time itself. She was vaguely
aware that they were still moving slowly along with the
procession and that they had drawn everyone's attention.
Molly's face was a distant blur, her mouth agape, her eyes
as big as saucers.

When someone came from behind and rode alongside
she came to her senses, feeling a slow, painful blush rise
up and stain her cheeks crimson. Anger and indignation at
the audacity of Lord Fox flared inside her. If she hadn't
been imprisoned against his chest and unable to move her
arms, she would have slapped his face good and hard for
his impertinence.

'Oh! How dare you? You are outrageously bold, sir. Too
bold.'

He smiled, his eyes scorching hers. 'Not as bold as I
would like to be, sweetheart,' he murmured, his voice reminding Prudence of thick, soft velvet.

Suddenly a voice rang out beside them. 'You, Lucas, run
true to form. Allow me to point out that this is no common
doxy—so now if you will be so kind as to release my baby
sister…'

Lucas looked quite taken aback, then he loosed his
laughter, his white teeth gleaming like a pirate's in his
swarthy face. 'Sister? Good Lord, Thomas. You are not
serious?'

'I am deadly serious. Now, unhand her, you reprobate.
Prudence is still a child and very impressionable.'

Prudence stared at the elegant figure of her brother, not
at all pleased at being referred to as a baby or an impressionable child. Thomas's features were tight and she knew
he was trying to make light of the situation, but she could
sense his displeasure on finding her out on the street with
the common folk.

Her eyes shifted to Lord Fox. With as much disdain as
she could muster in her humiliated confusion, she raised
her chin a notch. His eyes narrowed and gleamed, and a

strange, unfathomable smile tugged at the corner of his mouth as his gaze dipped lingeringly to her soft lips.

'Why, Thomas, I think I'm going to enjoy getting better acquainted with your little sister.'

Prudence, who had been paralysed into inaction by the unexpected arrival of her brother, wriggled out of Lord Fox's embrace and off his horse—exposing more than was decent of her slender, stockinged legs, almost choking on her ire while dozens of scathing remarks became tangled in her mouth. She glowered up at him, her cheeks stung with indignation. 'Why, you arrogant, insufferable beast—not if I can help it you won't. You can go straight to the devil for all I care. Now be so kind as to return my posy,' she demanded, holding out her hand.

'But you gave it to me,' he said soothingly, his imperturbable, dancing gaze studying her stormy amethyst eyes. 'Do you make a habit of bestowing gifts and then asking for them back?'

'The flowers were not meant for you.'

Lucas raised a quizzical brow, reluctant to relinquish the small posy of fragrant blooms. As quick as a flash Prudence snatched them out of his grasp, but not before Lucas had plucked the sprig of May blossom from behind her ear and secured it to the front of his doublet with a diamond-and-pearl encrusted stick pin. His eyes snapping with amusement, he reached down and with his fingers gave her a light, suggestive chuck under the chin.

Swallowing her outrage, Prudence turned from him and went to Adam, wishing he would snatch her off the ground on to his horse and kiss her the way Lord Fox had just done. But she knew he wouldn't. Adam wasn't like that, unless his years on the Continent had changed him. Secretly she hoped he hadn't changed. She couldn't bear to think of him kissing anyone but her.

Adam was clad in green and gold, his hair beneath his plumed hat as fair as Lord Fox's was dark. Gazing up at him with adoration and pleasure, Prudence handed him the posy. For three years she had been rehearsing what she would say to him when this moment finally arrived, and now all she could say was, 'Welcome home, Adam. I've missed you—we…we all have.'

A slow, appreciative smile worked its way across Adam's fair features. Touched by her simple gift, reaching down he took the posy out of her hand and tweaked her cheek fondly between his finger and thumb, as he would have done to a child. 'Thank you, Prudence. I'm looking forward to seeing you and your family later.'

The procession was moving past Maitland House and the crowd thickened about them. Prudence was forced to step back. Thomas nudged his horse towards her.

'I do not know the meaning of this, Prudence,' he said, his tone leaving her in no doubt of his deep displeasure, his eyes observing the creamy swell of her breasts, telling him that his sister was no longer the little girl he remembered, 'nor do I care to know. However, it will not do. Go and join Arabella and Aunt Julia on the balcony and watch the procession from there. I will see you later.' His curt nod dismissed her.

Mortified by everything that had happened to her in the last few minutes, and knowing that her indiscretion would not go unpunished, Prudence didn't look up to the balcony before entering the house, so she wasn't aware that the laughter had faded from Arabella's eyes, or how pale her face had become when she had watched the spectacle of Lord Fox kissing her sister, or how the colour had intensified when she had taken the posy from Lord Fox and given it to Adam.

Arabella felt physically sick with the force of the pain that attacked her, realising how blind she had been where her sister and her thoughts and feelings were concerned. Recalling the times over the past three years when Prudence often disappeared into a daydream, she now knew why and was deeply troubled and saddened by it—saddened because she knew Adam had quietly married Lucy Ludlow, their brother's sister-in-law, at The Hague.

Arabella was not alone in her disappointment. With his huge hands clenched into tight fists, Will Price's face had worked with fury as he had watched the powerful and infuriatingly handsome Lord Fox sweep Prudence off the ground and kiss her soundly in front of the entire population lining the Strand. When Lord Fox had done with her and she had taken her posy and given it to the flaxen-haired Cavalier following in his wake, Will had felt a rush of bitterness like he had never known before.

Will was obsessed by Prudence Fairworthy. Still in his early twenties, his face was already showing signs of debauchery and overindulgence in every vice. His lusts were easily satisfied by whores, but Prudence was different. She was the sister of a gentleman and not to be tumbled like a strumpet. Throughout the twelve months he had known her, he had oft anticipated not only the gratification of sampling the delights of her supple young body, but the time he would take over it. He had trailed after her like a besotted fool while she had kept him at arm's length, behaving like a prim little Puritan. And now he had watched her behaving like a brazen hussy, throwing herself at the preening Cavaliers like a shameless harlot.

'The bitch! The deceitful bitch!' he ground out between clenched teeth, his fury turning to cold, hard resolve. Her obvious indifference to him and his lowly station in life had made him keep his distance but, after what he had just witnessed, he'd be damned if he would do so any longer. When next they met he wouldn't show any consideration for her finer feelings—if the slut had any.

With rage burning inside him like acid, Will turned on his heel and headed away from the Strand, sickened by the spectacle of the arrogant, pompous, returning Royalists— silently damning each and every one of them to perdition, but somehow his curses proved less than satisfying.

* * *

With King Charles established in his palace at Whitehall, accompanied by Robert Armstrong, Thomas arrived at Maitland House to be reunited with his family. Having hoped that Adam would accompany them and awaiting his arrival with eager anticipation, Prudence was swamped with disappointment not to see him with her brother.

Thomas's meeting with his sisters was warm and emotional. After embracing Arabella, who wept copious tears of happiness and relief that he was home with them at last, he then enfolded Prudence in his arms, pressing his lips to her hair and infusing into her all the affection he had yearned to bestow on her since the day he had left England after the disastrous Battle of Worcester. The moment was deeply moving for them both, and Prudence was relieved that he was no longer angry with her for making a spectacle of herself earlier.

Thomas then drew Aunt Julia aside, carefully wording the circumstances of her husband's death, then helplessly watching while she dabbed at her tears before shoving her handkerchief into her pocket and smiling. Embracing her nephew, she then ushered him into the grand salon where a lavish banquet had been laid for an occasion never to be forgotten, glad that they were together as a family again at last.

With so much to celebrate the feasting began. With a desire to get to know Prudence, and better to keep an eye on her, Thomas insisted that she sit beside him. At the candle-lit banquet table he studied the young girl with a frown, her earlier misdemeanour not forgotten. The way she looked troubled him. All the other ladies seated at the table appeared muted and overshadowed by her vivid beauty. Though small of stature, she was miraculously lovely, her body ripe and perfectly proportioned.

Sensing the restlessness of her spirit, and letting his eyes linger on the stubborn, wilful thrust of her small chin, Thomas suspected that she had been given her own way in most things and allowed too much freedom for too long.

Feeling that she was in need of firm discipline, he was determined to curb this wild young hoyden, although what Verity would make of her he shuddered to think.

When the gentleman seated across from her enquired as to the whereabouts of Lord Fox, Prudence was relieved when she heard Thomas explain that his friend was busy settling himself into his quarters at Whitehall. Having no desire to lay eyes on that particular gentleman ever again, she sent up a silent prayer of thankfulness that she was to be spared his presence. Still trying to overcome her disappointment that Adam had not accompanied Thomas, she stole a glance with a touch of envy at Arabella seated beside her betrothed on the opposite side further along the table. She noted that her sister's spirits were uncommonly high, her face flushed and her light blue eyes as clear as crystal.

There was much revelry as everyone made merry. The air was sweetened with scented candles lighted in the chandeliers suspended above the table, casting their rosy glow on the assembled company, some invited, some not, but no one seemed to care. With free-flowing wine the atmosphere was loaded with gaiety and emotion. A couple of fiddlers were plucked from the street to perform, and endless toasts to King Charles were the order of the night.

Despite the disappointment caused by Adam's absence, Prudence joined in with the festivities, too happy to eat very much and content to gaze at her handsome brother as she drank her wine. Laughing and relaxed, with his dark good looks, he looked so noble, she thought, with a surge of pride.

As the evening wore on her cheeks became flushed, her eyes dark with wine. When Thomas became engaged in conversation with the gentleman next to him, she turned and looked at Robert at the moment when he gently took Arabella's hand resting on the table between them. Prudence saw him place it to his lips and look deep into her sister's eyes—as lovers do. She watched as Arabella responded with a smile of piercing sweetness, graciously inclining her shining head.

At that moment Adam's absence seemed all the more profound. Feeling a constriction in her throat and unable to stem her curiosity as to why he had not come a moment longer, she placed her hand on her brother's arm to claim his attention. 'What is it that keeps Adam away, Thomas? I expected him to accompany you.'

'Adam is staying at Whitehall tonight. He intends leaving at first light for Marlden Green.'

'But—why the haste?'

'To put his house in order for when his wife arrives from The Hague.'

As if from afar Prudence stared at her brother, unable to comprehend what he was saying. 'His wife?' she uttered, tonelessly.

'Yes,' he replied, his sister's sudden pallor escaping his notice as he carefully dissected an apple on his plate. 'Didn't you know? I'm surprised Arabella didn't mention it. Still, their marriage was only recent, and so much has been happening that she obviously forgot to mention it.'

'Who—who is she?' Prudence asked, trying not to sound too concerned.

'My own dear wife's younger sister, Lucy—which makes Adam my brother-in-law. She has remained at The Hague with Verity to take care of their uncle. Hopefully, when he is well enough to travel, we will all be reunited very soon.'

All Prudence's cherished illusions were destroyed in that instant. She stared at Thomas, unable to believe what he was telling her, that God was actually letting this happen to her. Clutching her wineglass, she looked around her in a dazed panic. The room began to spin and the world tilted crazily. Adam had married someone else! No. It couldn't happen. But it had. Oh, how foolish she had been to hope he would notice her when so many Court beauties surrounded him.

Thomas saw her white face. 'Why, what ails you, Prudence? Are you unwell?'

She forced a smile to her lips. 'It's nothing. Nothing at all, Thomas. I think I must have drunk a drop too much wine, that's all. If you don't mind, I'll step outside for a moment. Perhaps a little air will help clear my head.'

She left the house and escaped to the sanctuary and solace of the courtyard without any intention just then of returning to the party. She left just as a latecomer arrived, his sharp eye catching a swirl of petticoats and hyacinth-blue skirt disappearing down a passage.

It was dark when Prudence emerged into the courtyard, the only illumination coming from the lighted windows and a couple of lanterns. Feeling disconsolate, she crossed to the elm tree, which was the furthest point away from the house. Leaning against the stout trunk, she was oblivious to the din coming from the revellers in the street and of dozens of voices dining and drinking in the house. She felt so unhappy and miserable that she was sure she would die of it.

Suddenly her heart almost stopped when a dark silhouette appeared in the doorway, pausing for a moment and looking about. At first she thought it was Thomas come to look for her, but then she realised that this man was taller and broader than her brother. Suddenly she knew who it was, and in that moment of recognition all her senses seemed to be heightened almost beyond endurance. It was Lord Fox, looking just as sinister in the dark as he had looked carefree and relaxed astride his horse in the King's procession earlier. Praying he wouldn't see her and go away, she shrank beneath the tree's leafy canopy, but her dress must have caught the glow of the lantern light, because he descended the steps and began to advance towards her.

The haunting horror of his sharp footsteps when his feet

struck the cobbles congealed her heart with dread. The light behind him obscured the front part of his body and she stared at him transfixed, his features all planes and shadows. Dwarfed by his presence, darkness closed about her, stifling her breath.

When he finally stopped in front of her, Prudence felt his gaze glide leisurely over her, taking in every detail of her appearance. Her heart refused to obey her command to stop hammering in her chest, and as he drew even closer it became a test of nerve. She longed to dart past him and return to the safety of the house, but her legs refused to move. Looking up at him, she met the shining glimmer of his eyes.

He towered over her, tall, silent and mysterious, boldly masculine, his mane of jet-black hair falling to his collar. Gradually his features became clearer, his jaw lean and firm and stamped with iron determination and implacable authority, and Prudence was frighteningly aware of those brownish-green eyes above prominent cheekbones glowing down at her. Her instinct told her that everything Molly had revealed about his exploits and prowess in battle, of how he was feared by his enemies and admired by his friends, was true.

There was something attractive and almost compelling about his strong features, and certainly dangerous. She faced him boldly, his presence rekindling her anger when she recalled how he had outrageously singled her out from the crowd earlier and made a public spectacle of her.

'So, it is you,' she said ungraciously.

'As you see, Mistress Fairworthy,' he replied, his voice richly deep. 'And well met, yet again.'

'If you don't mind, Lord Fox, I came out here to seek solitude, and if you were any sort of a gentleman you would leave me in peace. Please go away,' she said, lifting her chin primly. 'Your company is not welcome.' More than anything she wanted him to leave. At the same time she wanted to conceal how deeply his kiss had affected her, how it had made her feel. And he had known exactly how she felt. Lucas Fox was undoubtedly an expert in making women desire him.

Lucas grinned lazily as his perusal swept over her up-turned face. It was like a pale cameo in the dim light, her eyes huge and dark, the warm, gentle breeze flirting with her hair. She was a truly fascinating creature. Proud, wilful and undisciplined she might be, but she also emanated a subtle quality that made him think of hot, sensual, tumbling love. Prudence Fairworthy was a fetching sight for any man, and the fact that she was Thomas's sister spiced his interest.

'No one should be alone tonight,' he murmured. 'The King's homecoming is an occasion for rejoicing, don't you agree?'

'Absolutely. And I was doing just that until you arrived. I am out here because it has grown exceedingly hot inside and I felt the need of some fresh air. I would have thought there would be enough celebration taking place at White-hall to keep you there,' she said tartly, trying to ignore his powerful, animal-like masculinity, which was an assault on her senses. But it was impossible to ignore the aura of absolute power that surrounded him, and it was more than the mere confidence of a soldier. Lord Fox was used to having things his own way, on every kind of battlefield.

'You are right. Celebrations are well under way, but I grew bored with viewing the ladies at Court,' he replied smoothly.

'So you came to see if the sights are any better at Mait-land House.'

'Precisely,' he said, the corners of his mouth twitching with humour. 'And I am happy to report that they are.'

'Can't you find anything better to do with your time than lust after women, Lord Fox?' Prudence said, her tone one of reproach.

Lucas grinned leisurely as his perusal swept her face. 'Forgive me if I appear forward, Mistress Fairworthy, but a man needs a diversion, and I've been a long time away from England.'

'Are you telling me there was a shortage of ladies at the Court in The Hague, Lord Fox?' she scoffed, knowing to her cost that this had not been the case, for hadn't Adam become smitten and married one Lucy Ludlow?

'My time was not spent at Court.'

'I see,' she replied, her interest pricked and sorely tempted to ask about his travels in the East. But she thought better of it, not wishing to become too friendly with this man who had publicly embarrassed her and disconcerted her in a way no other man had done before. 'Kindly say what you have to say and then go.'

Coolly ignoring her request, Lucas turned sideways so that the lantern light fell full on his features; with one shoulder propped negligently on the trunk of the tree, his arms crossed loosely across his chest, his gaze captured hers.

Prudence could not help but admire the way he looked. Clad in midnight blue velvet overlaid with silver lace, his appearance from the jewelled buckles on his shoes to his black hair was impeccable. Broad shouldered, narrow of waist and with long muscular legs, he gave the appearance of an athlete and, judging by his bronzed skin, of a man who had seen active service in some foreign land, a man who rode and fenced and hunted.

'I want to apologise for my behaviour this afternoon. It was highly reprehensible and I beg your pardon. I had no idea you were Thomas's sister.'

'And if you had, no doubt you would have forced your attentions on some other poor unsuspecting woman in the crowd,' Prudence said, averting her gaze, in danger of becoming entrapped by the compelling, incredible glow in his eyes.

Her chilled contempt hit Lucas in the face, and he answered with slow deliberation. 'I have never forced my attentions on any woman, and I am not in the habit of taking that which is not freely given. I assure you, Mistress Fairworthy, that when you threw your posy of flowers and it landed in my lap, when I looked and saw you, it was a temptation that I could not resist. You were by far the prettiest maid in the crowd.'

Prudence felt her cheeks grow hot and she was glad the darkness did much to hide her blush. There was an aggressive vitality in Lord Fox's bold gaze and an assertive arrogance in the set of his jaw that was not to her liking. 'I imagine you've said that to many women, Lord Fox. How many have you said it to and been sincere?'

Lucas's white teeth gleamed behind a lopsided grin. 'Only those I have a fancy for—and I never lie. I was hoping that since we are to be neighbours and you are Thomas's sister, when we return home you and I can be friends.'

Prudence gasped at his arrogance. 'I don't think we can ever be that,' she retorted ungraciously. 'Being my brother's friend does not give you some kind of claim on me.' Mutinously she glared up at him. 'The harm you did to my reputation today stands between us, Lord Fox.'

'I have no doubt that Thomas will take me to account over it, and he will be justified in doing so. There was a time when, for a gentleman to make a public spectacle of a young lady, he would have been obliged to marry her, but on such a day as this—with passions and emotions running out of control, and because we are about to embark on a more liberal age—I don't think your brother will demand that I do.'

'I shall see to it personally that he does not,' Prudence bit back.

Lucas relinquished his stance against the tree and edged towards her. His grin became wolfish, and he raised an eyebrow with an amusement that exasperated Prudence.

'Would you care for a repeat performance—without an audience this time?' he drawled softly.

Prudence saw the look in his eyes, and her heart began

to beat uncontrollably, while a warning screamed inside her head. 'Don't you dare come near me,' she whispered desperately, trying to deny the traitorous warmth seeping through her. 'I haven't forgiven you for the last time. If you kiss me again, I'll *never* forgive you,' she responded, panic rising inside her like a fluttering, trapped butterfly. She felt her face grow hot, the heat spreading at his nakedly desirous look. It was a look to assess her feelings and thoughts, an invitation, a need, and a certainty, and Prudence, who never had any perception of anyone else's thoughts, found herself floundering inside.

Her threat only seemed to please Lucas more. 'What a bloodthirsty little wench you are,' he chuckled. 'No matter. I can see I'm going to have my work cut out getting you to change your opinion of me.'

'Don't put yourself out. I have no opinion of you, Lord Fox.'

'Yes, you have. Tell me—didn't you like kissing me, Mistress Fairworthy?' he asked, his gypsy eyes observing her with frank interest, his gaze dipping to the rounded fullness of her breasts.

'I didn't kiss you,' she countered, crossing her arms protectively over her bosom, yearning to say or do something that would penetrate his imperturbable exterior.

Lucas's smile widened knowingly. 'You responded. Tell me, was that your first kiss?'

Prudence's cheeks burned even hotter and her eyes flamed. 'That is none of your business. Damn you for your conceit, sir. And I most certainly did not respond.'

'Yes, you did.'

'I—I was surprised, that's all,' she faltered.

The sound of Thomas's footfall was so soft that Lucas had the impression that he'd imagined it, but when he turned he was there.

Realising how insensitive and thoughtless he had been to tell Prudence of Adam's marriage after observing her

deathly pallor when he had delivered the words and recalling how she had given him a posy of flowers in the
procession earlier, Thomas had suddenly recognized that
she might have been nurturing a fondness for Adam
throughout his years in exile. It was his concern that this
might be so that had caused him to seek her out. However,
on seeing her alone with Lucas, he felt dismay rise inside
him. What mischief was the man up to now?

But his quick glance allowed him some understanding of
the situation, for he could see contempt in the dark eyes of
his sister staring defiantly into those of his friend, which
told him she was most unwilling to accept his attentions,
for which Thomas thanked God.

'Am I intruding?' he asked quietly, looking from one to
the other.

'No. Your timing is perfect, Thomas,' said Prudence.
'Lord Fox and I have nothing further to say to each other.
I was just about to return to the house.'

Lucas contemplated her with a half-smile. 'You don't
have to. You came to take the air, as I recall. Besides, there
is to be a celebratory firework display to welcome the
King's homecoming. It would be a pity to miss that.'

Prudence bristled like an outraged hedgehog. 'The air is
no longer to my liking,' she replied, with so much contempt
that his lids narrowed, his eyes gleaming with an expression
she could not define. 'And I can watch the firework display
just as well from the balcony.'

When she turned and flounced across the yard, Lucas's
admiring eyes followed her. He tossed a wide grin at
Thomas when she disappeared into the house. 'Ye gods,
Thomas! Your sister has the makings of a shrew and is a
natural-born rebel. Had King Charles a regiment of soldiers
such as she, Cromwell's forces would not have routed him
at Worcester.'

Thomas sent him a sardonic look. 'There are few things
that are beyond you, Lucas. And my little sister damned
sure isn't one of them. It was shameful of you to kiss her

like that earlier. Little wonder she is still bristling and angry with you.'

Lucas grinned. ''Tis nothing but a minor skirmish—besides, I found kissing her downright nice.'

Thomas saw a flash of the roguish charm that he knew was his friend's stock-in-trade. 'I'm sure you did. You seem to regard all women as objects for your pleasure.'

Lucas laughed, a rich, rolling sound deep in his chest. 'Perhaps you are right, Thomas. Why complicate life by thinking of them as anything else? Why confine myself to just one when I can make a whole lot happy?'

'Lucas,' said Thomas, the formality of his tone wiping the grin from his friend's lips, 'Prudence is a naïve eighteen-year-old. Do you comprehend that? You can't blame me for being concerned for her well being—with your hellhound reputation. Under normal circumstances the pressures of society would have dictated that I demand you marry her—so you can consider yourself fortunate that, in all the confusion of the King's homecoming, I have no wish to play the heavy brother and will overlook your public indiscretion. But mark me well, Lucas—I have no wish to see her become just another of your conquests.'

Until he and Lucas had parted company five years ago, when Lucas had left him to seek adventure and to savour the excitement of the East, his name had been linked with every beautiful female at the King's Court, but marriage had not been among the things he offered. Exactly where he had gone when they had parted company was as much a mystery to Thomas as it was to everyone else, and whatever had happened to his friend during those years of absence he kept to himself. His easy charm and his quick and sparkling eyes attracted as much attention as ever, but behind the sparkle they were forever watchful. However, despite their friendship, his unrestrained reputation made Lucas the last man Thomas wanted to show interest in Prudence.

Lucas grinned at him mercilessly. 'Small chance of that,'

he mocked, 'since your little sister seems to loath the very air I breath.'

'She scarcely knows you. However, you can be relied upon to change her mind,' Thomas replied drily. 'I know how adept you are at persuasion.'

'I like and respect you too much, Thomas. I won't abuse your friendship and trust by seducing your sister.'

'Then what are you doing out here with her—alone in the dark?'

'Apologising.'

'Good Lord! I'm happy to discover that there are some redeeming qualities in you after all. I did wonder.' Thomas spoke with a smile on his lips, but his voice held a hint of sarcasm that did not go undetected by Lucas. 'Did she accept your apology?'

'No—but I dare say she would have, had you not chosen that moment to come looking for her. Why did you?'

'Because of something I told her earlier, which I think may have upset her.' He frowned, clearly troubled. 'I strongly suspect she has a fondness for Adam Lingard.'

'But Adam's a respectable married man.'

'Unfortunately Prudence didn't know that. I suspect she's been carrying a candle for him since he left for The Hague—that she has feelings for him. To be told they will not be reciprocated—which I have just done—I sense has hit her hard and was her reason for coming out here. So go easy with her, Lucas.'

'You're asking me to behave myself. Is that it, Thomas?'

'That's it.'

Lucas looked at his friend hard for a long time and suddenly, to his own surprise, he said, 'You have my word.'

Thomas hesitated, searching Lucas's face. 'Then in that I am thankful. Of all the things you have been accused of, not even your worst enemy would dare imply that you were guilty of breaking your pledged word. I hope the same will apply when you finally take a wife. Will prayers and rings make a difference to how you conduct your life, Lucas?'

'When I marry I shall have a complete and abiding love for the woman whose life I share,' Lucas said calmly, his expression grave. 'I admit that I've done things over the years I'm not proud of, things that make me ashamed to think about, but somewhere along the way I began to see things differently. I'm home now, like every other Royalist who has been plotting towards this end, and there are many things that need to be done. I'm tired of wandering, Thomas. From this day I intend to live out the rest of my life at Marlden Hall.'

'And marriage?'

Lucas gave Thomas a rueful smile. 'I have given the matter considerable thought. Should I die childless, my estate will pass to my cousin Jeffrey—who, to my reckoning, is wealthy enough,' he said, his voice laced with dislike when he spoke of his cousin. 'Consequently I must provide myself with an heir, which is why I must take a wife. But I have no intention of adhering to custom by chaining myself to any woman I might only have a passing fancy for, in order to beget one.'

This came as no surprise to Thomas. Over the years Lucas's name had been linked to a long chain of beautiful women. He attracted them effortlessly, leaving a trail of shattered hearts and a host of furious parents of discarded and ruined daughters in his wake. Because his life so far had been one long adventure, the only part women had played had been to satisfy his sexual appetite. In Lucas's opinion they were irrelevant, dispensable and replaceable, and when a woman became too possessive he quickly became unobtainable. Thomas had begun to think that his friend would never marry, so he was pleasantly surprised by what he had just confided.

'Then whoever you choose will have to be quite exceptional to capture the heart of the elusive and extremely desirable Lucas Fox. But what of your uncle, George Fox? Does he still reside at Marlden Hall?'

'Unfortunately that is so. Like ourselves, many families

were divided during the war years. For those who had faith, believing that the things they fought for were right, then they deserve our respect. They were our enemies—but honourable enemies. I fear the same cannot be said of my uncle or his son. Unlike my father, who believed in the principles of the war, and that the King is the defender of the true church and his majesty sacrosanct, Uncle George had no such noble beliefs. Having no deep convictions for either side, he declared for Parliament because it was expedient for him to do so. By so doing he avoided the sequestrations imposed on Royalists, so I suppose Marlden Hall has fared better than most.'

'Knowing there is no love lost between the two of you, I don't suppose you will allow him to remain living at Marlden Hall when the property is returned to you.'

'No. In any case his position is threatened now the King has returned. It is almost certain that all Royalist properties gained by the regicides will be rescinded. My uncle may not have signed that notorious death warrant for the execution of Charles I, but it is widely known that he actively supported it. He will be lucky to escape with his neck intact. It is the reason why my estate, if I should die before him, would pass to Jeffrey. Uncle George believes I am dead, so I imagine my return will come as something of a shock.'

'I see,' Thomas murmured, curious to know more about those few missing years in his friend's life he knew nothing about, but something in Lucas's shuttered eyes warned him against it. It was something of a dark and sinister nature that had been there ever since they had become reunited at Breda before sailing for England. 'I'm not about to badger you into telling me what you got up to when you left me in France five years ago, but I have the feeling that the adventure you embarked upon was not all you hoped it would be.'

Lucas's jaw tensed and a hard glitter entered his eyes. 'You're right. It wasn't. Although I dare say there are those who would find it a vastly amusing tale,' he said with much irony. 'My cousin Jeffrey in particular, with whom I have a score to settle when next we meet. You were right when you said there is no love lost between my uncle and I, but there are no words to describe what my feelings are for Jeffrey.'

'Do you want to talk about it?'

Lucas was silent for a moment, his gaze fixed on some unseen image in the dark shadows of the high wall. Gradually his shoulders relaxed and then he shook his head, in jovial spirits once more. 'Not now, Thomas. It will keep. Come, tonight is for celebration. This is not the time to drag up our regrets.' He looked towards the house when people began to emerge to watch the firework display that had just begun—explosions of multi-coloured stars and soaring rockets lighting up the night sky and bathing the onlookers in a rainbow of colours. 'I will acquaint you with what happened to me another day.'

'I will be happy to listen. Now, unless you wish to remain and watch the fireworks, let us go inside. You must make your peace with Prudence. If there is to be harmony between us when we return to Marlden Green, it will not do for the two of you to be at each other's throats.'

Chapter Three

Unfortunately Prudence was nowhere to be found. Lucas made his excuses and left to return to Whitehall, unaware that she was on the balcony watching the firework display and saw him leave. Only then did she feel it was safe to return to the festivities. When Thomas saw her he drew her aside.

'Where is your friend?' Prudence asked innocently, giving no indication that she had watched Lord Fox leave. 'I don't see him.'

'Do you want to see him?'

'No. It's just as well he's gone. I think he is the most obnoxious man I have ever met.'

Thomas chuckled. 'I'm relieved to hear it.'

Prudence was surprised. 'You are? But Lord Fox is your friend.'

'So he is. But I am truly amazed. Grown men quake in his presence, but here you are, a mere slip of a girl, actually standing up to him. Be warned. Lucas is too much an experienced man of the world, Prudence, for a girl of your tender years. He thought nothing of making a spectacle of you earlier—for which I have berated him—and he would think nothing of seducing you now—if you were anyone other than my sister. You are far too young to challenge him. His skills of persuasion where women are concerned are renowned, so take care. Lucas would break your heart if you gave him a chance.'

Prudence wondered what her brother would say if she told him that her heart was already breaking over Adam, so it was unlikely that it would suffer from the same affliction twice. 'I won't, and if Lord Fox is as bad as you say he is, then I am very lucky to have had a narrow escape from certain disaster.'

Thomas gave her a look of reproach. 'You mistake me, Prudence. Lucas is not evil.'

'Is he not?' she declared adamantly. 'If he is called "The Fox", then he must have earned the name, and the not-too-flattering words such as cunning, deceitful and perfidious spring to mind—a true Machiavelli, in fact.'

Thomas frowned, not at all pleased to hear Lucas described so unfairly or severely by a girl who could have no comprehension of his friend's true character. 'Go easy, Prudence. Do not speak ill of him. Lucas is my good friend. I insist that you are civil to him when next you meet.'

Prudence bit her lip and her expression softened. It was clear to her that a special kind of friendship existed between her brother and Lord Fox, and she must respect that. If she had to endure his company, she would bear it for Thomas's sake without complaint—but that didn't mean to say she had to like him. And if he insisted on pursuing her, then by the time she had finished thwarting, frustrating and exasperating this arrogant lord, he would be glad to leave her alone.

'I shall try, Thomas—I do promise,' she conceded, knowing it would be difficult, but she was most sincere in what she said…at least, she was at that moment. 'But the nature of the man is not to my liking. He is far too full of himself.'

'Prudence.' There was warning in his voice. 'Have a care.'

'I will. And now, if you don't mind, Thomas, I would

like to go to bed. I've had enough of the celebrations for one evening.'

Turning over in his mind his encounter with Thomas's fair sister, Lucas was in a thoughtful mood as he made his way to Whitehall. He was sorry he'd missed saying good-night to her and sincerely hoped that on their next meeting she would be more amenable towards him.

With a glance he took stock of his surroundings, for the streets of London were a dangerous place to be after dark. Alone and attired in the fine clothes and jewels that bespoke a man of wealth and made him a temptation to the residents of the underworld, Lucas quickened his stride. When dusk fell over the city, once their day's work was done, decent folk went home and put up the shutters, but tonight, on the King's return to his throne, when every street flowed with wine, they mingled in their merrymaking with all manner of low life that crept out after dark to inhabit the streets: the preying ground of beggars, thieves and cut-throats, roving bands and bawds and their pimps.

Thinking of all this, Lucas became uneasily conscious of a chill feeling in the pit of his stomach and he had a compulsive urge to look over his shoulder. His hand went to the hilt of his sword, his instinct telling him that someone was stalking him. In a second he assessed the situation coolly, thinking it was most likely a robber, and he gritted his teeth at his own foolishness for not having brought Solomon with him or taken a chair back to Whitehall. He had been a fool once before to walk the streets of a city after dark, which had almost cost him his life. Tonight he had acted on impulse, without giving due thought to the consequences, which was something he had sworn never to do again.

The next moment his sensitive ears heard the heavy breathing of his stalker and the soft scrape of a dagger being unsheathed. The cold deliberation of it cleared his brain and made him think quickly and concisely, responses that had carried him through a thousand similar situations in battle unscathed. Drawing his sword from its jewel-encrusted scabbard he turned, his eyes catching the sinister flash of a blade. Convinced that the fellow's intent was to murder him, Lucas's reflexes were quick and he lunged at his assailant like an avenging demon.

The man had a small, straggly beard and bulbous eyes, which were obsessed by some grim purpose. He was a burly, lumbering shadow against the wall. He was also clumsy, for in attempting to dodge the deadly grace of the tall man's swift manoeuvre and the point of his sword, he fell back, placing his foot in a rut and stumbling to his knees with a grunt, dropping his weapon on to the ground. He had been a dangerous man with a dagger in his hand, but deprived of it he proved to be no match against such a powerful and towering adversary bearing a sword. Scrambling to his feet he bolted, disappearing into the underworld of rat-infested, foul and reeking back alleyways, a domain where no respectable man dared venture.

Breathing heavily Lucas sheathed his sword, just as a shower of silver stars burst above him in the sky, diminishing in their splendour as they gracefully descended in a magnificent cascade. The incident had all happened in the space of a moment, going unnoticed by the revellers in the street. Immediately he hailed an empty chair and ordered to be taken to Whitehall. As he sat back his face was grim, his mind going back over the unpleasant incident. He had many enemies, but he could think of only one who would want to kill him.

His cousin Jeffrey.

As Prudence went through the motions of preparing herself for bed, she was so confused as she tried to understand the turbulent, consuming emotions Lord Fox was able to arouse in her when they had only just met, and how he had managed to overshadow Adam in her thoughts by just a look—and a kiss. How could she ever think of him as her friend? Thomas was right. If he set his mind to seduce her, nothing was going to deter him from trying. She would be strong and rely on her courage and determination and her stubborn nature if she was going to avoid him, and she had an abundance of all three, which Lucas Fox had only glimpsed.

Her mind was in turmoil over Adam having married someone else. When he had gone to the Continent she had been just fifteen years old, but she had hoped that he'd noticed her, that he might have had some feeling for her. But he hadn't, she could see that now. That was all she had been to him—a silly young girl—and as soon as he'd reached King Charles's Court in exile, he had fallen for another. As she pulled the covers over her head she re-solved to banish Adam from her thoughts forever, but as she drifted into sleep her dreams betrayed her.

When she awoke the next morning she despised this weakness, and as she dressed she was determined to con-quer her infatuation. She wanted to talk to someone, but she couldn't talk to Arabella. She couldn't tell her sister the secret she had carried in her heart for three long years. Arabella would be shocked and grieved to know that Pru-dence could still want a man who was married to another.

Just as soon as she had eaten breakfast she would go to Mr Rowan's nursery to see Molly. Molly would listen to her. She always did.

As Prudence was making her way to Covent Garden through streets littered with the evidence of the previous night's revelry, she would have been concerned to know that Thomas and Arabella were discussing her. Thomas was angrily pacing the parlour with long, determined strides as he insisted on hearing more of her misdemeanours—some he'd already heard from cousin Mary earlier, who had gone out of her way to vilify Prudence.

'I wish I could say Prudence is a credit to you, Arabella, but I cannot,' Thomas said with a note of regret. 'I will admit to you that I am not best pleased. Our sister is a disgrace to our parents' memory, and I am relieved that neither of them lived to see what she has become—a hoyden, no less. Her behaviour seems to me to be quite reprehensible.'

'Do not judge her too harshly, Thomas. Perhaps if our parents were alive and you had not been forced into exile, our sister would not have turned out so wayward,' Arabella said quietly. 'But beneath it all, Prudence is a sweet girl with a soft heart and a generous nature. She may seem difficult, but she doesn't mean to be.'

'Rebellious and unbiddable is how I would describe her,' said Thomas, his eyes dwelling on his sister. Arabella was fair-haired, pretty and gracious and sweet-tempered, whereas Prudence was an exotic, vivacious firebrand—which brought to mind what Lucas had called her—a shrew and a rebel, which was hardly a flattering description of any well brought-up young girl in his opinion. 'Can you imagine how shocked I was to hear that her manners are outrageous, that she is the despair and embarrassment of the entire household, and that she frequently roams the streets in the company of a girl we know nothing about? And on top of all that she was seen kissing a youth who called at the house just the other day.'

Arabella smiled softly in an attempt to soften her brother's attitude towards Prudence. 'There's no need to be so shocked, Thomas, and I do try to keep a strict watch over her. The only time I allow Prudence on to the streets is to visit Mr Rowan's nursery in Covent Garden—and myself or one of the servants nearly always accompanies her. The girl you speak of is Mr Rowan's daughter, Molly, and the two have struck up a friendship.'

'Nearly always? So you do admit that she goes out by herself on occasion. She may intend no harm in her promenades, but by doing so she gives amorists the opportunity to meet her. And the kiss?'

Arabella sighed. 'Was completely innocent. The youth you speak of was James Lowther, who is just fourteen years old. His mother and Aunt Julia are good friends and James adores Prudence and would do anything to please her. He came to bring her some plants from their garden—for which he was rewarded with a peck on the cheek. That's all it was, and if Mary implied the incident to have been of a more passionate nature, then it was quite wrong of her.'

Thomas cast his sister a sceptical glance. 'Nevertheless, she should not bestow her affections so lightly.'

'Prudence is not wanton, Thomas. She loves life and has a spirit that makes her exuberant. If she has not turned out as you hoped she would, then I am sorry. I've done my best,' Arabella told him, annoyance creeping into her voice at her brother's readiness to berate her for not rearing Prudence to his satisfaction. 'It hasn't been easy for any of us these past nine years. But, as you know, Prudence does have a passion for gardening—which I have had reason to bless, for while ever she is tending her plants she is not getting up to mischief.'

'I'm sorry, Arabella.' Thomas relented, seeing his sister's dismay and admiring her readiness to spring to Prudence's defence. 'I don't mean to sound harsh or judgmental, but something must be done—and quickly. Does she have any suitors?'

'No—although unconsciously she does draw attention to herself wherever she goes, which is a constant worry. All the youths seem to notice her. There's something about her that intrigues them—Will Price in particular.'

Thomas glanced at her sharply. 'Will Price?'

'He works for Mr Rowan at his nursery where Prudence regularly goes to buy plants and to seek advice on gardening matters. Will certainly seems to find her appealing.'

'So does Lucas,' Thomas said with grim amusement,

standing still with his hands clasped behind his back as his features settled into thoughtful lines. 'It seems to me that we will have our work cut out guarding our young sister's maidenhead, Arabella. It's also clear that it's not too soon to think of marriage.'

'Marriage is not the solution, Thomas,' Arabella countered quickly. 'Prudence is not ready for that.'

He smiled grimly. 'Perhaps if Adam were still free she would feel differently.'

'So—you know about that, too. I had no idea until yesterday that she was so fond of him. She has given no indication.'

'Pity. Adam would have been eminently suitable—if a trifle quiet and reserved. Lucy, his wife, being docile and gentle, is just right for him and will make him happy, whereas Prudence is too volatile and would very soon become bored. I think what she needs is a man to gentle her, to take her in hand,' Thomas went on. 'A mature man, a man who will stand no nonsense.'

Arabella shook her head, prepared to disagree with him. 'I cannot deny that I am relieved to turn over the responsibility of Prudence to you, Thomas, but on this I matter I cannot agree. She has spirit, I know, but the kind of man you speak of would subdue that spirit. If you force her into a marriage such as that it would become a prison for her. It would be cruel and I would fear for the consequences.'

Thomas nodded. 'I hear what you're saying, Arabella, and I promise not to force her into anything that is distasteful to her. But marriage has to be considered some time— particularly when you and Robert marry and Verity comes to live at Willow House.' He frowned uneasily when he thought of his wife. 'I know you will like Verity, and she you, Arabella—but Prudence might very well prove to be a different matter entirely. Be so good as to go and fetch her. I think it's time I had a serious word with her.'

To Arabella's dismay, Prudence was nowhere to be found. She returned to the parlour just as Thomas was re-

ceiving Lord Fox, who had ridden from Whitehall Palace,
where he and his servant had managed to procure rooms.
Despite being their neighbour at Marlden Green, whose
family had lived at the magnificent Marlden Hall for generations, Arabella had met Lord Fox only once before last
night, and at that time she had been too young for him to
have formed any deep impression.

The same age as Thomas, at twenty years of age the two
young men had left Marlden Green together to join King
Charles at Worcester, for what was to be his final battle.
And now, like everyone else when they are first introduced
to this illustrious lord, she could not fail to be impressed
by his presence and bearing. Dreading having to tell
Thomas that Prudence had disappeared, she hoped her
brother's wrath would be somewhat tempered by Lord
Fox's presence.

'Where is Prudence?' Thomas demanded when Arabella
stared at him mutely, waiting for him to finish speaking to
Lord Fox. His voice bore an edge of sharpness that bespoke
vexation.

'She—is not in her room, Thomas. One of the kitchen
maids saw her leaving the house about ten minutes ago.'

Thomas's face was almost comical in its expression of
disbelief as he stared at Arabella. 'Not here? Do you mean
to tell me that she has been allowed out already?'

'She must have gone to Mr Rowan's nursery in Covent
Garden to see Molly. I'll go after her.' Arabella turned
towards the door but Thomas halted her.

'Stay where you are. I'll go myself. That young whelp
has just over-stepped the bounds of my endurance. I'll
teach her how to behave. It's high time somebody did.'

Anticipating that Thomas was going to unleash his wrath
on Prudence the moment he clapped eyes on her, Lucas
attempted to defuse the highly charged situation.

'Perhaps you will permit me to go after her,' he suggested calmly. 'My horse is saddled and I can be at the
nursery in a matter of minutes. Besides, the mood you're

in, Thomas, I don't reckon much to your sister's chances when you get your hands on her.'

Thomas threw his hands up in the air in frustration. 'Thank you, Lucas. You may go if you wish. But stand no nonsense. You have my full permission to drag her back to Maitland House if necessary.'

When Arabella had given Lucas directions on how to find Mr Rowan's nursery, he left the house.

It was still early, and Prudence was thankful there wasn't the usual crush of traffic to slow her down as she walked in the direction of Covent Garden, having no doubt that most people would still be sleeping off the effects of the previous night's celebrations. Covering her nose with a scented handkerchief to ward off the putrid smells rising from the gutters where dogs scavenged among the filth, she moved out of the way of a late reveller going towards Charing Cross in a fine carriage, escorted by liveried servants.

Shopkeepers were slow to open this morning. She heard the yodel of a milkman down an adjoining street, and a chimney sweep carrying a bundle of rods and a long broom scurried past. Water-carriers, their shoulders stooped from the weight of their yokes bearing buckets, went from house to house.

Leaving the Strand, the timber-framed buildings on either side of the narrow street were blackened by pitch and the smoke of sea-coal, the upper storeys jutting out and almost touching, shutting out most of the light. It gave the impression of passing through a tunnel. She managed to avoid the rubbish thrown out of upper windows and side-stepped worse.

At last, down a narrow twisting alleyway in Covent Garden, she reached Mr Rowan's nursery, which was closed in by high walls. The wooden gates stood open, indicating that Mr Rowan, who specialised in the supply of plants and seeds, flowering trees, fruit trees and shrubs, was already about his business. The yard where he could usually be

ALPENHOTEL ****
K R A M E R W I R T
Familie Kröll
A-6290 MAYRHOFEN, Am Marienbrunnen 346
Tel. 05285/6700 Fax 05285/6700-502

Restaurant T 83

RECHNUNG

1 x Juice 8cl   16.00 2
1 x Wodka   38.00 2

BAR öS   54.00
Betrag in Euro (3.92)

MC   NETTO   MWST   BRUTTO
20.0   45.00   9.00   54.00

Es bediente Sie HERR GUSTL

Elite-Term01 K15 21:28 15.08.01

found at this time of day was quiet. Only Will was there, watering some tender plants in tiny pots from a clay receptacle, which had tiny holes all over it to allow the water to sprinkle out so it did not drown the plants. Wishing there was someone else she could speak to, reluctantly she walked towards him.

'Hello, Will.' She was smiling as she drew closer, but gradually her smile faded. Normally Will welcomed her cheerfully, but today his face was drawn into sullen lines. His blue eyes looked dull and were almost hidden by folds of puffy flesh. Perhaps he was suffering the after-effects of the previous night's celebrations, she thought. It wouldn't be the first time she'd arrived at the nursery to find him red-eyed and rubbing at his brow, as if to ease the persistent ache that throbbed there, caused by drinking too much liquor the night before. He didn't stop what he was doing and she could tell from the surly glance he gave her that he had something to say. 'How are you this morning, Will?'

'Me? Never better,' he grunted. 'What the hell do you want coming here?'

Prudence's eyes widened and her lips parted, surprised by the viciousness of his reply. 'I've come to see Molly.'

'Then you've wasted your time. She isn't here.'

'Where is she?'

'Highgate—delivering some fruit trees with Mr Rowan.'

'Oh—I didn't know,' she said, disappointed. When Will looked away and carried on watering the plants, she edged a little closer to him, puzzled by his behaviour. 'Will—what's the matter? Has something happened to upset you?'

Will looked at the clay receptacle in his hand and suddenly flung it from him. Never had Prudence seen his eyes burn with so much wrath as they did at that moment when he fixed them on her accusingly, feeding on his own righteous rage.

'I'll tell you what's the matter—you slut,' he hissed. 'Did you think I didn't see you yesterday—pushing yourself forward to be seen by those bloody Cavaliers?'

Prudence was momentarily shocked into paralysis by his aggressive behaviour, but then she forced a small laugh and tried to sound nonchalant. 'I think you may be letting yourself be influenced by a purely personal resentment, Will. I know you have no liking for Royalists and do not welcome their return.'

'You're damned right I don't. I'm sick of you pretending to be little Miss Puritan—whiter than white—when all the time you have the morals of an alley cat. Shameless you were—flaunting yourself like a strumpet at the line of strutting peacocks. Did the memory of the kiss from the arrogant Lord Fox keep you awake all night,' he shouted, thrusting his face close to hers, 'or did you spend the night rolling around with him in his bed?'

Appalled, Prudence gasped, taking a step back. 'Oh! Oh—how dare you? How dare you say that? You have no right.'

'Mebbe not—but what I saw yesterday only proves that you're a better actress than I thought,' he growled scathingly. 'Not so angelic now, are you? What do you have to say?'

Something of the venom in his tone penetrated Prudence's mind. His arrogance and the injustice of the accusations he was flinging at her stirred her ire and her eyes flared. 'Nothing to you, Will Price. Nothing at all.' With a toss of her head she made a move to walk away, but seeing her intention, he stepped in front of her, barring her path.

He looked huge and intimidating as he glared down at her, his small eyes glittering hard, the broad expanse of his chest exposed beneath his half-fastened soiled shirt beaded with sweat. Gripping her arm in his large fist, words began to spill from his lips as though a long pent-up dam had suddenly burst.

'You can't say I haven't been patient—watching you come here time after time—wanting you. It isn't everybody who would have waited to be noticed. And don't look so surprised,' he laughed, with more than a hint of bitterness when her eyes widened with astonishment. 'Ever since I first clapped eyes on you I've wanted to tell you how I felt, to declare myself, but I thought you weren't for me.

'You've tormented me—do you know that? Coming to the yard all friendly like. I could've taken you time after time—but no, like a fool I thought, wait, treat her properly, and then maybe there'll come a day when she'll notice you. Now I know your pretty words are not to be trusted—your innocence is a sham. Aye,' he said, looking her up and down insolently, mentally stripping her of her clothing, which turned Prudence's blood to ice. 'I should've known the bitch was biding her time until those foppish Cavaliers came back so she could flaunt herself.'

Prudence stared at him, trying to comprehend what he was saying. How could she tell him the very touch of his hand repelled her? 'That's not true.'

He favoured her with a sneering grin. 'And would it have made any difference if you had? Aye—I know your brother was in exile, and that your family's poor—but not too poor to stoop so low as to take Will Price, eh? Not too poor to take to living in a hovel with a man with dirt on his hands, who stumbles and lurches around in his ugly boots.'

Prudence set her jaw and glared her anger at him. His words were as defiling as if he had violated her body. 'You're right, Will Price. If you think I would give myself to the likes of you then you are more addled than I thought. Now—let go of my arm and get out of my way.' She didn't believe that he would harm her, but she was wrong.

Will's eyes narrowed dangerously. His face was red and he was breathing like a winded bull. 'Beneath all your fine ways you're nothing but one of life's whores.' His lust overcoming his common sense, drawing himself up to his full height he hauled her furiously against his chest.

Pain as hot as pincers shot through Prudence's arms as she struggled against him. Suddenly something welled up inside her, a powerful surge of emotion to which she gave full rein. It was something larger than her own small self.

Because she was small and female Will misjudged her strength. When he planted his mouth on hers there was a sudden pain as her sharp teeth clamped down on his lip. With a yelp he released her and drew back, tasting blood. He raised his hand to wipe it away, just as her fist flew out and delivered a resounding blow to his cheek.

'You lout. You ill-mannered oaf,' Prudence cried, hotly irate, her dark eyes narrowed and sparking fury as she met his effrontery with a rage she had not known she possessed. 'Do you think I am that easy, Will Price? If I were a man I'd—I'd horsewhip you. I'd teach you not to go around ravishing respectable females with your revolting kisses.'

'Would you kindly explain what's going on?' Lucas's sharp bark came from the entrance to the yard.

Will dropped his arm in amazement, and in unison both he and Prudence looked towards the gates in mute surprise. The figure of Lord Fox, long of limb and lean of frame— six foot two of lean, hard muscle—strode towards them scowling darkly, his eyes flicking with distaste from one to the other. He halted a short pace away. The scene prompted Lucas to draw his own conclusions—Prudence's cry of outrage, accompanied by a resounding slap to her assailant's cheek, told him that this person's advances were not welcome. The young man was quite tall and muscular, with features grimly set and blue eyes narrowed into bitter slits.

'You are?' Lucas asked pointedly.

'Will Price,' he growled. 'I work for Mr Rowan.'

'And where is Mr Rowan?'

'He's not here this morning.'

'How convenient for you.' A mildly tolerant smile touched Lucas's handsome visage, but the glint in his eyes when they settled on Will was as hard as steel. 'However, I am sure your employer can find more worthy tasks for your attention than abusing his customers. If you do not choose to meet your Maker, I suggest you do not touch the lady again,' he warned in a tone of icy reproof. 'Sir Thomas Fairworthy would take it amiss if you hurt his sister.'

Slightly shaken, Will managed to draw himself up with nervous hauteur. The fact that his masculinity was about to be shredded by the older, more powerful and supremely confident Lord Fox, and that he would be brought down by his inability to control his lust for Prudence Fairworthy, overcame all other emotions. 'What's it to you?' he snarled.

'I'm the man who happens to be a close and personal friend of Sir Thomas Fairworthy. I am also the man who will speak to your employer and have you dismissed.' Lucas slid his gaze to Prudence, whose glower was hot enough to reduce him to a cinder. 'Are you all right?'

'He hasn't hurt me, if that's what you mean,' she ground out ungraciously, mortified that Lord Fox of all people must have witnessed the whole shameful, sordid incident. But then, wasn't he another who had dared treat her like a common trollop, kissing her in so casual, so cavalier a fashion?

'It is clear to me that Mistress Fairworthy finds your amorous attentions unwelcome,' Lucas said to Will. 'I think you should apologise.'

Will laughed derisively. 'I would sooner have my tongue cut out before apologise to that doxy.'

Prudence rounded on him, her face a mask of indignation. 'What did you call me? Why, you—' she cried hotly, but a sharp glance from Lucas silenced her.

'Perhaps you didn't hear what I said,' Lucas persisted, addressing Will once more, his voice cold and ominous. 'I think an apology to the young lady is in order.'

Stemming a string of foul curses that threatened to erupt from his mouth, Will glared at the Cavalier whose composure shamed him, the apology sticking in his throat. When Prudence saw he wasn't going to comply, she stepped back.

'Leave it,' she said firmly, unconsciously placing her hand on Lucas's arm when she thought he would raise it to strike Will. 'It was his own foolishness that led him to this. Let the matter end there.'

Lucas fell back a step reluctantly, looking down at Prudence. Her face was clear-cut and delicate, her hair all a-tumble about her slender shoulders, and utter contempt for the man who had molested her was manifest in her narrowed, translucent eyes. 'Am I to understand that you wish to ignore the fact that this man tried to ravish you?'

'Why, what will you do, Lord Fox?' she scoffed. 'Avenge my honour? I think not. No good will come of it.'

She looked at Will. The wretchedness of his family's existence was not unknown to her. They lived in a rented tenement up a filthy yard at Ludgate. Since the death of Will's brutal father several months ago, his mother and five young siblings were totally dependent on him. If Mr Rowan heard how he had tried to molest her, he would not tolerate his working at the nursery any longer. Will would never find work that paid so well and his entire family would suffer and be turned out on to the streets to grovel for a living as a consequence. Prudence had no wish for that to happen, and neither did she want to be the cause of it.

'I shall write to Molly and explain that I will not be coming to the nursery any more because I'm returning to Marlden Green with my brother and sister. To spare your family hurt, I shall remain quiet about what happened today. You were stupid and a fool to do what you did to me. I suppose passion can blind a man but, by my oath, Will Price, if you ever touch me again, I swear I will give you reason to regret it.'

'You are too kind-hearted by far,' Lucas drawled mockingly, but he shrugged. 'As you will.'

He looked at Will and his fists tightened. There was a time, not too long ago, when he would not have let a man off so lightly if he'd caught him molesting a young innocent. He would have killed the ravisher, no matter what. But the intervening years had taught him a tolerance, if not a wisdom, that his nature would once have condemned.

'Mistress Fairworthy is too forgiving. Consider yourself fortunate. Now,' he said, sweeping a hand in front of him in an invitation for Prudence to proceed. 'If you please.'

A trace of indignation still showed in Prudence's tight lips as she turned from Will and went ahead of Lucas out of the yard.

Standing alone, as Will watched them go he yearned for vengeance. He wanted to go after them and tear into the arrogant Lord Fox, to beat him to a bloody pulp, as he would anyone else of lesser rank who crossed him, and snatch the young woman from his side. But the taste of blood and the tender swelling on his lip where her teeth had punctured the flesh made him pause. Thoughtfully he stared after them. He would let the matter rest, for now, but if a chance arose in the future to get even, he would take it.

The man who stood just out of sight of the gates to Mr Rowan's nursery, his back pressed hard against the wall, had the air of a cautious animal as his eyes followed the two people who had just left the yard. A dim, wavering light penetrated the alleyway, and the dank smell of rotting vegetables and worse permeated the air. With his teeth drawn back across his lips and his eyes shining with an ugly inner glow, the man stepped furtively into the open, walking with the gait of a sailor as he followed the man and woman with stealth and at a discreet distance, stopping now and then, shadowy and motionless, out of sight of the couple who had no idea of his presence. Not until they stepped on to the Strand did he turn and retrace his steps back to Mr Rowan's nursery and Will Price.

Chapter Four

Prudence lifted her head haughtily and her mouth hardened to an unsmiling resentment as she glanced at Lucas
leading his horse a step behind her. 'I can't think how you
came to be at Mr Rowan's nursery, Lord Fox. It is off the
track, after all. Don't tell me you are out for a stroll for I
will not believe you. You either followed me or you have
an interest in gardening. Whatever the reason, do you have
to creep about?'

Lucas was incredulous. Good Lord! If the wench wasn't
trying to take the offensive by accusing him of spying on
her. 'If I had come accompanied by the London mob I
doubt you would have noticed, Mistress Fairworthy. And,
since you ask, it was for neither of the reasons you mentioned. Your brother sent me.'

Her eyes opened wide with alarm. She gasped.
'Thomas?'

Lucas grinned. Now he had her full attention. 'You do
have just the one brother, I believe,' he replied with an
underlying sarcasm. 'When he discovered you had left the
house he was quite beside himself with rage. Your sister
directed me to the nursery to fetch you home.'

His eyes were not without humour, but there was censure
in the firm set of his clean-shaven jaw. Prudence bristled

at his tone and glared her irritation. 'I can take care of myself.'

'After that delightful scene I have just witnessed, I disagree.'

Prudence ignored him and neither of them spoke for a full minute as they made their way down the narrow, deserted alleyway, entering a slightly wider street and going in the direction of the Strand.

'He's handsome isn't he, Will Price?' Lucas said at length, casually, watching for Prudence's reaction out of the corner of his eye.

'I suppose some might find him so, but he doesn't appeal to me.'

'Does anyone?'

'No, of course not,' Prudence replied, thrusting thoughts of Adam from her mind.'

'Your brother thinks you need taking in hand—and I tend to agree with him.'

'It's none of your business,' she retorted with cold hauteur, infuriated by his imperious tone. 'I do not have to explain what I do to you, Lord Fox.'

'Do you make a habit of leaving the house without telling anyone—unaccompanied?' Lucas persisted.

'Sometimes.' She tossed her head, the chestnut tresses dancing against her back. 'I do what I like.'

'Then don't you think it's high time you began to consider the consequences of such recklessness and tried harder at being a lady?' Lucas admonished, fighting the urge to turn her over his knee.

Prudence glanced up at him when he drew level and halted her by taking her arm at the end of the street. He was standing close, and though the shadow of his wide-brimmed hat hid part of his face, she detected a strong note of disapproval in his stance.

'Mistress Fairworthy,' he said curtly. 'When I came upon you just now you were about to be ravished. Your abuser accused you of being a doxy and I do not care to know why. I am here on behalf of your brother to escort you home—under force, if necessary. So let us, in common agreement, strive to be both gracious and mannerly until we reach Maitland House, where your brother will deliver the punishment you deserve, and soundly thrash that most tender part of your anatomy and render you incapable of sitting down for at least a week.'

Prudence's face burned, shamed and guilt-stricken because she felt she'd earned his condemnation—although the idea of being spanked like a naughty child went some way to shredding her confidence. Nevertheless she opened her mouth to challenge his statement, then closed it hastily. The expression in his eyes had frightened her.

'Do I make myself clear?'

Dejectedly, she said on a quiet note, 'Perfectly. Still—I am no doxy—and you, Lord Fox, should treat me with more courtesy and respect.'

'Courtesy and respect have to be earned,' he told her, satisfied by the lowering of her eyes and the droop to her soft bottom lip that she was adequately chastened.

'I confess that when I saw you in the Strand yesterday I mistook you for a female of a very different kind—which was why I did what I did,' he continued. When she made a move to carry on walking he took her arm once more and forced her to stand in front of him. 'Come here—and stop dancing about,' he said when she yanked her arm free and glared at him, mutiny returning to her dark eyes. 'Don't worry, I'm not going to kiss you again,' he told her drily, producing a handkerchief. 'You have blood on your chin. You don't want to face Thomas looking like you've been in battle, otherwise he will assume the worst.'

After placing the handkerchief to his lips and wetting it, he proceeded to rub Will Price's dried blood off her chin none too gently, aware of the effort it was costing her to stand there and let him. When the task was completed his generous, laughing mouth broadened into a lazy smile. 'I'm flattered you found the kiss *I* gave you more to your liking and did not feel the need to retaliate so cruelly.'

'Why, you conceited, overbearing—' She clamped her lips together in frustrated rage at the mockery playing in his gypsy eyes.

Lucas arched a sleek black brow. 'I know. Infuriating, isn't it? I have also been accused of being arrogant, ill bred and domineering. But I can be reasonable, polite and well mannered when the mood takes me,' he said agreeably, gazing down at her lovely, rebellious face. 'In fact, I can be rather nice on occasion.'

Prudence was thrown off guard by his unexpected gentleness. But then, with her meagre knowledge of men, she never did know what to expect from them. 'Did you mean it when you said that when you first saw me yesterday, you mistook me for a woman of a different kind?' she asked quietly.

Lucas studied her impassively for a long, silent moment, reading her perfectly correctly and sensing that this bothered her. 'No. That was unfair of me,' he said softly. 'Would you really like to know what I saw when I looked at you yesterday?'

She nodded, gazing up at him silently.

'I saw a lovely young woman with vibrant chestnut curls, wonderful eyes the colour of amethysts, and the smile of an angel. I will also tell you that you have an appeal—I can feel it. You have a fire burning inside you—and I find you the most enchanting creature I have seen in a long time. There is a freshness and warmth about you I find fascinating—in fact, you, my dear Mistress Fairworthy, are a veritable treasure trove of entrancing contrasts.'

'But I didn't know that was how people would see me,' she said, her voice a husky whisper, feeling utterly confused and miserable, not wanting to be any of those things if it made men behave towards her as he had yesterday and Will Price had done today. She swallowed and looked away, her glorious dark eyes sparkling with suppressed tears, shining with the pain his words had caused her. 'If I am like that I can't help it. But I don't want to be. There—there must be something wrong with me. It's nothing to be proud of.'

Lucas took her chin gently between his finger and thumb, giving it a small shake to bring her gaze up to his once more, and he looked with deep regard into the unwavering depths of her eyes. 'Let me assure you that there is definitely nothing wrong with you. I was paying you a compliment. You are a lovely, desirable young woman. It is hardly strange if the young blades find it hard to conceal their interest. You should be flattered by their attention rather than angry.'

Prudence stared at him in confusion, hardly able to believe the words he spoke or what she saw. Lord Fox's eyes were full of warmth, and he was smiling at her with gentle understanding. 'But how can I be flattered when it makes them behave like you did yesterday—and Will Price? It will bring me nothing but trouble.'

Realising just how hopelessly naïve and truly innocent she was, that she was unsullied and still a child in many aspects, Lucas sighed deeply. 'No, it won't. You might even begin to enjoy it. You can't change what you are,' he told her, envying the man who would one day unleash in her the sensual and passionate woman he knew she would be, 'so you might as well make peace with it.'

'Like you do, you mean,' Prudence said, startled by the gentle caress in his voice and feeling the need to lash out defensively when she felt herself weakening, 'by kissing every woman you meet?'

Lucas smiled ruefully, tracing his forefinger along the satin soft curve of her jaw. 'I don't. But if I did I wouldn't hate myself for it.'

The tips of his fingers on her cheek, and the deep, compelling timbre of his voice, were beginning to have a strange, seductive impact on Prudence's senses. Tingles of apprehensive excitement danced along her nerves.

Lucas studied her with heavy-lidded speculation, his gaze dropping to her soft lips and lingering on her mouth for a long moment before he slowly lifted his eyes to hers. 'I was right, wasn't I—last night—when I said you have never been kissed before.'

'Yes,' she confessed weakly.

'I knew it.'

Prudence tilted her head on one side, frowning up at him. 'How could you tell? Was I very bad?' she asked candidly.

Lucas's eyes were suddenly full of mirth, but he strove to keep a straight face to answer her question, which she had asked with the open curiosity of a child. 'No. In fact with a little practice you could become perfect. I—could show you how it's done. You will find me an excellent teacher,' he said, wanting more than anything to show her there and then, to kiss her until he had her clinging to him and melting with desire.

Prudence snapped her head up. His words and their meaning brought her spirits plummeting back to earth. 'Don't you dare touch me. I do not require lessons from the likes of you.'

'Are you not just a little bit curious to know how it feels to be kissed?'

'I do.'

'Properly, I mean.'

Prudence swallowed convulsively, heat coursing through her veins when she recalled how, yesterday, his mouth had taken full possession of her lips like a hot tidal wave that had almost swept her away. He had shown her how a kiss could be between a man and woman, and to pretend that she had not enjoyed the experience would be a lie. But under no circumstances would she allow him to kiss her again. It was unthinkable. Besides, that came under the category of abandonment and wantonness, which she must staunchly guard against where he was concerned. He was dangerous, and she knew there were not many women who could resist a virile man like him. Not when he was over

six feet tall, lean and muscular, with hair as black as jet
and as shiny as silk, and a face as handsome as a storybook
hero.

'No,' she said in answer to his question. 'Besides, I've
had enough kissing during the last twenty-four hours to last
me a lifetime—and if you must know, if that's all there is
to it then I can't see what all the fuss is about.'

Lucas quelled his shout of laughter, but with mirth
gleaming in his eyes he took her arm and walked on, shaking his head in disbelief at the absolute naïvety of this girl.

As they walked along Prudence glanced up at him tentatively. 'Was Thomas very angry?'

'I would be lying if I said he wasn't.'

She sighed deeply, mortified that she had thoughtlessly
left the house unaccompanied and without telling anyone
where she was going, rousing Thomas to such a rage when
he hadn't been in the house twenty-four hours. She looked
at Lord Fox with mute appeal, the prospect of facing her
brother's wrath nerve-shattering. She decided there might
be much to be gained if she were to appeal to her companion's better nature.

'Do you have to take me to Thomas? Can you not say
you couldn't find me?' she wheedled. 'When I appear I
could say I had been in the courtyard all the time.'

Lucas's handsome mouth twitched in a smile. 'And for
this could I expect some kind of reward?'

'If you like. I would accept your apology for making a
spectacle of me yesterday,' she offered magnanimously.

He frowned. 'Is that all? Your generosity astounds me.
I would call that a bribe. However, that is not enough to
tempt me, Mistress Fairworthy. It will take more—much
more than that,' he murmured, his eyes resting on the soft
swelling of her breasts where the low-cut gown revealed
the mysterious little valley between them.

Angrily aware of what his words and his look implied,
instinctively Prudence put up her hands, wishing she'd had
the presence of mind to bring her shawl. 'You will get

nothing more from me, Lord Fox,' she uttered scathingly. 'You can go to the devil for all I care.'

He laughed at that, throwing back his head and letting his laughter ring out to resound off the buildings in the narrow street, causing passers by to glance curiously in their direction. 'I probably will, Mistress Fairworthy,' he chuckled. 'But only when I'm ready. Now come along,' he said bracingly, stepping into the Strand, which was now congested with pedestrians and traffic. 'Better get it over with.'

The amusement in his voice made Prudence's blood boil. Tossing her head, she walked on ahead of him, biting back the angry words that tempted her lips. With a wolfish grin Lucas took his horse's bridle and followed, boldly admiring the gentle sway of her hips and the way her hair danced when she walked.

When they reached Maitland House Lucas went towards the kitchen to beg refreshment, but before he entered he turned and looked back at Prudence, seeing her—slender shoulders squared and head high—bravely enter the parlour to face her brother alone.

There was a charmed timelessness about the attractive village of Marlden Green, huddled around the little church. A wide stream, spanned by a humped-backed bridge, tumbled through its centre. With its timber-framed cottages, their first storeys jettied and hung with scalloped tiles, Marlden Green, once a Saxon settlement, was in the south of the Surrey Weald. The county had been secured for Parliament throughout the Civil War and had seen very little fighting.

Willow House, where the Fairworthys had lived for generations, stood away from the village down a leafy lane, a lane little used by anyone unless they were going to the house, and after months of disuse it was so overgrown that it was hard to believe there was anything at the end of it. When the coach passed through the tall wrought-iron gates and lurched to a stop at the bottom of a low flight of stone steps, Prudence stared at her home with brimming eyes. The windows of the large, rose-brick manor house were shuttered and a profound quiet and sadness hung over the place like a shroud, but for the three people inside the coach this was home.

Thomas had last seen it in '51, before he had gone to join the young King Charles at Worcester—the last battle of the Civil War, which had ended in defeat for the Royalists, and sent the survivors into almost ten long years of exile.

Memories came flooding back to all three of them of happier days, but they had been followed by years of hardship, when everything of value the Fairworthys owned had either gone to fund the King's coffers, pay off the creditors, or pay the fines imposed on them by Parliament. Though Willow House was still standing, it had not escaped the years of deprivation of its fields, the selling off of land and livestock, and other losses which had once kept the family in luxury.

When Arabella and Thomas entered the house, Prudence paused to let her eyes wander over the once well-kept garden, her heart wrenching at the rampant neglect. Withered stalks bearing last year's dead blooms were sad reminders of what she had missed. The rose bower where she had once sat on a summer's evening with Arabella and their father was overgrown, and the knot garden and box hedges unclipped, but beneath the tangle of weeds, vibrant orange marigolds peeked out cheekily, and a bank of purple rhododendrons, separating the kitchen garden from the rose garden, bloomed beautifully in open defiance.

Prudence sighed, thinking of the packets of seeds and cuttings she had carefully taken and raised which she had brought with her from London, knowing she was going to have her work cut out returning the garden to its former glory. But its fragrance smelled like home and the thought of getting to work filled her with joy, which added a light

skip to her step when she entered the black-and-white che-
quered hall of Willow House.

Arabella went from room to room, while Thomas threw
wide the shutters to let in the light, the clatter piercing the
stillness of the house. Prudence trailed her fingers through
the dust that covered the furniture. Brasses were tarnished
and there was the smell of mildew, but above it all was the
lingering aroma of her father's tobacco, which he had loved
to smoke after supper in his long-stemmed pipe.

Mr Trimble had kept his eye on the house and everything
was just as Arabella and Prudence had left it when they
had gone to London a year ago to live with Aunt Julia. Ned
Trimble, who had married a local girl and produced two
fine sons, had a dwelling in keeping with his position as
the Fairworthys bailiff and farm manager. Out of loyalty to
the Fairworthys and hoping for better times, Ned and his
family had stayed at Marlden Green. In any case it was
their home and they had nowhere else to go.

'There's so much to be done,' Arabella said, standing in
the centre of the kitchen with her hands on her hips, her
eyes surveying the large range where so many of the family's meals had been cooked in the past. 'We must get some
fires going and air the beds before we do anything else.
But dear me—it will cost us a fortune to set this place to
rights.'

'We are not destitute,' said Thomas, having followed her
into the kitchen. 'While we have been absent the tenants
have gone about their labours as usual and Ned has collected the rents. Nor did I spend my time in idleness on the
Continent.'

Arabella knew this to be true and she was proud of him.
To relieve the boredom of Court life he had fought under
both the French and Spanish flags, and to his credit he had
often sent money home. 'I know you didn't, Thomas, and
please don't think that I'm complaining. But we must employ workmen to repair the roof and paint the house—not

to mention a couple of servants and a cook, and eventually a housekeeper.'

Thomas came to stand beside her, placing an arm fondly about her slender shoulders. 'We'll take care of that to-morrow. The main thing is that we're home, all three of us, and for that we must be thankful. I'm only sorry Verity isn't here to share the moment—and that Father didn't live to see the King return to his throne.'

'I know. But he never lost faith that he would one day.'

'Robert spoke to me before we left London, Arabella. He told me that the two of you hope to wed in the autumn. Is that so?'

'Yes. But I don't intend leaving Marlden Green until things are back to normal here—and until Verity has ar-rived from The Hague. I'm so looking forward to meeting her, Thomas, and it's such a comfort knowing there will be another woman in the house when I leave. Because Rob-ert's law practice is in London, that is where we will live. But that doesn't mean to say I won't get down to see you all often.'

'I know.' Thomas gave her an affectionate squeeze be-fore crossing to the window and looking out at the garden, watching Prudence as she walked along a path, carefully inspecting every tree and shrub.

'At least we have our own resident gardener,' he chuck-led softly. 'Prudence will certainly take care of that side of things. I'll have a word with Ned and arrange for his sons to give her a hand with the heavy work. Economy must be the rule for some time. With haytime almost upon us it is important that we get the home farm up and running. That must be a priority. I know Ned has kept the fields cleared, and I sent him the means with which to buy seed to plant in the spring.'

'I know. Ned always kept me informed about what he was doing.'

'Because the income from the rents was insufficient to meet the fines imposed on Father by Parliament, I am aware

that before he died he sold some land to George Fox. I
must say that I deeply regret the sale of those fifty acres of
prime pasture by the river. We could do with them when
we begin buying stock.'

When he fell silent, after a moment Arabella came to
stand beside him. 'Have you given any more thought to
finding Prudence a suitor, Thomas?'

'Not much, but I will—when we are on our feet and
Verity has arrived.'

The poignancy of being back at Marlden Hall was almost
beyond bearing for Lucas as he entered the lofty hall of the
house where he had been born. An aching nostalgia swelled
inside him when he remembered years past, years before
the Civil War which had ripped the country and families
apart, when he had lived here as a child and then a youth
with his parents. He could still hear his father's voice, hear
his mother's gentle laughter, smell her elusive perfume.

When news of his father's death at Marston Moor back
in '44 had reached them at Marlden Hall, his mother had
never got over it and had died three years later. Lucas still
felt the aching wrench of their loss. He had been twenty
years old when he'd gone to join the King at Worcester in
'51, and after the Royalist defeat he had escaped to France
and had not returned to Marlden Hall until this day.

His eyes cold, his face impassive, Lucas watched his
uncle descend the grand staircase somewhat awkwardly.

His manner resentful and not engaging, slight of stature,
with narrow shoulders and fragile frame, at fifty-eight
George Fox looked a good deal older. His hair was sparse
and grey, his expression ascetic as his cold eyes, expressing
his dislike, became fixed on those of his nephew. The plain-
ness of his garb contrasted sharply to the flamboyance of
Lucas's own.

'So,' George said when he reached the foot of the stairs,
disadvantaged and resentful of the younger man's superior,
intimidating height. For obvious reasons his manner was

unwelcoming. He was also feeling out of sorts today. His gout was bad again, and he knew it would be a good deal worse before he reached London. 'You have come to claim what is yours, Lucas. I was surprised when it was brought to my notice that you returned to England with Charles Stuart. Word reached me some time ago that you were dead.'

'Then I am sorry to disappoint you, Uncle. 'Twas a rumour, nothing more—and both you and I know that Jeffrey was behind it. As you see…I am very much alive,' Lucas drawled. 'And I aim to stay that way.' He almost followed up his words by saying, Despite my cousin's obsession to get rid of me, but kept his silence.

Jeffrey Fox captained his own vessel on the high seas. Lucas did not believe his uncle knew much about his son's activities—that he and his crew were more interested in buccaneering than privateering, and that he himself had fallen prey to his viciousness. Nor did he intend telling his uncle or wasting his time maligning Jeffrey. No doubt he would find out soon enough the true nature of the scoundrel he had sired. Sooner or later Jeffrey would become a victim of his own ruthlessness and greed. He would meet his end either at the point of a blade or at the end of a rope.

'Exile has not treated you harshly, I see,' George said, having taken note of his nephew's fine physique and expensive garb, and the enormous ruby flashing on his finger like fire. He did little to conceal the grudging note in his voice. 'You look well—if a little older.'

'We all are,' Lucas countered with equal discourtesy, as his blistering gaze sliced over his uncle.

'I will not embarrass you by remaining at Marlden Hall any longer. As you can see, I am on the point of leaving,' the older man said, his voice hard and angry, indicating the trunks and baggage stacked near the door, ready to be loaded on to the coach which would take him to London.

'Far be it from me to detain you,' Lucas said drily, the

hate between them seeming to vibrate in the intense atmosphere. 'Do not appeal to me for an extension of stay.'

'Since I can no longer dispute your authority to be in this house I intend to leave within the hour. You will find everything in good order. The silver is still intact—nothing sold—or stolen,' George told him, his thin lips twisting with sarcasm. He bent closer and said savagely, 'Consider yourself fortunate that it was I who came to Marlden Hall when Charles Stuart dragged himself off into exile to lick his wounds. Anyone else would not have been so considerate.'

Lucas raked his uncle with a scornful glance and his drawl became clipped and abrupt. 'Considerate to whom, Uncle? You or I? None the less, despite your words to the contrary, no doubt you have had sufficient time to feather the nest you intend to retire to at my expense.' The glare his uncle gave him told him that this was indeed the case.

'You thought me dead, remember,' Lucas continued, 'and you, being my heir, considered the estate to be yours. How disappointing it must have been for you to find me still alive and well. But long before that—after Worcester, in fact—you sought to obtain premature ownership of my sequestered property by appealing to Cromwell—whom you went to great pains to insinuate yourself with by all accounts—and having it signed over to you by him personally.'

Turning, he strolled across the hall with long, purposeful strides, as cool and casual as any gentleman paying a call on another. Running his fingers over a magnificently carved table, his eyes did a slow sweep of all the familiar objects surrounding him. 'Where are you going?'

'I cannot rejoice in the return of Charles Stuart so I am leaving England. Jeffrey's ship is expected in the Pool at any time. When he sails I shall sail with him.'

Recalling the attack on his own person on the night of his return to England, all Lucas's senses became alert, but he gave no indication how much this information interested him. Mockingly he arched an eyebrow. 'Are you afraid, Uncle?' he jeered smoothly. 'You should be. The King has agreed to pardon all those of conscience who appeal for his grace and favour. A generous action, don't you agree?'

The flicker of hope that kindled in George's eyes was doused by his nephew's next words.

'However,' Lucas went on, his features relentless as he strolled back towards his uncle, the eyes he settled on him filled with a combination of accusation and icy condemnation, 'it does not extend to those who murdered his father—the forty-one men who put their name to that infamous death warrant. Your name might not have been one of them, but it is no secret that your support of that dastardly crime was profound. So you are wise to run, before you see the writing on the wall for yourself,' he added with deliberate cruelty, resisting an almost uncontrollable urge to murder this man, his father's brother, for his treachery towards his King and his family.

Chapter Five

After six weeks things began to take shape at Willow House and the Fairworthys settled down to a regular routine. Carpets were cleaned and rooms aired, dusted and perfumed. Workmen were deployed to work on the roof and the house, both inside and out. Thomas was constantly busy with Ned on the land, and Arabella, adept at managing work and money and the two women employed from the village to do menial tasks, worked wonders.

When Prudence wasn't needed, she was to be found in the garden doing most of the work herself, although she was glad when Ned's sons, Simon and John—two strapping youths of sixteen and fourteen respectively—came to give her a hand with the heavy work of clearing beds and borders and pruning overgrown trees and shrubs.

It was early one afternoon when they had their first visitor. A warm, gentle breeze ruffled the orange blossom and the sky was clear blue, the garden where Prudence worked offering a splendid view across to the woods and water meadows. With a kerchief covering her unruly hair she knelt on a small mat, with ruthless determination attacking a large tangle of weeds that were choking the marigolds. Thomas was with Ned somewhere and Arabella had walked into the village to see their old housekeeper in the hope that she could be persuaded to return.

Out of the corner of her eye Prudence saw a horse and rider come through the gates and ride up the path towards the house. Assuming it was Thomas and with her mind preoccupied with thoughts of Adam—even though she had accepted that any romantic dreams she had once cherished where he was concerned could come to nothing—she carried on working, uncaring that her hands were chafed and soiled as she struggled to dig out a particularly stubborn dandelion root.

When a shadow fell over her she paused, sitting back on her heels and looking up. It was Lord Fox; having dismounted and secured his horse, he was now drawing off his riding gloves. Immediately there was a resurgence in her of that awareness of the magnetism that had so affected her when she had seen him for the first time in the procession in the Strand, and then again when he had approached her in the courtyard at Maitland House. She had thought at first that it was the surprise and shock of suddenly seeing him, but now she knew it was more than that.

She hadn't laid eyes on him since that awful day in London, when he had rescued her from Will Price's odious advances and taken her back to Maitland House, where she had been given a severe dressing down by Thomas—it was an encounter she still hadn't recovered from. Lord Fox seemed preoccupied, flexing his fingers as if they were stiff.

Before Prudence had realised he was there, Lucas's eyes had passed with warm admiration over her shapely figure as she worked. She had rolled up the sleeves of her dress and the breeze teased the curling tendrils of hair that had escaped the confines of the kerchief. Intent on her labour his presence did not distract her from her task, so he took the opportunity to look his fill, noting how the bodice of her dress was stretched tight across her slender shoulders and back as she reached forward. He had ridden from Marlden Hall to see Thomas, and he was pleasantly surprised to meet Prudence again, whom he had often thought of since their last encounter.

With the sun at his back Prudence had to squint to see him better. He was bareheaded, the sunlight gleaming on his black hair. After years of people wearing drab clothes, it was a joy to see the Cavaliers still delighted in extravagant attire. With lace at his throat and wearing a maroon velvet jacket, Prudence noted that across his chest Lord Fox wore a sword band encrusted with jewels, which caught and flashed in the sun.

She recalled Thomas telling her how his friend had travelled extensively throughout the East during his years in exile, and for some reason it made her think of the glitter and shimmer of the Orient, of exotic smells, palm trees and deep blue seas. She gazed at the jewels with envy, thinking that just one would buy her a pony to enable her to ride into Dorking to buy more seeds and plants for the garden.

It seemed to Prudence as if Lord Fox's eyes never left hers. His powerful, animal-like masculinity was an assault on her senses. She made no attempt to get up as he stood looking down at her, his expression serious.

'So, sweet Pru, here you are. I've been thinking of you,' Lucas said without preliminaries, gazing down at her glowing features upturned to his. Any other young woman caught with her hands soiled, her curls rebelliously escaping the confines of a haphazardly tied kerchief and her faded, simple saffron-coloured dress having seen better days, would have been distressed that he should be witness to her undignified chore, but not so Prudence Fairworthy. She clearly couldn't care less, which Lucas found quite endearing.

Prudence stared up at him in amazement, thinking it was a peculiar thing for him to say. 'What on earth for? Why should you occupy your thoughts with me? After our last encounter, I'd have thought I would be the last person you would want to think about.'

A crooked smile accompanied Lucas's reply. 'On the contrary. Once met, it is impossible to forget someone as lovely as you.' He spoke quietly and without the usual mocking irony in his tone.

Prudence was all astonishment. It was not only because he had paid her a compliment, but also because she had never thought of herself as anything other than passably pretty—and certainly not beautiful. It was the second time he had remarked on her appearance, and although there was nothing lavish about his compliment, it made her feel unaccountably shy. She found herself blushing under his frank scrutiny.

'Do you have to stare at me quite so hard, Lord Fox?'

'Let us dispense with formalities. My name is Lucas. Actually, I was admiring you. Now, are you going to stand up? Or perhaps you would prefer me to get down to your level.'

Knowing this exasperating man would do just that, and never wanting to be as close to him again as she had been when he'd lifted her on to his horse and soundly kissed her, Prudence put down her trowel. 'I'll stand up.' Without more ado she got to her feet, accepting the hand he placed under her elbow to assist her, her heart sinking when she heard her skirt rip when it caught on a thorn.

'Damn!' she exclaimed softly without thinking, bending down to examine the tear.

Lucas gazed at her. 'It was my fault for unsettling you.'

'You don't unsettle me in the least, Lord Fox,' she said, finding it difficult to address him by his given name as she casually brushed her skirt.

'I told you that my name is Lucas—and, yes, I do unsettle you. You are blushing.'

'I am not,' she retorted, wishing she wasn't wearing her old tight-fitting saffron dress which she should have discarded or altered to fit her fast-developing body a long time ago.

'Your face is delightfully pink,' he teased.

It was, she knew it, for she could feel the colour tinting her cheeks despite all her efforts to prevent it. She glowered at him, taking refuge in anger. 'Are you always so annoying?'

To her surprise he didn't rise to her barbs. In fact, he looked amused and grinned rakishly. 'Always. Infuriating, isn't it?'

'Very,' she replied stonily. Meeting his penetrating green-brown eyes flecked with gold, with reluctance she thought that he looked wonderfully appealing with the shiny black wave tumbling carelessly over his brow. Her pulses seemed to pound and she found her bravado was about to expire. 'If you have come to see Thomas then I'm afraid he isn't here.'

'I have, but I also have another reason for riding over.'

'You have?'

Lucas answered with a smile, a slow, lazy white smile that creased his tanned face and made her heart leap into her throat. 'Yes. I've come to invite the three of you to dine with me at Marlden Hall on Wednesday next.' His eyes watched her, waiting to observe her reaction to his next words. 'Others are invited—including Adam Lingard and his wife, who I believe is expected to arrive in Marlden Green with Verity any day now.'

Prudence encountered a feeling of unease at the thought of meeting Thomas's wife for the first time, knowing very little about her sister-in-law. She also felt her heart skip a beat at the mortifying recollection of how she had made a fool of herself by giving Adam the posy of flowers in the procession. Knowing how it must have looked to Lucas and that he had known all along that Adam was married, she felt herself drowning in humiliation for her stupidity and gullibility. 'Oh,' was all she said, praying he wouldn't refer to the incident.

Mercifully he didn't. Instead Lucas reached out and took her hands, frowning when he looked at the soil-blackened flesh and a small cut on her right palm oozing a trickle of blood. 'Such lovely hands deserve better treatment. Gloves would help,' he said, stating the obvious.

The touch of his hands reminded Prudence of their strength when they had held her chin during their last encounter. When it looked as if he would retain her hands she pulled them away. 'I know, but they're clumsy, and I find it difficult separating the plants from the weeds when I'm wearing them.'

'Nevertheless you should wear them. Should you be doing this?' Lucas asked, glancing with distaste at the pile of weeds she had pulled out of the flowerbed.

'Why not? You may find it odd, but it's where I like to be best. I happen to love flowers and watching things grow. I'm hoping it will not take too long before I return the garden to how it looked before I went away. John and Simon help me sometimes.'

'And who are they?'

'Mr Trimble's sons—he manages the farm for us.'

'Yes, I know—and his father before him. I haven't been away so long that I forget our neighbours. Anyone who remains steadfast in their loyalty to the King I never forget,' he said quietly. Absently he detached a piece of dried grass from her sleeve, his look curious. 'Don't you think gardening is an unnatural occupation for a female?'

Prudence bristled, offended that he should ask this, that he might think it and consider her some kind of freak. 'Unnatural? No, of course not. I have very simple tastes. I am quite content to live here as we do, with the farm, the cows and the sheep—when Thomas can afford to buy new stock, that is—and take care of the people we employ, people who have served us faithfully for many years. Do you find that unnatural?'

'On the contrary. I find it admirable. Can I do anything to help?'

'What? Dig the garden?'

His eyes gleamed with laughter. 'Perish the thought. I would never be able to hold up my head again among my friends. Gardening is definitely not my forte. But I do have several gardeners at Marlden Hall. I would be happy to send one of them over.'

His offer warmed her heart and brought a smile of gratitude to her lips. 'Thank you. You are more than generous, but I can manage. As you can see, we have much to do,' Prudence said when his eyes did a quick sweep of the weed-choked garden, the peeling paintwork on the house and some of the shutters hanging askew at the windows. 'The house has been neglected since my father died and Arabella and I went to live with Aunt Julia in London.'

Lucas's expression became grave and was one of sympathy. 'I knew your father and was deeply sorry to learn of his death. As you probably know, my own father died at Marston Moor.'

'Yes, I do know. Father was wounded at Edgehill back in '42, the year I was born. It was a battle bravely won when the Cavaliers routed the Roundheads, but sadly he never fully recovered from his wound and was unable to take part in any further action.'

'Are you glad to be home?'

'Yes, very much so. And you?' she asked civilly.

'After almost ten years I am more than happy to be back. I had affairs to settle in London before coming to Surrey. I arrived here last week.'

'And your uncle?'

'I'm afraid Uncle George found my unwelcome appearance to be in bad taste,' Lucas replied dryly, recalling the unpleasant scene between them when he'd arrived home. 'He thought I was dead, you see, and had already settled down to a lifetime of ease at Marlden Hall—until he learned that I had arrived in England with King Charles.'

Prudence tipped her head to one side, looking up at him curiously. 'But why did he think you were dead?'

'It's a long story—one I will not bore you with just now,' he said, wondering how this naïve young woman would react if he told her how he had spent the last five years of his life. 'It was unfortunate that he and my father were on opposing sides throughout the Civil War. When the War was over, Marlden Hall and everything in it went to him for loyal service. He had the documents drawn up and signed by Cromwell himself to prove it. Ironic, really, since after myself Uncle George was—unless I married and provided an heir—next in line to inherit.'

Prudence had met George Fox when he had come to see her father to buy land, and she had found him to be a disagreeable man. He had one son, Jeffrey, who had chosen to make his life at sea. He was a man she had never met and knew very little about, only that people who had met him said he was pleasing to look at.

Because Lucas looked in no hurry to leave, common courtesy required she ask him to take refreshment. Besides, it was a hot afternoon and his home was a three-mile ride away. 'Can I offer you refreshment—lemonade, perhaps?' she asked hesitantly, carefully concealing her reluctance and hoping he would refuse…but knowing he wouldn't.

Lucas readily accepted her offer. Together they climbed some broad steps and walked along a tree-shaded beguiling path that meandered up to the house. Prudence showed him into the parlour.

'Excuse me. I'll go and wash my hands and pour some lemonade.'

She entered the kitchen, a cheerful room, with its lime-washed walls and brightly burning fire reflected in brass and copper pans, and pots of colourful nosegays standing on the windowsills to deter the flies. She quickly washed her hands and poured two glasses of lemonade from a huge earthenware pitcher Arabella had left to keep cool on the stone slab in the pantry, surprised when she turned round to find Lucas had followed her.

'Oh!' she gasped, almost bumping into the table to avoid him. 'You startled me.'

'I didn't mean to.' He took the glass from her out-stretched hand and looked around the kitchen with a quizzical expression on his face. 'The house seems quiet. Where is everyone?' he asked.

'Thomas is inspecting the fields down by the river and Arabella is visiting a friend in the village—but she will not be long,' Prudence told him in a rush, not knowing why she didn't want him to know that she was alone in the house, but for some reason she did.

'And your housekeeper and the servants?'

'Arabella hasn't appointed a housekeeper yet—that is to say, she might have,' Prudence corrected herself. 'That is where she is just now, you see—hoping to persuade our old housekeeper, Mrs Weatherill, to return. The servants, having finished their work for the afternoon, have gone home to visit their families.'

There was a childlike defencelessness in the way she said this and Lucas smiled slowly, his gaze capturing hers, an interested gleam glowing like fire in his eyes. 'Really? So, sweet Pru, I find you all alone?'

His voice was deep and seductive, like soft velvet—a voice that made one think of highly improper things. Prudence felt her face grow hot beneath his piercing stare, not liking his overly familiar use and shortening of her name which he seemed to be intent on doing. 'I—yes,' she murmured, lowering her eyes to hide her confusion and carrying her glass through to the parlour where she had originally left him. He followed her, like a panther stalking its prey, she thought nervously. Putting her glass down on the table, she turned and faced him, disconcerted to find him standing so close, the thought that he might take advantage of her being alone and kissing her rising to alarming prominence in her mind. But she need not have worried, for Lucas had no intention of doing anything that might earn him a rebuff.

He strolled across to the window and lifted his glass, looking at Prudence over the rim. He seemed deep in thought, as if he were turning a matter over in his mind that was of the utmost importance. He sipped slowly, savouring the lemonade as though it were the finest wine, gazing at her all the while with those seductive eyes of his. Prudence felt the power and provocation of that gaze and became extremely uncomfortable, beginning to wish she hadn't invited him in. His stance was leisurely and relaxed, and yet Prudence had the distinct feeling that beneath his relaxed exterior there was a carefully restrained forcefulness and power, and that if anyone should make a wrong move he would unleash that power to devastating effect.

'Do you usually invite men into the house when you are alone? Don't you consider it improper and that you risk soiling your reputation?' Lucas said, his face reflecting neither reproach nor condemnation, but Prudence gasped indignantly, no longer feeling any obligation to be courteous.

'No, I do not, and please do not misunderstand my reasons for doing so. I only invited you into the house because you are not just any man. You are known to me and you and Thomas are close friends. It would have been discourteous of me not to, but now I realise I was mad to do so,' Prudence flared. Just when she was on the point of ordering him out of the house, to her chagrin she saw he was on the verge of laughter.

Lucas gentled his voice as he crossed towards her. 'No, you weren't—and I was not criticising you. I'm glad you invited me in and gave me refreshment. I am grateful— truly. The day is uncomfortably warm and I have ridden some distance.' Quickly he drank the remainder of his lemonade and put the glass down. 'Thank you,' he said with impeccable courtesy.

All of a sudden Prudence was uncomfortably aware of how close he was, of the raw sensuality emanating from his tall, muscular frame, seeming larger in the small room. A tremor ran over her as his gaze moved slowly over her face, lingering on the inviting fullness of her lips.

Her face was a mirror of lovely confusion; taking pity on her innocence, Lucas gently traced his finger over the curve of her cheek, glad when she didn't draw back. His expression was soft as he gazed down into her melting amethyst eyes.

'My God, you are so sweet,' he murmured. 'You remind me of a wild flower, one that grows in the meadows and spreads at will. Uproot it and transplant it and it will wither and die.'

Prudence stared at him, thinking it was a strange thing for him to say and that he was talking to himself rather than to her. But his words touched an inner chord, for there was truth in what he said. Suddenly his manner changed. He frowned, a deep furrow above the bridge of his nose, and she could hardly believe her eyes when he suddenly turned and strode coolly towards the door. He looked back to where she stood.

'Do you ride?'

'Yes—I do. Why do you ask?'

'I'm going to find Thomas. Would you care to accompany me?'

'I—I'm afraid I can't,' she replied, surprised by the disappointment she felt at not being able to take up his offer. 'As yet we only have two horses here at Willow House. Thomas has one and Ned the other.'

Lucas nodded. 'Some other time, then?'

'Yes.'

Prudence watched him ride away, bemused by their meeting and prey to all the emotions he had aroused churning inside her. She could appreciate his virile good looks, his seductive scamp's eyes and sensual mouth, but that was where it must end, she told herself severely, and she sincerely hoped he was not going to fall into the habit of dropping in at Willow House whenever the fancy took him.

But then again, she mused, as she knelt on her mat to attack the offending dandelion root once more, pausing a moment and staring into space as she remembered how his expression had softened and he had looked at her with unbearable gentleness and traced the curve of her cheek just a moment ago, and how the simple touch had sent her emotions to war so fiercely inside of her that for one second, she had actually considered turning her lips into the palm of his hand.

She thought about their encounters, feeling a rush of righteous indignation when she recalled how he had followed her to Mr Rowan's nursery and reprimanded her for going there unaccompanied, but it dwindled away when she realised that she'd deserved it. A pink flush stained her cheeks as she also recalled how passionate his kiss had been on their first encounter, and the flush deepened when she remembered how angry and desolate she'd felt when his arms had released her. Picking up her spade, she sank it into the soft earth, utterly bewildered by her thoughts and feelings. She reminded herself that Lucas Fox might be the most handsome, exciting man she had ever met, but then she told herself that he was too conceited, too self-assured by far. He was both these things and more, and she must keep reminding herself of this, so that she could keep the fires of resentment alive.

But did she want to? She sighed unhappily, sitting back on her heels and shaking her head. She didn't know that, either. The more she delved into the exact nature of her feelings for Lucas Fox, the more confused she became, but feeling the way she did, it not only seemed silly, but wrong to go on resenting him. And why should she? Apart from kissing her on their first encounter—which she now knew had drawn the envy of every woman who had witnessed the incident—he had done nothing to deserve her bitterness and animosity.

Prudence would have been extremely perturbed had she been given an insight into Lucas's thoughts as he rode to find Thomas. Having met her again, he was finding that she wasn't easily dismissed.

Prudence Fairworthy was a natural temptress. Alluring and lovely, entrancing—and untouched. He found her virginal innocence strangely disturbing. The appeal of this young woman who was a virtual stranger to him he found hard to explain. Since returning to Marlden Hall he had seriously begun to consider marriage, and whenever he tried to think of a suitable candidate it was Prudence Fairworthy's image that lingered the longest in his mind's eye. Proud, wilful and undisciplined she might be, he admitted to himself, but she was also too lovely for comfort. She projected a tangible magic aura, and he could almost feel her vibrant inner energy and appetite for life. Her beauty in her home setting had fed his gaze and created a warm, hungering ache that would not be easily appeased by anything less than what he desired.

He did not pause to understand the reasons for what he was about to do. He wanted her, and that was reason enough. Little had he known when he'd embarked upon his journey from Marlden Hall to invite Thomas and his family to dine with him, that his visit would gain a dual purpose, for what he intended for Prudence was a much grander and more permanent coupling than a brief tumble between the sheets. He had never found anyone he wanted to share his life with until now, and that, combined with all Prudence Fairworthy's aforesaid characteristics, permitted him to make his decision.

It did occur to him that she might oppose him, but vainly assured of his own ability to lure her into his arms, into his bed, that did not worry him unduly. But, with a wisdom born of experience, he realised he would have to tread with caution. He did not want her to rebel and oppose him too fiercely, and he suspected that, if he presented his suit too soon, she would become as determined not to accept him as he was to have her. He would approach Thomas and offer marriage to his sister with typical speed and resolve, and take it from there.

Lucas laughed softly. Playing court to Prudence would be like paying court to a powder keg, in which case he must keep the arrangement secret until he had won her over, which shouldn't be too difficult once he'd secured

Thomas's blessing. But he was determined not to take too long. To fawn upon a woman in order to obtain her affection could prove to be a dastardly dull game.

Lucas found Thomas riding alone in the lush green water meadows, interlaced by a network of silvery streams of the winding river, where moorhens and swans were gliding gracefully between the rushes and birds hovered overhead. The two friends greeted each other warmly, and as they rode companionably together beneath the wide expanse of blue sky, they talked of friends and politics, of London and the King, before falling silent.

Rather like holding a carrot out to a donkey, Lucas purposely led Thomas over the land that had once belonged to the Fairworthys. He watched with interest as his friend's eyes did a slow sweep of the meadows, poignant memories of his family's own sheep and cattle grazing on the lush green grass evident in their depths. Lucas smiled faintly, feeling that the moment was right for him to put his plan to marry Prudence into reality. But he had not forgotten that on the eve of their arrival in London, Thomas had warned him to stay away from his sister. Lucas had promised him that where she was concerned he would behave himself, and in that he had been sincere.

Nevertheless, without false modesty, Lucas knew that when his friend realised that his intentions where his sister was concerned were strictly honourable, and never a man to turn away a bargain—be it in a matter of business or his sister's future—Thomas would listen to what he had to say and consider his suit fairly.

'I have a bargain to put to you,' he said quietly when they had paused their horses beneath the dappled shade of a leafy willow, looking at the panoramic view spread out before them.

Lucas had captured Thomas's attention. 'Then let me hear it.'

'This land meant a great deal to your family, didn't it, Thomas?'

'It did. As you know, it's prime pasture. I deeply regret that my father selected this particular stretch of land to sell to your uncle.'

'I've no doubt my uncle left him with little choice,' Lucas told him drily.

'I know. At the time, when money was desperately needed to pay the fines imposed on him by Parliament, Father was unable to draw on his long-held business assets—both here and in the New World—which was why he had to resort to selling several of his precious acres.'

'I am prepared to return to you all the land your father sold to Uncle George, Thomas—but it comes with a price.'

'I expect it does,' Thomas chuckled. 'But you'll have to wait. At present my financial situation does not extend to buying land.'

'I cannot believe you are so poor. Rents and income from your land are still provided.'

'That's true, but it comes in at a trickle. When my situation improves I want to increase my investments in the business ventures my father invested in before the Interregnum—so you see, Lucas, anything else will have to wait.'

'You will succeed. You have an intelligence and flare for business that will guarantee the prosperity for future generations of Fairworthys. But I can't wait, Thomas, and the price I would ask for this particular piece of land is not of the monetary kind.'

Thomas's curiosity was aroused. 'Oh? I'm interested. Enlighten me. What can I possibly give you that will compensate for the land?'

'Prudence.'

Thomas was unable to conceal his shock. 'Prudence? You want Prudence?'

'I will be willing to part with the land if you would allow me to court her with a view to marriage.'

'But why Prudence? Forgive me if I appear stunned by

what you ask, but you have known so many women that I cannot for the life of me imagine why you would want to wed Prudence.'

'I admit to having known many women, which is why I know I am choosing the right one to be my wife. I know this is sudden—indeed, 'tis so sudden that even I am quite astonished, for until I met her again a short while ago at Willow House I had no thought of marriage in mind—but Prudence is perfect. What I have to offer is worth your consideration, Thomas. I am an eligible man in the marriage market. I am not ancient, I am healthy and in possession of all my teeth. In fact, my merits are so impressive I surprise myself,' he joked.

'And you want my sister.'

'I do.'

'But Prudence is still a girl, Lucas.'

'If you think that then your eyesight is sadly impaired, Thomas,' Lucas said, giving him a brief, humourless smile. 'Your sister is a beauty—a rare jewel and quite unique.'

'That I do know. She is also a match for any man and accomplished in many things. Arabella has taught her how a house should be run, and she tells me that Prudence rides well, that she is conversant on most subjects, plays the virginals like an angel, and also turns a pretty foot in the dance. When I said she is a child, what I really meant was that she is a child compared to your age and vast experience with women.'

'I am twenty-nine and my experience with women is no greater than your own, Thomas.' His grin was rakish. 'Can I help it if women find me irresistible?' he joked. 'So tell me, what else do you have against me?'

'Your reputation for profligacy doesn't help matters.'

'Come now, you know that my reputation is not as bad as it has been painted. Not all my life has been devoted to the pursuit of pleasure—and certainly not during the last five years,' he said quietly, on a more serious note, which made Thomas glance at him searchingly. Lucas ignored the look and went on, 'I meant what I said when I told you that I am ready to marry and settle down, to spend the rest of my life with the woman of my choice, begetting children.'

'But why Prudence? Forgive me, Lucas, I applaud your taste, but I can't help thinking that if I were to consent to your proposal, it would be like feeding her to the wolves.'

'Do not underestimate your sister, Thomas. I strongly suspect that she has the courage to pit her will against any man—including me. I choose Prudence to be my wife, and in doing so I confess that I do not do so lightly. Despite all her accomplishments, which you were so quick to point out to me a moment ago, allow me to point out her deficiencies. I have not known her long, but on the occasions when we've met I have discovered that she has a temper. She has an unpredictable disposition, is hot-headed, wilful and rebellious, and will need gentling with a firm hand by the man she marries.'

Thomas agreed. 'That is our father's fault. Being the youngest she was his pet. He indulged her every whim and allowed her far too much freedom. Mother and I warned him—but he would only laugh and tell us not to worry, that his little Prudence would turn out to be so beautiful that no one would care how stubborn and wilful she was.' He cast an enquiring glance at his friend. 'And if I give my permission for you to marry her, do you intend to tame her wilful ways?'

Lucas saw Thomas's eyes were gleaming with wicked delight, as if unwilling to share some private joke. A smile tempted his lips. 'Nay, Thomas. 'Twould be a sin to tame such a prize. It is her spirit that I admire most in her. I intend to make her complaisant to my needs, but God help me if I do anything to change what's inside her. She is naïvety and innocence on the threshold of womanhood, and refreshingly virtuous—unhampered by caution or wisdom. Come, why do you quibble?'

'Because Arabella and I have discussed taking her to

London now the King has returned and presenting her at Court. I have no doubt at all that she will be a great success, with an abundance of admirers beating their way to my door.'

'And all of them impoverished,' Lucas countered truthfully. 'Why go to all that bother when I can offer her my name and an unassailable position in society? I am also willing to take her without a dowry. My desire to marry her was not inspired by thoughts of fortune. Come, Thomas, the matter could be over and done with, the land yours with your consent to a betrothal between your sister and myself and no one any the wiser for a few months— not even Prudence, for I suspect it will require considerable time and courtship to lure her into marriage with me. I have no wish to startle her by declaring my interest before she has developed a fondness for me.'

Lucas glanced across at his friend, who appeared deep in thought. Encouraged by Thomas's silence, he continued to press his suit. 'I am a wealthy man and prepared to settle any sum you care to name on Prudence. I promise you she will have no cause to complain as my wife. I shall not abuse her and will keep her as finely garbed as her beauty demands. Her life will be replete and I will give her every luxury in life within my power to grant her.'

Thomas looked at him gravely, aware that his friend was feared by his enemies for his formidable temper and rapier-sharp tongue, and that many people lived in fear of finding themselves on the wrong side of him. However, his courage on the field of battle, his intellect and dedication to duty and his friends, had earned him admiration from all who fought beside him.

Now his shock had passed, Thomas found himself warming to a match between his closest friend and his sister, a match that would unite the two families for all time. Furthermore, the Fox family was of old lineage and great landowners. Prudence had attractions enough to draw the attentions of dozens of returning Royalists but, in the way of the world, without money one must go abegging.

With Lucas's wealth Prudence would want for nothing—although as to what was the source of his wealth Thomas could only wonder. Owing to the funding of the war effort, Lucas had gone into exile as impoverished as every other Royalist, but when he had arrived at Breda after five years in the East, he had returned an extremely wealthy man. However, Thomas wondered with some trepidation how Prudence would react when she discovered what Lucas intended—with his blessing.

'You must want to marry her very much.'

'I do.'

'Then what can I say? I have no objections. You are probably the most stubborn, intractable human being I know, Lucas. You also have more character and substance than any man I know and, when you decide to be, you are the most loyal friend anyone could wish for. If Prudence is in agreement, she is yours with my blessing—and I could not be giving her to a finer man. I ask for nothing from you but the land, but you must realise that in the end the decision is hers to make. She is not easily persuaded. She also has some idealistic notions concerning marriage—and love plays a prominent part. I will not force her to marry you.'

Lucas looked at his friend with a combination of scepticism and absolute certainty. 'You won't have to.'

'You are too confident, Lucas. Prudence was precocious as a child—still is, for that matter—and no one was able to make her do anything she didn't want to do. From an early age she learned how to twist others round her little finger.' He chuckled deeply. 'I warn you to take care. You are in grave danger of becoming one of them. However, it has not escaped my notice that my little sister has developed an aversion to you that will not be easily appeased. She pushes you away like an offending plague.'

'I know. At present the plague and I are one and the same to her,' Lucas agreed on a note of irony.

'Yes, she is going to prove most unwilling. However,' Thomas said, quirking an amused brow at his friend, 'it will be interesting to see how you go about winning her over.'

'And succeeding,' Lucas replied, supremely confident that he would as he carefully disguised his delight that events were going his way. 'I shall woo her like her most ardent of suitors.'

'Not too ardent, I hope,' Thomas said pointedly. 'I have no wish to see you place Prudence in a situation where you will leave her with no choice but to marry you.'

'I shall strive to behave impeccably. And I shall start by doing so on Wednesday next when you and your wife and your charming sisters are to join my other guests at Marlden Hall. I am giving a supper party for the sole purpose of bringing a few of our neighbours together—those, like ourselves, who have recently returned from exile. Adam Lingard and Lucy are to attend.'

Thomas frowned suddenly. 'Knowing Prudence has a fondness for Adam, he could become a complication.'

'I don't see that. I'm not worried about him.'

'Then you should be. Compared to Prudence, Lucy is as plain as a pikestaff. Believe me, Lucas, if Adam weren't already married, now he has seen the change in my little sister, you would not be the only one pressing your suit. Still, she doesn't appear to be fretting and I hope she will soon overcome her infatuation, but there is no telling how she will react when she sees him again. It could prove awkward.'

A pair of cool green-brown eyes regarded him dispassionately. 'Which is why I want the meeting over and done with,' Lucas said in a tone that brooked no argument. 'I am aware that Prudence has taken a battering over this, that she is hurt and desperate to regain her pride, which she must be allowed to do with little fuss. I am prepared to be lenient. The sooner her youthful pursuit of Adam Lingard is over and she ceases to think of him in the romantic sense, the better it will be.'

Chapter Six

Thomas's wife arrived the following day. Having left her uncle in London with his sister, she travelled down to Marlden Green with Lucy and Adam, who had met them at Dover. Thomas collected Verity from Adam's home five miles away and brought her to Willow House.

Prudence was away visiting Mrs Trimble, and by the time she arrived home Verity had already made the acquaintance of Arabella and settled herself into her new home. Prudence became uneasily conscious of the woman who sat beside her brother, not knowing what to expect. Immediately the two of them rose and came towards her and Thomas introduced them.

'Why, Prudence. I am delighted to meet you at last,' Verity said, leaning forward and kissing her cheek, her lips barely touching her flesh.

'And I you,' Prudence murmured, sitting beside Arabella on the sofa when Thomas and Arabella resumed their seats. Studying her sister-in-law, she noticed a blankness in her eyes and that her smile was without warmth, which caused her to wonder what was taking place behind the cool exterior. She recognised an assertive person with nothing weak about her face, with her firm chin and the fine line of her brows. She was certainly attractive, with dark brown hair and eyes.

* * *

During the days that followed and she got to know her better, Prudence didn't know what to make of her, neither liking nor disliking her. Her manner was disconcertingly direct, and Prudence's impression was that behind the cool, serene exterior was a proud and obstinate woman. And yet she noticed how her features changed with every glance, every look, at her husband, which showed a love deeply felt.

But again Prudence felt a sense of unease, and she deeply suspected that Verity would not favour her presence at Willow House once Arabella was married.

From the moment Lord Fox had invited them to dine at Marlden Hall Prudence had been seeking frantically for an excuse not to go. She really didn't want to see Adam and his new wife, even though she knew she must eventually. She just felt that it was too soon, that it would be too humiliating, too painful. On the day she pleaded a headache and begged to be excused, which brought a concerned, suspicious glance from Arabella when she came to her room and noticed her glum face.

'But of course you must come with us, Prudence. I'll mix you one of my powders and you'll soon feel better.'

'Please don't make me go, Arabella,' Prudence implored on a note of desperation. 'I would much rather stay here.'

Arabella came towards her and studied her closely. 'What is it really, Prudence? What is the truth of why you do not wish to go to Marlden Hall?'

'I told you. I have a headache.'

'Oh, Prudence. Is it because Adam will be there? Is that the reason?' Arabella asked gently.

Prudence flushed, averting her eyes. The last thing she had wanted to do was admit to anyone that she'd been foolish enough to fall for a man who did not reciprocate her feelings, but it would seem that Arabella had worked it out for herself. 'Why on earth should my not wanting to go have anything to do with Adam?' she laughed nervously, trying to make light of her sister's question, but Arabella was not fooled.

'I think I know how you feel about him. I saw your face when you gave him the flowers in the procession.' She sighed at her sister's dejected demeanor. 'I have been extremely blind, Prudence. I should have seen it. I am right, aren't I?'

Prudence nodded miserably. 'Which is why I do not wish to face him. Oh, Arabella, I feel so stupid, so embarrassed.'

'Before Adam left for the Continent, did he give you any indication that he might feel the same?'

She shook her head.

'Well, then! If he didn't know, why be embarrassed about meeting him? You were very young and Adam was so much older than you,' Arabella told her gently, knowing how reluctant her sister would be to relinquish her dream. 'In fact, as I recall, you hardly knew him. I am sure that what you felt was nothing but a childhood infatuation for a handsome young man. It may have seemed enduring at the time, but it rarely lasts. It has been kept alive in you by separation, but now that Adam has returned I am sure you will find that your memories of him surpass reality.'

Prudence looked at her sister, knowing she was trying to make her feel better, but she didn't. Her face came close to an expression of defiance. 'What I felt for Adam went beyond infatuation, Arabella—or hero-worship. At least,' she said, her confidence beginning to ebb and uncertainty creeping into her voice, 'I thought it did. I may have seemed a child to him when last he saw me, but now he will see how changed I am, how grown up. Why, Lucas told me…'

Arabella jerked her eyes to her sister's flushed face in alarm, the look she gave her halting the words on her lips. 'Oh? Lucas? I assume you mean Lord Fox? And just what has Lord Fox been telling you, pray?' she asked tightly.

'Why—only that he finds me extremely pretty and has made a point of telling me so.'

Arabella paled, not blind to the brief flash of unchildlike ardour which lit her sister's eyes when she spoke of Lord Fox. That Prudence was ripe for love was evident to anyone who looked at her, and now Adam was no longer available to her it was inevitable that some other young man would come along and take her fancy—but Lord Fox?

Arabella had nothing against the man—in fact, she liked him—but his reputation was not unknown to her. Behind that handsome nobleman lay a trail of ruined young women and shattered hearts. He was the last man in the entire world she wished to show an interest in Prudence. Surely he would not have the temerity to interfere with the sister of the man who was his closest friend.

'I deeply regret leaving you alone the other day when Lord Fox came to call. Do not take anything he has to say seriously, Prudence. I understand from Thomas that where women are concerned he is no saint. He's a hard-bitten experienced man of the world with a well-deserved reputation for profligacy, whereas you are a babe in comparison. I warn you to be careful not to fall for his fatal attraction and become just another of his victims.'

'I won't. He's quite unlike anyone I've ever met before, and I confess to feeling a great unease whenever he and I are together. However, it's inconceivable that Lord Fox can ever be more to me than Thomas's friend. I don't know what it is that I want any more, Arabella, but what I do know is that I do not want Lucas Fox,' she said heatedly, doing her utmost to sound convincing in an attempt to quell the traitorous rush of warmth that suffused her whenever her thoughts turned to their illustrious neighbour. 'In my opinion he is arrogant and overbearing and too handsome for his own good. Nor do I approve of his reputation with the ladies—and if you must know, I go to dine with him at Marlden Hall with all the enthusiasm I would feel if I were on my way to being publicly flogged.'

To dine at Marlden Hall Prudence wore the same hyacinth-blue dress she had worn on the day of the King's procession through London. Arabella arranged her hair into a bun on the crown of her head, with side ringlets falling carelessly to her bosom.

On the journey she felt sick to her stomach at the thought of meeting Adam and being introduced to his wife, and even sicker when she thought of spending the entire evening in the presence of the intimidating Lord Fox. But for Thomas's sake she would endure it as best she could without complaint.

The area through which they travelled was heavily forested and rich in scenic beauty. The River Mole could be seen snaking its way along a valley bottom, the sloping sides clothed with box and yew. They approached Marlden Hall along an avenue of beeches, each tree decked out in summer splendour. When the house came into view Prudence was almost too apprehensive to take note of the huge, impressive building, built when Henry VIII was on the throne, with its many turrets and mullioned windows. The bulk of the house was built behind a frontal tower. It was set amid acres and acres of exquisite gardens and an enclosed park thick with ancient oaks and firs, where red deer browsed.

Their carriage halted behind a line of others at the bottom of a flight of wide stone steps leading up to a huge oak door. Green and gold liveried footmen stepped forward and opened the doors of the carriage. Suddenly Prudence's gaze was captured when a tall figure emerged from the house, for nothing in their brief acquaintance had prepared her for the Lord Fox who came forward with long, ground-devouring strides to receive them. Looking fiendishly handsome and elegant, he was dressed in black velvet, his coat slashed with gold. An unmistakable aura of calm authority was always evident, be it in the deep timbre of his voice or his confident stride.

'Welcome to Marlden Hall,' he said as they descended from the carriage, smiling as his gaze passed casually over the four of them before settling on Prudence. He looked straight at her, impaling her on his gaze, causing shock waves to ripple up and down her spine. 'Come inside and meet my other guests—most of them you will know.'

Noting Prudence's pensive expression and that she was looking at him with all the wariness of a nervous rabbit about to bolt down the nearest hole, Lucas knew exactly how her mind was working and sought to disarm her, to distract her from concentrating on her meeting with Adam. His expression was boldly admiring as he gazed down at the incredibly desirable young woman who fired his senses at that very moment.

'The dress is as exquisite as it was on the day of our first meeting—but barely worthy of the body it adorns,' he said softly, close to her ear as he stepped behind her, his long fingers deft and quick as he divested her of her satin cape himself, his hand sliding along the exposed flesh at her throat.

Unprepared for this attack on her senses or the touch of his hands, Prudence felt her cheeks burn and she turned her head to face him, a gasp escaping her parted lips. A half-smile twisted a corner of his mouth as his eyes warmly caressed her. There was a vibrant life and intensity in those incredible eyes that no one could deny. 'Lord Fox!' she admonished softly, preferring not to address him as Lucas as he had requested her to do. 'You are impertinent.'

'I fear that is so,' he sighed in overstated apology, the gypsy eyes sweeping her and catching her own, holding them with a smiling warmth.

Solomon, Lucas's personal servant, a brown-skinned young man from the Dark Continent who was meticulously garbed in a white turban, tight-fitting white satin trousers and a crimson tunic encrusted with gold embroidery, glided silently across the hall with kingly majesty and took the cape from him.

Double doors stood open leading to an inner salon, and as Prudence glanced uncertainly towards them, hearing voices laced with laughter, she felt the tension building inside her.

'Come and meet the others—although no introductions are necessary to you, Thomas. You know all the people here tonight.' Lucas placed his hand with possessive firmness beneath Prudence's elbow and led the four of them into the salon.

At any other time Prudence would have paused to gape at the exquisitely turned-out room in amazement. Her feet sank into plush green carpeting and the walls were hung with vibrantly painted Indian calico. Pedestals were set at intervals along the walls, upon which graceful white marble statues of semi-naked goddesses faced inwards to watch the assembled gathering, their expressions silent and watchful. But Prudence only had eyes for the slender, fair-haired man seated beside a dark-haired woman, the two dozen or so other guests milling around fading into the background.

When Lucas entered with his four guests, all heads turned their way and Adam and his wife rose to greet them. After introducing Lucy to Arabella, Adam turned to Prudence as Thomas and Arabella moved away to speak to Adam's father and others, all Royalists who had only recently returned from exile. Verity remained to speak to her sister.

Standing close beside Prudence, Lucas watched her, seeing a troubled clouding in the depths of her eyes. Then like a glow giving a false light she smiled, lifting her small chin and stiffening her spine with a show of being at ease and happy to see Adam. Pride swelled in Lucas to see how valiantly she fought for control—a fight she won.

'How nice to see you again, Adam,' Prudence heard herself saying, meeting his eyes. Her heart was hammering against her ribs and she was feeling unbearably self-conscious, but she managed not to flinch or drop her gaze. Facially he had changed little in the intervening years, but now there was a settled, contented air about him that had been absent before, and Prudence suspected this might have something to do with the young woman by his side. Unlike her sister, Lucy Lingard was small and frailly built. With a cloud of curly dark hair and a rather plain, round face, she had a shy look in her large, doe-like brown eyes.

Adam's eyes warmed with recognition and a pleasant smile curved his lips. 'Why, Prudence! How lovely you look. Allow me to introduce my wife, Lucy. Lucy,' he said, turning to the woman at his side and taking her hand, 'this is Prudence, Thomas's youngest sister. Prudence greeted me in the procession with a posy of flowers—grown by her own fair hands, I shouldn't wonder, for if I remember correctly she has a love of gardening. Is that not so, Prudence?'

'Indeed it is,' she smiled, aware that Lucas still had his hand firmly fixed on her elbow and that his fingers tightened slightly at Adam's mention of that day when Lucas had swept her into his arms and kissed her, an incident witnessed by more that one gentleman present, Adam included.

'Prudence was no more than thirteen years old when I left Marlden Green,' Adam told his wife.

Prudence looked at him sharply, her smile fading. 'Fifteen,' she corrected quickly, disappointed that he couldn't even recall how old she had been. That was the moment when she knew she had only made a shadowy impression on Adam Lingard before he had left for the Continent. She'd had nothing like the effect of the young woman who was regarding him with loving eyes.

Lucas took two glasses of wine from the tray of a passing footman and handed one to her, neatly leading her away from Adam and his wife to speak to his other guests, most of them couples and strangers to Prudence. She found it odd and rather disconcerting that he did not leave her side for a moment, which brought curious looks from other guests. Not even when they went into supper was she to be spared his close presence, for with Lucas seated carelessly and naturally in the high-backed chair that belonged to the master of the house at the head of the table, to her vexation she found herself directly on his left. To be within such close proximity of the man who played such havoc with her state of mind she found agonisingly unsettling.

Supper was a light-hearted meal over oysters, delicious salmon and roast duckling. Although conversation flowed easily between the guests, all of them having much in common and so many shared memories of their years in exile to discuss, Prudence, feeling very much like an outsider, merely toyed with her food, her normal healthy appetite having deserted her. The wine she had drunk was creating a slight haze all around her, softening the edges of everything and everyone close; glancing down the length of the table, miserably she saw that Adam only had eyes for his wife. As the meal progressed she began to wish she hadn't come.

She sighed for her disillusionment, for her shattered dreams and her misplaced devotion, which she had carried in her heart for Adam Lingard for three long years. But in fairness to Adam, none of it was his fault and she was glad he didn't know how she had felt, because now, meeting him again, she felt a strange feeling of guilt. When he had ridden away from Marlden Green to join his father on the Continent, she had said goodbye to a handsome, courageous young gallant, riding off to foreign lands and battles new. When he had slain all the enemies abroad, she had dreamed that he would return and carry her off like a knight in shining armour. It wasn't Adam's fault that he couldn't live up to her childish illusion.

She became aware that Lucas—who played host with a natural and relaxed manner that she reluctantly admired— was watching her, and when her eyes came round to meet his, she saw a half-smile curling on his lips.

'I'm sorry you don't care for the food,' he observed quietly.

'Oh, but I do. The roast duckling is quite delicious.'

'How can you know that when you haven't tasted it? Barely a morsel has passed your lips.'

'I'm sorry. There's nothing wrong with the food—it—it's just that my appetite appears to have deserted me,' she told him, pink-faced as she hurriedly stuttered her apology, stifled by his unprecedented efforts to charm and disarm her, his close proximity taunting and goading her.

'Is there nothing at all I can offer to tempt you?' he said, lounging back in his chair as she valiantly struggled to avoid his eyes, a smile playing about his sensual mouth, his long, slender fingers toying with the stem of his glass and the enormous ruby blazing with raw fire on his finger.

'No, nothing, thank you,' she answered, her pink cheeks turning scarlet. The double meaning to his question—one of which was abominably indelicate—heightened her embarrassment nearly beyond endurance. Under different circumstances she would have given him short shrift, but as a guest in his house and seated at his table surrounded by a host of other people she checked, with difficulty, the hot and angry words that bubbled to her lips.

Seeing the flushed, hurt look that she tried to turn away from him, Lucas leaned towards her. 'I did not mean that as it must have sounded to you, little one,' he said, lowering his voice so that in the chatter and excitement all around them his words came only to her ears. 'I beg your forgiveness if I have unwittingly caused you embarrassment.'

As he bent towards her, the soft scent of his cologne touched Prudence's senses with an acute awareness that made her almost giddy. She looked at him once more, undecided whether or not to believe him. More often than not there was mockery in everything he said, but there was also something warm and vital, something stimulating about him that in spite of herself drew her. All her energies rose to the challenge she saw in his attractive eyes. His sudden smile was arrogant and impudent and she desperately wanted to bring him down a notch, to topple him from his perch, and to do that she had more chance of succeeding by being all sweetness and light, rather than sour and po-faced.

'Thank you,' she said, flashing him a dazzling, animated smile that lit up her lovely face, a smile that was so sudden it took Lucas by surprise. 'An apology spoken so sincerely coming from the brave and famous Lord Fox is appreciated.'

'In that case, let me pour you some more wine,' Lucas said, observing that her glass was empty and ignoring the hint of sarcasm underlying her words. His eyes twinkled at her. 'You are very lovely, Prudence, and quite outrageous.'

'I cannot argue with that—particularly if it flatters me,' she replied, laughing softly.

'Flattery was not what I intended,' he murmured. 'I was merely stating a fact.'

Raising the glass to her lips, Prudence felt the wine melting her insides as she swallowed. An intimate atmosphere had fallen inside the room that was warm and almost tangible, bonding the people present.

'What are you two whispering about?' Thomas asked from across the table, when Verity, seated next to him, turned and laughed delightedly at something the gentleman across the table had said to her. Thomas focused his attention on Lucas, who had his dark head bent towards his sister.

'Only that we have been away too long, Thomas. An occasion such as this, to be together in peace, has been long awaited.'

'It's been a long time for all of us. There have been many changes in our absence.'

Lucas did not miss the hint of regret in his friend's voice, and he was not surprised by it. From Thomas's perspective, Lucas had emerged from the shambles of the Civil Wars and subsequent years more fortunate than most—like a phoenix rising from its ashes, surrounded by and able to afford every luxury money could provide.

'You're right,' Adam said. 'Many of us have suffered huge losses. Our gold and silver went to aid the war effort, our lands have been confiscated and many Royalists have had their homes plundered.'

'But some have secured promises of favours from the King,' Arabella said, picking up on the conversation, 'who has said that all they lost will be returned to them.'

'That is true,' Lucas agreed. 'Unfortunately, endless petitions have flooded in. Favours have been promised to so many exiles that there will not be enough to satisfy them all. The King has inherited heavy debts from previous regimes and he cannot afford to reward Royalists for past loyalties from his own pocket. Many who are impoverished find themselves at a disadvantage for, in seeking to obtain favours, they cannot afford the fees demanded by those in power at Court. Presbyterians, however—those who attempted to impose stern conditions on the King's return—can,' he finished with cynicism.

'It seems to me that the King has forgotten his own and his father's friends and seeks only to reward his enemies,' Prudence spoke out bitterly.

'Understandably the loyal should be rewarded,' Thomas said, 'and it is causing much bitterness among them that many of those who were against his father and himself have been given the highest places of authority and trust about his Majesty.'

Lucas nodded gravely. 'It certainly seems that way. The King has returned to England in a healing mood, and former foes are important in the healing process. He has set out with the highest intentions, which involves two considerations: conciliation and reward. However, the conciliation of the Cromwellians and reward of exiled Royalists is proving difficult—if not impossible.'

'Still, I thank God that we have not suffered as harshly as some,' said Thomas. 'Apart from the land my father sold to your uncle, Lucas, we are pretty well intact.'

'Perhaps when our situation improves, Lord Fox will sell it back to us,' Prudence said hopefully, flashing her eyes at Lucas. She hadn't intended to voice the suggestion and

she hadn't expected a reply, let alone the one he gave her.
Nor was she prepared for the way his gaze never wavered
from her eyes, but when it dipped down to her lips and she
saw the light that flared in the depths of his own, she was
unsettled by it.

'I will be more than happy to negotiate a price, sweet
Pru.'

Prudence's appetite was restored slightly when a footman
placed a raspberry syllabub in front of her. 'There you are,
Thomas. All is not lost after all,' she said jubilantly, spoon-
ing one of the delicious raspberries decorating the cold des-
sert into her mouth.

She did not see the amused, slightly smug glance that
passed between her brother and Lucas, but Arabella did.
She was puzzled and strangely alarmed by it.

As conversation ebbed and flowed across the table Prudence sipped her wine and turned all her attention on their
host, wondering why this man seated on her right at the
head of the table should disturb her more than Adam, the
man whom she had foolishly pined for three whole years.
With her mind fogged by the large quantity of heady wine
she had consumed, she decided there was much to be
gained from being nice to Lord Fox. After all, it was
Thomas's dearest wish that, in time, he would be in a situation to buy back the land their father had sold to George
Fox, so it would not help matters if she soured the waters.

Under the dark sweep of her sooty lashes she glanced at
him, the faint scent of his manly cologne—a strange aroma
of sandalwood and musk—sharpening on her senses, and
for an elusive moment the memory of the way he had removed her cape on her arrival, and whispered those intimate words into her ear, sent a thrill through her. She could
still feel the touch of his fingers on her neck, and the rock-
hard firmness of his well-muscled chest pressed against her
back.

And so, encouraged by the meanderings of her mind and
fortified by three glasses of wine, which had heightened the

colour on her cheeks to a rosy hue and deepened the warm glow in her eyes, after taking another swallow of wine for courage, the young and beautiful Prudence Fairworthy recklessly turned her attention from Adam and his wife—who had begun to sparkle so that she looked almost pretty—to their host, bestowing on him her most ravishing smile every time he spoke to her, and laughing and tossing her head until her chestnut ringlets danced.

At first Lucas acknowledged and welcomed her sudden friendliness and complete change in attitude with a gleam of knowing amusement, but after thirty minutes his eyes narrowed cynically and he began to grow more annoyed with her by the second as she continued to flirt with him, to play the coquette. He believed that she was using him to make Adam Lingard jealous, and that it was only because she was emboldened by the large quantity of wine she had drunk that she dared.

She looked like a beautiful, wild young temptress as she tried to dazzle him with her twin orbs of amethyst, her chestnut curls brushing her cheeks. However, whatever she had in mind, he had no intention of retaliating in kind by playing along with her.

His features perfectly composed, he shot a glance at a hovering footman, briefly conveying a message with his eyes. The footman stepped forward almost instantly and removed Prudence's glass when her head was turned away.

Later, when the guests had moved out of the dining room and were settling down to listen to the musicians playing lilting ballads up in the gallery and to play cards, in a deceptively casual move Lucas placed a restraining hand on Prudence's arm as she was about to move away.

'Excuse us,' he said to Thomas and Arabella. 'Prudence has expressed a desire to see the house.'

Prudence's eyes flew to his. 'I have?' she said unsteadily, swallowing her rising panic.

His casual smile hardened into a mask of ironic amusement. 'You have—the other day when I called at Willow House, if you recall.'

Try as she might, Prudence was unable to recall saying any such thing. 'I don't. Please don't trouble yourself on my account.'

'It's no trouble,' he hastened to assure her coolly. 'Shall we go?'

In alarm Arabella stepped forward to intervene, suspicious of Lord Fox's intentions where Prudence was concerned. 'I will go with you.'

'Oh, yes—please do, Arabella,' Prudence implored her sister.

Lucas's gaze slid to Thomas, who read the unspoken message in his friend's eyes and took Arabella's arm.

'If you don't mind, Arabella, I would rather you didn't leave just now,' he said stoutly.

'But, Thomas,' Arabella protested firmly. 'It is most irregular to—'

'Unfortunately Verity has disappeared to talk to Lucy and I find myself without a partner,' Thomas interrupted with a mixture of caution and irritation. 'I have promised Baron Sydenham and his wife that we will make up a foursome at cards. Come along. I see they are waiting.'

Arabella looked at him in confusion, amazed that her brother would permit Prudence to go off with Lord Fox alone. It really was most improper. 'But—Thomas—'

'Prudence will be perfectly all right,' her brother assured her in a tone that brooked no argument, seemingly quite unconcerned for the welfare of his youngest sister as he took Arabella's arm and led her away.

To Prudence's startled horror, Lucas clamped his hand on her elbow and propelled her out of the room, ignoring her indignation at being so familiarly handled. When the door had closed behind them she turned on him furiously, tearing her elbow from his grasp.

'Kindly take your hands off me. I never said that I wanted you to show me your house and you know it.'

Lucas looked down at her with undiluted anger. 'I thought to remove you from the company before you make an even bigger spectacle of yourself than you already have. I also want to speak with you alone. Before you leave this house tonight we need to reach an understanding. Now, come along. I said I would show you the house and I intend to do just that—starting in here,' Lucas said in a calm, authoritative voice, practically dragging her across the hall in his wake, opening a door and shoving her unceremoniously inside a comfortable withdrawing room.

Chapter Seven

Prudence stood before Lucas, enduring the icy blast of his gaze and taking judicious note of the taut set of his jaw, wondering what on earth she could have done to cause him to behave like this.

'What did you hope to accomplish by behaving like a foolish little flirt?' he demanded, his voice laced with steel.

No longer feeling reckless or defiant, Prudence stared in confusion at the man scowling darkly at her, unable for the life of her to understand how this situation had come about.

'Have you no thought for the consequences of throwing yourself at a man of my age and experience—that it is a dangerous game for an eighteen-year-old girl to play? I have fifteen years of experience with the opposite sex and I've had more affairs than I care to count. But I have never trifled with virginal innocents. I do not like playing games—and certainly not the kind that are played in the nursery with an outrageously impertinent chit who is completely foxed, and whose only reason for fluttering her eyelashes at me is to make another man jealous.'

'Oh, you beast,' Prudence retorted, angry and embarrassed at being hauled out of the salon in front of everyone and roughly shoved into this room, humiliated to the core by every hurtful word he flung at her.

'It was badly done, Prudence, and evident to me and

every one of my guests that the wine had loosened your maidenly inhibitions. There are a host of women at the Court of King Charles who are as bold and outspoken as the men with whom they openly flirt, and you have much to learn if it is your desire to emulate them. You chose to play your childish games with the wrong man. I will not be played for a fool.'

'Oh! How dare you?' Prudence flared, having listened to his furious tirade in angry, humiliating pain. The chastisement for her behaviour might well be deserved, but the rest of what he said wasn't. Plunking her fists in the curves of her waist, she struck a stubborn pose, the look in her eyes full of pure mutiny. 'Who do you think you are? And how dare you manhandle me into this room and speak to me like this? It's unfair and improper. You have no right to chastise me like a self-righteous, outraged husband. Only Thomas has the right to do that.'

'You were not flirting with Thomas,' Lucas remarked with scathing sarcasm. 'I have every right to speak to you as I see fit when you are in my house and you use me to make another man jealous,'

Prudence tossed her head haughtily, while feeling a stirring of alarm, for it was as if he believed he had some sort of power over her, which was why it would be so necessary for her to avoid him whenever possible in the future. 'I can't think what you mean.'

'Can you not? Then allow me to explain,' he said in a silky, dangerous voice, moving closer until he towered over her.

Prudence steeled herself for the rest of his verbal assault.

'I know all about your infatuation with Adam Lingard, and that you have cherished the hope that on his return to England he would marry you. I saw that when you handed him the posy in the procession. You are disappointed that he did not reciprocate your feelings—that he had failed to notice you even exist and married someone else. You feel hurt, angry and rejected, and cannot bear to see him bestow his affections on another woman. That is why you flirted with me, is it not—to make him jealous? But what you have to learn, sweet Pru, is that if a man does not care deeply for a woman, he will be immune from jealousy.'

His cold mockery and blistering gaze pierced Prudence's heart. 'You're hateful,' she whispered, tears burning behind her eyes.

'I agree, and I will give you fair warning, Prudence,' he enunciated coldly, 'although perhaps you would prefer to call it advice. If you ever use me again to make another man jealous, you will discover just how hateful I can be. And you won't like it. I promise you that.' His hand cupped her chin and he gave her a hard, penetrating look. 'Do I have your word on it that you will not do such a thing again?' he asked, in a tone that brooked no argument.

She swallowed, unable to look away from his hard gaze. 'Yes,' she whispered.

'I will not tolerate being made to look a fool. Is that understood?'

'I was not trying to make Adam jealous,' Prudence retorted, almost drowning in a sea of fury and mortification, finally tearing her gaze away from his. 'But think what you like. It doesn't concern me. You know nothing about me.'

'Yes, I do. You are wilful and quite outrageous, and tonight you have behaved like a silly girl who should have had some manners beaten into her when she was still a child.' When he saw her incredulous eyes shining with hurt, angry tears he was contrite and his expression softened. With his long fingers still curled under her chin, he turned her face up to his, a slow smile touching his lips. 'You are also very lovely. I find you quite enchanting and would like to get to know you better.'

'A snake would make a better friend than you,' she ground out, her temper restored. Knocking his hand away, she tried to retain a brave face, but she knew it was all her stupid fault for throwing herself at him earlier. Humiliated and deeply ashamed and with tears shimmering in her eyes, she stepped back.

Lucas stared at the scornful young beauty that was regarding him as if she would like nothing better than to scratch his eyes out. For a moment he studied her with heavy-lidded, speculative eyes. Candlelight glinted in her hair, gilding it with a copper sheen, the blue of her gown flattering her pink cheeks and turning her magnificent eyes luminous. He almost smiled. 'I can see you are extremely angry with me.'

She nodded. 'Yes.'

'But not nearly so angry with me as you are with yourself,' he said quietly.

Prudence lowered her gaze. He was right. She was ashamed and bitterly angry with herself for behaving so stupidly. Lifting her eyes to his, suddenly she saw something warm and alarming kindle in those mysterious depths. 'I am angry with myself,' she admitted tonelessly. 'It was irresponsible and childish of me to behave in that way. I am sorry and I promise that it won't happen again.'

Lucas nodded slowly, feeling admiration for her honesty and courage in admitting her wrongdoing. Folding his arms across his chest, he perched his hip on the edge of an intricately carved dark oak table, watching her with interest and deliberately blocking her way of escape.

'Now we have got that unpleasantness out of the way,' he said smoothly, an almost lecherous smile tempting his lips, 'perhaps you would like to continue where you left off in the dining room? Your flirtatious glances could only have one interpretation. After all your efforts at the supper table to seduce me, I think we should progress to something of a more intimate nature—at least while we are alone. So—what would you like me to do next? Or would you prefer to make the next move?'

Prudence eyed him warily, unconscious of the vision she presented as the candlelight washed over her. He was far too close for her peace of mind and automatically she took another step back. His eyes mocked her cautious retreat, but he made no comment on it. 'What do you mean?'

'That I won't mind in the slightest if you kiss me.' He had the distinct impression as he uttered the words that he was stirring a volcano that was about to erupt in his face. He was not disappointed.

All Prudence's wrath came rolling back and she faced him with the volcano blazing in her eyes. 'Why, you conceited ass. Kiss you? Why on earth would I want to do that? I'd as soon kiss a mule.'

'I assure you that it wouldn't be nearly as much fun as kissing me,' he chuckled infuriatingly, the sound low and deep in his chest. 'A mule, being a sexless beast, wouldn't kiss you back.'

Prudence stared at his arrogant features, at the mocking light in his enigmatic eyes, realising that he really did want her to take the initiative and kiss him. Silently she cursed herself for being so stupid as to flirt with this man in the first place, who was way beyond her sphere in both age and experience.

'Every day I learn things about you I don't like, and despite what my brother thinks of you I cannot share his opinion. I find you insufferably arrogant and overbearing. Your affairs are legendary. You are responsible for raising the temperatures of all the ladies at the King's Court, and by all accounts you are an unprincipled libertine who would think nothing of seducing a nun in a nunnery. And to make matters worse your behaviour is sanctioned by your friends, who seem to think you can do no wrong.'

Calmly, Lucas gazed down at her lovely, rebellious face. 'Have you quite finished?'

'Yes—but I'm sure there's much more.'

'Then don't stop now. I'm truly amazed. I didn't realise my amorous exploits were so well known as to cause so much interest. But you really shouldn't listen to gossip, Pru. And you must allow me to defend myself,' Lucas said with quiet implacability. 'For a start, rumour has grossly exaggerated my reputation. The things you accuse me of have travelled between here and the Continent and back again and have been embroidered many times. The first four years of exile I spent fighting in the French army. There may have been a dalliance or two, but I am no worse than others I know.'

'And the next five years?'

Suddenly his eyes became cold and his expression hardened. 'Some of them were not so pleasurably spent.'

Tilting her head to one side, Prudence regarded him quizzically. 'There seems to be a great mystery about you, my lord. I believe you travelled extensively in the East?'

'I did.'

His reply was brusque, all humour having left his face, leaving some battle-scarred remnants of something Prudence knew nothing about. She was curious and wanted to ask him more, but the look he gave her forbade it. He had his pride and his reasons, which he would not discuss with her.

'When I first met you I didn't like you then and I still don't,' she told him coldly—a statement that wasn't quite true, but she wouldn't give him the satisfaction of telling him so.

'I'm sorry you feel that way,' Lucas murmured quietly, looking at her with unbearable gentleness, 'because when I first saw you I thought you were the loveliest creature I had seen in a long time—if ever. And there was a moment when you were in my arms—when your mouth was warm on mine—that you seemed to enjoy being there.'

Prudence stared at him, surprised at the caress in his voice. She looked for mockery in his eyes but there was none. 'You—you took me by surprise that day.'

Letting his gaze slide over her, Lucas favoured her with a lopsided grin. 'But you did enjoy it, didn't you?'

Frantically she searched around for the right words. 'I—I found it—disturbing.'

'So did I. Shall we try it again and see if it still has the same effect?'

'Do you think that I've lost my senses?'

'Not yet. But you will. Who knows what might come of it?'

'Nothing will come of it because I'm not going to kiss you. Besides, you would be disappointed. I am not as practised in the ways of seduction as you evidently are,' she said sarcastically.

'Even amateurs have to learn.'

'And you think you can teach me?'

'I've had no complaints—and I'd be more than happy to give you the benefit of my experience. I am not letting you out of this room until I have your kiss, so you might as well get on with it. After leading me on so shamelessly, you owe it to me.'

The arrogance of his statement was so typical of the man that Prudence almost laughed. 'I do not owe you anything.'

'Yes, you do,' and, giving her no time to protest, he reached out and jerked her into his arms, pulling her between his thighs and full against his hard frame.

Prudence gasped at the intimate contact. 'Let me go,' she protested, squirming against him, unaware that she unconsciously increased his ardour with every movement.

'You are too proud and too foolish, my sweet,' Lucas murmured, his mouth hovering over hers. He knew he was gambling with an action that would, in all probability, deepen her dislike, but he was willing to chance it, hoping her heart and her lips would follow his lead. 'I need to change this problem you have of disliking me. You may fight me now, but soon you won't want to.'

He brought his mouth down on to hers, smothering her objections with a hungry possessiveness, his lips moving over hers with a ruthless intensity, punishing in their urgency, forcing her lips open from sheer pressure and shocking her senses. Prudence tried to wrench herself out of his arms, but they held her in a vice-like grip, and the more she struggled, the more punishing his mouth became.

The sensation of his lips on hers was achingly familiar, for she had lived it in her dreams a hundred times since that day he had kissed her in the procession. He had told her that she had responded to it, but this time she dare not. When she finally became still, trembling and defeated in his arms, he raised his head, looking down into her stormy eyes.

'That, my pet,' he whispered, his breath warm on her lips before he moved his mouth to her temple, trailing insistent kisses down the side of her face, 'was your first lesson. But I know you can do better.'

She stared at him, her breathing impaired, struggling against a painful knot of emotions in her chest.

Then he took her lips in a kiss so very different from the one before. Already disarmed, it was more than she could stand. His arms went round her, holding her tenderly now, bringing her body to vibrant life and splintering any resistance she had left. One hand curved round the back of her neck, his other encircling her waist. He kissed her thoroughly, insistently, warming her to the core of her being, his mouth coaxing hers to open, his tongue playing upon her lips before slipping inside to pluck and taste the soft, honey sweetness within. She surrendered helplessly, warming and yielding to the provocative caresses of his hands and mouth.

She moaned softly when he deepened his endless, drugging kiss, his mouth moving with persuasive insistence against hers as she became lost in a void of pure sensation, his knowledgeable fingers continuing to stroke the sensitive skin at the back of her neck. Something wild escaped within her, something too strong to fight against. Her hands crept up over his broad shoulders, and innocently and unconsciously she pressed and moulded her body to his, crushing her soft breasts to his chest, clinging to him as he continued to leisurely explore and taste the sweetness of her mouth.

Desire exploded in Lucas's body, pounding in his loins, when he felt the woman in his arms respond to his kiss with more ardour than he expected. The effect was devastating. When her low moan pierced his senses he dragged his lips from hers and raised his head, knowing he was in grave danger of becoming the seduced instead of the seducer. Placing his hands on her narrow waist, he held her away slightly and looked down at her flushed face, his senses filled with the fragrance of her hair. Slowly she opened her eyes, which were disorientated and dark and warm with passion, and he smiled, satisfied to see his kiss had had the desired effect.

'And that, my sweet,' he murmured, his voice low and husky, 'was your second lesson.'

Surfacing slowly from the haze of desire, Prudence looked at the sensual, finely carved mouth inches from her own—the mouth that had kissed her with such soul-destroying passion—from beneath her long sooty lashes and leaned against him weakly, unable to still the chaotic pounding of her heart or remove the look of wonder on her face as a tumult of emotions coursed through her. His kiss had seared through her resistance and left her shaken with the realisation of her own passion. Slowly reality began to return.

'Shouldn't we be getting back to the others?' she whispered, dragging the words from her constricted throat. She was a confusing mass of bewilderment and shame, unable to believe that she had just abandoned herself so wantonly in his arms.

'There's no hurry,' he said, his breath touching her cheek. 'I said I was going to show you the house.'

'But that was ages ago.'

'It's a big house,' he murmured. Bending his head, he lightly brushed her lips with his own, glorying in her purity, unable to believe he had just kissed an eighteen-year-old innocent who had been capable of almost sweeping him off his feet. She had touched a part of him that he'd never known existed.

When he had brought her into this room he had not intended to take advantage of her, only to take her to task for her unacceptable behaviour at the dining table, but she was so ripe and tempting, the scent of her too intoxicating for him to resist. In the past he had preferred to make love to women as experienced and enthusiastic in the art of love-making as he was—passionate, sensual creatures who knew how to give pleasure unashamedly, and to receive it— whereas Prudence was a virgin, which, in the world in which he moved, was something rare and extremely fine.

She seemed to contain all that he had ever wanted in a woman, and he had been startled by her passionate response to his sensuous kiss. His blood ran hot when he contemplated how it would be between them when she was his wife—of making love to her, of awaking all her desires and teaching her how to return his love in ways she could never dream existed. He tried to imagine her virginal, well-rounded body beneath his, her slender limbs entwined with his own, and the thought almost unmanned him. She was a lovely, exotic beauty he would never give up, and she had touched a tenderness and protectiveness in him he never knew existed.

'Are you still thinking of Adam?'

She shook her head. 'I wasn't trying to make anyone jealous. I swear it,' she said, her voice a strangled whisper. 'I was feeling miserable, I confess, and the wine made me feel better.'

'I believe you. But you're going to have the very devil of a headache in the morning,' Lucas told her, offering his wisdom freely. 'Are you no longer infatuated with him?'

'No,' she replied truthfully and without any hint of regret, wondering how it was possible to have put Adam from her mind so quickly. The part of her that she had dedicated wholly to him was gone. She had withdrawn her heart, which previously she would have laid at his feet. When

Thomas had told her that Adam had married someone else, her infatuation had faded with her emergence from adolescence. But she still liked and respected him. He was so genuine a person, so obviously in love with his wife—and she with him.

'Since he came back I realise we wouldn't have suited after all.'

'And after kissing me, do you think we would suit any better?'

With alarm bells beginning to ring inside her head, she drew back in his arms, her eyes snapping to his. 'Certainly not. Don't think that because of what has just happened it gives you the right to do it again.'

'I know Adam couldn't make you feel how I can when I kiss you.'

Prudence raised her chin a notch. 'You are conceited. You don't know that.'

He grinned. 'I know Adam—I know his tastes, which run to affection, not passion.' Lucas also knew that if Prudence had married Adam Lingard she would have been disappointed. By the time the honeymoon was over she would have been awakened to the pleasures of love and yet unfulfilled. 'I am experienced with women, Pru—experienced enough to know that when I kiss you and you respond the way you do, Adam Lingard has no claim on your heart.'

'That may be so, but Adam is a gentleman, whereas you are not,' she replied haughtily. 'If he were not married and if he liked me, he would never kiss me the way you have just done.'

Lucas's mouth twisted in sardonic amusement. 'Then he should,' he said softly, his eyes on her lips. 'You're the kind of woman who should be kissed—and often.' He regarded her with a thoughtful, almost tender expression. 'Judging from your words and that prim expression you're wearing, am I to understand that you intend avoiding any further romantic confrontations between us?'

Prudence began to wake up to what had just happened; the sensual spell he had put her under beginning to lift. She looked away, furious and ashamed of herself for having enjoyed his kiss, and furious with him for having kissing her in the first place, and for sweeping away so effortlessly her sense of decency and honour. She was reasonably sure his only interest in her was merely to add her to his many conquests, for she must not forget that this was a scene he would have enacted hundreds of times with women whose names he could no longer remember, and she had no intention of having her name added to that list.

'Yes. We're not compatible. I'm sure you know plenty of women who kiss better than me.'

'Not exactly,' Lucas said, his mouth quirking in a smile as he let his admiring glance roam over her glorious chestnut hair and voluptuous, restless figure still close to his own. 'Although, with practice, I have no doubt that you will improve. But worry not, my pet. There will be time enough in the future to teach you all there is to know about making love.'

Shocked to the core of her virginal heart when the full meaning of his words penetrated her mind, Prudence stepped back, out of his embrace, realising that after accusing her of playing a game with him, he had just done exactly the same to her. All he had wanted to do was humble her and humiliate her. His flat conviction that she had no choice but to yield to him again, coolly ignoring what she had just said and unconcerned for her feelings, was more than she could bear right now. He was smiling, but she was furious. If she had not been so furious she would have wept with shame. Outraged, she glared at him.

'Don't depend on it—you—you lecherous, amoral cad. Your barbaric attempt to seduce me will not be repeated. I will not flatter your vanity by allowing it to happen. I hope I have more sense than that. I hate you for this—and if you ever touch me again I swear I'll kill you.'

'I would be interested to see you try, my sweet,' he murmured, unperturbed by her sudden anger. Reaching out, he gently caressed the curve of her cheek with the tips of his fingers, smiling when she retreated and turned her face away. 'You may feel free to flirt with me whenever you like, providing you are sincere in what you do and not trying to make another man jealous.' He stood up to his full height, towering over her. 'Come. It's time we returned to the others before Thomas comes demanding an explanation. And try not to look so woebegone. Smile, little one, otherwise everyone will interpret it as something else and draw their own conclusions.'

Pasting a stiff smile on her lips, Prudence marched blindly out of the room ahead of him, but on entering the salon she was by his side, going through an extremely awkward charade of telling Arabella how splendid she found Marlden Hall.

Prudence's heightened colour and the glow in her eyes did not deceive Arabella. That Lord Fox was attracted to her sister was obvious, but that he should pursue her and take advantage of her youth and innocence was quite out of the question. It had to be. She had no desire to make an enemy out of Thomas's friend, but she would endeavour not to let them spend time alone together. When they got home she resolved to have a serious word with Prudence, and she would have more than a few to say to Thomas.

When the evening was over and they were returning to Willow House, a dozen or more conflicting emotions were at war within Prudence, among them anger, humiliation and wounded pride. Her feelings were in turmoil, but one stood out clearly above all the rest—that of frustrated desire. She now knew that everything she had heard about Lucas Fox was true, for she had been kissed by a man who was well practised in the art of seduction, a man with a wealth of experience her young mind could never begin to imagine.

He had known exactly what to do to arouse her to a fever pitch of desire.

Shame swamped her as she bitterly faced the awful truth. Physically, she was not immune to him. She was unable to withstand either his smile or his kiss. The sweet violence of it had wreaked havoc in her mind, her heart and her soul. Despite her resolve to stand against him and everything she knew about him, he could still rouse her body to a boiling cauldron of yearning.

Never had she been so confused in her life, for how could she dislike him as much as she thought she did, when above all the chaotic meanderings of her heart and mind was the realisation that she hadn't wanted him to stop kissing her? That made no sense at all.

It was during breakfast the following morning that Verity casually broached the matter of Thomas presenting Prudence at Court. She would have liked to add 'with the ultimate aim of finding a husband', but she knew she would have to tread very carefully in her new home. She found her husband's youngest sister an extremely wilful, stubborn young woman and far too outspoken for her own good. Prudence's presence in both the house and her own well-ordered life was a disruption she could do without. Fortunately Prudence had eaten early and was in the garden, so the matter could be discussed and put to her later when something positive had been decided.

Arabella looked sharply at her sister-in-law, who was coolly dissecting a piece of ham on her plate. 'I do not believe Prudence has any desire to be presented at Court, Verity,' she said, knowing her sister would resent being manipulated into doing anything that was against her will.

'I must stress that it is her future well-being I have in mind,' Verity said calmly, fixing Arabella with a shrewd, dark gaze.

'I'm sure it is, but Prudence has nothing suitable to wear

for such an important event,' Arabella told her, hoping this would put an end to the discussion.

But Verity was not to be deterred. 'I don't see that as a problem. Since Thomas and I are to take Prudence to town after your wedding in four weeks' time, we shall see to it that she is fitted for some new gowns—although it could take some time, for every dressmaker in London at this point will be swamped with orders from returning Royalists.'

'The kind of gowns you speak of will cost a great deal of money, Verity. Money we just do not have at this present time.'

Verity was not to be swayed. 'You can leave that for Thomas and me to worry about,' she said, in a tone reminding Arabella that after she was wed it would be her husband's affairs that would concern her and not her brother's. 'And anyway, these days everyone will be dealing in credit. It will be a great opportunity for Prudence—indeed, most people would deem it a great honour to be presented to King Charles. At Court she will meet all kinds of interesting people, and, in time, even a husband—a wealthy one, too, if she is fortunate.'

Unconsciously Arabella's fingers gripped the napkin on her lap, for she more than suspected that Prudence was a complication Verity hadn't counted on when she'd married Thomas at The Hague. 'At this present time I know my sister has no desire to plunge herself into Court revelries—and even less to look for a husband. And as Prudence's guardian, it is for Thomas to decide whether or not she is to be presented at Court—is that not so, Thomas?' Arabella asked her brother, who seemed unusually preoccupied with his own thoughts this morning.

Arabella was concerned by the influence Verity seemed to have over her brother, for although he was a strong, decisive man in matters of business, he was not so assertive where his wife was concerned, and he had wasted no time in giving her free rein in household affairs. Thomas had an exalted opinion of Verity. In his eyes she could do no wrong. That he loved her was evident—a gentleness and respect coming over his face whenever he looked at her. How Arabella wished she could be of the same opinion.

In an attempt to direct the conversation away from courtly matters, she raised the concern uppermost in her mind—that of Thomas allowing Prudence to disappear for half an hour alone with Lord Fox at his supper party. She accused Thomas harshly of being neglectful in his duty to their sister, leaving him in no doubt that she had considered it to be most improper and that she was most displeased.

Thomas looked at his sister directly, feeling that it was only right that both she and Verity should be made aware of the arrangements he and Lucas had made concerning Prudence. And so, without preamble, he told them the full facts of why he'd had no objections to Prudence being alone with Lucas.

'I didn't want to tell you just yet, Arabella. I wanted to wait and see how Prudence would react to Lucas's attentions. It is my hope that she will develop a fondness for him and in time will consent to be his wife.'

'But she cannot stand the man. Will you force our sister to marry a man she has no feelings for?' Arabella's voice was harsh as she tried to come to grips with what he had divulged.

Thomas frowned at the note of rebuke in Arabella's voice. 'Be assured that I will not force Prudence to marry Lucas without first giving her time to develop a fondness for him, and to get used to the idea of being his wife and mistress of Marlden Hall. However, I am confident that when she does marry Lucas she will do so willingly. When she gets to know him better she will soon change her opinion of him.' He smiled suddenly. 'There are few females who can resist Lucas's charm, Arabella, and I think we will find our sister is no exception.'

'Lord Fox is determined to marry her, isn't he, Thomas?'

'He is, and I cannot think of a more worthy suitor for

Prudence. He is quite taken with her. You must have noticed. He is also prepared to take her without a dowry.'

'How noble of him,' Arabella said, unable to keep the
sarcasm out of her voice.

'I did not think you would oppose a match between them
so strongly, Arabella.'

'Of course I oppose it. Prudence is eighteen years old,
Thomas—a child compared to Lord Fox's vast experience
of the world and its ways. Must I remind you that his reputation for profligacy is well earned? You should know that
more than anyone. I do not dislike Lord Fox—in fact, quite
the opposite. He is charming and his manners are exem-
plary. I am sure he will make some woman a fine husband,
but I cannot see that woman being Prudence. For all her
wilfulness she is true and loyal and has a passionate and
loving nature. When she marries she will settle for nothing
less than love. She will give all of herself to her husband
and will expect the same from him. I cannot see Lord Fox
being as singular in his affections, can you, Thomas?'

Judging from her brother's expression, he did not share
her opinion. He sighed deeply, for he could see that Arabella was clearly troubled by this and he would do his best
to allay any doubts and fears she might have concerning a
match between Prudence and Lucas.

'You are quite wrong about him and worry unnecessarily, Arabella. Lucas is a good man—indeed, I know none
better—and he is the most loyal friend anyone could wish
to have. He is a man who knows his mind, and he has more
character and substance than any man I know. I could not
see Prudence married to anyone finer. There are few who
have not heard of his exploits with women—but take it
from me that his reputation is not nearly as bad as it's been
painted. Despite the face he shows to the world, Lucas is
a sensitive man and capable of great gentleness.'

Arabella listened, with subtle changes of expression
crossing her face, ranging from anger and disbelief to uncertainty, ending with the realisation that perhaps she had

made a grave error about Lord Fox's character. 'Oh, Thomas. I do so want to believe you—for our sister's sake.'

Thomas was pleased to see a softening to Arabella's face and that she sounded somewhat mollified as he listed all Lucas's redeeming features. She was a sensible woman, if a trifle soft where Prudence was concerned, but he was confident that she would come to see the brilliance of such a match and be as eager for Prudence to marry Lucas as he was.

'But I have to say that he frightens me a little,' Arabella went on softly. 'He may be all you say he is, but I sense a ruthlessness inside him, a forcefulness. I believe he will stop at nothing when he wants something. I saw that last night when he removed Prudence from our protection. I can't help thinking he is not serious and that he will hurt her.'

'He won't. Lucas has committed himself absolutely to her.'

'How can you be so sure?'

'Because I know him. You're right, he is ruthless—and he has a temper to go with it, but he usually keeps it in check. He doesn't care what people think of him, and he does exactly what he likes, when he likes, and to the devil with the consequences.

'Initially I was against any kind of relationship forming between them—I even went so far as to tell Lucas to stay away from her. But when I discovered that his intentions were strictly honourable and that he wanted to marry her, I began to realise that it might not be such a bad thing. I will do everything within my power to encourage the match. If the truth be told, Prudence is more than a little obstinate. Marriage to a man of Lucas's no-nonsense character might temper our sister's wilfulness.'

Arabella's voice was laced with ironic amusement. 'Providing he learns how to handle her.'

'He will. Prudence will do his bidding.'

'Does this mean that when you accompany Robert and

me to London after our wedding, you will not be introducing her at Court as Verity suggests?'

'If she marries Lucas he will do that. He is respected, Arabella—and a man of importance. His family is of old lineage and he is also wealthier than most of the Royalists who returned with the King. He will give Prudence every luxury it is within his power to grant her if she becomes his wife. She will have no cause for complaint. Until he joined me at Breda in April, I had not seen him for five years. Whatever happened to him during those five years he has yet to divulge,' Thomas told his sister. 'But whatever it was I suspect it was of a violent nature and caused him great suffering. Something happened during those missing years that changed him. It was a different man who returned.'

'Then perhaps you are right and Lord Fox is ready to settle down.'

'Lucas wishes his intentions to be kept from Prudence until he's paid court to her and he thinks the time is right to tell her. I have given him my word that I will do this.'

'Then I suppose Verity and I must do the same. But I cannot say that I approve. Prudence will be angered and appalled to learn that you have discussed and made plans for her future without consulting her. When she finds you have given her hand in marriage to Lord Fox without her knowledge—then I fear for the consequences.'

Verity didn't. Bowing her head over her plate, she smiled quietly to herself. It would seem that everything would turn out far better than she had expected after all, and it wouldn't cost them a penny.

Chapter Eight

On reaching Dorking, an attractive market town set amid wooded hills where Arabella and Prudence were to do some shopping, they left Simon Trimble with the coach at the timber-framed inn and walked into the market place. After half an hour Arabella disappeared inside a shop to purchase some silks she required for a screen she was working on, hoping to complete it before her marriage to Robert. She left Prudence to carry an armful of packages back to the coach.

Prudence's attention was diverted by a commotion outside the inn. Two men were drunk and looking for trouble, already throwing punches at each other and causing a laughing, jostling crowd to gather around them to watch. Not looking where she was going, she crashed headlong into a post, scattering her packages on to the ground, one of them bursting open and allowing the apples to escape and roll around her feet. With an exasperated sigh she bent to retrieve them, grateful when someone stopped to help.

'Allow me. May I lend a hand?' The voice was soft and masculine.

'I would be most grateful,' she replied, standing up and arranging the packages in her arms once more. She raised her eyes to thank the gentleman who had been so kind as to help her, and found herself peering into the face of the man who had parted the throng on the day of the King's procession into London to allow her to see it better. He was calmly surveying her with considerable interest. 'Oh! It's you!' she gasped with surprise.

His smile was engaging, his teeth flashing dazzling white in his tanned face—a deep-baked tan that showed years of exposure to the weather. Sweeping off his hat, his dark brown hair fell forward. 'I, too, remember the occasion when we met. Your servant, ma'am,' he said, bowing with a courtly flourish. He was splendidly garbed in scarlet velvet, with white lace at his throat and dripping from his wrists.

His eyes, slightly veiled, raked her slowly from head to toe, travelling with a sort of insolent appreciation and with an odd look of amusement. Prudence did not understand the look, but it made her feel slightly uneasy. She took a step back, tilting her head to one side as she met his gaze. 'The last time we met I recall that you addressed me as *mademoiselle*.'

'I remember. It is my opinion that when it comes to manners the French can always teach the English a thing or two, and *mademoiselle* sounds so much nicer than ma'am or mistress, I always think. Once more I have the good fortune to help you by the wayside.'

'How strange that we should meet again like this,' Prudence murmured, noticing the small lines of ruthlessness around his mouth and the touch of arrogance in the set of his shoulders. 'I certainly never expected to.'

'I did,' he replied, with such conviction that her look became curious. 'And I'm glad we have. And you, dear lady, are just as lovely as I remember.'

Something about his eyes and his voice unnerved her. 'Do you always speak your mind, sir?'

'Always. It's best. That way we avoid misunderstandings—do you not agree?'

'Yes, I suppose I do. Thank you so much for helping me,' she said, balancing her packages and giving him her hand to shake, surprised when he kissed it instead. She felt the warmth of his lips as they lingered overlong on her flesh, and her instinct was to snatch it away. She withdrew it slowly instead, not wishing to give offence.

'It was my pleasure. Are you here unescorted?'

'I came with Arabella—my sister. I left her buying some silks,' she replied, studying his face—ostensibly a rogue's face, yet there was something far too confident—brazenly so—and clever in those darting, searching, piercing pale blue eyes. 'Do you live in Dorking, sir?'

'I'm just passing through. Captain Jeffrey Fox at your service,' he said, bowing once more.

Prudence started. Why did the sound of his name make her draw her breath in sharply? 'Jeffrey Fox? Then you must be Lord Fox's cousin—Lord Fox of Marlden Hall.' The curve of Jeffrey Fox's mouth tightened slightly and the lines at the corners grew deeper. His eyes hardened and something Prudence couldn't identify stirred in their depths, but his expression remained affable.

'You know my cousin?' he asked.

'He is our neighbour in Marlden Green.'

'I see. You have met him?'

'Yes. Lord Fox and my brother are good friends.'

'And you? Has Lucas been drawn by your bright eyes?' the Captain questioned with an impudent grin. 'He always was attracted by a pretty face.'

The words were lightly spoken, but they caught Prudence on the raw when she recalled all too vividly her last encounter with Lucas Fox at Marlden Hall. 'My bright eyes can be misleading, sir.'

'I take it you've not much opinion of my cousin?'

'I do not know him well enough to have formed an opinion, Captain Fox.'

He smiled thinly, looking at her closely and nodding slowly, seeming to read more into her reply than she was comfortable with. 'You will. There isn't a woman alive who can resist Lucas—always was good at breaking hearts.

He always had more luck than I—but then he is much better looking. I must allow him that,' he conceded.

'You are too generous to Lord Fox and too hard on yourself,' Prudence responded diplomatically. Jeffrey Fox was undeniably attractive, but his likeness to his cousin was slight. The rather drooping lids were the same, the curve of his mouth and the firm set of his jaw, but there the likeness ended.

He laughed good humouredly, a happy, ingenuous laugh that could have offended no one, so why was Prudence beginning to regret this encounter? 'And you, my dear young lady, are too kind.'

'However, you do have one thing in common, Captain Fox,' she said calmly. 'You both have the cheek of the devil.'

His eyes glinted. 'Aye—we have that. But 'tis said of my cousin that he is the devil's own child. Have you not heard?'

'I have heard something to that effect, but I cannot believe it.'

'Tell me, is my cousin well?'

'Yes—at least I believe so.'

'And is he in residence at Marlden Hall?'

'He was—the last I heard.' It was a normal enough question and his smile was quite infectious, so why did her feeling of unease persist and why did she sense a note of interrogation?

His eyes narrowed as they held her gaze. 'Will you tell my cousin that you've seen me, Prudence?'

'Do you want me to?'

He shrugged carelessly. 'It makes no difference one way or the other. I will not be visiting him. We never did see eye to eye. You can give him my respects if you like. Tell him I congratulate him on making a full recovery.'

Prudence glanced at him in enquiry. 'Why? Has he been ill?'

Captain Fox showed a change from his normal controlled

elegance. His eyes were much too bright, and an odd, rather sinister smile touched his mouth. He said in an undertone, 'It was not his health I was referring to.'

Suddenly the moment was one of awkwardness, bringing a tension between them. Glancing down the street, Prudence was relieved to see Arabella coming out of the shop. 'Forgive me,' she said, much too quickly. 'I have to go.'

He stood back to allow her to pass. 'It's been a pleasure meeting you again, *mademoiselle*,' Jeffrey said softly. 'I sincerely hope we meet again very soon.'

'Yes, perhaps we will. Goodbye.'

Arabella was accompanied to the coach by a female acquaintance she had encountered in the shop and they were chatting away animatedly. Prudence climbed into the vehicle, placing her packages on the seat, her eyes following Captain Fox's retreating figure. He must have felt her eyes on him, for he glanced back over his shoulder and winked an eye, an impudent, lopsided grin on his lips. When he walked on she observed how he swayed with the easy gait of a seaman, which reminded her that Jeffrey Fox was a privateer and the captain of his own ship.

He went towards a man who was holding the reins of two horses in the street outside the inn. She frowned, for there was something in the broad set of the man's shoulders and his stance that seemed familiar. Captain Fox swung up into the saddle and his companion did likewise. The man did not look her way, but Prudence had a clear view of his face. She gasped. It was Will Price.

For some reason she could not explain Prudence didn't mention the incident to Arabella, who talked nonstop about her meeting with her friend all the way back to Willow House and seemed not to notice how quiet her sister had become. Prudence hardly heard a word of what she was saying. It wasn't so much meeting Lucas Fox's cousin that brought about her feeling of unease, but seeing him in the company of Will Price. How had the two come to meet? And why had Will left his work at Mr Rowan's nursery?

And another thing she found quite disconcerting was that Captain Fox had addressed her as Prudence. How had he known her name? Had Will Price seen her and told him?

By the time the carriage arrived back at Willow House she was gradually recovering from the effects of her encounter with Lucas's cousin, but not from the shock of it. She distrusted the easy confidence of the man, which spoke of a determination to have his own way in all things. She did not like what she was feeling, and she did not like Jeffrey Fox either. Three minutes in his company was all it had taken. She had seen his eyes when she had asked if Lord Fox had been ill. Something of a dark and sinister nature that bordered on evil had moved in their depths. It was gone as quickly as it had appeared, but she did not ever want to see it again.

As she followed Arabella into the house, an uncanny and haunting fear had insinuated itself into her heart and mind that was going to be difficult to get rid of.

Two weeks following the supper party at Marlden House, it was Prudence's birthday. As soon as breakfast was finished, a smiling Arabella told her to go the stables where she would find her birthday present. When she arrived she found young John Trimble cleaning out a stall. Catching sight of her, he beamed, knowing why she was there. His grin widening, he immediately led an unfamiliar chestnut mare with a snowy white blaze from one of the stalls.

Overwhelmed, Prudence was speechless with pleasure as she ran her hands over her. The mare was the most beautiful horse she had ever seen, silky smooth and with a long flowing mane and tail, its eyes lively and intelligent. She knew it had to be for her because it was her birthday, and Arabella, who lived in constant terror of falling from the saddle, didn't like to ride. There was also a new bridle and a lady's high-backed side-saddle of padded purple velvet.

Immediately she went in search of her brother. He was in his study seated at his desk, looking through a leather-bound ledger at the records of rents Ned had collected in his absence. Unaware that he was not alone, she ran towards him and, throwing her arms about his neck, kissed him soundly on both cheeks, much to his astonishment and pleasure.

'Thank you, Thomas. Thank you so much,' she said, her heart swelling with gratitude. 'It's the best gift ever. She's beautiful.'

'That she is,' he agreed, laughing, this open display of affection from his sister leaving him in no doubt that she had found her horse.

'You told me you would buy me a horse, but I never expected it to be so soon.'

'I'm glad you like her. But what of the new saddle and bridle? Are they not fine, also?'

'The very best. I must find Arabella and Verity to thank them—and then I shall ride my beautiful mare into the village.'

'Prudence, wait,' Thomas said as she was about to scamper out of the room. 'We have a visitor.'

'Oh?' Still smiling, she turned.

With his shoulder propped negligently against the wall next to the window and his arms folded across his chest, Lucas was studying her closely. His black hair curled down to his broad shoulders, the wide lace collar offering the only relief to his black velvet short coat and straight breeches above his bucket-topped spurred boots.

Prudence hadn't seen him since that night when they had been his guests at Marlden Hall. Thomas had told her that their illustrious neighbour had gone to London on business, and she had sincerely hoped there would be pleasures and frivolities enough to keep him there.

Their eyes met across the room and her smile faded from her lips. Until that moment she had struggled to banish Lucas Fox from her thoughts, but she had not succeeded. It was like being on a hazardous obstacle course of emotions that left her weak. Secretly she had missed him more than she would have believed possible, for how could she ever forget how volatile, mercurial and rakishly good-looking this man was?

Instantly there was a resurgence in her of the magnetism that drew her whenever she saw him. It burned into her ruthlessly, making her heart turn over. Power exuded from his tall frame, making her feel quite helpless as she searched his dark features for some sign that this aloof, dangerously attractive man had actually held her in his arms and kissed her with such soul-destroying passion.

'I beg your pardon. I didn't see you there. I trust you've had an edifying look at me, my lord?' she snapped resentfully, unable to keep the venom from her tone, her look conveying the fact that she remembered their last encounter all too clearly and had not forgiven him for it.

Her sharp tone caused Thomas to glance from one to the other. His sister's aversion to his friend seemed to have deepened since their visit to Marlden Hall. Lucas's name never passed her lips, and when his name was mentioned she would look away—as if she were trying to forget he existed. It made Thomas wonder what Lucas had actually said to her on the night when she had drunk too much wine and flirted with him so outrageously, which had prompted him to take her aside and speak to her privately.

Prudence watched Lucas straighten from his stance by the window and move towards her. Warily, she eyed his approach. His gaze scanned her angry face, his half-smile revealing his amusement. When he took her hand and lifted it to his lips she snatched it away before it reached them, glaring at him. 'Don't do that. You take too many liberties where I am concerned, my lord. Do you make a habit of kissing the hand of every woman you meet?'

Lucas laughed out loud. 'The devil I don't. Only those I like.'

'Then you'll not kiss mine. I am most particular and I bruise easily.'

Totally unperturbed, his grin widened impudently. What

an enchanting creature she was—a combination between an angel and a spitfire. The sun from the narrow-paned window to the back of her shone directly on her hair, and he was filled with admiration for the rich vibrancy of its colour and texture. How he wished she would revert to the happy, smiling young woman who had come bounding into the room moments earlier, before Thomas had alerted her to his presence.

'When you've stopped snapping those eyes at me like a firecracker, I think we should start again. Good morning, Prudence. I came to discuss a matter of business with Thomas—and to wish you a happy birthday.'

'Oh! You knew it was my birthday?' she asked, standing poised, her nose tipped disdainfully high, her amethyst eyes opened wide, feeling completely dwarfed by this handsome, arrogant giant of a man.

'Your brother told me. Is there to be a celebration to mark the occasion?'

'I'm afraid not.'

He arched his brows, seeming surprised to hear this. 'No? I'm astonished. I thought every young lady enjoyed celebrations on her birthday.'

'And you would know all about that, wouldn't you, my lord?' she quipped. 'Considering your reputation for being an unquenchable rake and that half the females in Europe have apparently fallen victim to your charm, you must have attended simply thousands of ladies' birthday celebrations.'

Lucas gazed down into her wide eyes. 'That is a slight exaggeration,' he mocked lightly. 'Hundreds—not thousands.'

Prudence scowled at him. 'It might have slipped your notice, but the kind of celebrations you speak of have been forbidden in England for the past ten years.'

'Not any longer. Our country would shrivel up and die if we were to continue practising those wretched rules imposed on us by Cromwell.' When her expression showed no sign of relenting and that the twin points of her eye-

brows were locked together on the bridge of her delightfully pert nose, Lucas glanced at Thomas, clearly at pains
to control his laughter. 'Your sister is in a serious mood
today, Thomas. Can you not think of something to cheer
her on her birthday? A party, perhaps, or a trip into Dorking
to buy her a pretty dress?'

'I do not want a party, and Thomas has already given
me the finest gift of all.'

Thomas sighed, bestowing on his friend a feigned long-
suffering look. 'You must excuse my sister, Lucas. As you
must have noticed, she has no social graces and has a
tongue to rival that of a shrew.'

'I have had no need of social graces, and in no way do
I resemble a shrew,' Prudence retaliated sharply, burning
colour flooding her face. 'While the King and his court
have been living a life of self-indulgence on the Continent,
there has been no masques, no theatres for us to visit—in
fact, no merrymaking of any kind. But at least we can take
comfort in having lived a decent and moral life under the
Protectorate, without the decadence we hear contaminates
his Majesty's Court.'

Lucas rolled his eyes heavenward in mock horror. 'Good
Lord! What is this? Do I detect a malcontent in your house,
Thomas? Your own sister?' he said, one dark brow arched,
his eyes gleaming with derisive humour.

'This display of rebelliousness cannot be overlooked,
Prudence—and certainly not in front of Lucas,' said
Thomas, his face drawn into as convincing a facsimile of
stern disapproval as it was capable of just then, which
wasn't very convincing when his eyes were alive with
mirth. 'I will have you remember that he is a guest in this
house and I will not tolerate your rudeness.'

Very slowly Lucas smiled, his eyes gently taunting as
they settled on Prudence. 'Put it down to youthful exuber-
ance, Thomas. Perhaps your sister should be bled—or
might I suggest leeching,' he joked. 'If so, I can recom-
mend a first-class physician.'

'Oh, she'll be bled all right—' Thomas chuckled '—but not by a physician but a horse whip if she doesn't learn obedience and to conform to the new order of things.'

Prudence scowled at them both, her small fists clenched. 'Will you stop behaving like schoolboys? And please do not laugh at me…either of you. I do not enjoy being mocked. I am just as happy to see those days gone as everyone else.'

'Of course you are. Thomas and I were teasing.' Lucas lightly chucked her chin and grinned at her, and at that moment he did indeed look most endearing. 'And you are far too adorable to mock.'

'You won't get round me with your flattery, Lord Fox. I have no doubt that you can charm a snake out of its basket, but you won't charm me. You are insincere, your words sticky with the falseness of the Court.'

Thomas laughed softly. 'I think my sister has made a very accurate assessment of your character, Lucas.'

'Aye,' Prudence said, eyeing Lucas with deep distrust, feeling herself beginning to soften when he smiled in an attempt to mollify her—a devilishly engaging smile, those wonderful green-brown scamp's eyes full of lively amusement. 'I know him for a bully and a beast.'

'Lucas and I have finished our business, Prudence, so perhaps you would like to show this "bully and a beast" your horse before he leaves,' Thomas suggested.

Prudence didn't like, but with a supreme effort she forced a slight smile to her lips. 'I'm sure Lord Fox has more important things to do than look at my horse.'

Lucas exchanged an amused, knowing look with Thomas. 'Nothing would please me more than to see your horse,' he said, able to imagine her reaction if he told her he had already seen the chestnut mare, that he had chosen it because its coat was the same vibrant colour as her hair, that he had also examined it closely for any defects—and paid for it. 'And since I am in no hurry to return to Marlden Hall and there are many delightful things we might do on your birthday, perhaps you will allow me to be your escort on your ride. You might also like to accompany me to my home. The gardens are splendid at this time of year,' he added gently as bait. 'I'm sure you will agree.'

His invitation to show her his gardens was tempting, for they were renowned for their magnificence. She'd had a glimpse of them when she had been there two weeks ago and would dearly love to take a closer look, but her aversion to being alone with him outweighed her longing to see his gardens.

'It's quite out of the question. I couldn't possibly go with you alone, my lord.'

Not to be put off, Lucas turned to Thomas. 'What do you say, Thomas? Do I have your permission to take Prudence to Marlden Hall?'

'Of course,' Thomas replied without hesitation. 'Providing you see her safely home afterwards I have no objections.'

'Thomas! It would be most improper,' Prudence argued. 'Perhaps Arabella could accompany me. I'm sure she would like to see the gardens, too.'

'Arabella, I know, has made other arrangements for this morning. You'll be quite safe with Lucas.'

Lucas smiled smugly. 'There you are you see. It's settled.'

His eyes took hold of hers, challenging her to refuse. Prudence knew she couldn't, which did nothing but increase her smouldering resentment towards him.

'Will you not accompany us, Thomas?' she asked in sudden desperation, hoping that he would.

'Sadly I have no time for simple pleasures today. I have to visit two of my tenant farmers to discuss the rents, and mid-morning I'm meeting Ned to look over some cattle I bought last week.'

Prudence was disappointed. 'I see.' She looked at Lucas, who was smiling in the most infuriating way. 'Then if I'm to go with you to look at your gardens, my lord, I really should change my clothes.'

Lucas's gaze did a slow sweep of her apple green front-fastening jacket and matching full skirt, noticing how snugly the bodice moulded her rounded breasts and nipped her minuscule waist. Prudence reddened beneath his bold inspection.

'I find nothing wrong with the way you look,' he said softly, his eyes gleaming as they caressed her face. 'The clothes you are wearing are perfectly suitable.'

'Then since I am appropriately dressed, shall we go?'

Marching out of the room ahead of him, she didn't see the satisfied smile that passed between her brother and her antagonist, or her brother mouth the words 'good luck'. Passing the kitchen where Arabella and Verity were in conversation with Mrs Weatherill—their old housekeeper, who had been more than delighted to return to Willow House and take up where she had left off before the old master had died—she disappeared inside to get some lumps of sugar for her horse, slipping them into her pocket through an opening in her skirt. She paused in the hall to pick up a riding crop and to place a high-crowned hat on her head.

Lucas, watching her in fascination, considered it a sin to conceal those glossy locks from his eyes, but knew better than to comment. If the minx knew how much pleasure he derived from looking at them, she would make a point of covering her head whenever they met in future.

Without saying a word to her companion, Prudence walked stiffly through the garden towards the stables. Lucas followed, watching her swaying skirts, a smile sweeping across his features as he contemplated his impending ride to Marlden Hall with this enticingly lovely, albeit reluctant, young woman.

So far their relationship had been one of open combat, and it was clear that she was going to make him work hard to win her over. But he was not a patient man and already his patience was sorely strained by her constant sniping and

sparring, from which he derived a certain amount of pleasure, but eventually his patience would wear out and he
would be forced to subdue her rebellion in his arms—with
his mouth.

Determined to make her treat him with polite cordial-
ity—if not friendship—if they were to share each other's
company for several hours, he quickened his pace, matching his long stride to her brisk smaller steps. Reaching out
he grasped her arm when they were out of sight of the
house. With a gasp she stopped and glared at him.

'Now what is it?' she asked abruptly, giving him a look
that could have pulverised rock.

Placing his hands on her upper arms, Lucas managed to
get her to stand still. 'Simply this. Is it your intention to
remain in this quarrelsome mood for the entire day?'

Taking judicious note of the taut set to his jaw and feeling his fingers biting into her flesh, Prudence met his gaze,
beginning to regret her anger and her childish attempt to
distance herself from him. 'No. If you must know I hate
quarrelling, but you goaded me into it just now by mocking
me.'

'Thomas and I were merely teasing you,' he said gently,
releasing her arms from his grasp. 'I apologise if it upset
you, but if we are to enjoy today then do you think you
could amend your opinion of me? Must there be enmity
between us? Can we not at least try to be cordial to each
other and call a truce for now?' he asked with a soft, beguiling smile.

To his relief she took a moment to reflect upon the matter
before answering. Then, drawing a long breath as she felt
her antipathy towards him begin to melt in the most curious
way, she raised her magnificent eyes to his and smiled,
having decided that the most sensible and adult thing to do
was to capitulate to his demands, otherwise her sour mood
would ruin the day. Besides, she could find nothing in his
eyes or in his smile to stoke the flames of her animosity.

'You're right. I have behaved badly—although you are not entirely without fault,' she reminded him calmly.

Aware that she was referring to the time two weeks ago when he had invited her to his home and kissed her, he sighed. 'Let us put that evening behind us, shall we? Friends?'

'Friends,' she agreed. 'It would be churlish of me to continue behaving as if you are my enemy.'

Lucas lightly touched her cheek with his forefinger and smiled, adoring her spirit, admiring her sweet, fiery temper and her sense of fair play.

Reaching the stables, she found that while she'd been gone John had saddled the mare with the new side-saddle as she had asked him to. Her animosity towards Lucas was now forgotten as she lovingly ran her hand along the horse's sleek neck, laughing delightfully when it tossed its head and nuzzled her cheek.

Leaning against a wooden stall, Lucas watched her, totally enchanted, eyeing the chestnut mare as she happily acquainted herself with her new mistress. There was no denying the joyous blaze in the young woman's eyes when she looked at the gift he had brought from London for her birthday and gave it a sugar lump from her hand.

It was his unease following the attack on his person on the night of his return to London that had sent him back, with the sole purpose of going to the Pool of London to see for himself if Jeffrey's ship had docked. He had no desire to see his uncle, but after making discreet enquiries he had learned that he was still awaiting his son's arrival at a lodging house in Cheapside. Since the thirst for vengeance would not be easily slaked until all those involved in the death of Charles I had been punished in some way, he was keeping a low profile.

There had been no more assaults on Lucas's person, and as time went on and there was still no sign of his cousin's ship, he began to doubt that Jeffrey had been behind it and that he'd been too hasty to accuse him.

After purchasing the mare for Prudence's birthday, intending to be back at Marlden Green and to accompany her on her first ride, he had left London. But the deep feeling of unease persisted and he continued to watch his back, suspicious of every stranger's face and every shadow that moved.

It was unfortunate that he couldn't tell Prudence that the horse was from him and not Thomas as she thought, but if she knew the truth he had no doubt she would not accept the gift. In time, when he had won her over, he had every confidence that she would forgive both himself and Thomas the deception—and, if not, she would be so enamoured of her chestnut mare that, lacking the necessary power to part with her, she would be unable to find it in her heart to return the gift.

Reaching into her pocket, Prudence produced another lump of sugar, entranced as she watched the horse nibble it out of her palm.

'Have you thought of a name for her?' Lucas asked when John had disappeared to go and do some work in the garden.

Prudence raised her head, a clump of foxgloves catching her eye. The tall spikes with their purple, thimble-like flowers added a vibrant blaze of colour to a dark corner of the stable yard. Inspired, she looked at Lucas, turning the full force of her dazzling smile on him.

'Foxglove. I shall call her Foxglove. What do you think of that?'

Lucas seemed to seriously consider the name for a moment before he nodded, smiling his approval. 'It's a fine name—and appropriate.'

Prudence tilted her head curiously. 'Why do you say that?'

Unfastening the front of his doublet, he reached inside and quickly produced a small package tied round with a pink satin ribbon. Handing it to her, he said, 'You'll understand when you open your present.'

In puzzlement she looked from him to the neatly wrapped package, her fingers deftly unfastening the bow that secured it. The paper fell away to reveal a pair of expensive gardening gloves, reminding her of the day he had come to Willow House and found her pulling up weeds with her bare hands.

'Oh! I—I don't know what to say.'

'Thank you would be nice,' he suggested softly.

She looked at him and smiled. 'Yes—thank you. I promise I shall wear them.'

'I hope you do. You have lovely hands. When the time comes for you to go to London to be introduced at Court, it will be unacceptable to offer your hand to his Majesty to kiss if they are rough and callused from digging the garden and pulling up weeds.'

'I will remember,' she promised. Suddenly she realised what he meant when he said Foxglove was an appropriate name for her horse, and to Lucas's astonishment and absolute delight her smile widened, her small white teeth gleaming like pearls from between her softly parted lips. 'Foxglove! Fox and glove! Lord Fox, the giver of the gloves!' She laughed at her enlightenment. 'What a coincidence—and you are right. The name is most appropriate.'

Chapter Nine

Taking the reins, Prudence led Foxglove out into the yard. Climbing on to the mounting block, she settled herself in the saddle and arranged her skirts, watching as Lucas swung with the agility of an athlete on to the back of his powerful stallion.

'I suppose your stables are full of fine horses,' she said as they took the path away from Willow House towards Marlden Green, her apple-green skirt rippling against Foxglove's glossy flank.

'True,' Lucas said, riding beside her. 'Uncle George had the same eye for good horse flesh as my father. Fortunately, when I returned and he left Marlden Hall, he also left some superb thoroughbreds.'

'Where has he gone—your uncle?'

'London. Because of the hostility directed against the murderers of the King's father, and his own position—for it is no secret that he strongly supported that dastardly act— fearing for his safety and that vengeance will be allowed now King Charles has returned, he is lying low at a lodging house in Cheapside awaiting my cousin Jeffrey's arrival. His ship is due at any time in the Pool of·London. When he sails, Uncle George will sail with him. He intends making his home in America, where he has set up several business interests over the years. Were you acquainted with my uncle?'

'Not really. I met him once when he called at Willow House to discuss the selling of the fifty acres of land with my father. I cannot say that he made a favourable impression on either Arabella or myself.'

A wry smile curled on his lips, so faint it was barely discernible. 'That does not surprise me.'

Prudence turned and looked at him. 'You didn't get on with your uncle, did you?'

'No.'

'And Jeffrey—your cousin?' she asked tentatively, the man she had met on two occasions never far from her thoughts. 'Do you get on with him any better?'

'No.' His face was expressionless, his voice flat, but he was unable to conceal the bitterness that had been eating at him for five long years—which was the last time he had seen his cousin.

'On opposing sides during the Civil Wars, my father and Uncle George were constantly at war with each other. With my uncle living in Hampshire we saw little of him at Marlden Hall, but when we did you cannot imagine the quarrels that would always erupt between them. Their animosity towards each other was bound to affect Jeffrey, who was greatly influenced by his father. Although I must point out that when it came to supporting the King or Parliament, Jeffrey had no convictions for either side, as long as he could profit from it. It was a relief when he joined the navy and went to sea.

'He rose through the ranks to command his own ship. Later he left the navy and purchased his own vessel. He was issued with a ''letter of marque and reprisal'' and became a privateer.'

'What does that mean—a letter of marque?'

'That my cousin is in command of an armed vessel which is licensed to attack and seize the vessels of hostile nations.'

'That sounds like legalised piracy to me.'

Lucas grinned. 'There's a lot of truth in what you say. Originally the licence was issued to enable a merchant whose ship was attacked and his cargo stolen or destroyed to seek reprisals by attacking the enemy and recovering his losses, but since then the system has been used as a means of attacking enemy shipping in times of war—and it also saves the country the cost of maintaining a large standing navy. In theory, authorised privateers are recognised by international law and are not prosecuted, but the system is wide open to abuse, and privateers—which is the case with my cousin—are no more than licensed pirates, whose main objective is plunder.'

'I see. Were you and your cousin friends as children?'

'Sadly, no. Jeffrey was eight years older than I and considered me a nuisance. There was perpetual conflict and bitterness between us, which did not improve as we got older.'

And still is, Prudence told herself, wondering at the cause of the bitterness, sensing that the heart of the matter lay within the Fox family rather than the conflict that had existed in England for over two decades. Sensing Lucas didn't want to talk about it and not wishing to pry, although she felt uneasy having met Jeffrey Fox and not telling Lucas, she asked no more questions and concentrated her attention on her adorable Foxglove.

They rode through the sleepy village of Marlden Green and over the humped-backed bridge, attracting curious attention from everyone they passed. They were familiar with everyone in the village and acknowledged greetings cheerfully, but as they left the quaint huddle of cottages behind, Prudence knew that to be seen riding alone in the company of Lord Fox would give rise to much speculation and provide the gossips with plenty to talk about.

Surrounded by splendid scenery as they rode, warm sunshine washed over them. They turned off the main road, following a path through the woods, the many scents of the shadowy interior rising up to meet them. Lucas told his companion that it was a shortcut to Marlden Hall when she enquired as to why they had left the road.

After a moment of riding in silence, Lucas looked across at Prudence, admiring the way she handled her horse with confidence and ease. 'Are you enjoying the ride?'

'Yes,' she replied, thinking how elegant and relaxed Lucas looked atop his powerful black horse. She could hardly believe he was the same relentless seducer who had stolen a kiss from her the moment he had set eyes on her, and whose hungry mouth had again devoured hers at his house. 'It's so good to be on a horse again. I haven't ridden in ages.'

'Then it doesn't show. You, my dear Prudence, are a natural horsewoman. You have a perfect seat.'

Prudence glanced at him and smiled a slow, unconsciously provocative smile that sent a surge of pure lust firing through Lucas's veins. 'I've never had any complaints.'

Lucas grinned at her. 'Minx.'

'I can't for the life of me understand why you want to spend time with me. I'm not at all like any of those sophisticated ladies of your acquaintance.' Secretly Lucas thanked God for that. 'I've always thought of myself as being quite plain,' she finished with a little sigh of regret.

'I enjoy your company—when you aren't being stubborn and temperamental.'

'Me? Temperamental?' Prudence gasped, feigning offence, feeling strangely light-hearted.

Lucas laughed. 'There's no question about it. You, my sweet, have to be the most temperamental, intractable female it has ever been my misfortune to meet.' A slow smile tugged at his sensual lips. 'And since you were fishing for compliments, there is nothing plain about you.'

She flushed crimson. 'I was not.'

'Yes, you were,' he said, stifling a grin at the complete lack of contrition on her lovely face. His decision to ride directly to Marlden Hall was suddenly overpowered by a compelling need to be closer to her than riding allowed. The leafy glade, carpeted with woodland flowers through which they were riding, and the inviting soft green banks lining the sides of a silver stream were too tempting to resist. He halted, urging her to do the same. 'Now, get down off that horse,' he commanded.

'Why should I?'

'Because it's a perfect day for a stroll by the stream,' he said, dismounting and walking slowly, purposefully towards her.

Alarm bells started sounding in Prudence's head when she looked down into his sultry eyes. Already she was learning to recognise that look and what it meant when his voice became low and husky.

'I don't think we should,' she said, gripping the reins tightly.

Immediately he placed his hands firmly on her waist and lifted her down. Prudence fully expected his arms to entrap her and that he would try and kiss her, so she was surprised when he took the reins of her horse and his own and tethered them to the branch of a stout oak beside the stream. Turning, he held out his hand.

'Come.'

Prudence didn't take his hand, but she did stroll beside him along the mossy bank of the stream, watching the clear water as it tumbled over its rocky bed, aware of the seclusion of this place and her own vulnerability.

'I used to come down here often when I was a boy,' he told her. 'This was one of my favourite spots.'

Prudence looked at him and smiled as she envisioned a tall youth with shining black hair wading through the stream. 'And what did you do when you came here?'

'The usual things boys do—ride through the woods kicking up leaves, take off my boots and follow the stream all the way to where it joins up with the river. But most of all I used to daydream.'

He stopped and looked about him, going to a stout syc-amore and lowering himself on to the ground. He sat with his back resting against the trunk, one knee drawn up, and an arm dangling across it. His face curiously soft and his gaze never wavering from his companion, he patted the ground.

'Come and sit down.'

Hesitantly she obeyed, folding her legs beneath her skirts, but, like a stubborn child, she didn't sit nearly as close as he would have liked her to.

He gazed straight ahead, as if lost in thought. Prudence looked across at him, at the golden aura from a ray of light that fell across his handsome face. With its strong features and imperious profile, lean and finely drawn, it was almost as dark as Solomon's. She was drawn by the expression in his eyes, unable to identify any trace of humour or mock-ery. It had a yearning, almost nostalgic quality, as if at some time he had experienced some terrible distress and had come to this familiar, tranquil place to gain relief from it. She had never seen him like this. He had allowed the sardonic arrogance that was so much a part of him, and his intimidating self-assurance, to slip, making him strangely vulnerable and approachable.

'What are you thinking?' she asked softly, idly plucking at the grass with her fingers.

'Of Constantinople,' he said truthfully, his tone wistful. 'Of gold and white domes and minarets, and the wide ex-panse of blue water across the Golden Horn.'

'Oh!' she uttered in surprise, for his answer was totally unexpected. 'Won't you tell me about it?'

'If you wish to hear it. When I first approached the city up the Bosporus from the Mediterranean, the vista I first encountered held me in thrall. It was a magical sight. Its seven hills form an undulating line across the sky, and its domes and minarets seemed to float up out of a haze—like a mirage in the desert.'

Prudence tilted her head to one side, gazing at him with

a combination of awe and fascination, quite intrigued by this confounding man. 'Why were you travelling in the East?' she asked, questions about his mysterious past burning in her eyes.

He shrugged casually, reluctant to divulge the whole of the past five years, but deciding to enlighten her a little and do away with any misapprehensions she might have as to where he had been when he had parted company from Thomas. 'Pleasure—adventure. I was attracted by the beauty of the East and intended going to India.'

'And were you disappointed by what you found?'

'Disappointed? No. Anyone seeing Constantinople for the first time could not fail to be impressed by it.'

Prudence shuddered, her literary imaginings of the mysterious East having struck terror into her heart. 'You mean it's not steeped in medieval depravity and barbarism—that the Ottomans are not the bloodthirsty savages of legend, who slaughter or enslave those who cross their path?'

'Some are. Life at the Ottoman court is often brutal. It is a predominantly male world, and yet the influence and power of the Sultan's mother—or grandmother in the case of the present Sultan, who, when I first encountered him, was no more than a youth of seventeen, is enormous.'

'How long did you stay there?'

'Almost three years.'

'My—you must have been impressed.'

'I was. I lived in the Sultan's palace,' he told her, with a smile and a look of a shared confidence.

Greatly impressed herself by this revelation, Prudence's eyes opened wide with wonder. 'And to what did you owe this exalted position?'

'To the gratitude of the Sultan for having saved his royal life.'

Prudence was as captivated as a child listening to a fairy story. 'Oh! How?'

'From drowning. I was on a ship on the Bosporus when it collided with the Sultan Mehmed's barge. Unfortunately the Sultan was on it. All hell broke loose and in the confusion he and several of his senior officials were tossed unceremoniously into the water. Being the kind of person I am, I jumped in and pulled him out. I could see nothing brave in that, but the Sultan was grateful and rewarded me well. His Highness honoured me with his friendship and the freedom of the palace.'

A thought suddenly occurred to Prudence and her look became quizzical. 'What were you doing on that ship sailing for Constantinople when it was your intention to go to India? My education did stretch to the study of maps, and by my reckoning you were going the wrong way.'

Lucas suddenly looked embarrassingly uneasy and averted his eyes.

Prudence's eyes widened when realisation suddenly dawned on her and she scrambled to her knees. 'Lucas! Were you a slave?' She was so wrapped up in the story that she didn't realise she had used his Christian name for the first time.

When he met her insistent gaze his grin was almost sheepish. 'It's true. I was a slave. I was captured and sold to a Turkish pasha in Algiers. He was taking me to Constantinople.' His eyes twinkled roguishly. 'So—now what do you think of me? It's hardly the stuff heroes are made of. It's not something I want bandied about, either. With my outstanding reputation for courage and daring and feats of valour on the field of battle,' he chuckled, feigning a boast, 'if this comes out I'll never be able to hold my head up again among my friends.'

'No, I don't suppose you would.' Prudence smiled, a fetching little dimple appearing in her cheek as she fell in with his mood. 'But it wasn't your fault you were captured, and it's certainly an adventure well worth the telling.'

'An adventure I often think I dreamed up. But Solomon is living proof that I didn't.'

'When you saved the Sultan's life, did the Turkish pasha give you to him as a gift?'

'He did. To him it was an honour to bestow such a gift on the Sultan, but to me it was no such honour. And yet whatever our Western ideas of slavery, my bondage was far from wretched, and unquestionably more comfortable than that of the slaves in the West.'

'But it must have seemed terribly undemanding for a soldier.'

'I kept myself active by serving for a time in the ranks of the army of Islam—along with other Christian mercenaries. I also became one of the Sultan's favourites and was allowed the freedom of the palace. He was young and without friends.'

'And he saw you as his friend?'

'I think so.'

'Then why didn't he give you your freedom?'

'Why should he? He had no reason to. He was grateful to me for saving his life, but he was also selfish. He would call me his guest, not his slave, but I knew he would not let me leave willingly. I was most generously treated and he gave me much—a palace to live in, servants and jewels beyond compare, and as one of his favourites I acquired privilege. I refused nothing and became extremely rich by Western standards. Most of my wealth I secreted out of Constantinople to the West.

'However, I was wary and forever watchful. I knew my survival depended on the Sultan's friendship and that it wouldn't last. My time was limited. I knew it wouldn't be long before some jealous pasha poisoned my food or I'd find myself with a silken cord crushing my windpipe or a dagger in my back.'

'How did you escape?'

'When I learned that King Charles was to return to his throne in England, I decided the time had come for me to leave. My escape route was already planned. When there was no moon one night, Solomon and I disappeared from the palace. No one saw us leave.'

Prudence believed him. If what Molly had told her about

him was true, then she had no doubt that Lucas Fox could move like a shadow and disappear into thin air if he so wished. 'Is Solomon your slave?'

Offended that she should think this, his dark brows drew together and his reply was reprimanding. 'He is my personal servant, not my slave, Prudence. He stays with me from choice and he knows he is free to leave if he wishes.'

'But he won't, will he?'

'I doubt it. When I first met him he was just fifteen years old. The treatment he received as a slave was brutal. I befriended him, became his protector, and when I made up my mind to leave Constantinople he would not be left behind.'

Lucas went on to tell her about what life was like living in Constantinople, of the endless ceremonies and how time simply oozed away, and as she listened to his voice she closed her eyes, trying to imagine the glittering, waterside palaces at Stamboul, hidden behind massive walls with their marble halls laden with incense and exotic oils, the cool fountains and shaded terraces and blue seas, the heavenly sunsets and fragrance of flowers. When he told her of the thousands of craftsmen who worked to sustain this symbol of Ottoman magnificence, the whole visual message of the power of the sultans was brought home to her.

'The gardens you describe must require a considerable number of gardeners,' she said when he'd finished speaking of her favourite subject.

'Yes, they did. Almost a thousand, I believe.'

She gasped. 'That many? Heavens! With so many gardeners to look after them they must resemble an earthly paradise.'

'True, but these gardeners also have a more sinister role—when not tending the gardens,' he said, watching her fascinating facial expressions to everything he was telling her from beneath half-lowered lids.

'Oh?'

'They also act as executioners within the palace. A visit

from one of them carrying a sword or a silken cord is a sign of imminent doom.'

'Oh—how barbaric. How could you suffer living there for so long?'

'Suffer?' His expression became languid and a warm sensuality appeared in his eyes as his gaze caressed her face. 'I was not suffering, Pru. You see, there was another…more pleasurable aspect to life in the Sultan's palace. It was like an open heart, where the outer part was open to all forms of humanity. But the palace had a hidden heart—a separate world, which was reached through an entrance called the Gate of Bliss, where palace guards and servants rarely penetrated.'

Lucas paused and he studied her rapt expression in silence. His conscience chose that moment to suddenly assert itself and he had to remind himself that he was speaking to a gullible young woman who knew nothing of the world outside her own sphere. Anticipating that some of the things he would say if he continued might seem sinful to her, he said on a sharper note, 'And on that point I'm afraid our conversation must end.'

Disappointment clouded her eyes. 'But you can't stop now,' she protested.

'Yes, I must.'

'But why?'

His eyes captured hers and he laughed softly. 'Because the things that went on behind that particular gate are not for the ears of a virtuous young lady of the Western world.'

'What sort of things?' she asked, annoyed because he'd stopped.

'Wanton things, Pru. It would be pistols at dawn should Thomas discover I spoke of such things with you. They are not the kind of things a gentleman discusses with an unmarried woman.'

Clearly his explanation didn't satisfy her because her expression became indignant. 'Goodness! Do I have to wait until I'm married before such things can be discussed? It isn't fair.'

Lucas was well enough acquainted with her to know that neither the strictures of society nor Prudence herself could repress her natural curiosity about all things. He knew he ought to end the conversation right now, but when she looked at him as she was doing, watching him closely, a tiny, irresistible smile playing about her soft lips, he could not deny her. 'You're right,' he murmured, a glimmer of admiration in his eyes. 'It isn't fair. Very well, Pru—I will tell you. But I must warn you that some of the things I might reveal might shock you.'

Her eyes lit up and her interest deepened as she shuffled herself into a more comfortable position in front of him. 'No, it won't. I'm not easily shocked. What was this place?' she asked, sounding breathless.

'The Abode of Bliss—the seraglio—a word which refers to a palace within a palace, but to the Western world is synonymous with a harem.'

'A harem?'

'Harem—or haram—meaning forbidden, a system of se-clusion. The Christian peoples of the West, who conceive it as a place of lust, misunderstand it.'

Prudence felt her face grow hot, for what he was telling her conjured up a host of improper thoughts and images. He was right. He shouldn't be speaking to her like this, and she certainly should know better than to encourage him and to listen, but her curiosity was fit to bursting and she wanted to know more. 'And it isn't?'

'It's a political and social institution—of separating the women from the men. The Sultan's male offspring are raised within the harem in a suite of rooms called The Cage, entirely cut off from the rest of the palace. When one of them becomes sultan, as a result of this seclusion they know nothing of the world outside the confines of the palace.'

'But why are they kept so confined?'

'Harem politics can be ruthless, and young princes become the focal point of conspiracies among the imperial mothers, who all want their own offspring to become sultan. They are confined to keep them out of trouble. You could call hiding them away a humane alternative to the practice of murdering them all when a new sultan takes over.'

Prudence gave him an appalled look, horrified by what he was saying. 'But that's barbaric.'

'It is. But it happens.' His voice became quiet and seductive. 'The harem is also the place of the Sultan's happiness, designed for his sexual gratification—the female house of concubines,' he said, watching her closely.

She saw the look in his eyes, and her heart began to hammer a warning that he was about to lead her into uncharted territory. 'Concubines?' she whispered, her breath hovering somewhere between her lungs and her lips.

Lucas smiled slowly. 'Are you sure you wish to hear more?'

She nodded.

'Very well. Concubines are women who live and breathe only to give pleasure to a man. Her body is the font of his desire, and the delicate oils and scents she anoints her body with increase his desire. The only men who are allowed to enter the harem are eunuchs.'

Knowing perfectly well what a eunuch was, Prudence dragged her embarrassed eyes from his, her cheeks burning bright flames of crimson. Somewhere up above a skylark sang, and in the dark interior of the wood an animal scuttled in the undergrowth, but she was deaf to the sound, conscious only of the man and the enclave dappled with sunlight in which they sat.

Trying to think of something to say, she ran her tongue over her lips, and Lucas's gaze was captured, watching the unconscious provocation of her gesture, studying every detail of her face beneath the wide brim of her hat. A shaft of sunlight glinted on the wisps of hair brushing her cheeks, and turned her magnificent eyes to a dark shade of purple.

He smiled slowly. She was so innocent, so incredibly naïve. 'I see I've shocked you,' he murmured huskily. 'I did warn you.'

It was true, he had, but somehow she managed to drag her gaze back to his, her agile mind already leaping ahead. 'A little,' she confessed, 'but I now realise why you didn't try to escape from Constantinople sooner.' She was tempted to ask him how well acquainted he was with the women of the harem, but didn't dare.

Lucas smiled, but didn't expand on her assumption. He was both amused and intrigued by her genuine, unguarded reaction.

'Aren't these women permitted to leave the harem?'

'Yes, but tradition dictates that they must be veiled and accompanied by a eunuch.'

'Are all these women in love with the Sultan?'

'Good lord, no—although they do vie with each other to share the royal couch. Jealousy is rife—in fact, come to think of it, the harem resembles a nest of serpents, with oiled, supple bodies and rosy red lips that spit out venom. The vultures flying around the Executioner's Fountain, where executions take place on a regular basis, are more tenderhearted than some of the women in the harem. The sultan offered me the hand of one of his favourite houris in marriage,' he told her, explaining as gently and tactfully as he could that an houri was one of the beautiful virgins of the Moslem paradise.

'And did you accept?'

'No. To do so I would have had to become a Moslem. My Christian faith might not be what my dear mother intended it to be, but I would not change it for another.'

Prudence reflected on what he had told her when he fell silent. She was glad that he'd felt able to tell her about his past, about what had happened to him during those five missing years—even Thomas didn't know anything about.

It was as if it had drawn them closer, that a special bond had formed between them, and she had a peculiar feeling that this was what Lucas had intended.

But then she realised he hadn't told her everything. He'd only told her about three of those missing years. The two at the beginning were still a mystery and open to question. How had he been captured and sold as a slave? Before she could ask him he'd risen to his feet. Feeling the moment for questions had gone she did likewise, straightening her skirts.

'If you are to see the gardens at Marlden Hall we'd better go.'

For a moment Prudence thought he was going to draw her into his arms and kiss her, but instead he took her elbow and walked her back to the horses in silence. Gathering Foxglove's reins in her hand, she was surprised when Lucas lifted her effortlessly into the saddle. She looked down at him gravely, hardly able to believe what she was feeling.

'Thank you for telling me about what happened to you when you left Thomas in France.'

He smiled up at her, his eyes full of warmth as he boldly rested his hand on her thigh. 'You're welcome. Thank you for listening.'

Prudence could feel herself relaxing the closer they got to Marlden Hall. She found herself enjoying Lucas's easy ways and casual banter. His charm, wit, and manners were those of one born to wealth and position. What she had feared would be a tense, unpleasant ride had become an enjoyable outing, and the gardens were just as magnificent as she expected them to be.

For the first time in his life Lucas looked at them as he had never looked before. He was amazed that he could derive so much pleasure from simply walking along the paths with Prudence by his side, taking pride in the beautifully tended terraced gardens and the carefully manicured, geometrically laid out knot garden which stretched out like a beautifully worked tapestry, the many herbs and flowers delighting the eye and the nose. To the north of the house, before one reached the enclosed deer park, was the maze with its high box hedges, and the topiary, the distinctive clipped box and yew providing a series of shapes and colours that complemented each other.

As they strolled along a paved terrace, Prudence was spellbound as her gaze was captured by an ancient dovecote and woodland gardens in the distance, planted with azaleas, cherries and massive banks of rhododendrons.

'What a shame that you live here all alone, surrounded by so much beauty and no one to share it with,' she breathed, bending to take in the scent of a particularly beautiful shell pink rose.

Lucas watched her, completely captivated. 'It is true. Apart from the servants I live here quite alone.'

'Aren't you ever lonely?' she asked, straightening up and looking at him in questioning innocence.

He seemed to ponder her question before shaking his head. 'No—although I do not intend living here alone indefinitely.'

She tipped her head to one side and regarded him with open candour. 'You don't?'

Lucas met her gaze sagely. 'I do intend to marry at some time, Prudence.'

'Yes, I suppose you must. And have you a lady in mind?'

He regarded her piercingly, a barely perceptible smile forming on his mouth. 'You might say that. At present there appears to be several seemingly insurmountable hurdles in my way—but I have every confidence that they will be overcome.'

'Do I know the lady?'

He grinned. 'I believe you do.'

'And are you in love with her?'

'I—am fond of her,' he answered cautiously. 'She is extremely pretty, I enjoy her company and she makes me laugh.'

'That wasn't what I asked, and it isn't enough to base a marriage on.'

'Oh, she does have many other essential qualities, I do assure you,' he replied in an amused drawl. A slow smile tugged at his sensual lips. 'Do you suppose that if I told the lady that I love her, it would surmount all those hurdles in my path?'

'No, not if you don't mean it. She would find out and hate you for being dishonest. But you will still ask her?'

'That is what I intend.' He answered her impartial question in a calm, matter-of-fact voice, wondering what her reaction would be if he were to tell her there and then that she was the woman they were speaking about. His reasons for not doing so were influenced by two things. First, he wanted her to want him the way he wanted her before he made his intentions clear, and secondly, she would probably take flight and openly resist any attempt he made to go near her.

But it had been no idle statement when he had told her that he intended to ask the lady they were discussing to marry him. He would call on Prudence at Willow House and court her relentlessly. He would marry her, of that he was certain. The weeks in between would be agony, but he would have her in the end.

Pondering over what Lucas had told her, Prudence experienced something akin to disappointment, which both puzzled and surprised her. Something else puzzled her. Why had the lady he intended marrying not been present when they had dined at Marlden Hall? And if he was contemplating marriage, then why had he kissed her, and told her in no uncertain terms that he would kiss her again?

She sighed, realising that she was totally out of her depth when it came to trying to understand the workings of the male mind—especially when they were so much older and experienced than she was.

Mr Fletcher, the head gardener at Marlden Hall, was delighted to be introduced to Prudence, and more so when he realised she had a passion for gardening to rival his own. Lucas, whose enthusiasm came nowhere close, left her in Mr Fletcher's care and returned to the house, where he would wait for her to join him for refreshment before setting off back to Willow House.

But as he watched her happily walk away, he noticed how at home she looked against a backdrop of lilac and green lawns, of honeysuckle and roses. He felt an odd surge of protectiveness, an unusual twist to his normal desires whenever he was with her. The force of her attraction was like the pull of the moon on the tides. It was something that went beyond all earthly understanding. Her laugh was infectious, and her smile had the power to light up the darkest corners of his heart. She was also volatile, warm and elusive, and he was certain she would never bore him.

All these qualities, combined with her honesty, made her a prize above all else.

Chapter Ten

Prudence was quiet on the way back to Willow House. Lucas put it down to the excitement of her birthday and that she must have worn herself out looking at the gardens and trying to find her way out of the complicated maze, which she had insisted on entering. But he was wrong. When they had left Marlden Hall behind Prudence gave herself up to her thoughts. She found herself dwelling with a certain amount of curiosity on the woman he had told her about, the one he intended to marry, puzzled as to her identity. Lucas had told her that she knew her, so she must be local. Perhaps she belonged to one of the many important families in the district.

But it was what Lucas had confided to her when they had sat beside the stream in the woods that was prominent in her mind. It worried her that she hadn't told him about her meeting in Dorking with his cousin Jeffrey, and she felt that she should, but for some unknown reason she was uneasy about doing so.

No one was around when they reached the stables at Willow House. After removing Foxglove's saddle, Lucas turned to his companion, a worried frown creasing his brow.

'You are quiet, Pru. Is something wrong? Did what we talked about on our ride to Marlden Hall upset you?'

She gave him a nervous little smile. 'No—why should it have upset me? I'm glad you told me and I've had a lovely day. Thank you. You can go and find Thomas now. I intend staying here a while to groom and feed Foxglove.'

He nodded, giving her a long look. When he was almost out of the door her voice halted him.

'Lucas—wait.'

He turned and looked at her, waiting for her to speak. She was standing in front of Foxglove with her hands clasped tightly in front of her.

'There is something I should have told you but I—I didn't think it was important. It might not be, but I feel uneasy about it.'

Lucas walked slowly back to her, his eyes never leaving her face. 'What is it?' Already his voice had lost something of its gentle quality.

She licked her lips, which suddenly seemed to have dried up. 'Earlier—when—when you were telling about your cousin—Jeffrey…'

In an instant his whole body went rigid. She could see how white he had become, so white that a grey pallor showed through the bronze tones of his face.

'Jeffrey? What about him, Pru?'

Prudence swallowed hard, feeling that the delicate intimacy of their truce was about to crumble. She looked up at him, uncertain, searching his face. 'I—I have seen him,' she replied, hearing the reluctance in her voice, the admission dragging from her like a confession.

'Where? Where did you see him?' Lucas demanded, reaching out and gripping her arms.

'In Dorking when I was shopping with Arabella. I—I was returning to the coach alone when I dropped my packages. He—he helped me to retrieve them.'

Still gripping her upper arms, Lucas looked down at her for a long time without speaking, his eyes as hard and cold as steel. It was as though he was deliberating some inner problem and he could only find the answer in her eyes.

'How did you know it was Jeffrey?'

'He—he told me,' she stammered. 'I also met him on the day of the procession—just before you—well...' She lowered her eyes, too embarrassed to refer to the incident of him kissing her. 'He made a way through the crowd so that I could stand at the front.'

Prudence could see Lucas's mood had changed drastically—his careless, laughing manner was gone and his eyes were relentless, his mouth set firm. She couldn't read what lay behind this change, but one thing was clear. All likeness to his cousin had gone. This man was harder, more terrifying, and of a different breed.

'He was there? He was there that day?'

His voice had a dangerous edge. Prudence nodded, a prickling of fear beginning to escalate to panic. She tried to shake off his grip, but his fingers dug deeper into her arms like the teeth of a trap. 'I didn't know who he was—until we met again in Dorking. He—he was kind and quite civilised really.'

Lucas looked at her as if she had taken leave of her senses. 'Kind? Civilised?' he gritted, and Prudence actually flinched at the bite in his voice. 'My cousin is the most *uncivilised* villain I know, and he *never* does anything out of kindness. For God's sake, Pru, why didn't you tell someone you had seen him—Thomas or me—before now?'

'Because I didn't think it was important. In truth, I thought little of it at the time. I already knew he lived in Hampshire, and Dorking isn't so very far away so there was nothing unusual about him being there.'

'Not any more.'

'Pardon?'

'My uncle sold the house in Hampshire when he moved into Marlden Hall ten years ago.'

'I didn't know that. There—there is something else I should tell you. There was a man with him in Dorking, which I found quite unsettling. I still do. You see, it—it was Will Price,' she told him hesitantly. 'You remember Will?'

'Perfectly,' he bit back, unable to work out just then the connection between the two men or how their being together in Dorking had come about, but he had no doubt that it boded ill. Rage filled him. He ached with it. He felt as if it radiated to every part of his body and beyond. At one time he would never have imagined that his cousin's viciousness would override his common sense, but he had been mistaken. The methods Jeffrey had used to make quite certain he would never return to England and claim what was rightfully his had been chilling and brutal.

Until this moment he had assumed his cousin to be somewhere on the high seas, that he could not have been behind the assault on him on the day he had come to London. But he had been mistaken. Jeffrey could very well have set one of his henchmen on him. His cousin was here, had been here from the beginning, careful not to show himself to him.

Letting go of his captive's arms, Lucas combed his fingers through his hair and turned away, exasperated with her for not having told him of this sooner. 'Tell me something, Prudence. Are you always so secretive about what you do and who you see?' he said with cold reproach.

'Of course not. Lucas—what is wrong—and why does my seeing your cousin make you so angry? What's wrong with him? What has he done that's so terrible?' she asked, trying not to look as stricken as she felt. Why did she suddenly feel that she was caught up in the middle of something she didn't understand?

'Never mind,' he growled.

'He—he told me that if I should see you to give you his respects—and to tell you that he congratulates you on making a full recovery.'

Lucas swung round to face her, his handsome face livid. He was clearly furious, on the verge of an explosion. 'The devil he did,' he said. 'Don't be deceived by my cousin's charm, Prudence. His years travelling the world as a privateer, cultivating acquaintances among the Barbary corsairs and all manner of scum that sails on the high seas, have given him a pomposity, arrogance and cruelty that turns the stomachs of all decent, law-abiding men. You must never again have anything to do with him. You have no idea what he is capable of. You don't know him.'

Prudence looked at him with an awkward mixture of embarrassment and anger. So far her will to resist had been neutralised by her anxiety about telling him about Jeffrey and shock by his violent reaction, but now his wrath stirred her ire. What right did he have to treat her like this? She had told him about her meetings with his cousin because she felt he would want to know. She certainly hadn't expected to be made to feel as if she had done something wrong when she hadn't. Besides, whatever it was that had happened in the past to cause such enmity between Lucas and his cousin had nothing whatsoever to do with her. But the arrogance of the man, the autocratic and dictatorial manner with which he expected her to share his opinion of his cousin, was typical of him. Her eyes were mutinous as she jutted her chin.

'No, I don't know him—I couldn't possibly—not like you do, and I don't particularly want to. I don't know you either. You could be a scoundrel and a villain too for all I know.'

Lucas's eyes turned into shards of ice. They bored mercilessly into hers and a muscle began to throb in his cheek. 'You're right,' he bit out. 'I have been accused of being both those things and a hell of a lot more. I could be anything. I gave up on ethics a long time ago. Five years ago I experienced tyranny and injustice at its most brutal. I settled for survival because it was either that or death. That's all I knew then. One minute, one hour, one day at a time. Somehow I managed to survive one more sunrise, one more sunset, hoping that tomorrow might be an improvement on today. All I had was my will and my pride to see me through—and my pride was all I had left to me. Each new day was an added bonus when I awoke and found myself still alive.'

In contrast to the deadly quiet of his voice, his face was a mask of savage fury. His volatile anger was terrible and completely incomprehensible to Prudence, but she could sense in him a raw and quivering sensitivity. She realised that she had unwittingly unleashed in him all the hidden forces of a passionate nature, all the more hideous because the unyielding nature of the man made him normally able to master them. She stepped back and wrapped her arms around her waist, as if trying to fend off the hurt he was inflicting on her raw emotions.

'I don't understand what you're saying,' she whispered, alarmed by this new side of him—of the cold menace in his voice and on his face. More clearly than ever before, she realised that, despite their earlier closeness, they were still virtual strangers. Suddenly she felt that he had just given her an insight into those two missing years of his life no one seemed to know anything about. Images of all the horrors he might have suffered crystallised in her mind, and an icy chill stole through her.

'When did you see Jeffrey?' When she didn't answer his eyes slashed hers like knives. It was as if her silence put her instantly beyond all limits of his tolerance. 'I asked you when you saw him,' he repeated in a chilling voice.

'Sh-shortly after we dined with you at Marlden Hall,' she mumbled, never in her life having witnessed such controlled, menacing fury in anyone.

'And how did he appear to you?' he asked, finding it hard to take that, when he'd been in London looking for Jeffrey, Jeffrey had been in Surrey. If so, where was his ship? What was he planning?

'I told you he was helpful on both occasions—and extremely polite.'

'I can see my cousin impressed you,' he sneered, and Prudence wondered whether it was mockery she heard in his voice or reproof. Moving closer, Lucas raised his hand to cup her chin, his hold tightening when she tried to turn her head and pull it free. 'Prudence, I am using all the self-control I possess to keep from shaking you till your teeth rattle.' She met his eyes nervously. 'The next time you see my cousin,' he said in a tone that brooked no argument, 'I want to know about it immediately. Is that understood?'

'No, I don't understand. I don't understand any of this,' she said on a fresh surge of courage, stubbornly refusing to bend beneath the hard glitter in his eyes and submit to his authority, her heart screaming her resentment of his commands. 'You are making out that it was my fault—that I went looking for your cousin. I told you what happened and now I wish I hadn't. Why should I tell you anything? I am not some trained underling to do as she is told.'

'Do not use that tone with me,' he warned, his voice implacable. 'I am neither your brother nor your sister.'

'No, you are not, and I will speak any way I please. You have no right to order me to do anything. Do you challenge my brother's authority?'

For a long moment their gazes locked in combat as they assessed one another, and then Lucas let go of her chin. 'Very well.' His voice was tight. 'Then call it advice.'

'Advice often exhorts one to give up something one likes to do—to do something one does not wish to do,' she replied with a stubborn thrust to her chin.

His dark brows snapped together. 'I am asking you to trust me, Prudence. I do not speak lightly when I ask for your co-operation on this matter. It is imperative that, should you see Jeffrey again, you will tell me—or Thomas. Pru—do not play with me.' His voice was soft with warning.

Meeting his gaze, Prudence drew a shaky breath. 'I'm not,' she whispered, wishing she knew what all this was about.

Lucas gave her a long, penetrating look, hardly knowing how to cope with the emotions raging inside him at the thought of Jeffrey and all his evil getting close to this young woman, who was quickly becoming the most precious thing in his life. 'I want your word that should you meet Jeffrey again, you will tell me.'

'I give you my word.' She was breathing in shallow, suffocated breaths. 'You speak as if I kept my meeting with your cousin to myself deliberately.'

'Of course not.' Reading the hurt and confusion in her expressive eyes, Lucas realised that he'd probably done the utmost damage to the relationship he'd been trying to build between them all day—the happiest day he had spent in a long time because of her presence. If he had wanted her to hate him, he had accomplished his goal brilliantly. He despised himself for it and yearned to beg her forgiveness. The fury within him died abruptly and, as he gazed down at the pain in her eyes, his stomach clenched at the thought that he had put it there.

Today he had discovered she was a mass of contrasts, all of which he found vastly appealing. Not only was she fiery and skittish, temperamental and stubborn, she was also intelligent, witty and fun to be with. She was also refreshingly devoid of pretension and artlessly sophisticated—although no doubt she would argue with that. She had listened and gazed at him in wonder when he had told her of the three years he had spent as a slave in Constantinople, and he had been humbled by her innocence and ignorance when he had told her of life within the Sultan's harem. He was ten years older than she was, and a thousand times more experienced and harder, and yet her very closeness and the way she had of looking at him softened him, making him want to love and protect and cherish her, emotions he had thought long since dead.

Suddenly the rage was gone from his voice, replaced by a tone Prudence had never heard in him before, and there was in his eyes something like an involuntary tenderness.

'I'm sorry, little one,' he said quietly. 'I didn't mean to be angry with you—at myself, maybe, but not with you.

Of course you're not to blame, but since you seem to have attracted the likes of my cousin I am deeply concerned. It tears me apart when I think he might hurt you. I implore your forgiveness if I have caused you pain?'

Prudence raised her eyes and looked at him, trying to understand the turbulent, confusing emotions he was able to arouse in her. 'I should find it easier to forgive you if you told me what terrible deed your cousin is guilty of.'

He shook his head slowly, his fingers lightly caressing the curve of her cheek, as he became preoccupied with her rosy lips. 'You are too young to become caught up in the quarrels that exist between my cousin and I. Now is not the time to speak of it.'

The gentle touch of his fingers on her cheek caused a flame to flicker to life within her, and she felt her breath come a little quicker from between her parted lips. His closeness did something to her heart that she could not bear to contemplate or try to understand. She could only gaze at him as a tumult of emotions coursed through her. There raged within her a memory of an evening spent at Marlden Hall, when his kisses had seared through her resistance and left her shaken with the realisation of her own passion. All those feelings came tumbling back as she stood there, trembling in anticipation of another kiss as his face came closer and she heard a sudden hoarseness in his voice as he spoke her name.

'Pru…'

He never said anything else, for at that moment they heard voices outside the stable.

'Prudence? Lucas?'

Thomas's and Arabella's voices broke the spell and Prudence, moving quickly, lowered her gaze and walked blindly around Lucas. He drew near and caught her hand, halting her with her back turned to him.

'Do not be angry with me,' he begged, his whisper brushing close against her ear, sending a warm, tingling shiver through her. 'I was sore, and I said more than I meant to. I'm sorry, Pru.'

'I'm not angry,' she replied simply, pressing his hand without turning to look at him. 'And I'm sorry too, Lucas. Please forgive me.' He released her hand and she went out into the stableyard to meet her brother and sister.

Prudence paused on the brow of a hill, which gave her a clear view of the water meadows below. Her eyes followed the lazy swathe of the river as it meandered its way through the valley bottom. The air was cool against her face, which she found invigorating and inhaled its freshness.

In one week's time Arabella was to marry Robert, who was to travel to Marlden Green for the ceremony the day before the wedding. He would take his bride to his home in London the following day. Prudence would also be leaving for London at the same time with Thomas and Verity for an indefinite period. Thomas had some business affairs to sort out and Verity was eager to see her uncle. Gently she patted Foxglove's neck with a rueful sigh, for she was going to miss her dreadfully.

Prudence knew that Lucas was to call on Thomas that morning and would undoubtedly have accompanied her on her ride. Having no wish to give people reason to gossip should they be seen riding alone together a second time— and the lady he intended to marry very much on her mind— she had purposely set out early to avoid him, and to bring some rest to her roiling thoughts. She wondered what he would say when he found she wasn't there. Would he wait a while for her to return, or would he go home? Perhaps he might ride after her, thinking that she would want him to—and part of her did want him to, and that was the problem. She was beginning to enjoy being with him—enjoy having him close.

She found her thoughts carrying her away. In fact, from the moment Lucas had left her at the stable a week ago after their ride to Marlden Hall, they had tumbled and crashed and refused to give her rest. She had tried shrugging them off, but they reappeared like grey shimmering ghosts, to maul and shred her peace of mind. Images of Lucas's face constantly invaded her memory, along with the moments they had talked together, walked through his magnificent gardens at Marlden Hall together—and when he had kissed her. She saw again the strange expression in his eyes when he had looked down at her in the stable. What had he been about to say when they had been interrupted?

On a sigh she touched Foxglove gently with the whip and she responded instantly, moving eagerly as she retraced the path towards home. Prudence had to pass by the home farm where Ned Trimble lived with his wife and sons. She rode into the rickyard, which was a hive of industry, for harvest was almost upon them. It started when the wheat was ready in August, when men, women and children from the nearby hamlets and villages rose with the Harvest Horn each morning at five o'clock, and worked until the sun went down.

She found Ned plastering the axles of a wagon with thick yellow cart grease, for he was unable to bear the squeaking of the dry guides when the shaft horse turned the wheels. She stopped to tell him that some of the cattle Thomas had recently acquired must have broken through the fencing, for they had somehow found their way on to the land near the river, the land her father had sold to George Fox.

Ned stopped what he was doing and scratched his head, looking up at her queerly. 'Nothing wrong with that, miss—and nothing wrong with the fencing either. Sir Thomas told me it was quite in order that I put them there.'

'Really? Oh—I see.'

Prudence didn't see—not at all; all the way home it continued to puzzle her. Their finances being what they were, she knew Thomas hadn't bought back the land—besides, he would have said. Perhaps Lucas had agreed to rent it to him.

When she returned to the house she found Arabella and Thomas in the parlour. Verity was taking a nap, which she always did at this hour of the afternoon. Arabella was working on her screen close to the window, and Thomas was sitting in his customary place beside the fire, which was lit despite the warmth of the day. He looked up from the book he was reading when Prudence entered, and he smiled.

'Did you enjoy your ride, Prudence?'

'Very much,' she answered, seating herself opposite him. 'Thomas, I didn't know you were renting the land off Lord Fox our father sold to his uncle.'

'I'm not. Why do you say that?'

She shrugged. 'It's just that the cows you bought recently are grazing on Lord Fox's land. I thought perhaps they had wandered there of their own accord and called to tell Ned. He said you told him to put them there.'

Thomas shifted uneasily and cast a furtive glance at Arabella, who had stopped sewing and had her needle poised in mid-air. She was watching her brother closely. Prudence did not miss the knowing glance that passed between them, but before she could comment on it Arabella said, 'Lord Fox called to see Thomas while you were away, Prudence. He was sorry to have missed you. Had you waited, he would have accompanied you on your ride.'

'I know. That's why I went early,' she told her sister quietly.

'Why? Does his presence displease you?'

'No. He makes me feel uneasy, that's all. Lord Fox has told me that he is to marry, and if this is so then he would be committing an unforgivable breach of decency should he be seen riding with me alone.'

What she said brought startled glances from both Thomas and Arabella. 'Marry!' they exclaimed simultaneously.

Prudence looked from one to the other. 'Didn't you

know?' She shrugged, assuming by their silence that they didn't. 'I'm surprised. I thought he would have been sure to tell you, Thomas. He told me just the other day. Perhaps he hasn't mentioned it to the lady he wishes to marry yet, so it might be best if we don't mention his forthcoming nuptials to anyone for the time being either.'

'And did Lucas, by any chance, tell you the name of the lady he intends to wed?' Thomas asked cautiously.

'No. But he did tell me that she is not unknown to me. Do you know who she could be, Thomas? She must be someone who lives in the area.' She looked across the room at Arabella, bewildered by the stricken look on her face. 'Why, Arabella, is something wrong?'

'Yes—something is very wrong,' Arabella replied, ignoring the look of caution her brother threw at her.

'Arabella,' he said, his voice tight. In keeping with the plan, he sent her a warning look, cursing perverse fate for making what had already been a difficult situation into one that looked fit to worsen. 'Don't say—'

'No, Thomas,' Arabella broke in sharply, meeting his eyes. 'You know I've been against this subterfuge from the start. It's not right to keep it from Prudence. She should be told.'

'Told? Told what?' Prudence echoed in bewilderment.

'That you are the woman Lord Fox intends to marry,' Arabella told her as gently as she could.

For a moment Prudence's mind went completely blank. She stared from one to the other in confused, disorientated shock. What colour remained in her face drained away. When their words finally sank in, shock and horror brought her surging to her feet. Her eyes blazing, she glared at her brother, and when she spoke her voice shook with the violence of her outrage.

'Of all the conceited, vile, despicable, underhand knaves!' she seethed, unable to think of any more expletives to portray her animosity. 'How dare Lucas Fox play games with me? What sort of man is he, anyway? When was he going to tell *me*?' she demanded, her hands clenched into fists at her sides, a spasm of pure disgust forming a tight knot in her stomach.

Thomas had half-expected a bout of tears and recriminations, but he hadn't expected such tempestuous aggression. 'When he had won your affections and when he thought the time was right.'

'The time will never be right. I am obliged to Lord Fox for his *interest*, but I cannot—no—I will not marry him. The man is completely heartless, and I cannot believe I let myself be taken in by him when he so gallantly offered to show me his home on my birthday. I will never be able to forgive my stupidity for trusting him. Do not try to make me marry him, Thomas. I would do anything to please you and Arabella—but not this. I do not feel particularly complimented by his intentions and even less flattered.'

Arabella got up and came to her in alarm, placing an arm about her tense shoulders, saddened that their blundering had caused Prudence so much distress. 'No one is going to force you to do anything you do not want to do, Prudence. Is that not so, Thomas?' she said, looking for reassurance to her brother.

Thomas frowned, disappointed that things had turned out this way. 'Of course the ultimate decision lies with you, Prudence. But do not be too hasty in your rejection of Lucas. This is a great opportunity for you. What matters is that Lucas wants to make you his wife. He has a large estate—and you would still be close to Willow House. You would also be able to indulge your passion for riding and gardening—and Lucas would be most generous. He is a wealthy man—beyond most—'

Prudence glared at Thomas in disgust. 'I care nothing for the man or his wealth,' she told him, sounding harsher than she had ever sounded when she addressed her brother. But considering the circumstances, it was important that her feelings had to be made plain to Thomas and Arabella, so they wouldn't browbeat her into marriage to Lucas Fox.

'Next you will be telling me that the matter is already settled.'

'Of course I gave him my permission to go ahead and court you. Lucas knows I have no objections to the match. I never thought I would see the day when a woman would captivate him the way you have. You cannot hope for a better offer. Lucas has known ladies of great beauty and wealth, but all they did was amuse him for a time, while you have gained the very thing every one of those females desired above all else—the offer of his hand in marriage. He's a fine man, Prudence, and he has many qualities to commend him.'

'Good heavens, Thomas, why do you make it sound as if I'd been offered a kingdom? I find the manner in which he has hatched a plot to marry me behind my back—arrogantly expecting me to fall in with his wishes without argument—both insulting and degrading. He may not be so willing when he realises there is no dowry,' she stated coldly.

'You have qualities in abundance that will make up for that. Lucas is willing to take you without a dowry.'

Prudence was stricken. 'And you agreed to this? You agreed for me to marry this man, who was a stranger to me until not so very long ago, without consulting me? Oh, Thomas, how could you do this? Please don't tell me you made a settlement on me.'

'No, Prudence,' Arabella said gently. 'Lord Fox made the marriage settlement on you.'

Prudence stared at her sister through eyes enormous with disbelief. 'He did? Arabella—what are you saying?' Suddenly, through the turmoil in her mind something penetrated, something so awful and humiliating that she fervently hoped Thomas wouldn't confirm it. It was a picture of a lush green meadow full of strawberry roan cows munching contentedly on the grass.

'How much does Lucas Fox want to marry me, Thomas? Is he willing to buy me?' she asked, her face a stiff mask as she fought the anger and shame churning within her, and the unbelievable hurt that this might be so. 'Has he promised to return the fifty acres of land our father sold to his uncle if I agree to become his wife?'

Unable and unwilling to conceal the truth, Thomas nodded. 'He did make that offer.'

'I see,' she replied, feeling more hurt and degraded than she cared to admit. 'Then you were somewhat premature in grazing your cows on those fertile acres, Thomas. I will not be bought by any man—and least of all by Lucas Fox. Did he promise you anything else?' As soon as the question left her lips she knew there was. She felt a terrible, unexplainable premonition of dread that mounted by the second. All of a sudden the whole gruesome picture fell into place in every profane detail. With heartbreaking clarity she thought of Foxglove, and she knew the beautiful little mare had been Lucas's gift to her on her birthday, that it was not from Thomas and Arabella, as they would have had her believe.

In the ensuing silence she stared in burgeoning horror at her brother. 'It was Lucas who bought Foxglove, wasn't it?' she whispered brokenly, blinking back scalding tears that threatened to flow.

'Yes.'

'I knew it.' Prudence stared at her brother as if she thought he was as evil as Lucas. 'Oh—how could you?' she cried, her voice shaking with bitterness and pain. 'How could you let me go on making a fool of myself? I was gullible to the point of stupidity. Why did you let me believe she was from you?'

'Because you would have refused to accept such a gift from Lucas.'

'You're right. I would. I still can.'

'What are you saying?' Thomas demanded.

'Just this. I shall give Foxglove back,' Prudence informed him firmly. 'I want nothing from him. Absolutely nothing,' she said tonelessly, the repetition with which she issued this statement already beginning to ring a note of insincerity in her mind, the weakening increasing her anger. Her eyes speared her brother's like shards of steel. 'I will not be paid for—and certainly not by a man whom I know will demand value for his money. I have my pride, Thomas, and when it comes to the truth of the matter, I consider myself above the price of fifty acres of land and a horse.'

Thomas came to his feet, finding it all he could do to bridle his temper while Prudence was determined to be as difficult as she could be over this. 'That's quite enough, Prudence. Control your tongue. Your attitude is unacceptable. I think you had better go to your room and calm down. I am aware that you have a penchant for foolishness and wilfulness that outweighs all the considerations of common sense. However, I will ask you to consider long and hard Lucas's proposal. We will speak of this again when you are more rational.'

With her heart screaming her resentment, and feeling more hurt and degraded than she cared to admit, Prudence held her chin high as she walked towards the door, and without so much as a backward glance she jerked it open and closed it firmly behind her.

Thomas and Arabella looked at each other, each silent and thoughtful. When Arabella made a move to go after her sister, Thomas halted her.

'Leave her to calm down, Arabella. She'll come round.'

Chapter Eleven

Battered, humiliated, and deeply hurt, when Prudence reached the privacy of her room, she felt the full weight of her misery and succumbed to her tears. She cried for her foolishness, for her gullibility, and for the time she had wasted trying to understand the turbulent, all-consuming emotions Lucas was able to arouse in her.

After a night of tearful self-recrimination, unable to think of anything but her mortifying predicament and her mind tormenting her with images of her own folly, blind to everything but going for a ride on her beloved Foxglove, she went to the stables.

When Thomas came up behind her she turned and looked at him directly.

His eyes travelled with concern over her pale face and his brows drew together beneath the brim of his high-crowned hat.

'I hope you do not intend riding far, Prudence—not with a storm threatening.'

'I only intend going as far as the village. I'm hoping the ride will clear my head.'

'You seem on edge—and it is no wonder. Are you still upset about what you learned yesterday?'

She shook her head. 'No. Not any more. But I wish you hadn't kept it from me, Thomas. It was wrong of you to do that.'

'I apologise, Prudence—but Lucas considered it more appropriate to wait a while before making his intentions known—to allow you time to get to know him.'

'I realise now that that is the reason why he's been so attentive towards me of late.' She frowned, looking at her brother steadily, clearly troubled by events. 'Thomas, I don't know what to do.'

He smiled, understanding what she was going through and that it was all a part of becoming a woman. Prudence was growing up at last. 'I can see that. Do you feel anything for Lucas?'

Her frown faded to be replaced by a sad introspection. Whenever she was with Lucas she felt that something deep inside him was reaching out to her. Finding an answering response, like a strong magnetic pull, it was slowly, relentlessly drawing them closer together. She almost cried out at her predicament and shook her head wistfully. 'I don't know what I feel. Whenever I think of him I'm so confused. What I do know is that I respect him enormously—and—he disturbs me greatly.'

Thomas saw the truth of her words in her lovely eyes and he sighed. 'If you were to tell me that you love him I would say that you have excellent judgement. Lucas is the most loyal friend anyone could wish for—and he has more character and substance than any man I know. Take it from me, Prudence, he is a fine man. I know of no one finer. He has an undoubted charm to which few females are impervious. Every unmarried woman at the King's Court would be honoured and flattered to receive a proposal of marriage from him—so why do you hesitate?' She lifted her eyes and looked so pleadingly into her brother's face that he took both her hands in his own. 'What is it? What is holding you back?'

Swallowing hard she spoke with difficulty, quietly. 'I'm so scared, Thomas.'

'Of Lucas?'

She nodded. 'He is a man of so many contradictions—a soldier, an adventurer. The kind of life he has led I cannot even begin to comprehend. He is so much older than I, with a wealth of experience and a knowledge of people and places I could never know. I am quite bewildered as to what he can possibly see in me.'

Thomas's face was tender. 'Can you not? I can—and he has indicated his joy at this marriage. You will have a whole lifetime before you to get to know each other—and I advise you not to try to understand what is outside your comprehension. Just remember that he chose you for his wife above all others, and be happy knowing that, even if the methods he used to procure you do not meet with your approval.

'But you are right. There are many things about Lucas even I don't understand. He does not give of himself easily or lightly, but locked inside he has an ocean of love to give to the right woman. I truly believe that you could be that woman. No one could desire the happiness of a true marriage more that Lucas. Despite the face he shows to the world, he is a sensitive man and capable of great gentleness. But after saying that I would not force you to do anything against your will, Prudence, and that includes marrying my closest friend.'

'You want me to marry him, don't you, Thomas?'

'It is my dearest wish that you develop a sincere affection for him and are willing to honour his proposal. And remember, it could be worse, for it is not uncommon for young women of your station to marry without meeting their betrothed. Usually it is a matter for their families, and it is not for the daughter to raise objections to the match. But this need not be your own fate.' Suddenly his eyes twinkled teasingly. 'Come now. You cannot tell me that you don't enjoy defying and provoking my friend.'

A touch of Prudence's humour returned, and with a playful smile dimpling her cheeks she admitted, 'Yes, sometimes. It can be stimulating.'

'There you are, then.' His expression became grave once more. 'You are very dear to Arabella and me, Prudence, and we would not see you unhappy. In the end the decision is yours. But will you promise me something?'

Knowing what he was about to ask her she straightened and, in a small voice, conceded, 'Yes. What is it?'

'Yesterday you made your refusal to marry Lucas in an emotional gesture which, though understandable, I urge you to reconsider.'

'I was angry, wasn't I? I will do as you ask—but you must understand what this decision means to me. Ever since you told me of Lucas's intentions, I have been unable to think of anything else. I can't make up my mind and I need time to think about it, Thomas—and to let him know that I object most strongly to his method of going about it. Not once has he said he cares for me. Marriage is important and serious and not something to be undertaken lightly—especially for me.'

A slow smile touched her brother's lips. 'Of course not. But don't take too long. Lucas is not noted for his patience. He wants you to reach an understanding before too long.' He took the reins and led Foxglove out into the yard, frowning at the clouds rolling in from the west. 'Those clouds look menacing and I've already heard the rumble of thunder in the distance. Don't be away too long and ride no further than the village.'

Prudence had no intention of riding far, but after skirting the village she was unable to resist the temptation to go to Marlden Hall and confront the man who had had the effrontery to enter into a contract of marriage with Thomas without consulting her. However, when the tall chimneys of his house came into view her confidence disintegrated. Dismounting, she sat on a log and removed her bonnet, and with her hands clasped together around her knees she gazed at the house in the distance, attempting to imagine what it would be like to be its mistress.

She sat without moving for half an hour or more, trying to force all emotion from her mind and use reason when she thought of her predicament. Thomas certainly had logic on his side when he argued that she should marry Lucas— with his title, his splendid house and gardens, to say nothing of his wealth that would enable her to live in the lap of luxury for the rest of her life. She would want for nothing, and Thomas would be spared the trouble and expense of presenting her at Court and get his fifty acres of land.

She shivered when a cold wind blew through the trees and the first spots of rain fell, but so lost was she in her musings that she continued to stare at the house, ceasing to think rationally and turning to emotion. She resurrected the image of the man who wanted her for his wife and reconstructed the times when they had been together. The joy she had felt when he had held her in his arms was shattered by tearing disappointment that he had bartered for her as he would a horse. The only result of this was to bring tears to her eyes, which ran down her cheeks in icy trails. Unhappily she brushed them aside. So much for emotion.

But what of duty? Did she not have a duty to Thomas? He wanted that fifty acres so much. Already his cattle were grazing on those fertile pastures. What would Lucas do if she refused to become his wife? Would he ask Thomas to remove them? Oh, she thought bitterly, how could he put her in this situation? It wasn't fair. His deception was unpardonable. He had been arrogant in his belief that he could gradually seduce and persuade her into falling in with his wishes, and what vexed her more than anything else was that he might be perfectly correct in assuming that she would.

She sighed unhappily. She certainly wasn't indifferent to him, so she couldn't pretend that she was. In fact, when they were apart she missed him more than she would have believed possible, so did she really hate the thought of marrying him? Could she swallow her pride and go to him and tell him that she would surrender unconditionally—to simply say that she was willing to marry him and yield without a struggle? It would please him immensely to hear her say it. However, it wasn't that easy—but how she wished it was.

She failed to notice until too late that the sky had darkened and the wind had risen, whipping her hair into a frenzy and sending her bonnet up into the air. With dismay she watched it go soaring over the treetops, quite irretrievable. The raindrops came steady at first but in no time at all the heavy clouds unleashed a torrent of water that was relentless. Her clothes were ill suited to withstand such a heavy downpour, and she was soon soaked to the skin. Getting to her feet, she looked around her in despair. She couldn't possibly ride all the way back home. It was much too far, and even the trees offered little in the way of shelter.

Climbing back on to her horse, she realised she had no alternative but to beg her would-be suitor's hospitality. A faint twinge of doubt about what she was doing pricked her, but setting her chin and trying to decide what tone she would use when she saw him, she laboured on. Gripping Foxglove's reins she rode past startled gardeners sheltering beneath the trees. Seeing her, they paused in their conversation, their mouths agape. Reaching the house, she slid from the saddle at the same time that a groom, having observed her riding up the drive, came to take her mount. A footman opened the door and she walked in, knowing she must look a fearful sight. Pausing in the middle of the hall she looked around at the rooms leading off, wondering behind which closed door the master of the house was lurking.

'Would you please inform Lord Fox that I am here?'

The footman's eyes travelled over her bedraggled appearance, unable to believe this was the same lovely young woman his master had brought to Marlden Hall a week ago.

'He is in his study, Mistress Fairworthy,' he replied, trying to maintain an imperturbable façade as he indicated a door opposite. 'I will announce you.'

'Thank you, but please don't bother. I will announce myself,' she told him, ignoring his shocked expression and walking towards the closed door with all the dignity she could muster. After knocking, lifting her resolve and taking a firm hold on her courage, she entered, closing the door behind her and resting her back against the hard wood.

Having discarded his jacket, Lucas was seated at his desk working. Her heart lurched at the sight of him. All her resolutions of confronting him had momentarily mellowed to a desire just to see him. His white shirt partly open at the front revealed the strong muscles of his neck and upper chest, with its crisp matting of hair just visible. Broad shouldered and with his black hair curling darkly about his bronzed face, and with his wicked eyes and lazy smile, he would have made the most handsome pirate, she thought.

If only he hadn't gone behind her back and hatched a scheme to marry her. How could she ever forgive him for his supreme arrogance in assuming that she would be so flattered by his glib proposal that she would meekly fall in with his plans without argument? Which only went to show how little he knew her, and that he cared nothing for how she felt, and that he was only concerned with what he wanted.

When Lucas looked up and saw Prudence standing in front of his desk, looking for all the world like something that had just been pulled out of the river, he stared in appalled surprise, coming slowly erect and rigid in his seat. 'Prudence! What in God's name are you doing here—and in this weather?' he said, getting to his feet and walking round the desk to stand in front of her.

He cocked a handsome brow as he gave her a lengthy inspection. In sharp contrast to her bedraggled and saturated appearance, her pert nose was tilted to a lofty level and her eyes were riveted on his like hard flints as she courageously faced him down. But where she had displayed frivolity on their last encounter, he now perceived an air of seriousness about her—and his instinct told him why. She looked cautious, wiser, no longer like a puppy that had slipped its leash.

'Well,' he said, his eyes locked on hers with a frowning intensity, 'you certainly know how to make an entrance. You take me wholly by surprise.'

'No doubt it will fill you with perverse satisfaction on seeing me appear before you like this, but I was out riding and got caught in the storm. Unfortunately I had ridden further than I realised and found myself closer to Marlden Hall than Willow House. I had no alternative but to beg your hospitality,' she explained, at first apologetically, but then she realised that she had no reason to be contrite.

'I see.' His eyes were probing. 'I thought there might have been another reason for bringing you here.'

'I admit that when I reached the village I did decide at that point to come and see you, but when I reached your drive I changed my mind. The rain changed it back again.'

'And what was the reason that *almost* brought you to my door—before you lost your nerve about confronting me?'

Prudence's trembling chin raised to a lofty level as she eyed him coolly. 'I did not lose my nerve. As a matter of fact, there were two reasons,' she told him, feeling the damp chill of her wet clothes and shivering. Her skirts felt like dead weights about her trembling legs but she refused to give in to her discomfort. 'First of all I was coming to return your horse. Secondly, to tell you that I do not think much of your methods of procuring a wife. What you did was vile and contemptible—and your deviousness and deceit do you no credit,' she told him bluntly.

With no small amount of admiration, Lucas watched her struggle to maintain her dignity as she walked into the centre of the room, dripping water all over his carpet. He should have known that a defiant Prudence Fairworthy, with an infuriating stubborn streak and an unpredictable disposition, would resent and oppose a proposal of marriage having been made secretly between the prospective suitor and her guardian, instead of quietly accepting and letting the betrothal run its course until the wedding. Clearly it had been an affront to her pride, and her pride would force her to retaliate by making the whole ordeal as difficult as possible for him.

'Thomas told you,' he said, his words more of a statement than a question.

'As a matter of fact it was Arabella. Unlike my brother, she was of the opinion that I should be told what you intend.'

'So—you know it was I who bought you Foxglove for your birthday?'

'Yes—and you should have told me. How could you let me believe she was a gift from my brother and sister? That was quite despicable, deceitful and underhand.'

'I agree. It was. But would you have accepted the gift had you known it was from me?'

'At what price?' With humiliation and renewed wrath shining in her magnificent eyes, she faced him squarely, the sudden glint that crept into his look telling her that that question could be settled with no discussion at all. 'I will not be indebted to you, Lucas,' she said quietly.

'I would not want you to be. Can I not persuade you to keep Foxglove?'

Prudence found her legs carrying her towards him. Lucas Fox was capable of persuading her to do anything. 'I care little for your methods and even less for your kind of persuasion. You insult me, Lucas—fifty acres of land and a horse?' she retorted, tossing her head haughtily and spraying him with droplets of water from her hair. 'I consider myself to be worth far more than that. Thomas should have negotiated a better deal—a whole herd of cows to go with the land, perhaps? A stable full of thoroughbreds? By all accounts you can afford it,' she said, her voice threaded with sarcasm.

Despite her haughty stance, Lucas saw that her beautiful dark eyes, which were blazing scornfully at him, were also full of hurt. 'You're right,' he said gently. 'Anyone knowing you would agree that you are worth much more.'

'When you brought me here on my birthday and you told me there was a woman you intended marrying, why did you not tell me it was me?' she asked, looking at him steadily.

'Because it was too soon.'

'Yes, it was. It was arrogant of you to assume I would accept a proposal of marriage to a virtual stranger like an idiot. I do have a mind of my own, Lucas.'

His eyes captured hers and held them prisoner. 'I know. That is one of the things that attracted me to you in the first place.'

His admiration unnerved her. 'And I am more than capable of taking care of myself.'

Lucas leaned forward until the wide amethyst eyes came to meet the mocking smile in his. 'Were you able to do that, Prudence Fairworthy, you would not be here,' he pointed out.

Prudence's face burned with the truth of his statement, and it goaded her. As dearly as she wished to throw an angry denial at him, she could not. Her hauteur faded and was replaced by an expression of pained sadness. 'You may think you know me, Lucas, but you don't. You have much to learn.' Her voice was small and oddly strained. 'You cannot buy me for fifty acres of land and a horse.'

Refusing to believe that all his romantic plans were about to be demolished, Lucas folded his arms across his chest and perched his hip on the edge of the desk, arching his brows as he looked at her, at the way her wet hair clung to her face and hung about her slender shoulders and down her back in limp strands, making her look like an adorable waif.

'When I asked Thomas for your hand in marriage, I was not buying you, Prudence. If you believe that, then condemn me for it if you must—but I beg you to pardon me afterwards. I was clumsy, and in too much of a hurry. I should have approached the subject of marriage between us more cautiously, not rushed in without consulting you first. Clearly my mishandling of the situation has put your back up, and I cannot, in all fairness, say that I blame you for being angry. I confess to being drawn to you on our first encounter. I tried to discount it and put it down to infatuation, but when I returned to Marlden Hall and visited you at Willow House that day, I had to finally face the truth—that I wanted no other woman but you for my wife.'

A warmth was growing within Prudence that had nothing to do with the heat of the room. She was surprised when tears she could not restrain came to her eyes.

'Why—Prudence Fairworthy!' Lucas murmured as he confronted her moist gaze. 'What am I seeing? Tears? Is this the same young woman who has courageously stood up to me in the past and said her piece, who has told me that I have the morals of an unquenchable rake, and to go to the devil on more than one occasion?'

'Yes,' she whispered. Her eyes dried and her ire had fled, but was replaced by a tightness in her chest.

'And does the prospect of being my wife distress you so much, little one?'

She was so startled by the gentle caress in his voice that she stared at him, searching for a hint of sarcasm in his expression, but unable to find any. Not daring to answer his question, she averted her eyes. She wanted to appear indifferent, cold and remote—anything but distressed, but she could not say that the idea of being his wife distressed her. It would be a lie and he would know it. They both knew how her traitorous body responded to his attentions.

Seeing her shiver in her wet garb and realising that she must be experiencing immense cold and discomfort, Lucas's eyes swept over her dripping form and, standing straight, he arched a dubious brow. 'Enough of this for now. We will talk later when you've bathed.' With long strides he walked to the door. 'We had better get you out of those wet clothes before you take a chill.'

'There is no need to concern yourself,' she whispered. 'I have no intention of removing any of my clothes. I shall return home just as soon as it's stopped raining.'

'There is no sign of the weather improving, and you cannot remain like that. Did you tell Thomas you might come here?'

'No,' she said, giving him a sullen look. 'I—I didn't tell anyone. Anyway, he wouldn't have let me come alone.'

'Little fool,' he growled.

To her consternation he opened the door and went out, leaving her standing there. After a moment he returned, carrying a towel. Gratefully she took it from him and began rubbing at her hair.

'Mrs Witham, my housekeeper, is preparing you a bath. I've sent Solomon in my coach to inform Thomas where you are and to ask your sister to send you some dry clothes. There is every possibility that you will have to remain here until morning.'

His words, though spoken in soft tones, tore through her. She was extremely uneasy at being alone with him for the entire night and of what he could do if he set his mind to it. 'Please don't trouble yourself,' she said in a rush. 'Just as soon as the rain subsides I shall leave. I insist on it.' As if to mock her, at that moment the rain drove itself against the window panes and a rumble of thunder came crashing over the house, followed by a streak of lightning that lit up the room. Her legs trembled and she shivered, acutely aware of the icy chill encasing her body.

Lucas noticed and sighed. 'Prudence, be reasonable. I am only trying to help you—and you do seem to be in need of my services. There is some logic in you staying here until after the storm. Now come along and I'll escort you to your bath. The sooner you are out of those wet clothes the better you will feel. Come, don't be foolish,' he said when she drew back a pace.

'Foolish or not, I would rather not.'

'It will be unfortunate for you if you don't comply.'

'Unfortunate? What do you mean?'

'That I shall just have to divest you of your clothes my-self—right here.'

He regarded her with an intensity that made Prudence shake her head and back away, eyeing him warily. His statement had brought a bright hue creeping into her cheeks.

'Lucas! You wouldn't.'

'Try me.' His jaw clenched and his eyes narrowed. 'I find it curious that you have not yet made a more accurate assessment of my character. When I say a thing I mean it, so don't you think it would be wiser to allow me to escort you to your bath?'

Prudence hesitated, quite certain that he was more than capable of carrying out his threat. She dallied over the tempting idea of turning her back on him and marching out, storm or no storm, but she was not yet ready to leave the warm comfort of the house. Seeing that there was no moving him, she let out a sigh of defeat.

'Very well. But do you promise to let me leave just as soon as the rain stops?'

His chuckle was low and deep. 'I give you my word,' he conceded, confident that the storm would rage all night.

'And I can trust you to behave like a gentleman at all times?' she asked as she turned from him and placed her hand on the door handle.

Reaching out a long arm, he slammed it closed just as she opened it. With one hand still on the door, with his other he gently brushed back her damp hair and bent his dark head to her ear, drawing a gasp from her.

'I am willing to agree to any reasonable terms you state, but that, my sweet, is another matter entirely,' he breathed softly.

Startled, Prudence whirled to face him, but immediately realised her mistake. His broad, muscular chest was far too close and his head bent to hers. Leaving one hand resting on the door, his other arm snaked round her waist and he pulled her close. Her hair tumbled in disarray around her creamy-skinned visage. Her lips were soft and her eyes dark and sensuous, and beneath the fabric of her dress—with her warm body and nipples that seemed to burn into his chest, and her heart hammering like a wild, captive bird—was the undisguised fullness of womanhood.

He brushed his lips against her cheek, admiring the soft blush on the skin, and the delicately formed lips, which seemed to beckon his own. 'Prudence, understand this,' he murmured, speaking against her flesh. 'You are in my house alone, and if I choose to take you I will and there will not be a damned thing you can do about it. But somewhere, beneath my less than honourable reputation, some part of me still remains a gentleman, and I am also a man of my word.'

'What do you mean?' she whispered, unable to steady the chaotic pounding of her heart, her dark, heavy lashes fluttering downward self-consciously as he continued to stare. He laid his long fingers alongside her jaw, tilting her face to his and plumbing the innermost depths of her liquid bright eyes.

'I gave my word to Thomas that, where you are concerned, I would not step beyond the bounds of propriety. But that does not rule out persuasion.'

A tremor went through Prudence as his hand caressed her cheek, claiming the softness of her. His eyes above her own glowed intently, as his caresses grew purposefully bolder, the tips of his fingers tracing a burning line down her neck. A shocked gasp caught in her throat. She wanted to push away the brand that seared her, yet wanted it to go on. She swallowed, trying to keep her voice from shaking in reaction to his lips. 'It would appear that my brother is not the most proficient of wardens if he intends to leave me here for the entire night alone with you,' she said in a breathless whisper. 'Perhaps Arabella will return with Solomon to act as my chaperon.'

'She won't,' he whispered back, brushing her lips with his own, his warm breath mingling with hers, and moving on to nuzzle aside the scented tresses. Finding her ear, he touched it lightly with his tongue.

The heat of this gentle caress seared through Prudence, setting fire to every nerve. 'But how can you be sure of that?' she gasped, wishing he wouldn't do this to her, and yet at the same time not wanting him to stop.

'Because after this latest escapade of yours,' he murmured, tracing a molten path with his lips over her cheek once more, 'I suspect Thomas is extremely irate and can think of nothing he would like more at this moment than to get you off his hands for good. Arabella would only get in the way of things if she were to return with Solomon.'

Prudence's ears were temporarily deaf to what he was saying because of what he was doing to her. His face was so close that she could discern every handsome detail, and the way he was looking at her awoke burning memories she found extremely disturbing. A trembling warmth ran through her, completely disrupting her composure. She turned her face away to try and hide what she was feeling, at a loss to know how to deal with what was happening to her. That Lucas Fox was a man of extraordinary skill and prowess she knew, but she could not continue to withstand further attacks of his ardour and escape unscathed. This wily knave would not be content until he'd whittled away all her self-control and had her trembling at his feet.

Warned by an instinct she didn't understand, Prudence pulled back in his arms and shook her head dazedly, wanting him to release her and yet at the same time desperately wanting him to kiss her properly.

'If you please,' she whispered, drawing a shaky breath, 'I would leave you now. You forget that we are alone in here and that servants gossip.'

'A fact which seems to weigh more heavily upon your

discretion than mine, my love. You do want me, Pru—admit it.'

'I don't know what I want,' she whispered, closing her eyes with sheer bliss when his lips once again seared her flesh.

Lucas was becoming increasingly aroused and her resistance only sharpened his desires. He knew he should feel guilty for having taken advantage of the opportunity presented to him by the storm, that she deserved his protection and respect, not his lust, but his brain and his body seemed to be hypnotised by her face—and he was being ruled by an arousal that was almost painful. Realising that he was in danger of losing control, and amazed by the fact that this untutored girl was responsible for his condition, he reluctantly loosened his grip and drew a long breath.

'Prudence, we're going to have to stop. Come. Your bath will be getting cold.'

Prudence's swirling senses slowly began to return to reality. She nodded, allowing him to open the door, then take her arm and escort her up the elaborately carved wooden staircase to a room on the first floor of the three-storied house.

'Enjoy your bath,' he said in the doorway, gazing down at her, noting the telltale flush on her cheeks and the soft confusion in her searching dark eyes. 'If there is anything I can do to make your stay at Marlden Hall more pleasant, please don't hesitate to ask.'

Alone on the landing Lucas shook his head to clear it, telling himself he should have put Prudence inside the coach and returned her to Willow House with Solomon, but he also told himself he couldn't possibly have sent her back in that sorry state she was in when she arrived. His conscience shouted at him that he had another selfish reason for keeping her at Marlden Hall, but he ignored it.

From the very first, when he had realised that he wanted her for his wife, he had known she would oppose him if he made his intentions known too soon—and he had been

proved right—but he was supremely confident that her op-
position could be broken with very little effort. Prudence
was here now, beneath his roof, in his bedchamber, and he
had the whole night to persuade her.

His smile became one of almost lewd satisfaction when
another clap of thunder burst over the house, then he
laughed out loud. Never had he welcomed a storm as much
as he did just then.

Mrs Witham was a small grey-haired woman dressed in
black, with a white lace cap covering most of her hair. A
maid was just pouring the last of the hot water into a tub,
which had been placed in front of a fire blazing in a huge
stone hearth, when Prudence entered. She scuttled out when
her task was done.

'You'd best take off your damp things before you catch
a chill. I'll leave you to bathe while I see about getting you
something to put on until your clothes arrive,' Mrs Witham
told her, the friendliness in her voice as plain as it was in
her eyes and smile. 'Solomon should return with them before supper is served.'

'I—I may not be here for supper, Mrs Witham. If the
rain stops I shall return home.'

'Oh, but the master was most firm about you dining with
him later and having a room made ready. He was most clear
about that. I'll leave you to get out of your wet things—
unless you would like me to stay and give you a hand…or
one of the maids, perhaps.'

'No. I can manage to undress myself. Thank you, Mrs
Witham.'

When the housekeeper had left, Prudence looked at the
tub with longing. An enormous cloud of fragrant steam rose
from the water, and she was unable to resist the temptation
to relax in its warmth. After stripping off the wet garments,
she climbed in, quickly soaping her body and hair, before
relaxing with a blissful sigh and letting the hot water caress
her. It was wonderfully soothing, and she could feel warmth

gradually taking away the chill her damp clothes had imbued into her body.

Resting her head on the back of the tub, she took stock of the room, which showed excellent taste. Her eyes absorbed the extravagance and unaccustomed luxury of the furnishings and ornament. Several were Oriental in design, she noticed. Some of the apple-green and Chinese-blue vases were painted in intricate patterns of peacocks and other richly plumed birds and flowering trees.

The huge ornate bed made of cherry wood, with silk coverings and maroon velvet drapes hanging from the tester and tied back to the posts, was impressive. At night when the occupier of the bed was sleeping, they would be drawn to shut out the cold chill of the drafts invading the room.

Her eyes dwelt on the crest heavily embroidered in gold silk into the fabric—a hart and a falcon supporting a shield, both creatures favoured by the Fox family for generations because they were synonymous with the hunt. The mullioned, diamond-paned windows, upon which the rain was still beating relentlessly, had drapes to match the bed, and the room was lined with elaborately worked tapestries, each one depicting a hunting scene.

The chamber was predominantly masculine, fit for a noble lord—the lord of the house.

Lord Fox!

When Prudence realised whose room this was, all her emotions marched to war, propelling her upright. His room, indeed! Of all the rooms in this great pile, he had to put her in his. He had tricked her, duped her, and now how smug he must be feeling, how he must be laughing, knowing she was naked in his room—in his tub.

Hot colour mounted high in her cheeks and warmed her ears, but as quickly as her ire rose, so it died, and she smiled slowly, settling back into the water. As the image of a chiselled profile and warm green-brown eyes floated before her, she was past chiding her will into obedience. She could still feel the heat of his gaze that set her blood on fire, and his lips, which had stirred her to impassioned heights, twisting her insides into burning, tight knots of yearning.

Stepping out of the bath, she towelled herself dry and picked up a flame-coloured velvet robe she saw draped over a chair. Thrusting her arms inside the wide sleeves she wrapped it round her naked body. It was enormous, covering her completely and falling about her feet like a pool of shimmering water. Her nostrils caught the manly smell of the fabric. The pleasant, spicy scent of sandalwood was familiar and stirred a memory—a disturbing memory of the times she had been close to the owner of this robe, when he had held her, and kissed her. The memory softened her mood and she sighed. The huge bed beckoned seductively to her but, too afraid to recline on those silken covers, she curled up instead in a chair by the fire and let her mind wander aimlessly.

On a sigh she rested her cheek against the upholstery, unable to fight what Lucas was doing to her, and no long certain that she wanted to. When they were apart she was confident she would never feel anything for him, and all it took was a smile or a touch to make her surrender to his will. She was as susceptible to him now as she had been when he had plucked her out of the crowd on their first meeting and kissed her.

'Dear Lord,' she breathed aloud. 'What am I to do? What kind of sorcery does the man possess that he can have this effect on me?'

Chapter Twelve

Thomas was livid when Prudence didn't return from her ride. He knew perfectly well where she had gone, and he was just about to follow when the storm broke and Solomon arrived. Quickly his eyes scanned Lucas's note, which explained everything, also suggesting that Prudence stay at Marlden Hall until the storm passed over. If it failed to do so, then the most sensible thing to do would be for her to remain there overnight. A house full of servants should be more than ample to uphold the proprieties.

'To protect her, you mean,' Arabella couldn't help retorting when he passed the note for her to read. She was appalled at the idea of Prudence staying away all night. 'Lord Fox says that he will send her home when the storm passes over, but just listen to it, Thomas,' she said as another rumble of thunder broke over the house with an almighty crash. 'It may not pass over until it's too late and Prudence will have no alternative but to stay the night. She cannot possibly remain at Marlden Hall alone with him. Why, it's quite outrageous and not to be considered. There is nothing else for it. I must return with Solomon.'

Thomas's anger had lessened on the arrival of Solomon and he had become thoughtful. 'No, Arabella. We will do as Lucas suggests and send some of her clothes back with Solomon. I am sure Lucas knows what he is doing. Maybe after spending a little time alone with him, and a little tender persuasion from my friend—' he smiled '—our sister will find herself falling for his legendary charm.'

Arabella stared at her brother in disbelief, and it was clear to her when she saw Verity's quiet smile that she was in agreement with her husband. 'I am not sure I care for his methods of persuasion. Prudence won't know how to deal with him. Compared to Lord Fox, our sister is a babe in arms.'

'Don't you believe it, Arabella,' Thomas chuckled softly. 'Prudence will hold her own—of that I am certain.'

'But something like this could ruin her reputation.'

'Hellbent on defying me and going to visit Lucas alone, she has already brought censure upon herself. It's too late to do anything about that now.'

'And you can trust Lord Fox not to harm her—that he won't ruin her?'

'Absolutely. Be assured, Arabella, Prudence will be safe enough. Lucas has given me his word.'

Mrs Witham came to take Prudence's clothes away to launder, bringing with her a warm spicy brew in a cup and urging her to drink it.

''Twill ward off a chill,' she told Prudence when she saw her place it to her nose and grimace at the smell with distaste. 'The master instructed me to make it for you. It's not nearly as bad as it smells, I promise you.'

Prudence was not convinced but did as she was directed and sat and drank the brew, having no idea what it contained—hoping it wasn't some kind of potion Lucas had concocted from some strange Eastern recipe that would render her senseless and make her unresistant to his advances. When she had drained the contents she sighed. Whatever it contained, its effects were quite pleasant. Already she could feel the tension easing out of her aching muscles.

Solomon returned from Willow House with her clothes and no Arabella. Prudence was swamped with disappointment. It was as if her family had abandoned her to her fate—although she realised that fate had intervened in her life the moment she had seen the supremely arrogant Lucas Fox riding in the King's procession, resplendent in his fine clothes and sparkling with jewels.

She wondered what madness had made Arabella agree to letting her stay at Marlden Hall alone with him, and then she realised that her sister was in no better position to stand against Thomas and Lucas Fox than she was herself. No doubt once Thomas had recovered from the shock and fury of her disobedience, he would see that her defiance could be turned to his own and his friend's advantage, and she had to admit to herself that this thought didn't worry her as it once would have.

She was relieved to find the dress her sister had sent was a good choice. The colour was pale indigo blue and it was modest in style, being square-necked, not too low, full-sleeved, with the pointed bodice and a full skirt. Having dried and brushed her hair, she left the long silken tresses to hang free. Mrs Witham came to inform her that his lordship was waiting for her to join him for supper.

Unable to suppress her eager curiosity to see Lucas, she took a deep breath and, gathering as much courage as she was able, went downstairs. One of the footmen showed her to a smaller, more intimate room than the one where she had dined when she had been one of his guests on his return to Marlden Hall several weeks ago.

Standing in the doorway, she waited for him to notice her. He was at the opposite side of the room with his back to her and one hand resting on the chimney breast. His head was slightly bent as he watched the flames leaping and dancing in the hearth. He'd taken off his jacket, and beneath the white cambric shirt his muscles flexed when he stood up straight, lifting his hand and combing his fingers through his dark tresses.

His stance was sombre, as was his expression, and Prudence wondered what he was thinking. She took in the sheer male beauty of this man who wanted to make her his wife, feeling her blood run warm. He was everything a man ought to be. She was aware of the aura of calm authority and strength that always surrounded him, that was evident in his voice and lent purpose to his movements.

As if sensing her presence he turned, and his features softened into a wry smile when he saw her standing in the doorway. With long agile strides he came towards her. Taking her hand, he drew her inside the room, closing the door firmly behind her. She felt his gaze slide leisurely over her, taking in every detail of her appearance. Her eyes had to lift to his slightly, and when she met the shining glimmer of his own she trembled.

'I compliment you. You look lovely, Pru—although my heart is already pining for the adorable young waif who sought my hospitality earlier—if a trifle damp.' He laughed softly when her cheeks flamed scarlet. 'Come, let us eat. I was beginning to think you would leave me to dine alone. I hope you're hungry.'

'Yes. I'm ravenous,' she admitted, trying to ignore the tug of his eyes.

After considering her a moment, Lucas poured wine into two silver goblets and handed one to her. 'Here, you look nervous. Perhaps this will help.' A mischievous twinkle appeared in his eyes. 'It certainly helped enliven your spirits and increased your feeling of well-being the last time you were at Marlden Hall,' he said meaningfully.

His gentle reminder of the wine she had consumed that night and its dire consequences made Prudence's cheeks burn with embarrassment. She was determined not to repeat that mistake and to keep her wine to a minimum but, feeling the need of something that would still the quaking inside her, she nervously raised the goblet to her lips and drank, wishing the room was bigger, for then she would not feel so swamped by Lucas's regard.

'You are rested, I hope?' he asked congenially.

'Yes—thank you. Although I confess to having felt a

little uncomfortable on finding myself installed in your room.'

'The reason why I told Mrs Witham to prepare a bath for you in my bedchamber is quite simple. You arrived here looking for all the world like a drowned rabbit. It was clear to me that you were cold and in danger of catching a chill. My room was the only room with a fire in it. The state you were in, it would have been quite remiss of me to have you placed in another that is cold and unaired.'

Prudence tilted her head sideways and looked at him, a smile tempting her lips. 'That was most considerate of you, Lucas. But why is it that I mistrust your intentions? How do I know you won't intrude on my privacy?'

Lucas was torn between laughing and kissing her, because to intrude on her privacy was exactly what he wanted to do. 'You don't. But if that is what you are afraid of, then I will point out that there is a lock on the door you could use to keep me out. Would you have preferred me to have placed you in a less hospitable room to take your bath? If so, then I would begin to suspect that you might be some kind of masochist. Now come along and eat.'

He held a chair for her at a small table large enough to seat four people. Perched rigidly on the edge like a bird poised for flight, Prudence suddenly felt uncomfortable beneath his look that was too personal, too possessive. Her mind was tumbling over itself as to how she was going to survive until morning. Seating himself across from her, Lucas saw her gaze flicker repeatedly around the dark panelled room and he sensed her panic mounting by the second at being alone with him. But she was a plucky little thing, he thought, like a skittish colt.

'Try and relax,' he murmured, wisely suppressing the urge to reach out and take her hand resting on the table.

'If I am to remain,' she said uneasily, 'I would be grateful if you would agree to observe all the proprieties.'

His smile was one of condescension. 'If you are afraid that there will be a repetition of my earlier conduct, I will set your mind at rest. I am hungry and, until my appetite has been appeased, you are quite safe.'

She glanced at him warily, her cheeks warm. 'And afterwards?'

His eyes gleamed with wicked amusement. 'We shall see.'

A sharp retort tempted her lips, but further discussion was prevented when one of the servants entered the room to serve them supper. The food was excellent and the cook of exceptional ability. Not having eaten anything since breakfast—and then only very little—Prudence ate hungrily, enjoying the meal. When they had finished eating they moved from the table and sat on either side of the fire, to enable the servants to clear the table.

'My chambers are at your disposal, but I knew you would feel uncomfortable about using them, so I have asked Mrs Witham to have another made ready,' Lucas said, relaxing in the high-backed chair with his goblet of wine, his long legs stretched out and crossed in front of him.

'Thank you. It was kind of you to give up your room for me,' Prudence said quietly, 'but I would prefer to sleep elsewhere—preferably at home.'

'Then it is unfortunate for you that the storm prevents you from doing so. It seems destined to continue throughout the night.'

'You could send me back to Willow House in your coach,' she suggested hopefully.

'That would be most unwise. The heavy rain has swelled the river and raised the level of the stream to a dangerous height. Solomon only just managed to cross the bridge in the village. By now it will be under water. Thomas sent a message saying he will expect you back in the morning.'

Uncomfortably aware that the young female servant who had just carried out the last of the dishes had looked at her oddly, becoming positive that the entire population of

Marlden Green would be gossiping about her tomorrow, Prudence frowned.

'I do hope your servants can be relied upon for their discretion. I have no wish to be the object of scorn and ridicule in Marlden Green. If it gets out that I've spent the night at your house alone with you, my reputation will be quite ruined.'

Lucas shrugged indifferently. 'As Lady Fox you will be able to do as you please.'

Prudence's reaction to that was swift and unguarded. She glared at the arrogance of his statement. 'Don't be so presumptuous, Lucas. I haven't decided anything yet.'

'Nevertheless you will be,' he said with absolute finality. 'So you might as well accept the inevitable.' He raised his goblet. 'To our happiness,' he said, watching her over the rim as he drank the deep red liquid.

Watching him place his glass on a small side table, Prudence was struck by his monumental gall and she stiffened, determined to stall for time. 'I've told you—nothing is decided. You'll just have to wait for my answer.'

'Not too long, I hope. And besides, I sense you are uncomfortable living at Willow House with Verity. When the two of you are together it is evident that you don't get on. It would seem a husband is the only solution to that particular problem.'

Prudence lowered her eyes. Wasn't there anything this infuriating man didn't know? He was right—she and Verity didn't always see things eye to eye, and Prudence knew that her sister-in-law would not be content until she had Thomas and the running of Willow House all to herself. But the problem was minor and she would not tumble into marriage to solve it.

'I didn't have any problems until I met you,' she told him quietly. 'And if Verity and I are experiencing difficulties in getting to know one another, then a husband is certainly not the solution. Besides, if the situation becomes intolerable for me to continue living at Willow House, I know Aunt Julia wouldn't mind if I went to live with her in London. I would also be close to Arabella when she and Robert are married. As you know, they are to be married in a week's time, and we are all journeying to London the next day.'

'I am to go to London myself shortly, so it is inevitable that we will see one another.'

'Is it?'

'Yes. I will not give up, Prudence,' he stated firmly, refusing to even consider such a thing, no matter what he had to do to keep her.

'Even though I might be an unwilling wife?'

One dark eyebrow rose in a measuring look. An almost lecherous smile curved his lips as he rested his elbows on the arms of the chair and steepled his fingers in front of him. 'Unwilling? There was nothing unwilling about your reaction to my embrace earlier, my sweet. I won't change my mind.'

Prudence flushed, unable to quell the peculiar sweet stirring of pleasure his endearment caused. He meant it, she knew, and she was flustered by his possessive remark. 'But—you must know hundreds of beautiful, sophisticated and experienced women. Why me?'

Lucas gazed across at her, noting the soft confusion in her searching dark gaze. 'Because I don't want an experienced woman as my wife. I want you, Pru. No man of sound mind could resist so much temptation set before his eyes. You have captured my fancy and I have become hopelessly entangled in my desire.'

His eyes never left her—they seemed to scorch her with the intensity of his passion. Prudence was bewildered by it and lowered her gaze, afraid to meet that penetrating stare. She was already too well aware of the beguiling quality of his smile. 'That's an exaggeration,' she said at last. 'Lucas, you can't force me to marry you if I don't want to. Even if you drag me to the altar, you can't make me say I will.'

'I won't have to force you. When you are my wife it

will please me greatly to give you gifts—which it did when I gave you Foxglove. Don't deprive me of that pleasure.'

'What—will you do with the fifty acres of land if I don't marry you?' she asked tentatively.

One dark brow flicked upward in a measuring look. 'If? You mean you are considering it?'

She became flustered beneath his penetrating gaze that never wavered from her face. 'Why—I—I—marriage is a great step, and not to be undertaken lightly. Naturally I shall give the matter a good deal of consideration.'

'Then in answer to your question, I will ask Thomas to remove his cows from my land if your answer is no,' he told her calmly.

'Won't you consider selling him the land?'

'There is only one way that land will ever belong to your family again. If you have any love for your brother, knowing how desperately he wants it, it might be difficult living at Willow House knowing you are the one keeping it from him. But if you don't share your brother's desire to own the land once more, and feel no guilt, then I don't think we need concern ourselves over it.'

The subject was dismissed with this statement, leaving Prudence feeling guilty and thoroughly miserable. But she wouldn't let him see.

After saying goodnight to Lucas, ignoring the warm glow in his eyes, Prudence undressed and put on her nightdress in the chamber allotted to her. The noise of the storm had passed over, but a steady rain continued to fall. She lay down and thought sleep would evade her, but she soon drifted away, only to find her mind invaded by a vague world of dreams, dreams that involved a tall manly form pursuing her, dreams that were like fleeting shadows flitting across her mind.

It was some time after midnight when she woke, wondering what had disturbed her. To her abject horror, when she half-opened her eyes she saw the shape of a man across the room by the door. With a gasp she sat up abruptly, clutching the bedclothes beneath her chin as she faced the intruder. His awesome presence seemed to fill the room. In the gloom she watched as the tall, ghostly figure moved towards the bed, looming large and sinister over her. She was as if paralysed, her breath constricted in her throat; in fact, she was very near the precipice of hysteria. His face was only faintly discernible, but she had no need to see the man's face to know who he was. It was Lucas who stood by her bed, looking down at her.

He was covered in the flame-coloured robe she had worn earlier. Instinctively she knew he was naked beneath it, and she could imagine his lean hard body, and the gleam of his bronzed skin. She could sense his eyes on her, sense his penetrating gaze stripping her body bare. She watched him with the same rapt attention a rabbit gives a stalking fox, feeling his presence with every fibre of her being and, despite her shock, a growing warmth suffused her, melting her wariness.

'Are you afraid?' he asked, his voice deep and husky.

She stared up at him, her mouth agape, his shadowy form making her achingly aware of her own vulnerability and helplessness. 'No—but please go away, Lucas,' she whispered, her voice holding a desperate appeal as she shuffled further away from him.

His response was to sit on the bed. His features were clearer now, and Prudence fancied there was an expression on his face she had not seen before. His hair was tousled, his jaw lean and firm, and his dark eyes glowed down at her. Reaching out, he took one of her hands still clutching the bedclothes to her chin and kissed her fingers very gently. Her heart was pounding a deafening beat. She was tense and still, her brain racing as she tried to think of a way out of this.

'Lucas—please, I—'

'Pru,' he murmured, 'shut up.' Looking into her eyes as

he caressed her fingers with his mouth, Lucas could feel her melting, feel it in the way her fingers trembled.

'But I—'

He stopped her sentence with his thumb gently pressed against her lips. 'Shut up.'

The tone of his voice was so soft and inviting that for one mad moment Prudence almost surrendered. She felt herself tremble with the need that he always invoked in her when he was close, but she must not let him come closer. 'You cannot mean to do this.'

Taking her shoulders, he drew her lithe form towards him, capturing her in a fierce embrace, his eyes feasting on the delicate creaminess of her face and her shining hair spilling down over her shoulders and the soft bedding. The sweet fragrance of her body drifted through his senses, and the throbbing hunger to possess this woman began anew.

'I mean it,' he whispered, his mouth against hers. 'The attraction between us has been denied for too long, my love. I think we need to reach an understanding before you leave my house in the morning.'

'There is nothing to understand,' she whispered, suddenly afraid of the purposeful gleam she saw in those heavy-lidded eyes looking down at her.

'There is, my love,' he said, his voice a ragged whisper as he slid his tongue across her lips. 'Let me show you.'

Drawing her closer still, his parted lips took hers in a kiss like no other. His hands sank into the thickness of her hair, holding her head immobile as his mouth slanted across her lips and devoured their sweetness, languidly coaxing and parting, his tongue probing and plundering the honeyed cavern, as if he had an eternity to explore and savour.

The sweet urgency of it made Prudence lose touch with reality. It filled her soul. The embers that had glowed and heated her rebellion earlier now burned with passion, her protestations having become raw hunger. It was a kiss so exquisite that whatever conscience she had left died, as she became imprisoned in a haze of dangerous, terrifying sensuality over which she had no control.

At first she returned his kiss timidly, with an uncertainty of innocence, and then with an eagerness that astounded Lucas. Parting her lips, she welcomed the continued invasion of his tongue, sliding silken arms tightly about his neck and pressing herself to the hard contours of his virile form, little realising the devastating effect her softly clad body had on him as her lips blended with his with an impatient urgency. She threw back her head and arched her back when his lips left hers to draw a molten trail down the slender column of her throat.

Impatiently his fingers plucked at the tiny buttons securing her gown, sliding it down over her shoulders to her waist. Prudence gasped when she realised she was almost naked, hearing a small voice of sanity echo somewhere in her mind. In futile protest her hands came up flat against his chest and she tried to push him away, but she was neatly imprisoned. He had the advantage and he used it. He wanted her willing and quivering beneath him, begging for what he burned to give but must withhold at the last, even though it would be sheer torture for him.

With potent desire pouring through his veins, stretching his long lean body out beside her he pressed her back against the pillows, taking both her hands and rolling over slightly to pin her lightly beneath him. Prudence closed her eyes and let the hot, flickering flames of desire sweep through her when he bent his head and his warm mouth caressed the warm mounds of her breasts, his tongue flicking like a searing brand over their hard, rosy peaks, drawing each tip against his teeth until she arched and whimpered against him, the pulsing heat this created spreading to her loins like white fire through her veins, tearing the restraint from her world.

Finding her lips once more, his tongue lightly traced her lower lip, his kiss deepening with all the persuasive force at his disposal as he slid his free hand down and forced back the bedcovers, working her nightdress up over her thighs, slipping his hand beneath and touching her bare skin which felt like liquid satin, wanting to know and caress every part of her, to let his lips wander at will over the contours of her, wanting to claim her as his own.

As his hands explored every inch of her body, Prudence was on fire. With a low moan she stretched alongside him, the hard pressure of his loins making her all too aware that this was a strong, virile, healthy man. So lost was she in the desire he was skilfully building in her that, when his hand travelled along more intimate ground, her thighs loosened of their own accord and quivered beneath his questing hands. She almost drowned as wave after wave of pleasure washed over her.

Hesitantly she half-opened her eyes and met his intense gaze, hearing the drumming of her heart until her ears were full of the sound. Faintness drifted on the edge of her vision. She wanted him. She ached for him, and she clutched at him with the awkward desperation of inexperience, when a change came over him and he stopped what he was doing, drawing her nightdress down over her slender legs.

Fighting his rampaging desire, Lucas leaned over her and took her face tenderly between his hands, caressing her cheeks with his thumbs and gazing down into her passion-bright eyes, knowing she would willingly surrender her virginity if he asked her to. The moment his lips had touched hers and he'd felt her body mould itself to his, he knew she wanted him. She was too young and inexperienced to conceal her feelings, too genuine to want to try.

'My God, Pru. You are so sweet,' he murmured. 'You are temptress, angel and courtesan all in one. 'Tis my dearest wish to stay with you tonight and be damned to your virtue. You torment me. I am beset with wanting you. You twist and pluck at my insides so that I am driven to forget the promise I made to your brother and indulge my appetite further—if I thought you would not hate me forever.'

With her lips parted, Prudence was too dazed to do anything but gaze up at him as a multitude of emotions coursed through her. A growing apprehension widened her eyes. She was shaken by the realisation of her own passion, and she was seized by a raging fear that if he stayed a moment longer she would dishonour herself and her family. Tenderly he kissed her lips.

'I like to have you near me, and it is my desire to have you near me every morning I wake. Now—'tis late. Goodnight, little one,' he whispered, slipping off the bed and silently leaving her alone.

When Prudence opened her eyes to the cold light of day, she felt as if she was a different person from the one who had come to Marlden Hall yesterday. Lucas had awoken feelings inside her that she had not known existed. She was no longer a naïve young innocent but a woman, with a woman's wants and needs that could match those of any other—and she knew that only one man could fill those needs.

What she had felt for Adam had not been like this. That had been warm and gentle and pure, whereas what she felt for Lucas she couldn't begin to analyse or understand. It was dark and mysterious and all consuming, a highly volatile combination of terror, danger and excitement, and the force of it terrified her. Last night he had come to her room to seduce her, to make her want him, and he had succeeded. Her face exploded in a blaze of scarlet when she thought how she had lain with him and kissed him, had let him fondle her in the most intimate places, and she felt the pleasurably wanton feelings tearing through her again at the memory. More than anything in the world she had wanted him to make love to her—and he had known it—and she still did—and he would know that, too.

She almost died at the predicament in which she found herself. 'Oh, dear Lord,' she whispered, covering her face and squeezing her eyes closed. What had she done? Never again would she misjudge Lucas's strength or his ardour.

She could still hear his voice in her head, strong and vibrant, and feel the strength of his hands exploring the secrets of her body with the sureness of an experienced and knowledgeable lover. The smell of his elusive scent still lingered, and she could still taste his kisses and remember how urgent and hungry his mouth had been on hers.

Instead of trying to stifle the feelings, she allowed them to flow through her. Not even in her wildest dreams had she imagined that a man could make her body come to life like that, and she doubted that anyone else ever would but Lucas Fox. It was instinct with him and, being a demanding male, with a dominating sensuality, it was the most natural thing in the world for him to make love.

Was it possible that she would marry him after all? Her heart—that small beating organ that had always ruled her head and been her undoing—was whispering, *yes—perhaps*. She climbed out of bed and began to dress, her body still warm from its contact with his virile flesh, and no matter how she tried to calm her trembling limbs, she was unable to turn away the memory of how wonderful it had been to have him hold her—and that she could have him hold her like that every night of her life if she so wished.

When she was dressed and Mrs Witham came to tell her that Lord Fox was about to have breakfast and would like her to join him, she went downstairs in a state of spiralling apprehension at the thought of seeing him again. How would they react to one another, and how could she appear calm and matter of fact when she could remember every intimate detail of what she had done with him?

When she reached the hall she stood and looked around, wondering which way to go.

'Prudence,' Lucas said from the shadowy doorway of the room where they had dined the evening before.

She spun round, finding it difficult to hide her treacherous heart's reaction to the deep timbre of his voice. Why, she wondered desperately, did she feel different from the way she had felt yesterday? Why could she still feel his hands on her bare flesh and his kisses on her lips? Slowly she walked towards him, trying to still the trembling in her legs. He seemed extraordinarily tall and broad-shouldered to her this morning, his face more striking and handsome than ever.

As he stood looking down at her, there was a small quirk of a smile on his lips, and though his gaze travelled leisurely from the top of her bright head, lingering meaningfully on her soft mouth, it lacked the roguish gleam that oft brought a flush to her cheeks.

He stood aside to allow her to pass into the room, closing the door behind her. 'I trust you slept well?' he enquired softly.

Prudence lifted her large liquid eyes to his, praying fervently that he wouldn't mention his nocturnal visit to her room. 'Eventually,' she answered, relieved that her voice sounded calm, although his warm, masculine voice brought her senses to life. She glanced at the table laid for breakfast. 'Have you eaten?'

'Not yet,' he replied, gazing down at the incredibly desirable young woman, who even now was setting his body on fire. 'I waited for you.'

'There was no need. I—I really would like to go home.'

'When you've eaten, I'll take you back.'

Realising it was useless arguing, Prudence sat at the table, and while Lucas ate what she considered to be a disgustingly hearty breakfast, she toyed with a cup of chocolate and some bread and butter.

When they were ready to leave, Prudence stood on the steps of Marlden Hall waiting for Lucas to bring their mounts from the stable. The storm had passed, leaving the land drenched and sparkling beneath a blazing sun shining out of a speedwell-blue sky. When she saw Lucas cantering towards her from the direction of the stables, her breath caught in her throat. She was ashamed of how much the sight of him mastering that huge, sleek and beautiful animal

excited her. With the sun shining full on him, turning his
hair to polished ebony, he was devastatingly attractive.

Dragging her gaze from his bronzed features, she turned
her attention to one of the grooms leading Foxglove. Lifting
her skirts she descended the steps, and when Lucas stopped
in front of her and dismounted with an enviable agility, her
eyes flew to his. They were watching her closely.

'Do you still wish to return Foxglove?'

Filled with indecision, she looked towards the beloved
mare and sighed.

'Prudence, it is I you are angry with, not the horse. Whatever has transpired between us, accept her for what she is.
A gift from me to you. Besides,' he said, stroking the
mare's mane, 'she's become so attached to you that I fear
the poor animal will pine away if you don't. She may not
survive the trauma of being apart from you.'

Foxglove flicked her ears at the sound of her name and,
thrusting her nose at her mistress, whickered for attention.
Unable to resist, Prudence placed her cheek against the
horse's warm neck, certain that Lucas had had a word in
Foxglove's ear in the hope of persuading the clever mare
to play on her emotions. She swallowed back her tears, her
eyes shining jewel bright.

'Damn you, Lucas Fox. You know I can't refuse. In this
instance I concede victory to you. I suppose I was a little
hasty in wanting to bring her back.'

She didn't see the tenderness in Lucas's slow smile as
she planted a kiss on Foxglove's nose.

They were both quiet on the ride to Willow House. The
road was soft with mud and precarious in places and took
some careful negotiating. Crossing the bridge in the village
and seeing that the water level of the stream was nowhere
near as high as Lucas would have had her believe last night
when she had asked to be taken home in the coach, although Prudence managed to throw him a look of severe
displeasure, she couldn't stifle her smile. It was a look that

told him she knew precisely why he had told her the false-hood.

Lucas halted in the lane just out of sight of the house, grasping her reins as she was about to ride on.

'What is it? Why have you stopped?' she asked, panic entering her eyes.

'Before you face your brother I think we should talk.'

'Oh! What about?'

'Prudence, we cannot avoid speaking of last night and what happened between us.'

She turned her head and met his gaze full on, her face burning with embarrassment. 'I—I didn't invite you into my room last night, Lucas—for you to force yourself on me.'

He arched his eyebrows in wry amusement and chal-lenged her with a mocking grin. 'Nay, Prudence. I may have entered uninvited, but I don't seem to recall forcing myself on you. In fact, to tell the truth, I confess to being somewhat frayed by your eagerness. You melted in my arms, as I remember, and made me most welcome. Your passions were in grave danger of running out of control. Still, I'm not complaining,' he said softly. 'I confess to enjoying the moment. Your eagerness astounded me. Noth-ing you can say or do will change what happened between us. You do want me, Pru,' he told her with a knowing smile. 'You cannot deny it.'

She swallowed nervously and stared at him, memories of what he had done to her, memories of his passion, his gentleness and restraint filling her mind—and added to that were memories of her own urgent desire, how she had wanted him to dispense with her virginity and make love to her in the same way that he had made love to countless other women before. She opened her mouth to utter a de-nial, wanting to hurt him, to humiliate him, but her con-science chose that moment to assert itself and strangled the words in her throat. She had gloried in his loving, and she could not bring herself to tell him otherwise.

'Yes—yes, I do want you,' she replied fiercely. 'But can you not understand that there is a part of me that doesn't want to want you? I hate myself for enjoying what you did to me last night. I don't understand it and I don't want to feel like this. It's unendurable.'

Reaching out, Lucas tenderly caressed her cheek, relieved when she didn't draw back. 'My poor little Pru. It needn't be. It could be something wonderful if you would let it.'

It was his tone, not his words, that conquered her. 'I know,' she whispered shakily.

'Then don't fight me, little one. You will tire yourself out with the effort,' he said, his heart wrenching at the way she was looking at him. 'In the end you will succumb to what is in your heart and you will not want to fight me any more.'

Prudence breathed deeply, looking at him steadily. 'You are so sure of that, aren't you, Lucas? You are so arrogant in your assumption. Don't you ever get tired of playing the lusting rake, of having women fall at your feet—of having them worship and adore you as if you are some kind of God? I don't want to be like them.'

Lucas smiled on hearing her refer to him as a lusting rake, but then his smile faded and he grew more serious as a deeper feeling took over. He looked at her steadily. 'You won't be. I admit there have been many women in my life, but I have always been single-minded in my pursuits. I speak the truth when I tell you that you are the only woman I have offered for. You are the woman I want to spend the rest of my life with, and I will not be satisfied until I have you. Surely that must count for something in your estimation of me.'

Prudence swallowed and averted her eyes, feeling confused, her spirit bruised. 'Yes—yes, it does.'

Lucas reached out and placed his fingers on her chin, turning her face to his. 'It was wrong of me to make bargains with your brother without first speaking to you—and your reaction was exactly the reaction I would expect a proud, rebellious, lovely young woman to make. Pru, I apologise,' he conceded quietly. 'I have behaved badly. I deserve your anger—but not your hatred.'

To Prudence's mortification, tears stung her eyes. 'But I don't hate you,' she whispered. 'Please don't think that.'

'I know you don't,' he said feelingly.

Lucas escorted her into the house, taking Thomas aside when Arabella ushered Prudence upstairs to her room to reprimand her. Thomas sighed deeply, frustration written all over his face as his eyes followed his youngest sister up the stairs.

'I swear that girl will be the death of me, Lucas. She tests my temper to the very limits of my endurance.' He returned his gaze to his friend, looking at him levelly. 'I trust you behaved yourself?'

Lucas grinned. 'I give you no cause for complaint, Thomas. I behaved like the gentleman I am. Take Prudence to London after the wedding as planned and I will join you there.' His eyes twinkled wickedly. 'I think she is beginning to see things my way.'

Chapter Thirteen

Arabella and Robert were married in the church at Marlden Green. It was a quiet affair and a happy one, made happier because they were able to be married in church and the ceremony conducted by a priest, and not, as had been the case during the Interregnum, by a Justice of the Peace and without God.

The following day they journeyed to London. Still concerned over her uncle's health, Verity insisted that she and Thomas reside with him and her aunt—her uncle's sister—in Long Acre. Prudence was most relieved when Thomas gave his permission for her to stay with Aunt Julia, who was more than happy to see her back. Cousin Mary, who was heavily pregnant, was less so, although she wasted no time insisting that her young cousin should help her mother look after the children during her confinement. Arabella and Robert were to live with Robert's father until their own house was made ready for them to move into in High Holborn.

Nothing was changed at Maitland House, and the flowering tubs in the courtyard, which Prudence had planted and tended so lovingly, were flourishing. Her days established a pattern. In the mornings Verity called to take her shopping, and during the afternoons, Arabella would often call and take her and Aunt Julia in her carriage to the park at St James's. Later, and with great excitement, they would all go to one of the newly opened theatres to see a play.

Thomas and Verity, whose names were on the King's guest list, went to concerts, banquets and masques at Whitehall Palace. Prudence would listen in rapt attention as they told her all about the revelries, the scandals and intrigues, which were all very much a part of the Court. She was appalled by the abandoned behaviour of some of the courtiers and their ladies.

Observing her horror—and her open curiosity to know more—Thomas would laugh humorously, promising her that very soon she would go and see for herself, and Prudence accepted the imminence of this without protest. Thomas went on to tell her that the King, deprived of merry-making for too long and wishing to rid his Court of the melancholia that had shrouded it for all those years of exile, was more indulgent towards his courtiers than he otherwise might have been.

Thomas had forbidden Prudence to leave the house alone, so when she went to Mr Rowan's nursery she was always accompanied by one of Aunt Julia's servants. Molly was her usual merry self and more than happy to see her friend back in London, if only for a short time. Prudence enquired after Will Price, and was not surprised when Molly told her that Will had suddenly left her father's employ on the morning after the restoration of King Charles. Prudence knew his leaving had something to do with her, but didn't say so to Molly. However, his association with Jeffrey Fox remained a mystery.

Lucas was constantly on her mind, and it amazed her just how much she was missing him. All through Arabella's wedding she had thought of him, imagining what it would be like for them to be standing before the priest and having him declare them to be man and wife together, and her body had warmed with the thought. At night she fell asleep dreaming of his strong arms embracing her tightly, of his whispered words and demanding kisses that stole her breath, of her desire that had been uncontrollable—and of his caressing hands that had set her body aflame and made her forget that it was wrong for him to touch her so intimately.

His image had followed her all the way to London. She saw the way his smile swept across his bronzed features, the way his ebony hair dipped over his brow, and the tender way he had held her chin and looked at her on parting. His lightest touch had the power to reduce her body to a quivering mass within seconds. Warmth flooded her heart and she smiled when she recalled how touchingly sincere he had been in his apology for his ungallant proposal, and again when she recalled their interesting conversations on the day of her birthday.

He was a hard, arrogant male, with an indomitable will— yet he was also tender, caring and persuasive, and what he was offering was beyond anything she could have imagined. She did care for him, deeply, and he must care for her to choose her above all others to be his wife.

After spending an hour or so with Molly, when they had chatted and strolled arm in arm by the river beneath the warm sun, Prudence returned to the house where aunt Julia met her with great excitement.

'You had a visitor while you were out, Prudence. The gentleman waited, but when you didn't come back he left.'

'A visitor? Who?'

'Lord Fox,' Julia said with a knowing smile. 'He said to tell you that he will call again.'

Prudence's heart slammed into her ribs, although she couldn't for the life of her have said why she should be so surprised by his visit, for he had told her himself that he was to come to London and that they would meet. Feeling as if the world was beginning to spin and tilt around her, she was unaware that she was holding her breath as she stared at her aunt. She was so disappointed that she'd missed him. 'He did? When will he call again? Today, to-morrow—the day after? When?'

Catching a glimpse of the unaffected warmth her niece must feel for Lord Fox, Julia smiled. 'Tomorrow after-noon.'

Prudence looked at her aunt with profound dismay. 'Oh, but Mary is expecting me to visit her. With her confinement due at any time, I've promised to bring Jane back here with me.' Three-year-old Jane was Mary's youngest child and the most troublesome. She wore Mary out with her tan-trums and constant crying. Julia had taken pity on her daughter and offered to look after the little girl until Mary's baby was born. Prudence had promised her cousin that she would collect her the following day.

'If you set off early you'll have plenty of time to get to Bishopsgate and back before Lord Fox arrives.'

'I do hope so.'

Julia gave her an understanding look. 'So—that's it.'

Prudence glanced at her aunt. 'What do you mean, aunt Julia?'

'I mean, my dear, that Lord Fox is responsible for the change in you.'

'Change? Is there a change in me?'

'You may take it from me that there is. You are posi-tively glowing. I can see he has made an impression on you.'

Prudence beamed. 'I never could hide anything from you, could I? It would be difficult for Lucas not to make an impression on anyone. He is an impressive person.'

'I can see that,' her aunt chuckled.

'Oh, aunt Julia. I am so happy—and at the same time afraid of the feelings he has awoken in me.'

Julia smiled. 'Nice things, I hope.'

Prudence flushed beneath her aunt's soft gaze. 'Oh, yes. I—I wasn't going to say anything until I've seen him, but he—he wants to marry me,' she blurted out. 'He intends to marry me, I realise that now—and I want to shout it to the whole world.'

'And how do you feel about that? Are you ready for marriage to Lord Fox, Prudence?'

A wistful look entered Prudence's eyes when she thought of Lucas and what marriage to him would be like. She no longer knew herself, but what she did know was that despite everything—his reputation as a rake, and that he was a supremely arrogant male—she loved Lucas Fox with all her heart, and she wanted his love above all else. Achingly she wanted to look on his beloved face, to have him hold her again, and she was afraid of the violence of her tumbling emotions. 'To remain at Willow House riding my horse and tending my garden was an illusion on my part,' she whispered. 'All my illusions are gone now. How could I have been so foolish—so incredibly naïve?'

'And have you accepted Lord Fox's proposal?'

Her cheeks dimpled into an enchanting smile. 'Not yet. But I will. It took me a long time to admit to my feelings, but I now know that I love him—desperately. Say you're happy for me, Aunt.'

Julia's smile was one of profound pleasure. She gave her niece a hug and wept a little, but she assured her, with pure happiness, 'It is my dearest dream come true. If only your father were alive. He would be so pleased to know you were making such an excellent match, and delighted at the prospect of the two families being united.'

Prudence heard what she was saying with an inward burst of pride. 'I know he would. Initially I refused to flatter Lucas's ego, his vanity, by professing that I wanted to marry him—because he was arrogant in assuming I would simply fall in with his plans without argument. He has never doubted for one second that I would marry him, and I wanted him to realise that I don't like being bullied. I intended keeping him waiting a very long time before I gave him my answer to his ungallant proposal.'

'Ungallant?'

Quickly Prudence told her aunt of the deal Lucas had struck up with Thomas without consulting her, and how, when she found out, she had been determined to oppose it.

Julia listened in complete absorption, chuckling softly when she had finished. 'I don't suppose Lord Fox has met with any resistance from females before—and certainly not from one as young as you are. So you no longer intend keeping him waiting?'

Joy suffused Prudence's face and her eyes sparkled. She clasped her hands, smiling. 'Oh, no. Lucas can be very persuasive. I've missed him so much, aunt Julia. I can't wait to see him again.'

Julia sighed. 'You've grown up at last,' she told her, and it was true. Prudence felt as though she had been born anew of some unaccustomed new process of gestation. Some time, perhaps on the night she had stayed at Marlden Hall, that naïve young girl with her head full of childish fancies had vanished forever. Very little remained of the innocent Prudence Fairworthy, who had fallen with such blind infatuation into the illusion of calf-love with Adam Lingard.

Prudence wasn't destined to see Lucas the following day. On the journey to Mary's house in Bishopsgate, the carriage had developed a problem with one of the wheels; by the time a new wheel had been found and fitted, it was dark when Prudence arrived back at Maitland House with her young charge.

When Lucas called on her and left after waiting over an hour, saying he would return the following afternoon, he looked so disappointed that Julia felt sorry for him. Unfortunately, on arrival at the house young Jane became extremely fractious and would not settle without her mother. She became so distressed that, afraid the child might become ill as a result of so much weeping, the adults agreed that she must be taken back to Bishopsgate. Concerned about Mary, Julia said she would take her, but Jane clung to Prudence and dissolved into loud fits of wailing every time someone tried to take her from Prudence. And so it was agreed that Julia and Prudence should go together.

When they arrived at the house a flustered maid on her way out met them on the doorstep.

'What is it?' Julia asked in alarm. 'Is it Mary?'

'Her pains started three hours ago. I've sent word to her husband at the Exchange to let him know. I also sent for Mrs Bundy, the midwife, but she hasn't come. I'm going to see if I can find her—the mistress's waters have broke, you see.'

'Yes, you go. I'll do what I can for Mary until she gets here.' Julia looked at Prudence in alarm as they entered the house. 'Dear me, I do hope everything's all right. The other births were long and drawn out—never as quick as this.'

Julia and Prudence, who was carrying a now-sleeping Jane in her arms, went up the stairs. Placing the child on her bed, Prudence followed her aunt into Mary's lying-in chamber, assailed by the stench of sweat and vomit. Mary was hunched over the birthing-stool, groaning. Her hair hung in limp strands about her shoulders, and her face was the colour of curdled milk. It contorted with pain as a contraction knifed through her.

'Thank God you've arrived, Mother,' Mary gasped between fractured breaths, gripping her mother's hand as she strained her distended abdomen. 'The baby will be born soon—I know it.'

A stout young maid called Beth placed a lavender-scented compress on her head, uttering words of encouragement.

Immediately Julia took charge of the birthing. Never having been in a lying-in chamber before and knowing little of birthing procedures, Prudence held back, shocked by what she saw. The birthing stool looked more like an instrument of torture instead of an aid to deliver new life. Julia bent to examine her labouring daughter; when she was satisfied that the birth was progressing as it should, she glanced sharply at her young niece and smiled when she noticed her white face and large eyes, the pupils dilated with fear and anxiety.

'Don't look so worried, Prudence. Everything is as it should be. Unfortunately the same cannot be said of the children, if that dreadful din coming from the nursery is anything to go by. Go and quieten them. Beth and I will manage here until the midwife comes—although she may not be needed. I think the baby will arrive before Mrs Bundy.'

Only too eager to make her escape, Prudence went to the nursery, disappointed that she would miss seeing Lucas that day.

Riding beside Solomon from Maitland House towards Whitehall, his temper already splintered by his failure to locate Jeffrey, Lucas scarcely noticed his surroundings. Having found Prudence absent from home on his second visit, a disappointment that he'd never known swamped him. In his impatience to see her, to feast his eyes on her face one again, he had behaved like a besotted idiot, racing to Maitland House the minute he'd arrived in London the previous day.

He was regretting not having secured a commitment from her before she'd left Marlden Green. Knowing just how obstinate and headstrong she could be, by now she'd probably worked herself into a fresh state of rebellion because of the marriage arrangement he'd made with Thomas without her knowledge. She did feel something for him, it had been there from the start, and if she weren't so young or so stubborn she would have known it then. He wanted her, and he wanted her to want him—and he did want her, more than anything he'd ever wanted in his life.

His brow became furrowed with a deep frown as a suspicion that Prudence might be avoiding him began taking root in his mind. When she had left for Bishopsgate yesterday, knowing he was to call on her, why hadn't she left him a note? And today the same thing had happened. Maitland House had an army of servants, so why had it taken both Prudence and Lady Julia to return a troublesome child to its mother? Unless she didn't want to see him. Anger that this might be so consumed him, and by the time he reached Charing Cross he was almost convinced of it. His anger turned into a cold, hard resolve. Turning in the direction of Long Acre, he was relieved to find Thomas at home.

Subjecting Lucas to a brief scrutiny, Thomas said, 'You, my friend, look like hell.'

'Thank you, Thomas,' he said drily. 'It's good to see you, too.'

Thomas handed him a goblet of wine. 'Here, you look as though you need it.'

Stony faced, Lucas took it, drinking it in a single draught.

'Now, what brings you to Long Acre looking like a thunder cloud?' He listened patiently while Lucas told him, then he laughed in disbelief. 'Good Lord, Lucas! Prudence would be delighted to see you. I know it.'

Lucas threw Thomas a look of unwavering distaste. 'I am certain that if your sister wanted to see me, Thomas, she would have been there. I did leave a message informing her that I would be calling on her yesterday and again today. '

'That can easily be explained. Mary's confinement is due any day, and Prudence has promised to help with the children. I've been out of touch with what's happening at Maitland House, but since it is clearly troubling you, I will call on Prudence myself. Although I must say I'm surprised. If you're so impatient to see her, why didn't you ride to Bishopsgate to see her there?'

'I would have done, but my time is limited. I have come to London to find my cousin,' he said in calm, measured tones, 'but he's lying low. So far he has eluded me, but I will track him down.'

Thomas looked at his friend's grave countenance steadily. 'On the night we returned to England, I told you then that I would be happy to listen if you wished to tell me what happened when you left me in France to travel in the East.'

'And I replied that I would acquaint you with the facts another day.'

'And will you? There's…no time like the present,' Thomas prompted hesitantly.

Lucas shrugged. 'Why not? There is no harm in the telling.'

'You met up with Jeffrey didn't you, Lucas, when you went south?'

'Yes—in Marseilles. I was there to obtain a passage on a ship to Alexandria. Being at the crossroads of several commercial routs, it was my intention to go to India. Jeffrey's ship was in dock and we met. One night something of a vicious nature occurred—it was an attack on my person, which almost cost me my life, which it was meant to do,' Lucas said quietly, his voice trembling slightly with memories he would rather forget. 'For two years I was deprived of my freedom and tortured to the brink of madness. Deep in my innermost self I know that the identity of the person behind it was Jeffrey, and it is important to me to prove it.'

Thomas was astounded. 'Good Lord! I knew nothing of this. We may not be acquainted, but I would not believe it of your cousin. No matter how badly you were treated, you are not a man of vengeance, Lucas,' he said, wary of his friend's unfathomable mood.

'What you say is true, Thomas. I am disinclined to avenge myself, but that is not the same thing as an inclination to forget what my cousin is guilty of where I am concerned.'

'But how can you be certain it was Jeffrey who tried to kill you?'

'Because with my death he had much to gain. I know he wants to give up the sea and settle down. And what better place to do it than at Marlden Hall, where his father—with Cromwell's blessing—had already insinuated himself?'

'And with so little evidence you accuse and convict your cousin of trying to murder you?' asked Thomas, still not convinced.

'No. Make no mistake, Jeffrey is a dangerous foe. The enmity between us goes back to childhood. It became more virulent with the passing years—but I never believed he was cold-blooded enough to commit murder. It was in Marseilles that I discovered these were the depths to which my cousin was prepared to sink, to have me removed in order to get his hands on my estate.

'Jeffrey conceived a scheme to get rid of me, hiring a couple of ruffians to do his dirty work. Unfortunately, after taking his money, the men he hired doubled their takings and sold me to a Barbary corsair. When I awoke I was on a Muslim galley, and what I learned from the captain of that ship was damning. I spent the next two years of my life chained to an oar. It seemed as if death stalked my every waking minute. The hatred I felt for my cousin and my determination to survive that—and the next three years and escape—was the only thing that kept me alive and sane.'

When Lucas spoke, his voice was deep in the tragedy of the past. Thomas flinched, catching his eye and seeing something of his inner torment, imagining the hell that must have been for a man as proud and noble as his friend. It explained the carefully held ferocity of the energy of all his movements, which Thomas had noticed when he'd met up with him in Breda before returning to England. Lucas seemed to find it difficult being in any one place or still for any length of time.

'Then I can understand how important it is to you to find out the truth,' Thomas said quietly.

'It is. I am also determined that never again will I be subjected to the experience of humiliation—of absolute helplessness.'

'But if what you suspect is true and Jeffrey did attempt to kill you, do you think he will try again when he discovers his scheme failed?'

'He has—on the night of our return to London.' Lucas quickly gave Thomas the facts about what happened that night.

'Good Lord!' He was astounded. 'I had no idea.'

Lucas's expression was grim. 'How could you? I told no one. Jeffrey is ruthless. On board ship his rule is supreme. Like any judge he deals swift justice. Any man who goes against him will be found floating in the ocean with his throat slit before the day's end. When he discovered his plan to have me killed had failed, he will have been brooding and seething ever since. I know my cousin, Thomas. The longer his resentment goes on, the more dangerous an enemy he could become.'

'Then take care, Lucas. Be extra vigilant. After surviving Worcester and ten years in exile, I should hate to see you slain by an assassin's blade now peace is restored. How will you find him?'

'I have my contacts—and hired men are scouring the wharves and taverns. They will employ any means to obtain information.'

'Surely it would be easier to look in the Pool for his ship?'

'My enquiries so far have revealed that his ship was sunk when it was attacked off Gibraltar by corsairs—which explains why I was unable to find the vessel in the Pool when I was last in town. He was due to arrive in London back in June or thereabouts. Desperate to escape the outcry for revenge against the men who put to death the King's father, uncle George was waiting for Jeffrey to take him to America, but after visiting his lodgings in Cheapside, I have learned that he has taken passage on another vessel.' His expression became grim. 'Jeffrey is here, Thomas. I can feel it. If I have to turn London upside down in search of him, I'll find him.'

'Have there been any sightings of him?'

Lucas made his friend the object of his penetrating gaze. 'Two. Prudence has seen and spoken with him on two occasions.'

Thomas stiffened. He was astounded, unable to believe what Lucas was telling him. 'Prudence? But surely you are mistaken. How could she? Where?'

Having told Thomas all the facts about Prudence's encounters with Jeffrey, Lucas left. Thomas was furious that she hadn't told him. He was so furious that it prevented him from being able to decide on her punishment just then, but he would. By God, before tomorrow was out he would see her wherever she happened to be.

When Mary had been delivered of another girl, and with enough servants and aunt Julia to look after the children, Prudence returned to Maitland House the following day. She was ill prepared for the arrival of her brother. One look at his rigid stance and unsmiling mouth when he stopped in front of where she was seated, reading a book, told her he was extremely vexed about something. She rose to receive him.

'Why, Thomas! I—'

'So, here you are,' he interrupted sternly. 'Might I ask what is happening here? Yesterday I received a visit from Lucas, and he informed me that he has called to see you on two occasions and both times you have been elsewhere.'

'I know. I'm sorry, Thomas—but I can explain. Was he very angry?'

'He was not pleased. Prudence, are you deliberately trying to avoid him?'

'Of course not.' She looked at him, dismayed. 'Oh, Thomas—I sincerely hope Lucas doesn't think that. The first time he called I had gone to Bishopsgate to collect Jane.' Quickly she gave him an account of all that had transpired that day, and how she'd had no choice but to return the child to her mother the next.

'Couldn't one of the servants have taken her—or Aunt Julia?' Thomas argued, knowing he was being unreasonable, but ever since Lucas had told him of his sister's encounters with Jeffrey Fox, all rational thought had fled.

'Aunt Julia was very busy, Thomas, and had made arrangements to go and stay with Mary during her confinement. Jane was clinging to me, and to have given her over to one of the servants would have distressed her even more. Anyway, aunt Julia accompanied me, and it's a good thing she did, because when we got there Mary's baby was about to be born. I returned to Maitland House this morning.'

'And Mary?'

'Was delivered of another girl.'

'Good. Philip will be pleased,' Thomas said in clipped tones, accepting the news of another of Mary's offspring being born into the world with scant interest.

'Yes—and aunt Julia. She's relieved it's over. But—tell me about Lucas, Thomas. Was he very vexed not to find me here?'

'Aye, he was,' Thomas revealed, omitting telling her that his friend's vexation was not all her fault, and that it had been intensified by his failure to locate his cousin. 'The least you could have done was to have left him a note explaining. He assumed you would.'

Prudence bristled at his reproach. 'I confess I didn't think. But Lucas always does assume too much where I am concerned.'

'He assumes too much because the man loves you—you blind little fool,' Thomas told her brusquely.

'He does?' she whispered, completely disarmed by his revelation.

'Of course he does. I sincerely hope you will not refuse to marry him?'

'I—I…' It was on the tip of her tongue to tell him that there was nothing in the world she wanted more than to be married to Lucas, but she was in such an emotional turmoil that she couldn't trust herself to speak.

Thomas misread her reaction and took her hesitation to mean no, she would not marry Lucas. His face darkened. Grasping her by the shoulders he gave her a slight, angry shake. 'I told you in the beginning that I would not force you to do anything you do not want to do, and I meant it, but why does the thought of being Lucas's wife bring you so much misery? Why?' he demanded, his face twisted with angry regret. 'I thought you were softening to the prospect.'

Close to tears she shook her head in mute appeal. Never had she seen Thomas so angry, and she had no idea why he was behaving like this.

'Is your rejection permanent? Is it that you haven't got over your infatuation with Adam Lingard?'

'No,' she gasped. 'Of course not. Please believe me when I say Adam means nothing to me any more. I never think of him—ever.'

'I'm glad to hear it. Then is there someone else you have a fancy for?' he demanded. 'A young man here or in Marlden Green?' Suddenly his eyes narrowed with suspicion. 'Or Jeffrey Fox, perhaps?'

Her head shot up and her eyes opened wide with surprise. 'Jeffrey Fox! Why on earth should you say that?'

He glowered at her. 'I know of your encounters with *that* particular villain. They may have been accidental, but you should have told me.'

'I—I didn't think it was important. I still don't—and by your tone I sense that where Captain Fox is concerned, you share the same opinion as Lucas.'

'I do. Lucas has often said that his cousin was born to be hanged, and damn me if I don't believe it to be the truth.'

'Maybe you're right. I can't say because I don't know him—and I have no wish to. There was something quite sinister and unlikeable about him that made me nervous. But personally I have nothing to reproach him for. He was both kind and extremely helpful to me on both our encounters.'

Thomas's sharp, derisive voice rang out. 'Was he, by God?' he jeered, his face almost purple with fury at what he considered to be her lack of familial loyalty. 'And did Lucas tell you why he has such a low opinion of his cousin? Did he tell you of the evil he perpetrated against him?' he demanded, his voice gathering emphasis.

Prudence shook her head, feeling stupid.

'Then let me set you straight,' he said, his eyes narrowing, a hard gleam in their depths when he pinned them on his sister's. 'Lucas won't thank me for telling you, but I think you should be told. Jeffrey Fox's hatred of Lucas was so deep and so vicious that, when they met in Marseilles almost six years ago, he arranged to have him killed. But instead of killing him, the men Jeffrey hired to carry out that evil act—lacking the courage to do it himself—doubled their stake and sold Lucas to a Barbary corsair—a ruthless, bloodthirsty savage, a man fabled for his ferocity and skill at attacking and plundering Christian vessels in the Mediterranean.

'Lucas spent the next two years of his life chained to a fifteen-foot oar of the corsair's galley—vessels that required a steady supply of oarsmen, due to the fact that they expired either from the cruelties inflicted on them by their captors or exhaustion. There were times when Lucas all but died, and it was sheer grit and determination—and hatred for his cousin—that helped him to survive those two tortuous years.

'The corsair fought off all attempts by government forces to destroy him, but eventually he was attacked by one of his own kind. After a fierce and bloody encounter off the Maltese coast, his vessel was destroyed and most of the slaves captured. Along with the others, Lucas was taken to Algiers and sold to a Turkish pasha.'

Silent, wide-eyed with horror, Prudence listened to her brother, a memory of the time when she had told Lucas of her encounters with his cousin resurrecting itself. She recalled how, in his anger, Lucas had given her a brief insight into the two years of his life she knew nothing about—of his sufferings—but never had she imagined he had been subjected to anything as monstrous as this.

When at last Thomas finished speaking, she felt the blood drain from her face, then she slowly shook her head. 'No,' she whispered as a scream of hysteria and denial rise in her throat. 'No,' she cried again in wild disbelief, her emotions veering from hysterical panic to madness. 'Oh, my God.' Mortification tore through her and she moaned, wrapping her arms around her waist, but the image of Lucas—that proud and noble man, being subjected to such pain, humiliation and torment—wouldn't cease.

Trying to cling to a single thread of control, battered, she shook her head, unable to speak past tears of shame and sorrow choking her. Her head drooped in defeat, her hair falling forward and hiding her face as her body began to shake with silent, anguished weeping. She covered her face with her hands in an attempt to shut out the picture of Lucas being so humbled, an immense pity welling up from the bottom of her heart towards the man whose sufferings must have been intolerable.

'Oh, Thomas—I—I didn't know. I didn't know.'

Her tears and her terrible anguish doused Thomas's wrath and he pulled her into his arms, clasping her tightly to him, his hand soothing the back of her head. When her sobbing subsided and she finally stopped shaking, she raised her tear-streaked face to his.

'I have to see him, Thomas.'

His voice was kind and sympathetic. 'Of course you must. I'm sorry, Prudence. I didn't mean to tell you like that. It was unforgivable.'

'I'm glad you did. Lucas told me about his time in Constantinople—of the three years he spent as a slave of the Sultan—'

'He did?' Thomas smiled wryly. 'That's more than he told me.'

'But he left out those two awful years.' She shuddered.

'Now I know why. I must go to him at once. I am most anxious to see him—to explain my absence when he called. I pray he will forgive me,' she whispered. 'If he doesn't, I don't think I shall be able to bear it.'

Thomas tipped her chin, gazing down into her tear-bright eyes in amazement. 'Are you telling me that you are in love with Lucas?' When she nodded he gasped, smiling with incredulity. 'And you have no objections to being his wife?'

She smiled at him sweetly. 'None whatsoever.'

Thomas laughed out loud, crushing her to him. 'You minx. You exasperating, adorable, incredible minx. There are doubtless many skirmishes ahead for the two of you. You are a virago, Prudence—but you also have a magic quality when you choose to use it. Should you use it on my poor friend, he may well become lost.'

Chapter Fourteen

When Prudence was ready, Thomas took her in his coach to Whitehall, where Lucas had acquired pleasant lodgings. In fact, the house was so much to his liking, Thomas told her, that he was thinking of buying it for his town house.

Darkness was falling over the city when they left Charing Cross and proceeded along King Street. Thankfully it was devoid of its daytime congestion of traffic. Feeling nervous about her meeting with Lucas, Prudence looked about her, straining her eyes and just making out the ghostly, octagonal turrets of the Holbein Gate ahead of them. The coach turned off to the right down a narrow street, halting before a massive door.

After assisting Prudence out of the coach, Thomas rapped loudly on it, the sound resonating deeply inside the house. The door was swung open, and in the flicker of flames from the many candles lighting the hall, Prudence saw the impassive features of Lucas's black-faced servant, Solomon. He stood aside to allow them to enter, but Thomas held back, taking his sister's hand.

'I won't come in with you. I think you should see Lucas by yourself. He will see that you return safely to Maitland House.'

Speechless, Prudence watched him go before turning and

entering the house. Handing her cloak to a bowing servant, she nervously turned to Solomon.

'Tell Lord Fox that I am here, will you, Solomon?' Despite her nervousness of facing Lucas, Prudence was struck—as she always was when she was in the presence of Solomon—by the splendour of his dark features and splendid bearing. He faced her with a dignity that she found impressive. There was a moment's silence before he answered her, his voice rich and deep and heavily accented by a strange foreign tongue that fascinated her.

'He knows you are here already, and I would not wake to draw breath in the morning if I were to send you away without first announcing you. But I feel that I must warn you,' he murmured, his lips breaking into the broadest white smile Prudence had ever seen, 'that his temper has been better—but I know he is glad you came.'

'Thank you, Solomon.' Taking a deep breath, Prudence followed Solomon in his Oriental garb into a splendid salon. She came to a halt just inside when her eyes beheld the man she had come to see.

Dressed in a loose white shirt tucked into his black breeches, Lucas was standing in the open doorway to another room across the salon, his shoulder propped indolently against the frame, arms crossed over his chest, looking for all the world like some sinister spectre. He looked unbearably handsome. He also looked absolutely furious. Prudence felt her confidence melting away. How could she have deluded herself into believing this man could be swayed from his purpose? He was no love-smitten youth to be put off by an indifferent smile.

'Leave us, Solomon,' he said in an ominously low voice. 'Mistress Fairworthy and I have something to say to each other that is best said in private.'

Silently Solomon slipped from the room like a black ghost.

Frozen to the spot, her heart hammering in her chest—although she couldn't for the life of her think why it should,

for she had done nothing wrong that she could think of—
Prudence looked at the man across the room. During the
time they had been apart she had hoped she had managed
to conquer the debilitating effect he always had on her
senses, but his potent sexual magnetism was like a palpable
force. How had she allowed him to do this to her? She was
scandalised by the stirrings inside her that the mere sight
of him always commanded. She could not understand this
hunger, this need, which held her captive to her emotions
where he was concerned. In silent, helpless appeal she
stared at his granite features.

Lucas looked at her cold and dispassionate and in complete control, while he strove to tame his rampaging emotions.

'Well? To what do I owe the honour of this visit?' he
asked, his voice heavily laced with sarcasm. 'You are
alone, I see.'

Prudence jumped, hurt and appalled by his biting tone.
'Thomas brought me—'

'I thought he might. Where is he now?'

'He—he has returned to Long Acre.' Slowly she began
to move uncertainly towards him.

Calmly Lucas observed her graceful movements as his
gaze sliced over her in her periwinkle-blue gown, her
lustrous hair tumbling in waves and curls over her shoulders.

Swallowing past the awful lump of contrition in her
throat, she said in an aching whisper, 'I have come to explain why I wasn't at Maitland House when you called to
see me—why I couldn't see you.'

'Couldn't—or wouldn't?' His soft voice was more intimidating than a raised one. Relinquishing his stance in the
doorway, he took a couple of strides into the room, the
ruby ring he always wore glowing blood-red in the candlelight. Pinning her eyes with his, he hooked his thumbs into
the leather belt around his waist and remained several feet
away from her.

'Couldn't, of course,' she replied in answer to his question. 'Lucas, why are you making this difficult for me?' she asked, with such quiet dignity that Lucas felt his heart begin to melt. Her glorious dark eyes, sparkling with suppressed tears, were looking at him with no trace of defiance and without guile. The skin beneath them was smudged with faint mauve shadows, and her normally glowing complexion was drained of colour.

'Am I?'

'Yes. This is silly. I have done nothing wrong that I know of, and you are being unreasonable.' Quickly she told him why she had not been at Maitland House to receive him, and she was relieved to see his features soften and that he looked contrite.

'I see. I understand perfectly why you had to be with Mary, but you could have left me a note explaining all this. The servants at Maitland House were not exactly forthcoming with information.'

'When we took Jane back to her mother yesterday morning, neither aunt Julia nor I knew we would find Mary about to give birth. Lucas—I—I would do anything to try to atone if I have angered or upset you in any way—but it was not my fault.'

One dark brow lifted in questioning arrogance and his firm lips twisted with irony. 'Anything?'

'Yes,' she whispered, looking into his fathomless eyes. Her throat ached, and she was trying hard not to cry. 'Lucas—please don't be like this. You have no reason to be. I cannot bear it,' she whispered wretchedly. 'Please don't shut me out.'

Her soft plea wrung his heart. 'Is there anything else you wish to say to me?'

Prudence was relieved to hear the harsh edge of his voice was tempered at last. 'Yes. I—I've come to tell you that I've considered your proposal and I accept. I want to be your wife, Lucas—very much.'

He saw the tears shimmering in her dark eyes, and one

that had traced unheeded down her cheek. His heart wrenched and, unable to go on torturing her when he had no reason to, with a raw ache in his voice he said, 'Why, Pru? Why do you want to be my wife?'

She gazed at him, knowing he wanted nothing less than her unconditional surrender. 'Because—because I love you.'

'Then if you come here, you can say it again and cry in my arms. And while you do, I will tell you just how much you have come to mean to me—and how much I love you, and that I will never let you go. I will tell you that I have loved you from the minute I lifted you on to my horse during the procession, and that within just a few short weeks of our meeting I knew I wanted you to be my wife. And when I've done that and we are of one accord, I will kiss you.'

Tortured by her tears and loving him so much, Prudence moved the few steps towards him, but unable to wait he reached out and snatched her into his arms, wrapping them about her as she wept happily against his chest, wetting his shirt with her tears. He clasped her tighter, kissing the top of her shining head, inhaling the sweet, familiar scent of her perfume.

'Dear Lord, I've missed you,' he told her, his voice a ravaged whisper.

'I'm sorry,' she whispered brokenly, still sobbing. 'I've missed you too—so much. I couldn't fight my feelings if I wanted to. They are too strong for me.'

'Don't,' he begged, unable to bear her tears. Turning her face to his, his mouth touched hers with an aching tenderness. 'Don't cry any more, sweetheart. You're tearing me apart.'

'I don't mean to. I don't seem to be able to help it,' she said, smiling through her tears as he proceeded to kiss the droplets from her cheeks.

Without a word he scooped her up into his arms and carried her to a large couch, gently setting her down on the carmine and gold damask upholstery as if she were a treasured prize. Sitting beside her, he gathered her into his arms and brushed her hair back from her face. An instant later he was kissing her face, her eyes, her throat. Finding her mouth, tasting of salt and tears, he cherished it with his own, feeling it moving under his, moving and clinging, as her sobs ceased and her body began to respond to his kiss and the strength of his hands moving over her shoulders and back, and the sides of her breasts.

When he bowed his head to place his lips to their soft mounds partly exposed above the bodice of her gown, she pressed her lips against his neck. The gentleness of it triggered off his passion. Avidly, like a man starving, he again crushed his lips over her proffered mouth in a drugging kiss that went on and on until both of them were aflame. Without taking her mouth from his, Prudence raised her feet on to the couch and lay back, taking him with her, almost conquering the last shreds of resistance in him as she wound her slender arms around his neck, pressing herself against him so that almost every inch of her body was under his.

She became a living spell, a temptress, a triumphant siren, as Lucas very nearly admitted defeat and was almost tempted to strip her clothes away. Dragging his lips from hers, he looked down at her adorable face. Her eyes were dark and languid with passion.

'Please,' she whispered, her voice shaky with awakened desire.

'Please what, my love?' he murmured, glorying in the gentle passion in her eyes. 'Make love to you?'

She stared up at his bronze face close to her own, savouring the exquisite happiness of being with him. 'I want to be yours, Lucas—now—tonight.'

Lucas sighed, gently brushing away a hair caught on her lip. He wanted to take her—and warm, passionate creature that she was, she was ready to be taken, as the throbbing ache in his loins was telling him. Taking her hand he placed his lips to her palm. 'Nay, love,' he said in a deep, quiet voice, wistful with regret. 'I cannot take you until you are my wife—much as it tortures me not to. We must wait.'

She sighed, basking in his closeness. Laying her hand against his hard chest, she could feel the beat of his heart and the heat of him. 'But that could take for ages.'

Covering her hand with his, he laughed softly, tipping her face and kissing her lips as he delighted in the disappointment that crossed her face. 'Brazen hussy,' he teased. 'Your eagerness pleases me, my love—but you will have to temper your ardour as I must temper mine. Besides, if I take you now, Thomas will know it.'

'But how? What we do is between us and no one else.'

'Until you become my wife he is still your guardian, my love. If we were to make love he would see your radiance and guess the cause.'

'Are you afraid of my brother?' she teased.

'No, but I gave him my word that you would retain your virtue until you are my wife—and if I were to break my word it would spoil my enjoyment,' he added with a grin. Cradling her chin in his strong fingers, he looked deeply into her shining eyes. 'I love you, sweetheart, and I am not prepared to wait overlong for our wedding. However, if you are going to insist on getting married in Marlden Green, it will take time. I have commitments that could keep me in London for several weeks.'

'I don't mind where we marry, just so long as it is soon.'

Tracing her jaw and cheek with his forefinger, his gaze was compelling. 'How would you feel about getting married in London? And how does a week from now sound?'

Her lips broke into a smile of delight. 'What? No bans?'

'No. Besides, I have no intention of allowing anyone to come forward to ban a union between us.'

'They wouldn't dare,' she laughed. 'What will you do?'

'Apply to the bishop of whichever diocese we intend to marry in for a special licence,' he murmured, his gaze fastening on her moist lips once more.

'And do you have a church in mind, my lord?'

A slow, roguish grin dawned across his features. 'There is one particular church that appeals to me.'

'Oh? Well—since I am to be the bride, do you mind telling me which one?'

'St Brides.'

'What? The Fleet Street St Brides?'

'The same.'

When it dawned on her why he had chosen this particular church, a knowing smile broke on her lips and her eyes shone with warmth. 'St Brides is very old.'

'I know. The first Christian church there was founded by St Bridget, a sixth-century Irish saint from Kildare. Her feast day is celebrated on the same day as that of Bridget—who is—'

Prudence flushed scarlet. 'Thank you for the history lesson, Lucas, but I do know who Bridget is,' she interrupted.

Lucas's lips quirked and he arched his brows. 'You do?'

'Yes.'

'Then tell me. Who is she?' His look was one of teasing as he waited patiently for her reply.

The rosy hue on her cheeks deepened. 'The pre-Christian Celtic goddess of fertility,' she laughed, glad when he laughed with her.

'Do you like children, Pru?' he asked after a moment, still smiling.

Her smile became soft when she remembered how it had felt to cradle Mary's newborn infant in her arms. 'Of course I do.'

'Good, because I would like us to have several. And what better place to begin our lives together than to wed in St Brides with the Celtic goddess of fertility watching over us? A week from now you will be my wife, irrevocably and forever.'

Threading his long fingers through her hair, his strong hands were gentle as they cupped her face. Lowering his head, Lucas let his sensual mouth claim hers once more in a kiss of violent tenderness. Prudence returned his kiss with unselfish ardour, all the love that had been accumulating through the days of being without him infused into that kiss.

'Tell me what it is that keeps you in London,' she murmured when he finally dragged his lips from hers.

He sighed and looked down at her, his expression grave. 'I am trying to track down my cousin, but he's proving damned elusive. I have men looking for him everywhere, but as yet they have no leads.'

Prudence became alert. 'Jeffrey?'

'The same. He is here in London.'

'But—how do you know that?'

Lucas's features tightened, his expression grim. 'I know. I feel it.'

Prudence blanched at the change that came over his features. Suddenly she was afraid for him, without knowing why. 'Must you look for Jeffrey, Lucas? Is it so important that you find him?'

'If you knew what my cousin is guilty of, you would understand.'

'I do,' she whispered.

His eyes snapped to hers. 'How? Who told you?'

'Thomas. He—he thought I should know.'

Naked pain sliced across his features before his body went rigid. 'When? When did he tell you?' he demanded harshly. 'Tonight?'

She nodded. 'Yes.'

That one syllable word brought Lucas to his feet in one lithe, furious movement. His eyes glittered down at her from a face that was tense with rage. Prudence struggled to sit up, bracing herself for an argument.

'Lucas—please—don't look at me like that. If only you had told me, I would have understood why you hated Jeffrey so.'

'Told you?' he seethed. 'How could I tell you something so bitter and evil I couldn't even bring myself to think about? Prudence, when I was captured, everything was taken from me but the beat of my heart. I suppose you could say I was lucky because I was able to gather a containment about me and shut the world out—concentrating on one more pull on the oar, one more battle, one more day, waiting for a miracle to release me. For two years I was a man without dignity. I was no more than a log rotting away.'

His face remained an impenetrable mask. Leaning towards the young woman who was looking up at him with an expression of horror and love, he gripped her shoulders with fingers of steel. His fearful dread that she had come to him out of pity made him savage.

'When, Prudence? When did you find out you loved me? Was it after Thomas told you of my two miserable years as a galley slave or before? Because, before God, I will not endure sympathy or pity from you. Never from you.'

The look of anger glaring in his eyes was frightening. 'It was before, Lucas—I swear it. It just made me realise how much I do love you—how much you have come to mean to me. It also gave me the jolt I needed to swallow my stupid pride and come to you—which I have wanted to do ever since the night I stayed at Marlden Hall. Please say that you believe me when I tell you that my heart is full of love for you and I will never go away.'

Breathing hard, Lucas looked into the depths of her eyes, and what he saw was a love so intense he was humbled by it. He felt the tension in his body begin to relax. 'I believe you.'

'I don't pity you and I am not giving you sympathy. When I knew what you had been through—of your suffering—my own was unendurable. I wanted to have been there with you to share your ordeal, your sufferings. But what Thomas told me also made me angry. I still am, and my anger is directed at your cousin for what he did to you. I cannot blame you for wanting revenge.'

His breath jerked in his throat and he stared at her. 'Revenge? Is that what you think? Pru, I do not want revenge. I am not a vengeful man. My reason for wanting to drag Jeffrey out of whichever hole he is hiding in is to make certain I can live out my life without the fear of being brought down by an assassin's blade.'

When the full meaning of his words hit her, Prudence gasped, thoroughly alarmed, the threat Jeffrey Fox posed to this man she loved above all else having acquired a horrible reality. 'No, Lucas. Jeffrey wouldn't.'

'I have no illusions about my cousin. Since I returned to England, I believe he has tried once and failed.'

She stared at him with a pale, stricken face, his words causing fear to course through her. 'What? When?'

'On my return to London—when I left Maitland House and was making my way back to Whitehall. I overpowered the man who attacked me, but he managed to get away before I could question him. I suspected it was somehow the work of Jeffrey, but when his ship failed to turn up I believed I was mistaken. However, when you told me you had seen him on two occasions—that he was in London on the day I rode into the city—I became certain he had hired the man to kill me.'

'Can you remember what the man looked like?'

'Unkempt—a burly fellow with a small beard and bulbous eyes.'

'That sounds like the man Jeffrey was with on the day of the procession. Why does Jeffrey hate you so much?'

'It's a long and bitter tale,' he said, sitting beside her and gathering her into his arms. Reclining on the cushions, his eyes looked back over the distance of the years. 'When my parents married and the years passed and no children came along, everyone believed my mother was barren. Uncle George, ten years my father's junior, was my father's heir and began to realise that Marlden Hall and the estate would pass to him and his heirs. He married, and soon after Jeffrey was born. When Uncle George was grooming Jeffrey for what he was certain would one day be his, just when it was thought my mother was past child-bearing age, she conceived and I was born. Jeffrey was eight years old at the time.

'Neither Uncle George nor Jeffrey forgave me for that. Whenever Jeffrey came to Marlden Hall afterwards, he would ride around the estate, filling himself with more and more hate. And then he stopped coming altogether and joined the navy. But he was bitter and still coveted that which he had lost. I didn't realise just how much until we met in Marseilles.' He sighed, looking down at Prudence's upturned face. 'You know the rest.'

He stood up, taking her hand and pulling her off the sofa to stand in front of him. 'And now, my love, you will share my supper and then I will take you back to Maitland House. Tomorrow will be a busy day for you. When I present you at Court as my wife, it is imperative that you have a fashionable wardrobe. I am sure Verity will know the best dressmakers to take you to.'

Standing on her toes, Prudence placed a playful kiss on his lips. 'That could prove to be an expensive business, my lord.'

His eyes twinkled. 'An expense I can well afford, my love. I told you I did not leave Constantinople a poor man. As my wife, you will have nothing but the best—speaking of which, I have something to give you.'

The sheer size and beauty of the ring he slipped on to her finger took her breath away. It was composed of a circle of diamonds of an extraordinary size, its centrepiece an Oriental topaz exhibiting a lustre like the sun. Lucas's dark gaze held hers when he had placed it on her finger, telling her how it had once belonged to one of the wives of the King of Siam, and which he had acquired, from a Free Merchant who had arrived in Constantinople, with just such a day as this in mind.

Later, after enjoying good food and superb wine as they talked of all the years ahead of them, with her head in the clouds and her happiness almost complete, Lucas took her back to Maitland House. Aunt Julia was with Mary at Bishopsgate, but Thomas, Verity, Arabella and Robert were all eagerly awaiting their return. There were kisses, laughter, smiles and toasts to the newly betrothed couple, and the following morning, with marriage plans the order of the day, Verity and Arabella whisked Prudence to the finest, most fashionable dressmakers in town.

Chapter Fifteen

Reeking of fish and cordage, the sailor town of Wapping on the Thames embankment was made up of filthy passages and alleys, of ramshackle tenements and lodging houses, bars and brothels, stinking tanneries and breweries, and teeming with poor labourers, beggars and all manner of low life. The taverns were mean, dingy establishments and dangerous, with an air of casual disrespect for the law.

The Black Cod was no different. It was just one of hundreds of establishments where mariners were accommodated and entertained while they were ashore. It also catered for the men who worked the river—and the women who lived off the mariners and the river men. Every night someone was beaten or knifed, and their bodies would later be found floating in the Thames.

The Black Cod was full and noisy, the language profane—another ship having spilled its crew, too long at sea, into the taverns of Wapping. Two scantily clad whores—the redness of their nipples exposed above their filthy bodices—wandered in off the street. A couple of sailors, their speech drink-slurred, dragged them unresisting on to their laps.

Sitting beside his untouched mug of ale was Jeffrey Fox, deaf and blind to all that was going on around him as he watched the night come down over the murky waters of the Thames. His mind was concentrated on the man he loathed above all else. The hatred he felt for his cousin had festered in his mind for so long that it took all the self-discipline he possessed to stop himself hunting him down with his pistol and openly blowing his head off.

For weeks Jeffrey had been scheming for a way to get rid of him. He had tracked his movements from the moment he had arrived on English soil, and even employed Phineas Frost—a murderer and a thief—to attack him on his way back to Whitehall on the night of his return, but the attack had failed and Phineas had disappeared back into the underworld from whence he came.

Following the incident where Lucas had swept Prudence Fairworthy off her feet in the procession and soundly kissed her, Jeffrey had made a point of finding out her identity. The following morning he'd followed her to Covent Garden. Observing everything that had taken place in the nursery yard and the surly youth's rage at his failed attempt to seduce Mistress Fairworthy—and then, to add insult to injury, being bested by Lucas—Jeffrey had realised that to form an alliance with the youth, Will Price, might work to his advantage.

He cursed Lucas, with his wealth and his fine estate. And he cursed the beautiful Prudence Fairworthy, who troubled his dreams. He savoured the memory of her face and pictured himself making love to her, pleasuring her. Suddenly his eyes hardened, his mind seething with her shifting image. But she was his cousin's woman—this, too, he had discovered—and as such deserved no pleasure. He would do what he wanted with her, roughly, until she begged for mercy, and then he would hand her over to Will Price to do with as he pleased.

For the next week everything was rushed and planned and ordered and contrived to make the wedding occasion a memorable one. Prudence was kept so busy she hardly saw the man she had committed her life to as her vast wardrobe was arranged.

The list of garments she was measured up for, in shades to match her creamy skin and the vibrant, autumnal tones of her hair, was endless—day dresses, evening dresses, dresses for balls and masques, riding dresses, cloaks, hats and petticoats, and all the necessary accessories that were required to complete the extensive wardrobe of a lady of quality. At first Prudence maintained that it was all an unnecessary extravagance, but soon realised that it was quite useless voicing her objections when Verity and Arabella were being carried along on the crest of some gigantic wave, and when she was marrying a man as wealthy as Lucas Fox.

When the day of the wedding arrived, and they were surrounded by a large gathering of family and friends—and several curious ladies and gentlemen of the Court, who were eager to see for themselves the woman who had succeeded in securing the affections of the popular Lord Fox when hundreds of others had failed—Prudence and Lucas gazed lovingly into each other's eyes as they spoke their vows; afterwards, Lucas took his wife in his arms and kissed her with a passion that left her breathless.

Lucas was unable to believe that the exquisite creature in a gown of ivory satin and silver lace, with a white petticoat edged in delicate pink and silver rosebuds, was his wife. With her large amethyst eyes and her hair cascading in abundant chestnut curls and framing her enchanting face, she was a vision of radiant, breathtaking beauty. Delicate pearl drop earrings and a single strand of pearls given to her by him as a wedding gift were her only adornment. And, of course, she carried an arrangement of roses she had grown herself, all held together with ivory and silver ribbon to match her gown.

The wedding feast was a truly joyous affair. They drank from the loving cup and endless toasts were drunk to their happiness and long lives together. It was not until they returned to Lucas's town house that the couple got the privacy they needed. Lucas poured a glass of ruby red wine for his bride and handed it to her, then poured one for himself. He raised his glass.

'To us, my love.'

'To us,' she whispered, raising her glass and gently tapping his before taking a sip of the wine. She was surprised when Lucas suddenly removed the glass from her fingers and bent down, placing his arm under her knees and scooping her up into his arms. She gasped with delight, seeing a wicked light dancing in his gypsy eyes as she locked her arms about his neck, and she knew precisely what he was going to do next. 'Lucas—'

'No objections, my sweet. This is our wedding night— and you are my adorable bride. I do not intend wasting one minute of it.'

'I'm not objecting. Take me to bed,' she murmured, kissing his mouth of her own volition, her look one of tenderness, love and wanting as he carried her to their bedchamber. Quickly he dismissed the maids waiting to help Prudence out of her bridal gown, determined to divest her of every article of clothing, from her gown to her silk stockings, himself.

'You are an inviting, haunting temptress,' he murmured against her lips as his fingers deftly began to unfasten each tiny button at the back of her gown, 'and you are about to experience a night of passion and sensual delights such as you cannot have imagined.'

When she lay between the cool sheets, Prudence watched her husband remove his clothing, feeling a tremor of alarm and embarrassed admiration pass through her as his body was exposed to her. He had the bronzed body of a tall, lithe athlete. His shoulders and thighs were firmly muscled, his belly flat and taut, and a thick mat of springy black hair covered the wide expanse of his chest. He was splendid, magnificent, and as she stared at him her heart gave a tremendous leap, unable to believe how handsome he was. He laughed when she flushed and averted her maidenly eyes away from his manhood, and his teeth gleamed white from between his parted lips as he threw back the bedcovers and joined her, pulling her against him.

In the light from a single candle and the sanctuary of their bed, Lucas gloried in her beauty—her tiny waist and rounded hips and full breasts. He lingered over his wife of a few hours as he began to seal their vows securely in a physical knot of passion, determined that he would make her body sing with rapture before he was done. But it was no easy matter ignoring the urgent heat and throbbing in his loins, and as her gentle fingers shyly began to explore his naked body, slowly gathering courage, they ignited too many fires for his rapidly splintering restraint.

Prudence could not believe the flood of warmth and the pain of ecstasy increasing within her when his mouth devoured her own and seared her flesh with a melting hunger. Lost in the desire he was skilfully building inside her, she writhed against him as his hand slipped down and slowly stroked the smooth curve of her hip and wandered over her lower abdomen, feeling consumed by heat and an almost driving urge to rise and press her body against his. Where his hand had gone before, so his lips followed, journeying randomly over her belly and lower still to tease the triangular reddish-gold tangle of hair between her thighs, rousing her sensations and persuading her heart to beat in a frantic rhythm. His hands stroked downwards over the curve of her hip and then upwards along the velvet softness inside her thighs, his fingers entering that most intimate part of her.

She gasped at his invasion, opening her eyes. Above her she could see his face was hard, his eyes dark with passion, and yet there was so much tenderness in their depths that her heart ached.

With his blood flowing through his veins like molten lava, Lucas gloried in the joy of the woman in his arms,

feeling her yield to his caress. Bending his dark head, his
mouth covered hers in a long, drugging kiss as his knowledgeable fingers teased and toyed with deliberate slowness,
exploring her dark velvety warmth until she was moist and
moved her hips against him. Unable to fight back his rampaging desire, he eased himself on top of her, and she
parted her legs to receive his rigid hardness.

Anticipating the pain she would experience in the next
moment, Prudence stiffened her body, her arms going
round him. When he plunged into her, when the moment
of pain had subsided, in its place was a hungering, throbbing ache. He filled her fully, touching all of her. It was
incredible, something new that burst inside her, and as she
slowly began to move as he moved and arched to meet him
to the full, she was so carried along on a rapturous glow
of passion by the driving force of his powerful strokes deep
within her that she was almost delirious. When the explosion came and he poured himself into her, it broke in a
wave of ecstasy and she felt her body soar.

When the weight of his strong body lifted off her, sated
and happy, Prudence looked up at him, fighting her way
back from oblivion. Lucas was on his side, resting on his
elbow, the fingers of his free hand gently brushing strands
of hair from her face. He was looking at her with part
reverence, part awe, unable to believe this woman, his wife,
had succeeded in sending him to unparalleled heights of
satisfaction and desire. He had always known that when he
finally made love to her they would be a combustible combination, but what he had just experienced had been the
most splendidly erotic sexual encounter of his life.

When she sighed and closed her eyes, he lowered his
head and ran his tongue provocatively over her lower lip.
'Are you happy, my love?'

'Mmm,' she breathed without opening her eyes.

'What are you thinking?' he asked with a tender smile,
stroking her satiny skin.

On a sigh, like a kitten she nestled close beneath the

sensual onslaught of his caressing hand and mouth. 'My thoughts are most unladylike, my lord. I will not offend your ears by airing them.'

Opening her eyes, she saw the gleam of a thin silver scar—one of several, she noticed, on the side of his chest. She felt him stiffen when she reached out and touched one with her fingers, tracing its smooth line and knowing there would be more on his back. Her heart almost broke in two when she thought of the torment he must have suffered at the hands of those brutal Barbary corsairs, and their liberal use of the lash. She lifted her head and looked at him, her eyes shining with unshed tears.

'Oh, my love. How those barbarians have hurt you,' she whispered.

'Nay, love. My torment was in not being able to hit back.'

As if to heal his scars she kissed each one before wrapping her arms around him, and Lucas thanked God she was not repulsed by what she saw, although the scars were now faded.

'Have I told you how much I love you, Lucas?—and if every night is to be like this one, then I shall be well satisfied.'

'You speak as if this one is already over and done with, sweetheart. If that is what you think, then you are mistaken,' he said and, as if to prove it, he took her lips in a devouring kiss, renewed desire already pouring through him as he proceeded to kiss and caress her into mindless insensibility.

Two days after her wedding, after visiting a milliner's along Fleet Street, where there were pleasant shops of every kind, Prudence and Arabella were about to return to their coach when a haberdasher's displaying some particularly fine embroidered French ribbons in the window caught Arabella's eye. She insisted on going inside to take a closer look. The shopkeeper was a pleasant young woman who immediately began showing them samples for their appreciation. Finding the interior of the shop stuffy and impatient to return home to Lucas, Prudence excused herself to Arabella, telling her she would wait for her inside the coach.

Unfortunately, when she stepped outside she could just see their coach disappearing down the street. The streets, being narrow and incommodious, left no room for coaches to loiter and they were forced to move on. She knew the sensible thing to do was to wait for Arabella and her maid, but she was tired from shopping and her limbs ached to sit down. And so she began to follow the disappearing coach, sidestepping oncoming pedestrians, knowing it would be waiting at the end of the street.

When a man stepped in front of her she was about to pass him by, but when he spoke she stopped. Her heart almost ceased to beat when she recognised Jeffrey Fox. Sporting a gold-knobbed walking cane, he was bare-headed and not so finely garbed as the last time they had met. His purple jacket and breeches were badly soiled, as was the white linen at his neck and cuffs. Prudence went numb when she met his gaze. The charismatic façade that had once attracted her was now arrogant, saturnine, and cruel, and the cocksure smile had acquired a malevolent twist.

In a split second dreadful suspicions leaped into her mind—did Jeffrey Fox intend to harm her? Did he intend to get at Lucas through her? No—that was too fanciful by far, she told herself severely. She tried to compose her features, but the trembling in her limbs persisted, and the opening to a street on the left of her was far too empty and much too quiet.

Making her an elegant bow, Jeffrey smiled, a smile without warmth. 'Lady Fox! What a pleasant surprise. I congratulate you on your marriage to my cousin. I wish you a happy life together at Marlden Hall—while it lasts,' he said, his meaning plain to Prudence. 'Perhaps I shall visit you there one day.'

'Our life together at Marlden Hall will be a *long* and

happy one, Captain Fox—and I think you know that you will not be welcome there,' Prudence said coldly, wishing Arabella would hurry up and join her.

He smirked. 'That may be, but you will have to put up with me being there one day.' His eyes narrowed as they locked on hers. 'Unlike the last time we met, you do not seem happy to see me.'

She glared at him, contempt written broadly in her eyes. 'I think we both know the reason for that.'

Jeffrey laughed, the sound an unnerving rumble deep in his chest. 'I can see my cousin has changed your opinion of me. But your beauty is still the same as when I first saw you.'

'You have not changed,' Prudence countered. 'You are still the same blackhearted villain who tried to kill his own cousin.'

'So—he told you that, too. And you believed him?'

'Every word. Our meeting today is not a coincidence, is it, Captain Fox?' she said, suspecting he had been watching her movements for days.

He gave what he presumed to be a charming smile. To Prudence it was a grimace. 'Call it what you wish. We have matters to discuss—in private—private matters.'

'I have nothing to say to you.' She made to turn but his hand shot out, his fingers closing round her arm like a steel band.

'Ah, but that is where you're wrong.' His smile left no doubt about his meaning.

'Take your hand off my arm. At once.'

He chuckled. 'Nay—I am not your husband, madam, to order about. You are beautiful in temper—does Lucas tell you that? I can't explain it, but I've never wanted a woman as much as I want you.'

'And you've always coveted everything Lucas has. Is that not so?' she spat.

The meaning of the words and the force with which they were delivered hit home. Jeffrey's veneer of sham politeness crumbled and the smile on his face disappeared as he thrust his face close to hers. 'That is true, and I aim to leave him with nothing. I like you, Prudence—and I am not the only man who likes you. Maybe I will give you to him—after I have taken you myself.'

Prudence paled. She didn't know fully what warped memories this man harboured against her husband, but she knew that every rebuff Lucas had given him must have festered for years inside his head, and that he was dangerous. The street around her was alarmingly empty of people, and when a coach suddenly appeared out of the quiet side street and drew alongside, she was about to appeal to whoever was inside for help. But the door was flung open and two callused hands reached out and grabbed her.

She spun about to flee, but Jeffrey Fox came up behind her, cutting her intended scream short by clamping his hand over her mouth. And then everything happened so fast as she was hauled and pushed roughly into the interior of the coach. She moaned when the gold knob of Jeffrey's cane came crashing down on her, striking her temple, and before a black miasma of unconsciousness descended, it was Will Price's face she saw bending over her.

When Arabella and her maid emerged from the haberdashers, they could find no sign of Prudence. Puzzled by her disappearance and distraught, Arabella immediately went to see Lucas, breathing a sigh of relief to find him at home.

As Lucas listened to her his face darkened. Jeffrey had Prudence! He knew it. When Arabella had left to alert Thomas, he looked straight ahead, considering that one overriding fact—Jeffrey had Prudence—and the equally overriding conclusion—he intended to get her back. Calming the rage inside him and forcing his mind to a cold analytical bent, he and Thomas and the men he'd hired to look for his cousin began trying to work out where he would have taken her, but all their searching yielded nothing.

Lucas would know neither rest nor peace until Prudence was safe in his arms. The thought of her in the hands of his half-crazed cousin, of the indignities he might force on her, caused a dull rage to fill his being, which increased when all their efforts to find her came to nothing. It was as if she had vanished into thin air.

Prudence had no idea how long she had been unconscious or where she was. It was dark and she had no way of knowing how late it was. By the light of a single candle she could see that the room, with its low ceiling and black beams, was dingy and cramped and that damp plaster was hanging off the walls. She was lying on a pallet stuffed with straw and covered with foul-smelling blankets.

With her head pounding fit to burst from the blow Jeffrey had given her, she dragged herself off the bed and went to a small gable-end window. The room was high up in a building—a tavern, she thought, if the noise of revelry coming from below was anything to go by. She could hear the distinctive sounds of the river traffic—the coracles and ferryboats and barges that filled the waterway at all times of day and night.

Straining to see through the window's grimy panes, despite the smoke erupting from the many chimneypots that clogged her vision, to her right she could just make out the ghostly shape of the Tower and the skeletal masts of tall ships and the bobbing of lanterns on the decks of seagoing vessels on the Thames, which meant she was somewhere below London Bridge. The bridge, under which the Thames made its turbulent passage, was an obstruction to all incoming ships, and as a result the shipping kept to the Pool of London. This was where the quays and the custom house were located, and it had been London's main port from Roman days.

Making a quick exploration of her prison, she saw there

was a cupboard and broken chairs and a filthy closed stool in a corner, and it didn't surprise her to find that the door was locked. She huddled in a ball on the bed like a small, captive animal awaiting her fate. A stench rose up from the streets to permeate her prison and seemed to touch with cold fingers upon the deepest part of her fears. It was the stench of flotsam, of decay and poverty, the rotten, unacceptable smell of humanity at its meanest level.

Panic and helplessness almost choked her as she struggled to come to terms with what had happened to her. She was tempted to bang on the door in an attempt to attract attention, but she was too afraid that she might alert Jeffrey or Will Price. Tears stung her eyes, but she dashed them away, setting her teeth in a determined effort not to give in to despair. No matter what Jeffrey intended, she would fight him with every ounce of her strength.

As the night wore on and no one came, it was thoughts of Lucas that sustained her. She thought of him with a poignant, painful longing, which gave her comfort and strength. He would be looking for her, worrying about her. She bowed her head to her drawn-up knees. Please God, let him find her soon.

It was over twenty-four hours since his wife's disappearance when a short note arrived for Lucas, informing him that something he had lost and was eager to find could be located in a tavern close to the river at Wapping.

'We must take care, Lucas,' said Thomas, glancing at his brother-in-law's tense features. The strain was taking its toll on them all, but Lucas seemed to be in the grip of a nightmare. '*You* are Jeffrey's objective. If you are right and he has taken Prudence to get at you, then clearly the note has been sent to lure you into a trap. By waiting this length of time to contact you, he will expect the suspense to have worked you into such a state of frustration and worry that it will send you dashing blindly off to Wapping. No doubt he or one of his henchmen will be waiting for you in some dark alley.'

Lucas nodded, his sense of rage subdued beneath a firm grip of will. 'I know—but from past experience I know it pays to be bold in matters such as this. Anyway, we have no choice. We have nothing else to go on. Peter Fennor— one of the men I hired to look for Jeffrey when I arrived in London—used to be a mariner, which was why I hired him in the first place. He is familiar with most of the shipping areas around the Pool—Wapping and its taverns in particular. I'll send him there to see what he can find out. I think we should wait until he returns and go ourselves after dark.'

'It might be wise for us to go by river,' Thomas suggested quickly. 'To take your own transport will attract undue attention and alert your cousin, and a hackney will be slow.'

Lucas nodded. 'You're right. Although I strongly suspect Jeffrey will have someone watching the house, waiting for me to leave.'

'In that case the most sensible thing to do will be to leave by a back entrance. We can take a boat from the stairs at the palace and go as far as Upper Thames Street, where we will leave the boat and take another at Billingsgate and go on to Wapping. I have no mind to shoot the rapids between the piers of London Bridge during daylight hours and certainly not after dark,' he said drily, knowing too many people who had perished that way.

That evening, when it was quite dark, Peter Fennor returned to the house, and the news he brought to them after his visit to Wapping was not unencouraging. With all the skill of a born actor, Peter had casually mingled with the mariners in the bars and taverns close to the river, and had discovered that a man fitting Captain Fox's description was known to be a regular customer at the Black Cod—one of the meanest, most dangerous taverns in Wapping.

* * *

Prudence must have slept, because when she awoke a watery light filtered through the grime on the windows into the room. Feeling hungry and with her head still aching from the blow, her nightmare was renewed. Her heart was pounding as her imagination began working feverishly. What did Jeffrey, with his capricious nature, intend doing with her? If she were to perish at his hands, then no one would know what had happened to her.

Later, when the light was beginning to fade and she was about to face her second night of captivity, she heard a key grate in the lock. All her senses became alert; her eyes were huge as they stared at the door, fully expecting Jeffrey to appear. It was Will Price. He was exactly as she remembered, but he had put on weight and his face was flushed, his eyes red and bleary from drink.

'Do you remember me, Prudence?' His voice was coercing as he looked at her ardently.

Prudence scrambled off the bed and faced him angrily. 'Aye, Will Price, I remember you. But I'd as soon forget. Whatever villainy you are up to with Jeffrey Fox, you will come to no good. How dare you forcibly abduct me and keep me prisoner in this hovel?'

'It's what Captain Fox brought you here for—for me. We have an agreement, you see. He gets your husband—I get you.'

His arrogance roused her temper. 'You're mad, Will Price. Go away. I have no wish for your company. It disgusts me.'

'But I have a wish for yours. You're more beautiful than I remember. Just looking at you warms my innards. The pain of wanting you will not go away.' He edged closer, but she moved back. His ardent gaze turned to a leer as he positioned himself between her and the door. 'Are you angry with me for neglecting you all these hours?'

'Get out,' she cried as he advanced towards her, revolted when his sweaty hand shot out and caught her arm. His breathing was laboured as he pulled her towards him, and her stomach heaved at the disagreeable aroma of sweat that assailed her nostrils.

'Don't scream,' he warned, his body trembling with pent-up desire, unreleased for too long. Suddenly he let her go when the figure of Jeffrey Fox appeared in the doorway.

The two men faced each other, a sliver of steel gleaming evilly in Jeffrey's hand. 'You're drunk, Will. Leave her be.' Jeffrey smiled thinly at Prudence. 'Will gets like a lust-crazed beast when he's drunk.'

Will cursed profanely. 'The woman is mine,' he growled. 'We agreed.'

'Of what use is a woman to a dead man?' Jeffrey sneered, wielding the blade threateningly. 'You fool. I brought her here for two reasons: to lure The Fox into my lair, and to take his wife when and if I feel like it. Afterwards, if she doesn't please me, you can have her. Now get out. You know what you have to do if you want to earn your shillings.'

Will's eyes narrowed above a greedy snarl. 'You'll owe me more than a few shillings and a passage to America on your ship *if* I pull this off. Aye, a lot more.'

Jeffrey picked up on what he said in a flash. '*If?* There is no *if* about it. You'd best have a care, Price. Whoever interferes with my plans now risks his life.'

Will shrugged. 'Aye—and then you'd have to hire another cutthroat to get rid of me—knowin' you haven't got the stomach to do the job yourself,' he sneered contemptuously. 'You don't frighten me, Captain—never have.'

Prudence looked at Will. 'His ship? Is that what he told you, Will? You fool. You've been duped. You've let Captain Fox deceive you with his tricks. Didn't he tell you that he was attacked off Gibraltar and that his ship and most of his crew are lying somewhere at the bottom of the Mediterranean Sea?' she goaded deliberately, feeling a surge of triumph when her revelation registered in his dull eyes. 'There is no ship, is that not so, Captain Fox?'

Will's eyes went from Prudence to Jeffrey as this new

light of knowledge began to dawn. 'What's she sayin'?' he
roared in outraged disbelief. 'Do you play a double game
with me? You told me your ship was moored at Deptford.'

Jeffrey's eyes glittered hard as he threw Prudence a look
of anger, but he mastered himself so that only a very careful
observer would have seen that something was seriously
amiss. 'And so it is,' he answered glibly, with a twisted
smile of arrogance. 'Go and see for yourself if you don't
believe me.'

Will didn't believe him. With only an arm's length between the two men, Will's eyes blazed with savage fury
and an abrupt state of sobriety ensued. 'You're lying. You
hired me to kill Fox with the promise of his wife, a handsome purse, and a passage to America. You tricked me,
you dog. All the time you intended double-crossing me
when the deed was done.'

Jeffrey's eyes fairly crackled with rage. Despite all his
efforts and his carefully laid plans, things were going
swiftly awry.

A growl started rising from the innermost depths of
Will's being and blood-red hate filled his sight. Forgetful
of the knife Jeffrey was holding, with a bellow of rage, he
launched himself blindly at the other man. They grappled
ferociously, and Will had his hands locked round Jeffrey's
throat when suddenly he gasped and fell back, blood oozing
from a flesh wound in his side where Jeffrey's knife had
penetrated. Will looked at the wound and then at Jeffrey
still wielding the knife.

'God rot your eyes,' Will swore. 'I'll get you for this.
You'll not escape me the next time,' he hissed, before
stumbling through the door.

'It would appear that you will have to find yourself another assassin to kill Lucas, you coward,' Prudence sneered
at Jeffrey contemptuously. 'Are you not man enough to
perform the deed yourself? Has what happened in Marseilles slipped your mind already—and that assassins are
not to be trusted?' she scoffed.

Breathing heavily, Jeffrey glared at Prudence, who was rubbing her arm where Will's grip had been. 'You're right. This is something I will do myself.' His manner suddenly changed, and he smiled, shoving the knife down the top of his boot. 'You should thank me. I have saved you from a terrible fate. Come, Prudence,' he coaxed. 'I have grown quite fond of you, you know, and it pains me to keep you in such mean conditions.'

'If you are trying to convince me of your gentle manner, abusing me is not the way to go about it.'

'I must keep you here until your husband comes looking for you. When he is out of the way we can get to know each other better.'

Prudence tensed, unable to hide her loathing. Approaching him, she looked him squarely in the eye. 'And do you think I will be so easily won over by the man who has killed my husband? Lucas will not be so easy to dispose of a second time. He will never be snared by your trap—which, I assume, is to lure him down some dark infested alley and slit his throat.

'He will find me and kill you for this—and if he doesn't, my brother will. You should heed my warning, Captain Fox, for if you pursue the killing of my husband—your cousin, I would remind you, your own flesh and blood—I shall live to see you hanged for it. So whatever you hope to achieve by using me as bait to catch my husband, it will prove pointless in the end.'

Her eyes glittered with a coldness that almost chilled Jeffrey to the bone. He stared at her, wondering at the courage she had found. His own was punctured by sharp twinges of apprehension, for he was convinced that she meant every word she said.

Without another word Jeffrey went out and locked the door. Regret was a worrisome thing as he made his way down the narrow stairs to the tavern below, especially when he began to realise that what he had done could lead to serious consequences for himself. He had been too hasty—

he should never have abducted Prudence, for by doing so he had openly challenged his cousin and risked losing everything he coveted.

He had sent a message to Lucas's house at Whitehall, telling him that his wife had been taken and the vicinity in which she could be found. That should bring him to Wapping straight away—and if Will Price wasn't waiting to dispose of him as planned, it gave him more reason to worry, for Lucas would come looking for him.

Jeffrey considered doing the deed himself, but that would mean leaving Prudence unguarded—and besides, he had never killed anyone, and the thought of doing so brought bile to his mouth.

Chapter Sixteen

Having staunched the flow of blood from his wound, which wasn't life threatening, Will Price watched from the safety of the shadows as the lighting from the ramshackle dwellings and taverns outlined the three figures standing on the jetty. When he had agreed to Captain Fox's proposal to dispose of his cousin for a sum of money that had staggered him, he'd had no scruples about doing so—especially when he remembered how the arrogant Lord Fox had humiliated him on their previous encounter at Mr Rowan's nursery. But now things had changed. It was not Lord Fox who would be found floating face down in the Thames come daylight.

Lucas surveyed the waterfront with distaste, knowing that only desperate men and fools ventured into this quarter after dark. It was teeming with a motley assortment of low-bred individuals, many of them living on the streets, along with the garbage, the sewage and the vermin. When Will Price approached him, Lucas recognised him immediately. Recalling what Prudence had told him about seeing him with Jeffrey in Dorking, he quickly alerted Thomas and Peter to the danger. As well as swords, all three of them had pistols concealed beneath their cloaks.

When Will halted in front of them, instead of plunging his knife into Lord Fox's heart, he told him in a low, conspiratorial voice that the only danger he could expect would come from his cousin. Lucas was by no means convinced and studied him with open suspicion. Nevertheless he listened as Will Price quickly told him where he could find his wife, before turning and vanishing into the network of alleyways well known to him. Lucas made no attempt to go after him, having recognising an element of truth in what he had said.

On reaching the Black Cod, Thomas and Peter began searching the crowded rooms for Jeffrey Fox, while Lucas, all his senses alert and his fingers on the butt of the pistol tucked into his belt, climbed the narrow, winding stairs up two floors.

When the door was forced open to the room where Prudence was imprisoned, she could not believe her eyes when Lucas burst in, an irate innkeeper's wife hurling abuse at him as she followed in his wake. Immediately Prudence tumbled headlong into her husband's arms, which closed around her with stunning force, his hand cradling her tear-streaked face against his chest. She clung to him in silence, holding him fiercely to her, too happy and deeply moved to speak. Her recent shock, terror and fear, and feeling faint with hunger, had used up all her resistance.

Gently Lucas held her face in his strong hands and looked wonderingly down into her face. When he touched her lips with a kiss, she looked at him with eyes brimming with love.

'Don't talk now, my love,' he said hoarsely, overcome with an emotion which threatened to unman him. 'Time enough for that later. You are alive and I thank God with all my heart.' Anger burned in his eyes as he traced the bruise on the side of her face with his finger, and when she winced with the pain he drew in his breath. 'I might have spared you this had I refused to let you out of my sight. I see the evidence of my cousin's abuse, but has he abused you in any other way that I cannot see, little one?'

She shook her head, gripping his hand. 'No. Lucas—

we've got to get out of here. Jeffrey intends to kill you,' she whispered urgently.

He laid his fingers gently against her lips as she gratefully leaned into his embrace. 'Don't fret, sweetheart. I did not come without help,' he told her. 'Thomas and a man I hired weeks ago to look for Jeffrey are with me. We'll come out of this safely. I promise you.'

Someone else had come into the room. It was Thomas. He took his sister in a fierce, emotional embrace before handing her back to Lucas.

'There's no sign of Jeffrey.'

'Now *that* doesn't surprise me,' said Lucas drily. 'Come, let's get out of this hovel. The very stench of the place sickens me.'

Ignoring the innkeeper's wife, who continued to screech obscenities at their backs, they went down the stairs to the tavern below, which was overflowing with rogues, thieves and scoundrels; the noise of inebriated singing was deafening. Prudence was unable to avert her eyes from so much depravity, of giggling whores being dragged down upon men's laps, their bosoms exposed to be fondled.

Supporting his wife, Lucas went outside, pausing to wait for Thomas who went in search of Peter. Suddenly, mocking laughter echoed from the gloom of an alley, bringing their startled attention to a shadowy form standing a short distance away. They were unable to see his features clearly, but they both knew it was Jeffrey. He stepped forward, arrogant in his demeanour, confident with a pistol in his hand.

'And what do we have here?' he jeeringly questioned. 'Lord and Lady Fox? How nice to see you both together.'

Lucas's eyes were like cold pieces of flint as they met his cousin's amused smile. Quickly he shoved Prudence behind him, eyeing the pistol warily. 'So—we are face to face at last, cousin. I had grown up knowing of your insane hatred and jealousy—but I had no idea what such bitter resentment might lead you to do, until we met in Marseilles. And now this. If I ever catch you on my property or in close proximity to my wife again, I will arrange your judgement day to come sooner than you expect.'

'You—threaten me?' Jeffrey's tone was mockingly incredulous. 'I am the one holding the pistol. It's your life hanging in the balance, not mine.'

'I am stating what our future relationship will be,' Lucas said coldly, feeling his wife's trembling form sagging against his back as she fought to remain upright.

'Considering what is past, I cannot say that I blame you,' Jeffrey conceded with a sneer.

'I have had many enemies, but how was I to know that the most dangerous of them all was my own kin? My cousin.' Lucas smiled, his eyes glittering with ironic amusement. 'So—does my murdering cousin think to confess the truth I have known all along—that it was you who hired those men to kill me in Marseilles, only to have them sell me on to double their take?'

'I have no reason to deny what you know to be the truth, cousin. I admit to wanting that property of yours, and I might have had it, had those villains not double-crossed me in Marseilles—and had Charles Stuart not returned to England. I thought I had truly bungled when you turned up at The Hague and came back to haunt me. But I've got you again, just where I want you. And this time, there'll be no one to save you.'

As he met his cousin's tolerant stare, Jeffrey ceased his prattle, finding no evidence that he worried the other man, who looked completely unruffled. He began to experience a feeling of unease, and his fingers clasping the pistol began to shake, which Lucas noticed.

'You had your chance to get rid of me and failed. You are a sad excuse for a man, Jeffrey. I pity you.'

Thwarted of triumph, Jeffrey's fury burst. 'Pity? You pity me?' His face darkened with rage as he watched his cousin begin to move closer. Lucas's face was carved from granite, and as calm now that he stared death in the eye as it had ever been. His absolute contempt for the man who was bent on killing him was manifest in his narrowed eyes, the lift of his arrogant head and the curl of his lip.

At that moment Jeffrey envied him more than he had ever done. He had everything—looks, wealth, power, a magnificent house and a woman any man would gladly die for—while he had nothing. He was nothing. The galling, frustrating truth pounded inside his head, it throbbed in the centre of his soul and fed his hatred. Lucas should be dead and everything should be his—and now he had the chance to kill him. He laughed, but the sound failed to convince him. That was the moment when he remembered what Prudence had said—that he was not man enough to perform the deed himself.

He breathed deeply, his face relaxing. So that was what she thought, this woman who had not the wit to keep her tongue still, for if she had, Will Price would have been standing here as planned. The bitch! She thought she was so clever. But look at her now. She could do nothing but hide behind her husband and tremble with terror. He would show her. He had waited too long, spent too much of himself to turn away now. But still his hand trembled and his will would not obey his mind.

At that moment providence chose to intercede for Lucas and Prudence when a crowd of disorderly revellers poured out of the tavern on to the street, creating a loud diversion as they snaked their way between Lucas and Jeffrey. In a flash Lucas dragged Prudence back inside the tavern, just as Thomas and Peter elbowed their way through the throng.

Quickly Lucas told them what had happened. Careful for their lives, they drew their pistols and stepped outside the tavern, but Jeffrey had disappeared into the dark network of alleyways. Unwilling to remain any longer in that place, Thomas found a hackney carriage to take them back to Whitehall. Peter remained behind to look for Jeffrey Fox.

When the crowd spilled out on to the street from the tavern, separating Jeffrey from his cousin, he drew back into the shadows of the alley. He would never know if he would have had the courage to kill his cousin, for at that moment a fist was slammed into his gut, winding him and doubling him over with the pain of it. He groaned in agony as a vicious knee sank into his groin and brought him to his knees.

'That's for your trickery, you crawling bastard,' a voice rasped.

A hand gripped his hair and jerked his head back so he was looking full into the enraged face of his attacker, a face with matted hair and lips parted in the crazy, delirious smile of a man possessed.

It was Will Price.

A punch in the face burst Jeffrey's nose and sent blood spurting in all directions and tears streaming from his eyes.

'And that's for lyin'. And this,' Will hissed, 'is for Prudence Fairworthy—the fairest maid this side of heaven… and hell.'

A knife pricked his neck, and Jeffrey felt a burning, searing pain as it entered his throat and ripped and tore. Blood poured into his mouth and his eyes glazed over, and death was all around him.

When Lucas and Prudence arrived at their house in Whitehall, her whole family was there, waiting for her, wanting to enfold her in the protective warmth of their arms and love. Arabella wept copious tears of relief, and aunt Julia hugged her, crying and smiling at the same time, saying 'Thank God' over and over again. Verity did the same, with so much feeling that Prudence guiltily regretted any ill feelings she had held towards her sister-in-law.

She was fed, then bathed and finally put to bed, and only when everyone had gone to their respective homes and the house was quiet did Prudence nestle wordlessly in her husband's arms, her hand resting against his chest.

He smiled and kissed the shining top of her head. 'How perfectly your body fits into mine,' he murmured.

'I was thinking the same thing,' she murmured, hesitant to mention anything of her ordeal, but there was just one question she had to ask him that puzzled her. 'Lucas—how did you know where to find me?'

Her husband's brows drew together. 'I received a note from Jeffrey informing me you were being kept at a tavern in Wapping—but not which one. When we arrived on the jetty, Will Price materialised and told us where you were. I must say I was surprised, considering our previous, unpleasant encounter—and knowing he was hand in glove with Jeffrey. I had every reason to mistrust him, but something in the way he looked and spoke told me that their relationship was not as harmonious as it might be.'

'You were not mistaken. Jeffrey hired Will Price to kill you with the promise of a generous reward and a passage on his ship to America. I believe I was to be thrown in as an extra.' She smiled. 'When I told Will that Jeffrey's ship was lying at the bottom of the sea, Will—whose temper always was volatile—became enraged and accused him of trickery, and refused to have anything further to do with him.'

With a low chuckle, Lucas tipped her face up and placed a light kiss on her lips. 'It would seem I have you to thank for getting Will Price off my back. I am indeed grateful.'

'How grateful?' she breathed, nuzzling his neck with her lips and pressing her body closer to his.

His eyes narrowed and he smiled slowly. 'How grateful would you like me to be?'

'Very, I'm afraid,' she said, with such a deep sigh that, despite this being one of the most achingly poignant moments of his life, Lucas burst out laughing and clasped her to him, burying his face in her sweet-scented hair, before desire began to course through him, fuelled by two nights of abstinence. His mouth closed over hers and she wrapped her arms around him.

'Welcome home, my love,' he whispered.

The following morning Peter Fennor arrived at the house to see Lucas.

'I came as soon as I could. I thought you might like to know,' Peter said to Lucas alone in the reception room.

'Know what?'

'A boatman found Captain Fox just after sunrise.'

'Where? Where did he find him?'

'Propped against his boat in the mud—with his throat cut. No doubt he'd been left there to be sucked into the river with the incoming tide.'

'And do you know who is responsible?'

'It's said at the Black Cod that his accomplice, Will Price, could have done it.'

'They're probably right. And where is Will Price?'

'He enlisted on a vessel which left the Pool for the Caribbean at first light.'

Combing his fingers through his hair, Lucas sighed and lowered his head. Despite everything Jeffrey was guilty of where he was concerned, this was not the end he would have wished for him. But his demise removed forever all threats to his future happiness with Prudence.

With the summer behind them and King Charles II settled into his own routine, although no Act of Parliament could wipe out twenty years of civil strife, he showed little inclination to embark on any radical changes. Debates in both houses were a long and ugly business of deciding who should be left out of the general pardon. It was accepted that all the regicides who had condemned Charles I to death, and others who had helped bring about his death, were to suffer in some way, but, whatever the outcome, it was an ocean away to be of any threat to George Fox in the Colonies.

London's parks and pleasure gardens were decked in au-

tumnal glory on the day when Prudence, escorted by Lucas,
was presented at Court. There, in the sprawling splendour,
was lodged the Court, and there, at its heart, lived the King
with his Privy Servants and Councillors. Here and at Parliament, the kingdom was ruled, and Prudence was overcome with a sense of majesty.

Along the Privy Gallery, from which a complex network
of small rooms opened off the broad, impressive space,
people wandered freely and at ease. Entering the stately
Presence Chamber, Prudence was met by a magical combination of visual splendour and power. A burst of light
from an extravagant glitter of candles dazzled her, a wave
of perfume engulfed her, and the scene was of shimmering
gowns, sparkling jewels, of fluttering fans, the hubbub of
conversation and the soft swish of trains as they trailed over
thick piled carpets.

Here was allowed a flamboyant intimacy with the King
that occasionally overstepped the bounds of decency. It was
a hotbed of intrigue where courtiers vied for supremacy,
and for some, who had fallen from grace, where insecurity
became a fact of life.

Prudence's first instinct upon entering the Presence
Chamber—where she was surrounded by all the pomp and
ceremony that was royalty, where the very air was charged
with the King's person—was to turn on her heel and run,
but she was as one hypnotised.

Lucas was overwhelmed with profound pride at the picture his wife presented. She had been lovely before, but
now, looking like a porcelain figurine in her shimmering
long-trained dress of gold silk, her chestnut hair dressed to
perfection and gleaming like a shining light, her lovely face
aglow with anticipation, she was exquisite. Sensing her nervousness, he smiled and squeezed her hand reassuringly.
His very nearness gave Prudence the courage she needed
to approach the dais upon which the King sat, where pres-
entations were taking place.

The King was in conversation with his brother, the Duke

of York, who was standing beside him, and whose dark head was bent as he listened with quiet amusement to some witty comment his Majesty had just made, but the beautiful young woman on the arm of the devilishly attractive Lord Fox arrested both their attention.

Smiling, Lucas took his wife's hand and with due ceremony led her forward. Prudence thought her heart would surely burst, it was pounding so hard.

'Sire—may your Majesty grant me the honour of presenting to you my wife, Prudence,' said Lucas.

Keeping her eyes lowered, Prudence sank into a faultless curtsy while Lucas knelt, and when she rose she looked directly at the King, meeting dark, sombre eyes. His face was lean and lined with the tribulations of exile, his expression grave, even severe, but which softened when he spoke. His eyes were languid and full of appraisal—a betrayal of his weakness for beautiful women.

'Why, Lucas,' the King said, with the familiarity of long acquaintance, 'this is surprising. Your wife? Then the honour is mine. I am charmed to meet her.' Taking her hand, he raised it to his fleshy lips. 'Welcome, Lady Fox. You will be a beautiful addition to the Court. It is always a pleasure to see a new face—particularly when one is blessed with so rare a beauty.'

The intimacy in his voice caused Prudence to flush softly, for she was unused to such adulation—except from her husband.

Lucas observed the effect his wife was having on the Duke of York—a man renowned not only for his expert soldiering, but also for his love of women. He took his love where he could find it, and now, when Lucas observed the slow smile of appreciation on his lips as he looked at Prudence, and the way his eyes swept over her, absorbing every delectable aspect of her slender form, his gaze lingering overlong on the tantalising display of creamy flesh, he experienced a new, shattering pain. For by this very deed the Duke of York had given him cause for jealousy, and made him determined to remove himself and his wife the very next day from the licentiousness of the Court to Marlden Hall.

Prudence was self-consciously aware of the rush of attention she had aroused, that every eye in the room had become focused on her in curiosity, and it was with immense relief when they stood back and mingled with the throng of courtiers who lined the way to the dais. But she could see that she was not the only one who had drawn the eyes of everyone present. Lucas's commanding presence was awesome, and there were far too many ladies looking at him like predatory felines for her liking. A blinding streak of jealousy suddenly ripped through her.

'Everyone is looking at us,' she whispered.

Completely impervious to the stir they were creating, Lucas looked down at her lovely upturned face, feasting his eyes on those glorious twin orbs of amethyst. 'I know. I have no intention of spending much of our time at Court where you will have every lord who is not in his dotage panting after you.'

The possessive words added to Prudence's sense of euphoric well being. An unconsciously provocative smile broke across her lips and her eyes twinkled mischievously. 'Are you worried that I will encourage them, my lord?'

Lucas looked down at her intently. 'Should I be?'

'No—because if I do, I am quite certain you would retaliate by panting after one of these ladies whom I observe looking at you as if they have been starved for at least a week and you are their next meal.'

'That, my love, is very astute of you,' her husband complimented quietly. Suddenly he took her hand. 'Come with me,' he said, heading for the doors.

'Where are you taking me?'

'Somewhere quiet.'

A slow, disbelieving smile broke across her face. 'I like quiet places.'

His chuckle was rich and deep. 'I'm glad to hear it, because tomorrow, my love, I will be taking you home to Marlden Hall.'

* * * * *

MILLS & BOON®

Makes any time special™

Mills & Boon publish 29 new titles every month. Select from...

Modern Romance™   Tender Romance™

Sensual Romance™

Medical Romance™   Historical Romance™

MAT2

FREE

2 BOOKS

AND A SURPRISE GIFT!

We would like to take this opportunity to thank you for reading this Mills & Boon® book by offering you the chance to take TWO more specially selected titles from the Historical Romance™ series absolutely FREE! We're also making this offer to introduce you to the benefits of the Reader Service™ —

★ FREE home delivery
★ FREE monthly Newsletter
★ FREE gifts and competitions
★ Exclusive Reader Service discounts
★ Books available before they're in the shops

Accepting these FREE books and gift places you under no obligation to buy; you may cancel at any time, even after receiving your free shipment. Simply complete your details below and return the entire page to the address below. *You don't even need a stamp!*

YES! Please send me 2 free Historical Romance books and a surprise gift. I understand that unless you hear from me, I will receive 4 superb new titles every month for just £2.99 each, postage and packing free. I am under no obligation to purchase any books and may cancel my subscription at any time. The free books and gift will be mine to keep in any case.

HIZEC

Ms/Mrs/Miss/Mr ....Initials ....
BLOCK CAPITALS PLEASE

Surname ....

Address ....

....

....Postcode ....

Send this whole page to:
UK: FREEPOST CN81, Croydon, CR9 3WZ
EIRE: PO Box 4546, Kilcock, County Kildare (stamp required)

Offer valid in UK and Eire only and not available to current Reader Service subscribers to this series. We reserve the right to refuse an application and applicants must be aged 18 years or over. Only one application per household. Terms and prices subject to change without notice. Offer expires 31st December 2001. As a result of this application, you may receive further offers from Harlequin Mills & Boon Limited and other carefully selected companies. If you would prefer not to share in this opportunity please write to The Data Manager at the address above.

Mills & Boon® is a registered trademark owned by Harlequin Mills & Boon Limited.
Historical Romance™ is being used as a trademark.

'Who are you?' Jack pleaded.

She looked up and met and held his gaze. 'I'm Colin Forbes,' she said, laughter bubbling on her lips and glowing in her face.

'You are not Colin Forbes,' he stated categorically. 'For one thing, I interviewed Colin Forbes for this position and I know what he looks like and, for another thing, you're a woman!'

'We swapped,' Kelly replied. She then lifted her fingers in a mocking salute and said, 'Kelly Jackson at your service, Dr Gregory!'

GW00372123

Having pursued many careers—from school teaching to pig farming—with varying degrees of success and plenty of enjoyment, **Meredith Webber** seized on the arrival of a computer in her house as an excuse to turn to what has always been a secret urge—writing. As she had more doctors and nurses in the family than any other professional people, the medical romance seemed the way to go! Meredith lives on the Gold Coast of Queensland, with her husband and teenage son.

Recent titles by the same author:

WINGS OF SPIRIT
WINGS OF CARE
WINGS OF PASSION
WINGS OF DUTY
COURTING DR GROVES
PRACTICE IN THE CLOUDS

WINGS OF DEVOTION

BY
MEREDITH WEBBER

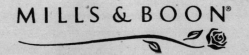

MILLS & BOON®

*All the characters in this book have no existence outside the imagina-
tion of the author, and have no relation whatsoever to anyone bearing
the same name or names. They are not even distantly inspired by any
individual known or unknown to the author, and all the incidents are
pure invention.*

*First published in Great Britain 1997
Harlequin Mills & Boon Limited,
Eton House, 18-24 Paradise Road, Richmond, Surrey TW9 1SR*

© Meredith Webber 1997

ISBN 0 263 80212 4

*Set in Times 10 on 11 pt. by
Rowland Phototypesetting Limited
Bury St Edmunds, Suffolk*

03-9708-49775-D

*Printed and bound in Great Britain
by Mackays of Chatham PLC, Chatham*

CHAPTER ONE

JACK heard the commotion as the doors slid silently open to allow him access to the lobby. One glance at Mrs Katinski's flushed cheeks as she leaned across the reception desk, arguing volubly and flashing be-ringed hands in the face of some hapless guest, warned him that this was not a minor tenant-management tiff, but an eruption of Vesuvian proportions.

He hesitated in the blast of cold air which rushed from the building. His head was pounding and every bone in his body seemed to ache, although he knew, technically, that this was most unlikely.

Could he back away unseen and head for the basement car park? He could go directly up to his floor from there—if his legs would carry him that far! He glanced quickly at Mrs K's opponent before he began his retreat, wondering if it was someone he should rescue from the receptionist's wrath.

The guest was a stranger—a slim, dark-haired woman—but even from this distance the upright stance and defiant tilt of her head suggested that she could handle Mrs K.

He rubbed one hand across his face, feeling his palm catching on rough, unshaven stubble as he tried to ease the gritty feeling in his eyes. A hectic twenty-four hours on call had culminated in a five-hour evacuation flight and he'd driven like a robot from the airport, thinking only of crawling into bed—and staying there as long as possible. He eased one foot cautiously backwards, not wanting to attract attention to his retreat.

'Ah, here's Doctor now. Dr Gregory! Gregory!'

Too late for escape! Mrs Katinski had a voice that could reach the outskirts of Rainbow Bay—hard to pretend that he hadn't heard her!

He straightened his shoulders, gritted his teeth and marched into the fray.

Two minutes, that's all he'd give her. If what she foolishly perceived to be his 'authority' hadn't worked in that time, he'd excuse himself and go straight up to his apartment.

'What's the trouble, Mrs Katinski?'

Striding—authoritatively, he hoped—towards the desk, he noticed that the receptionist's colour was almost dangerously high and her fingers were shaking. He'd have to speak to her daughter again and emphasise how important the blood-pressure medication was.

'It's this woman, Doctor. She wants to go into your apartment and I tell her no, and she says yes, and I say only Colin Forbes, are you Colin Forbes or Mrs Colin Forbes, and she say no but that's where she wants to go and am I going to keep her standing here all day when she's tired and dirty and needs a bath.'

The words, tumbling out in high-pitched hysteria, were barely discernible, and the one in four he'd understood made no sense at all. Mrs Katinski paused for breath, then added, 'Loose woman,' in a condemnatory undertone which was heard by most of the onlookers now gathered in the lobby.

Professional concern had kept Jack's attention on the woman behind the counter, but Mrs Katinski's final admonition made him turn towards her antagonist.

She stood very straight, blue eyes flashing with fury and cheeks pink with anger, not high-blood pressure. Her wide, full-lipped mouth was held tightly shut, as if she were holding a string of uncomplimentary words behind her teeth.

As he watched her shoulders lifted—taking a deep

breath, he realised. His eyes took in, then lingered on, raven-dark hair that hung to just below her chin and moved like ebony silk—all in one piece. . .

Then her head tilted up, and she confronted him.

'I explained it all very carefully to this. . .woman!' she enunciated carefully, spacing the words to pretend that she was in total control. 'Explained who I was and why I was here, and asked for a key. . .' he turned to glare briefly at Mrs Katinski '. . .as instructed.'

Mrs Katinski, frowning ferociously, muttered a few of what Jack assumed were Middle European curses, then switched to rapid-fire English.

'You think I let her in your apartment? You think I let any woman who walks in off the streets into your apartment? What would you say about that?'

'Oh, for heaven's sake, you make it sound like an illicit assignation. What kind of—?' The stranger rounded on the receptionist, but Jack had begun to catch up with the conversation and interrupted.

'You were trying to get the key to *my* apartment?' he demanded. 'Why?'

'To ravish you, of course!' the woman snapped, throwing her arms into the air to emphasise the irony. 'And, if you really are Jack Gregory, could we continue this discussion somewhere else?' She waved a hand around the crowded lobby. 'Privately?'

She shot another frosty glance at Mrs Katinski before she added, 'I've already explained to your morals' guardian here that it's a business arrangement!'

A hoot of laughter from one of the onlookers and a smattering of applause brought a scowl of withering scorn from the stranger, but it also alerted Jack to the fact that they were attracting more and more attention.

'You're right,' he muttered, reaching down to grab a small overnight case which was resting by her feet.

'Is this all you've got?' he asked, totally perplexed

by the situation but anxious to escape the
now-crowded lobby.

'It's more than enough, I'd say!' some wag called
out and, glancing at the cause of all this trouble, Jack
saw the lovely mouth tighten again and the slim figure
stiffen with wrath.

Thinking that she was going to back away, he took
hold of her arm.

'I have four matching cases in my car,' she said
frostily, and allowed him to lead her, head held high
and shiny black hair swinging slightly, towards the bank
of lifts at the rear of the lobby.

Clutching her bag, he herded her into the first available lift then closed his eyes for a moment. It was a
dream—a nightmare—and when he opened his eyes
again she'd be gone!

She wasn't, of course. She was standing right where
she'd been all along, her face tight with impatience.

'Well?' she demanded.

He frowned at her, confused by the peremptory
tone—by her demands—her anger—her presence!

'What floor are you on?' she asked, with mock
patience. 'We need to press a button to make this
thing work.'

It was a living nightmare!

'You weren't serious about coming up to my apartment, were you?' He stumbled over the words, pressed
the button for the top floor and forced his scrambled
and exhausted brain into action. Someone had done this
as a joke. Peter and Katie had left for the United States
yesterday. . .

'Peter sent you!' he declared, turning triumphantly
to face the woman who was clutching the support bar
and looking pale. She certainly didn't fit his image of
a prostitute. Not that he imagined prostitutes often!
Maybe she was what they called a 'hostess'.

'Has he paid you already? I don't want to upset you, but I'm really not into this kind of thing.'

For someone who'd been so vocal only minutes earlier she was strangely silent. He looked more closely at her, seeing the white bones of her knuckles through her skin where her hand gripped the bar and the tense set of her face, her rigid shoulders. She was terrified.

The lift jolted to a halt, and he watched as she stepped hurriedly out then glanced nervously about her.

'Hey, don't worry,' he soothed, disturbed by such a sudden transformation. She'd gone from fighting tiger to timid kitten in the time it took the lift to rise fifteen floors.

'I don't want anything of you—' hell, that might hurt her feelings '—although you're very lovely.' He tried a conciliatory smile. 'Actually, I've been up most of the night and all I want to do is sleep.' He considered adding 'alone' but decided that it would sound pathetic.

She ignored him so he led the way to his apartment door and unlocked it, wondering why he was so intent on apologising—and on reassuring her.

'No one mentioned the fifteenth floor!' she murmured, her strong voice now a husky whisper. And, tired as he was, Jack felt a stirring in his blood, a spark of desire so unfamiliar that it was followed by a shock wave of denial.

'Come in and sit down,' he said gruffly, and led the way inside.

Light flooded the big lounge-dining-room from the floor-to-ceiling windows that allowed panoramic views of the bay. His visitor glanced at this spectacular vista which held most newcomers spellbound, then shuddered. She sank into the nearest chair, resting her head on one slim, well-manicured hand and muttering to herself.

'Are you feeling faint? Do you want a glass of water?'

He was concerned and puzzled at the same time. Was she new at this game and genuinely upset now she was alone in an apartment with her 'client'? He studied the bent head for a moment then walked through to the kitchen for water. Or was this some act she put on to save herself the bother of. . .performing?

He'd always believed that he was broad-minded, accepting of other people's behaviour and preferences, and totally non-judgemental. Yet he could almost taste his own discomfort.

He made his way back to his unwelcome visitor, clutching the glass of water. Her head was still bent, but he could tell from the movement of her shoulders that she was breathing deeply again—almost literally gathering herself together.

He cleared his throat, then groaned inwardly at his own behaviour. What a stupidly theatrical way of attracting her attention.

Theatrical or not, it worked! Her head lifted, and the laser-like eyes swept over his unshaven face, down his dusty, untidily clad body and finally came to rest, with bitter scorn, on his outthrust hand.

'I want an apartment on a lower floor, not a glass of water.' She flung out each word with a crisp venom. 'I can't stay here!'

The glass slid from his nerveless fingers and smashed onto the tiled floor, splashing water on the smart tan sandals and smooth calves of his visitor.

'You can't *stay* here?' he croaked.

He remembered her saying something about four more suitcases! Surely Peter couldn't have booked her for any length of time! He tried to recall more of Mrs Katinski's lament but all he could remember was that the woman had demanded access to his apartment— and that she wasn't someone? Wasn't who? Or was it whom? The pounding in his head was replaced by a vice-like pain in his temples.

'No, I can't stay here,' she repeated carefully, mopping at her legs with a fine white handkerchief. 'It's too high up! I don't like heights.'

He looked into her face, which lifted to see his reaction to her statement, and saw her stiff-necked pride. It had taken some effort for her to make that admission. And, remembering her white-knuckled grip on the bar in the lift, he guessed that 'don't like' was a piece of masterly understatement.

'Then I suggest you leave as quickly as possible.' He felt the throbbing in his head ease slightly. It was the relief of having found so simple a solution to this macabre situation.

Or was it the solution? The blue eyes blazed scorn at him.

'Are you sure you're Jack Gregory?'

'Why wouldn't I be?' he demanded, annoyed that she wouldn't go—and even more annoyed because he found her attractive and part of him didn't want her to go.

'Because I can't believe someone so pea-brained could possible be in charge of the Rainbow Bay Base of the Royal Flying Doctor Service!' she stormed. 'I arrive in this town after driving thousands of miles. I'm greeted by that virago at the desk, put through the third degree and refused admission. Then you turn up and I'm hauled into the lift like a bag of potatoes, dragged up here, have water thrown all over me and then told to go! I can't wait to see what you do with your other employees!'

'Employees?' He heard the word falter out of his mouth, and quite understood why she thought him pea-brained. An aching pea-brain—that's what he had at the moment!

'Employees—people who work for you,' she said helpfully, her voice so full of sarcasm that it made his skin prickle.

It was definitely time he took control of the situation!

He straightened up, kneaded his temples, brushed his hand across his face again to clear the fuzziness of exhaustion and stepped forward.

'Look, Miss Whoever-you-are—'

He felt a dampness round his foot, but was too intent on his 'there's obviously been some terrible mistake' speech to take any notice until he saw her glance downwards and heard her gasp.

He followed her gaze and saw the pool of water reddening around his feet. He'd forgotten the broken glass! A piece must have sliced neatly through his light-soled sneaker and now he was bleeding all over the floor.

'Definitely pea-brained,' he heard her mutter, but, when she looked up he saw that her lips were twitching and her eyes were sparkling with irrepressible mirth.

For a moment he gazed at her, unable to breathe. His heart had stopped beating, too, he realised. Stopped for an instant then gone into palpitations.

'Sit down, take your shoe off and let's have a look at it,' she said firmly, and he found himself obeying meekly while the intruder carefully knelt and collected all the pieces of glass. She looked around, obviously working out the plan of the place, then rose and headed unerringly for the bathroom.

Jack pulled off his crimson-stained sock and tried to angle his leg around so that he could see the bottom of his foot. Blood seeped over his fingers so he gave up trying to inspect the wound and pressed his far from sterile sock against it. Behind him, he could hear cupboard doors opening and closing.

Make yourself at home! he thought grumpily, acutely

aware that he'd lost the first round with this abrasive and unsetting stranger. He lifted the sock away and tried to contort himself again.

'Most men have poor flexibility,' she said cheerfully, returning to stand over him and watch his antics with mocking eyes.

'I doubt that women's flexibility is any better than men's,' he argued, infuriated by her attitude—not to mention her presence and the effect she was having on him—and his own feelings of inadequacy as the situation escalated out of control.

'Oh, no?' she challenged. She dropped gracefully to the floor, sat cross-legged and drew one foot up to inspect the sole of her sandal with sinuous ease.

'I don't believe any of this!' he complained. 'I'm sitting on the floor bleeding to death while a total stranger, who's obviously as mad as a hatter, proves she can look at the bottom of her feet!'

'Stop whining,' she ordered. 'You're the one who didn't believe I could do it.'

She untangled herself as she spoke, revealing far more shapely leg than he was quite prepared to see.

'And, for a doctor, you keep a very scrappy medicine cupboard. Three Mickey Mouse sticking plasters and a tube of gunky green stuff I wouldn't put on a dog! Mind you, you're very well prepared for other eventualities.'

She lifted her head from her examination of his injury and looked appraisingly at him.

He remembered Peter's last but one practical joke and knew exactly what she'd found in the bathroom cabinet—hundreds of them! He writhed uncomfortably beneath that challenging blue regard and wondered if thirty-six-year-old men could still blush. From the heat throbbing in his cheeks, it certainly felt that way.

'I've always got a medical bag with me if I need

first-aid stuff,' he countered, hoping that this defence would hide his embarrassment.

'Oh, good!' Cool hands wrapped around his foot and gentle fingers pressed into his skin. 'Where is it?'

He closed his eyes and prayed as he'd never prayed before. He considered himself a good man—kind and helpful—fond of dogs and small children! Surely a merciful heaven would let him wake up now?

There was no flapping of wings as angels rushed to rescue him.

'I left it at a friend's place,' he muttered. 'Leonie's daughter, Caroline, had cut her hand. It needed a stitch. I took the bag inside, then—'

'Obviously other things happened,' the visitor finished for him, casting a derisively knowing look over his unshaven face and rumpled clothing. 'Hope you took along some of your supplies.'

He opened his mouth to argue again, then slammed it shut. How dared she judge him this way? Or was she deliberately provoking him to anger?

Bizarre thoughts flashed through his mind—followed by incredible images. He wanted to shake her—to take his anger out on her physically—and that shocked him for he didn't consider himself a physical man! But there was a sexual element in his reaction, which was even more startling—more intriguing—more repellent.

'Well, it looks like Mickey Mouse to the rescue.'

She'd been back to the bathroom while he sat on the floor with weird erotic fancies dancing in his head. He watched her as she knelt in front of him and lifted his foot to rest it on her upper leg. A dark-haired stranger in a washed-out denim button-through dress. A dark-haired stranger whose touch was sending tremors along his nerves.

'I'd say your shoe suffered more. If I dry the wound

well and pull the band-aids tightly across it, it should heal without a stitch.'

She reached out towards the small overnight bag he'd carried upstairs, unzipped a side pocket and withdrew a small leather case. More zips slid, and she produced some antibiotic powder which she puffed efficiently onto his foot.

He watched her neat, unfussy movements while his brain tried to rerun what he could remember of their conversation. She knew who he was—she spoke of 'employees'. If she was what he'd thought—would she call herself an 'employee'? There was one way to find out.

He leaned forward as she sat back to examine her handiwork.

'Please! Who are you?' he asked.

She looked up and he saw the thick, spiky lashes that framed those incredible eyes flicker down, then up again. She met and held his gaze, grinning at him.

'I'm Colin Forbes,' she said, laughter bubbling on her lips and glowing in her face.

Infuriating witch! He'd have to strangle her!

He tried to stand, but she pushed him back.

'Don't get that foot wet,' she warned. 'Wait there while I mop up the water and find a clean sock for you to put on.'

'I'll get my own clean sock,' he growled. 'You stay right there until I get back.'

'Scared of what I might find in your bedroom?' she taunted. 'After the bathroom, I doubt anything could shock me.'

He pushed himself backwards across the tiles before he stood, avoiding the pool of water. The woman had produced a towel from her small bag and was intent on cleaning up the mess he'd made.

As if aware that he was watching her, she glanced

up at him, then looked away again—towards the wall
of glass. He saw a shudder cross her expressive face,
and the faint colour in her cheeks began to seep away.

'I don't suppose you could close the curtains while
you're on your feet?' she murmured. 'I'm OK while
I'm doing something to take my mind off where we
are, but I wouldn't like to go into a catatonic state of
shock before we've introduced ourselves properly.'

Introduced ourselves properly? He must be exhausted
for his body to be reacting so vigorously to that husky
suggestiveness!

He limped away, first to his bedroom where he lifted
his leg so that he could see his foot in the mirror. Having
pulled on a sock to keep the plasters in place, he made
his slow way back to the living-room, where he drew
the curtains. They cut off his magnificent view but were
fine enough to allow the warm winter sunlight to filter
into the room.

'Is there a blind in the kitchen?' she called from her
chair near the front door.

He shook his head in disbelief, walked into the
kitchen and pulled down the blind—surprised to find
that it worked. He certainly hadn't used it in the seven
years he'd lived here.

Time to take control, he told himself, then vaguely
remembered thinking something similar earlier in this
encounter. His head was still aching. Should he find
some pain relief first?

Procrastination—that's all that would be—and he
doubted he had any aspirin or paracetamol in the place
anyway! He prodded the glands beneath his jaw-bone
to see if he could find an explanation—apart from
tiredness—for his headache, felt the unshaven stubble
again, sighed heavily and returned to the fray!

'You are not Colin Forbes,' he stated categorically,
returning to the front foyer and looming above her in

what he hoped was a taking-control kind of way. 'For one thing, I interviewed Colin Forbes for this position and I know what he looks like, and, for another thing, you're a woman.'

He didn't need to see the faint movement of her lips to realise that he'd sounded ridiculous. Maybe he was delirious!

'I did wonder if you'd notice,' she mused. 'Colin tried to tell me that you were so absorbed by your work and so devoted to the Service that I could be here for a month before you realised we'd swapped.'

'Swapped? What do you mean, swapped? I run a diverse and difficult service to people who are made especially vulnerable by distance. It's not some inner-city twenty-four-hour clinic where doctors work to fill in time until something better comes along. It's hard and tough and requires dedication, even from locums. I explained all of this to the locum service and to Colin Forbes and I had hoped they understood. Now you sit there and flippantly tell me that you swapped!'

'Lecture over?' she drawled, her blue eyes no longer laughing, but snapping with anger. They mesmerised him long enough for her to snatch the advantage.

'If you've read your agreement with Locum Managers you might remember that they have the right to substitute a doctor with similar training and experience with or without notice to you, the client. I think you'll find the ''notice'' is somewhere in your office, because the decision was made three days ago.'

Her tone deepened with anger, unusual in a woman's voice. He'd always thought they became shrill. . .

Hell's teeth! This was no time to be thinking of voices. He had to sort out this mess.

'And you've the same training and experience as Colin Forbes, I assume?' He hoped he sounded cool and business-like.

'Kelly Jackson at your service!' She lifted her fingers in a mocking salute. 'Same high school, same university, same training wards—even similar country towns where we did GP work as well as covering the hospital.'

'You speak as if you know him well,' Jack muttered, intrigued and somehow disturbed by a new nuance in her voice.

'Not as well as I thought I did,' she said crisply. 'Now, what can we do about finding me somewhere to live?'

The change of subject confused him for a moment— but when hadn't he been confused since this farce began? Again he rubbed at his face and ran his fingers through his hair. Even touching it made him aware how tender his skull was. And lack of sleep was making the simplest of decisions difficult.

'A flat, or house—a room somewhere?' she prompted, and the 'how can this idiot run anything?' look was back on her face.

'It's winter,' he explained. 'That's why I told Colin he could stay with me.'

'Do you get cold in winter?' she enquired in silky tones. 'Need someone to warm the bed? Prefer male company? Or will a female do equally well?'

He'd have to strangle her, he decided, as her jibes prodded his irritation back to life. Some time when he didn't feel so peculiar.

He tried counting to ten, got lost at about six, hauled in some air and expounded, in what he hoped was a voice iced with disdain, 'It's the tourist season. Southerners flock north to escape the winter, staying for any length of time from a week to four months. You can try to find alternative accommodation, but unless you fancy shifting on a weekly basis, in and out of rooms when cancellations might leave something free, you're stuck here.'

He watched her cast a nervous glance towards the windows and, for a moment, felt a twinge of sympathy towards her. Then, as she swung back to fix him with an accusing glare, he reminded himself that he'd be as well off feeling sorry for a school of piranhas.

'*I* can try to find alternative accommodation?' she repeated, emphasising the 'I' just enough for him to guess that she was going to quote the Locum Managers' contract at him again. Had she memorised the damn thing?

'I'll talk to Leonie—she might have some ideas,' he offered, realising that the last thing he wanted was to share his home with this aggravating woman for the next two months. 'And, in the meantime, I'll keep the curtains closed.'

He went back to his bedroom to phone, praying that Leonie would be at home. She'd take this cantankerous female off his hands and he could get some sleep.

Kelly watched his tall, unkempt-looking figure shuffle away. Had there been a glimmer of humour in his eyes when he'd mentioned the curtains—or was it a practical statement of fact?

Great start to a new job! she thought gloomily. First the argument, then finding that she was expected to live way up here in the sky. She shouldn't have let the woman downstairs upset her. After all, she'd come to Rainbow Bay to avoid being upset. And as for Jack Gregory! She glanced towards the bedroom, hearing the murmur of his deep voice but unable to distinguish the words.

First impressions could be wrong, but how could such a mixed-up guy—even a good-looking mixed-up guy—run a service as far-reaching as the Rainbow Bay Royal Flying Doctor Base? Colin had been impressed by him, she remembered—but, then, she was beginning to think that Colin might be easily impressed!

She heard the click of a phone being replaced, and straightened in her chair.

Was Leonie his girlfriend?

The thought irritated her even more, although she didn't know why.

'Leonie will be here in ten minutes,' he announced, emerging from the bedroom. The relief showed on his stubble-darkened face. 'She's the base manager. She'll look after you.'

Kelly curbed the 'I don't need looking after' that flipped onto her tongue. She certainly needed somewhere to live, and a local would have more hope of finding something than a stranger. Besides, the man sounded genuinely concerned.

'Passing the buck?' she teased, noticing the long, strong fingers that kneaded at his unshaven chin.

'Only 'till I've had a bath, an aspirin and some sleep,' he assured her. 'I'm sorry, but you've caught me after a bad twenty-four hours.'

He rubbed at his eyes, and she recognised—belatedly—the drawn greyness of exhaustion.

'Well, go and have your shower and get to bed,' she told him. 'I'll let this Leonie in.'

He hesitated, then turned away.

'Don't get your foot wet,' she called after him. 'You'll need something waterproof to pull over it. Try the bathroom cabinet!'

He swung back to face her and she knew from the black scowl he directed at her that he'd seen her laughing. The door slammed shut, blocking him from view.

CHAPTER TWO

KELLY stayed where she was, surveying the room and
telling herself that it could just as easily be on the
ground floor. She heard shower water running, then the
noise ceased and she looked apprehensively towards
the door. It had been a long drive north and she was
tired herself, and not up to another round of confron-
tation just yet!

A bell chimed musically and she opened the door to
admit a petite blonde with a charming smile and clear
grey eyes that studied her intently.

'No wonder poor Jack sounded harassed on the
phone,' the woman said. 'You don't fit my image of
Colin Forbes either.' The smile widened as she stretched
out her hand. 'I'm Leonie Cooper.'

Poor Jack, indeed! What about poor her? Kelly
thought, but she accepted the proffered hand and introduced herself.

'I'm Kelly Jackson, and I'm sorry about the mix-up.
The secretary at Locum Managers assured me that she
would let you know.'

Leonie shrugged.

'These things happen. As long as you're here, and
willing to do the job, I can't see any problem.'

Another bell rang—insistently!

'It's Jack's mobile,' Leonie said, looking around
anxiously as she tried to track down the source of
the noise.

'Here!' Kelly picked it up off the floor near the chair
she'd been using. Jack must have taken it out of his
pocket when he sat down to examine his cut foot.

21

Leonie answered, her voice discreetly low. Kelly heard repetitions of 'yes' and 'no', then a reassuring, 'I'll see what I can do.'

She terminated the conversation and folded the little case shut.

'That was Nick Furlong—our third doctor. He wanted to let Jack know he's on his way back from an uncomplicated evac job—ETA about an hour and a half.'

'Is that the rule?' Kelly asked. 'Do we have to report in to his lordship at all times?'

She nodded her head towards the bedroom door as the irritation over her strange reception surfaced again.

Leonie ignored her tartness and explained calmly, 'Jack hasn't been well and, to exacerbate matters, he's been working double on-call shifts while Nick was on his honeymoon. Nick phoned to tell him to get some sleep as he'd be able to take any but the most urgent of call-outs. Do you know about our priority ratings?'

'I read up on them in the information the Locum Managers gave me,' Kelly told her, remembering the examples given for Priority One, Two and Three ratings of emergency evacuation. 'Priority One is go immediately, isn't it?'

Leonie nodded. 'And Priority Two means go when you can. Even with a Priority One, the best time we can ever do from call to take-off is half an hour. It takes that long for the pilot to get to the airport, do pre-flight checks, send off his flight plan and for the medical staff to gather up the equipment they might need. Knowing the ETA, Jack can work out if Nick will be back in time to take the flight or if he will have to go himself.'

'Makes sense,' Kelly agreed, ashamed that she'd leapt in to pre-judge the man. 'Will you tell him?'

She indicated the bedroom with a slight movement of her head.

'I'd better,' Leonie murmured, and moved away, leaving the mobile phone on the chair.

Kelly watched her open the door and peer inside, then heard her quick intake of breath.

She looked back towards Kelly and whispered, 'He's sound asleep, and he looks dreadful,' before disappearing into the room.

When the phone began ringing again it was an automatic reaction to answer it.

'It's Sister Joan Campbell, from Wyrangi,' an unfamiliar voice said. 'Who's that?'

'Kelly Jackson, the new RFDS locum,' Kelly replied, crossing her fingers and hoping it was true. Surely she wouldn't be fired before she'd been given a chance to prove herself? Leonie reappeared, frowning with concern. She stood beside Kelly and listened.

'I've a young woman, thirty-four weeks pregnant, with quite severe blood loss. She tells me this has happened twice in the last twenty-four hours. It could be a placenta praevia but, with no ultrasound, I can't tell. I daren't do a physical examination because if the placenta has moved I'll cause more bleeding! I'd like her in a proper hospital ASAP in case she needs an emergency Caesar.'

'We can't send a nursing sister on her own in case she needs the operation before she travels. I'll have to wake Jack,' Leonie whispered.

'Jack's awake,' a deep voice growled. 'How's a man expected to sleep with people coming in and out of his bedroom, phones ringing and women whispering outside his door? What is it?'

'Possible placenta praevia at Wyrangi,' Leonie told him while Kelly finished her phone conversation with a firm, 'We'll be on our way at once.' This one couldn't wait for the doctor called Nick to return, and she didn't need that sore-head hovering in the bedroom door to

confirm that decision. The sore-head with the great
'abs'! she amended, as her gaze was drawn to his
bare torso.

'What's this "we"?' he demanded, pushing one arm
into the sleeve of an olive-green cotton shirt.

'You're exhausted,' Kelly pointed out. 'I'll go with
you and you can correct me if I go wrong. Although,'
she added, catching a glimpse of his red-rimmed eyes
as he came closer, 'a ten-year-old child might be
more use.'

'He's used to going without sleep,' Leonie said,
taking the phone out of Kelly's hand and pressing in
some numbers. 'I'm paging the pilot,' she explained.

'Most doctors are used to it,' Kelly argued. 'Which
doesn't alter the fact that if it was my operation I'd
prefer someone who was conscious opening me up.'

She waited for a rebuttal, but Jack Gregory appeared
to have lapsed into a coma.

'I have to start some time; it might as well be now!'
she added, ignoring the clenching and unclenching of
her stomach.

Leonie was regarding her with astonishment, while
Jack's attention was now concentrated on his shirt
buttons.

'I really am a doctor, you know,' Kelly told Leonie.
'Locum Managers were supposed to fax up all my information to you, but I've a copy of my résumé here.'

She dug into her overnight bag and thrust the folder
at the older woman.

'Now, shouldn't we be going?'

Leonie looked from her to Jack, who shook his head
and shrugged as if to say, she's mad—humour her.

'Well, I suppose it's an opportunity for you to see
the way things happen,' Leonie agreed.

She sounded dubious but she couldn't be any less
certain than Kelly herself was. Her heart quailed at the

thought of getting in the plane, but these new colleagues couldn't see her heart!

'Well, if you're coming, you can drive. Your car or mine?'

Jack had returned to conscious life!

'Mine!' Kelly said decisively. She had enough problems at the moment without tackling the idiosyncrasies of a strange vehicle. 'It's parked out the front.'

She watched as he leant on the wall and pulled on a loose, rope-soled, canvas shoe, wincing slightly as he eased the injured foot into it. His movements, even in his tired state, had an economical grace. He slipped on the second shoe.

'Good!' he said crisply, and, picking up a fistful of keys and the mobile phone, he led the way towards the door.

Kelly followed, puzzled by his ability to become so instantly alert. They travelled downwards in the lift with stomach-swooping swiftness, then out through the foyer—past the dragon behind the desk.

Kelly unlocked the car doors while Jack said farewell to Leonie, then he climbed in, issued brief but concise instructions—go to the end of the Esplanade, turn left, follow through to a main road, turn right—rested his head against the seat and appeared to lapse back to sleep. Instantly alert, then instantly unconscious!

She drove carefully, ignoring the fluttering in her stomach. One of the reasons she'd given in to Colin's suggestion to take over his locum job had been the opportunity to finally conquer her aversion to flying. Her fear of heights had kept her out of planes until now, but if she was making changes in her life and overcoming one weakness she might as well overcome this as well, she'd decided.

The airport was well signposted, and she swung confidently off the main road, following blue RFDS arrows until she reached the glistening silver hangar with the winged emblem above its wide doors. A plane stood on the tarmac, shining in the bright winter light. Her very fine veneer of courage vanished!

I must be mad, she thought as her stomach heaved convulsively. She pulled into a parking bay beside the hangar and, while she hesitated for a moment—fighting her internal upheaval—her passenger returned to life.

'We'll take a humidicrib and blood products. I'll get the equipment while you get back onto Joan and find out the patient's blood type. You'll find the Wyrangi number under 'hospitals' in the teledex on the office desk. If it's a common type we might have a match, but I don't think we should waste time waiting for a blood-bank delivery. If we don't have the type we'll take red blood cells.'

Maybe he hadn't been asleep! Kelly pushed open her door and hurried after him into the cool hangar. He'd simply been resting his eyes while his brain kept busy, planning what they would take.

'Our keys are marked to show which cabinet they open,' he pointed out, waving his hand towards the storage section in the big building. 'Non-refrigerated drugs in here, dressings beneath them, splints, stretchers and other bulky equipment over there.'

Kelly glanced at the cabinets, then remembered his earlier order and walked through to the small office beyond them. If the patient haemorrhaged badly they would need blood, and plenty of it! She found the number and rang through to Wyrangi, noting down the information Joan must have read from the patient's file.

Returning to where Jack surveyed a neat pile of equipment, she passed him the note. It would be easier for him to find the blood products they required than for her to go searching through the cold storage.

'A doctor with legible writing?' he said, turning

towards her, one eyebrow raised in mock surprise.

'I can't see the point in keeping records if no one can read them,' she contended, watching him open the refrigerated cabinets and search through the contents. His movements were deft and deliberate, despite his lack of sleep, and she found herself envying his certainty.

'Do we have an external electronic foetal monitor?' she asked, turning her mind firmly back to work.

'I've put it with the humidicrib. Did you know that all our planes are fitted with oxygen, and suction, and each one has a portable vital signs monitor?'

'I went over the new RFDS plane in Brisbane and saw the medical equipment installed especially for it,' she told him, and he turned to face her, squashy bags of fluid in his hands.

'Why look surprised?' she demanded, disconcerted not by the questioning glance but by the colour of his eyes—a soft, hazy green shot through with gold—like sun splashes on new wheat fields.

'Ready when you are,' a voice called, and they turned in unison to see a man in the neat uniform of the RFDS pilots standing by the door of the hangar. 'Wyrangi, right?'

'Wyrangi, and ready in about two minutes, Michael,' Jack replied, introducing Kelly to the rangy young man. 'When you've faxed through your flight plan you could take some of this lot on board.'

He turned back to Kelly.

'Always lock every cabinet before you leave the hangar and, as soon as you get on board, make a note of what you've taken. It saves a lot of mental effort when you're filling out requisitions at the end of a flight.'

He packed the blood products into a cool-box.

'Do you always carry this much gear?' Kelly asked,

as fascination with the process conquered her nervous qualms.

'Even when we're going to a small hospital the rule is to take what we might need. Who knows what emergency they may have faced to deplete their own stocks?'

It made sense, she realised, and an unfamiliar excitement skittered through her.

Jack straightened up, cool-box in hand.

'This fits into a portable freezer on the plane. We could be back here two hours after we operate—if we decide to operate out there. One unit should do, but I've put in two—stupid to get out there and find you need more.'

His voice was rough and rasping and she sensed that this rational conversation was causing him a great effort. She remembered Leonie saying that he hadn't been well. Was he one of those men who kept going, regardless of their own physical or mental well-being? Interested in spite of her determination not to get involved with these people, she studied him as he locked each cabinet and double-checked by pulling on the door-handles. A careful man!

The pilot reappeared. Jack handed him the cool-box, then picked up the humidicrib and waved his hand towards the other equipment bag.

'You take that,' he suggested. 'Pop it under your seat when we take off, then you can look through it on the flight so you're familiar with what we carry.'

He led the way out of the hangar, still talking, and Kelly realised that he was teaching her the things she would need to know when it was her turn to be on call. Was this official acceptance?

'Drugs and equipment are kept in special packs which fit into the equipment case, so today I've grabbed the obstetric emergency pack. You'll find it has everything we need.'

They reached the foot of the steps that led up into the plane.

Her legs stiffened but determination carried her forward. Then Michael pulled the door shut behind him and Kelly felt the walls begin to close in on her. She breathed in and out very carefully, telling herself that it would be all right—that she was not going to panic!

'Would you like to sit up front? See something of the country?' Michael asked.

Sit up front? Where she could see how impossibly high they were above safe, solid, oh-so-familiar ground?

'Not this time,' she stuttered, hoping that her voice didn't sound as breathless as she felt. 'I want to go through all this gear and make sure I remember how to use it.'

Jack growled something she took to be disgust at her attempt at humour, but she was feeling too panic-stricken to worry about his reactions.

'I'll sit up front and sleep,' he announced, moving out of the cabin into the cockpit.

Michael watched him go, then turned to smile reassuringly at Kelly.

'As my wife would say—he's having a bad hair day.' He grinned and Kelly found herself smiling back, although she couldn't imagine why. She was locked into a metal cocoon and was about to be whisked thousands of feet into the air on her first plane trip in thirty-one years of considerably enjoyable life!

'Strap in until we get up,' Michael added, waving her into a seat. 'I'll sing out when you can move about. We've got the wind with us, so Wyrangi's about ninety minutes' flying time.'

He went through to the cockpit, whistling cheerfully, and Kelly tucked the equipment bag under one of the seats. Michael had strapped the bulky items into place at the rear of the cabin and she realised that this would be standard procedure. If the plane hit turbulence they wouldn't want things flying around the cabin.

If the plane hit turbulence she would probably drop dead on the spot, she decided, then remembered the young woman waiting for help at the strange-sounding town.

Could people die of fear? Surely not! She continued a silent debate on the subject until Michael called out that she could move about.

Move about! That was a laugh. Her bones had turned to jelly, and her hands were shaking so much that she couldn't open the clasp on the equipment bag. What an idiotic thing to do—taking on a job like this! She'd resign tomorrow—or today, as soon as she got back! Her fear of heights that led to fear of flying shouldn't worry her—she could learn to exist without putting it to the test. Simply not fly anywhere! Ever! Or walk near windows in tall buildings!

But she had taken on this job, she reminded herself. And commitment was important to her. If you accepted a challenge you carried it through—that was a creed by which she lived. And what if she had a patient on board who needed her assistance? Would she have put on this same pathetic jellyfish act?

The thought sobered her enough for the shaking to stop, but her stomach churned uneasily. Nausea she could live with, she decided, and made her now-steady fingers open the clasp on the bag.

As she examined the emergency obstetrics pack she managed to forget that she was thousands of feet above the earth's surface, and went through, in her mind, the operation she might be called on to perform. Or assist while Jack Gregory performed!

She thought of her ridiculous introduction to the man who ran the Rainbow Bay Base and wondered about him. She'd certainly teased him until he was close to anger—but he'd have been weakened by tiredness and the confusion of her unexpected arrival. He seemed too controlled. . .

She was still thinking about Jack when the plane dropped into an airpocket, sending her heart plummeting even lower and her stomach into acute upheaval. Jack's face, wrathful or otherwise, was forgotten for the remainder of the journey.

'You OK?' Michael asked, exactly ninety minutes after take-off, when they were safely on the ground and he walked through to open the door.

'I'm not used to small planes,' she muttered, knowing that she must look like a pallid ghost. She'd had to make use of three of the tough paper bags she'd found in the pocket of the seat in front of her, and now had the evidence of her weakness concealed in a sealed plastic rubbish bag. At least, on a medical plane, such things were provided for waste disposal!

Michael's glance flickered to the bag, and back to her face.

'Leave it under the seat,' he murmured. 'I'll take care of it.'

She flashed him a grateful smile.

'The ambulance isn't here so I expect your patient is waiting for you at the hospital.' He spoke in a louder voice, alerting her to the fact that they were no longer alone.

'I spoke to Joan Campbell on the phone,' Jack explained as he appeared from the cockpit, looking even more tired than he had earlier. Perhaps it was the rumpled dark hair, or the lack of colour in his lips. 'She didn't want to shift the patient until we've seen her. We may have to operate here before we bring her back.'

At least he's using 'we' not 'I', Kelly thought, snapping the locks closed on the equipment bag.

Jack grabbed the cool-box and disappeared out of

the door, while Michael picked up the humidicrib and headed for the tarmac. Kelly, pleased that they'd both left before she had to put her legs to the test of standing upright, dragged the equipment bag out from under the seat, and followed, her knees shaking with relief.

A small sedan was waiting for them, driven by an aide Jack introduced as Mary. Michael helped pack the gear into it.

'I'll be ready to take off again whenever you get back,' he told them. 'Get someone to phone when you leave the hospital so I can have the engines running.'

Jack nodded, then climbed into the back seat and appeared to fall asleep again.

Would she remember all these procedures when she did a trip on her own? Kelly wondered, realising how necessary it was to co-ordinate movements in order to achieve optimum success. Then excitement gave way to doubt. Would she ever do a trip on her own? Could she take responsibility for a sick patient if she was going to be paralysed by her fear? Had her decision to take on this job been totally irresponsible?

She dragged her mind back to the present. Mary was pointing out the prawn trawlers moored along a jetty in the inner harbour and the old pub which had been here since 'the olden days'!

'Mining company put in the new harbour to export their stuff,' Mary explained, gesturing towards the mouth of the narrow bay where a long pier stretched out to accommodate the huge ships which carried the ore from the nearby mines.

'Hospital!'

Kelly was glad Mary had announced it. It was even smaller than some she had visited while on duty in the bush.

'I'm Joan Campbell.'

A large, capable-looking woman emerged from the

building and introduced herself. She cast a professional glance at Jack, who had heaved himself upright and was rubbing at his eyes.

'Is he conscious?' she asked, winking at Kelly.

'Is it possible to tell?' she retorted. 'This is all I've seen so far.'

There was another growling sound, then Jack straightened, glared at the pair of them and said carefully, 'I am perfectly all right.'

'You look it!' Joan told him, taking the cool-box from his limp fingers. 'I told you that flu would catch up with you if you didn't have some time off. You can have a quick look at Alison—from a distance and wearing a mask—then you will lie down in the ward and sleep. I'll call you if I think Kelly needs help.'

'Bossy bloody women!' the man muttered, taking the humidicrib from Mary and following Joan into the hospital. Kelly brought up the rear, her thoughts now concentrated on the man in front of her. She should have realised that it was more than exhaustion. Even through the masking stubble earlier in the day, she'd been conscious of a flush on his high cheek-bones. Only she'd taken it to be anger!

Joan paused on the verandah and explained to Kelly, hurriedly but with great precision, exactly what had happened.

'The previous episodes were what made me think of placenta praevia. Bit of a show, then a clot forms and it stops. No pain or contractions at all with the first two episodes, but since I phoned you earlier contractions have begun.'

'Uterine aggravation will often bring them on,' Kelly offered, deciding to follow Joan's lead and take charge of the situation. 'What have you done?'

'I've got her in a left lateral position with her legs raised to ease pressure on the cervix. She's on oxygen,

I've put a Foley catheter in to drain her bladder and check urine output. I didn't want her moving around if she wanted to urinate as any movement seems to accelerate the haemorrhage. I've started an IV of lactated Ringer's to replace the fluid she's losing. So far there's no sign of hypovolaemic shock and her capillary refill is good. Blood pressure's OK with the diastolic rate low but—'

'But she mightn't show signs of shock until a blood loss thirty percent has occurred. How's the foetal heart rate?'

'Still strong,' Joan told her, leading her through a small waiting-room with a ward off to one side and into a small but functional operating theatre.

'This is Alison Walters,' Joan said, introducing the patient, 'and Nancy Biggs, who is relief nursing sister at Wyrangi.'

Jack Gregory, a mask held across his nose and mouth, was talking quietly to Alison.

The young woman tried a smile but it did little to relieve the concern on her face. Nancy reached out and shook hands in welcome.

'Shall I leave you to it?' Jack swung towards Kelly. His mesmerising eyes, the colour emphasised by the mask, repeated the question.

'I'll call you if I need you,' Kelly promised, feeling nearly as weak-kneed as she had on the plane. It must be the after-effects of the flight, she decided.

He nodded once then left the room.

Explaining everything she was doing, Kelly began her examination—unobtrusively comparing her findings with those on the chart Nancy had handed her. Alison had been admitted at eight. According to the file, she'd woken late and seen the bright show of blood. Her husband was away at one of the mines so she'd asked a neighbour to drive her to the hospital.

'Did you have breakfast?' Kelly asked her, knowing that she'd prefer not to have to use a tube to drain the stomach.

'Didn't feel like it,' the young woman said.

'And she's had nothing here,' Joan said quietly. Kelly glanced at her, realising that the older and more experienced nursing sister had guessed that an emergency operation at this hospital was the most likely scenario.

Turning her attention back to the patient, Kelly outlined exactly what they would do and why she felt it was necessary. Alison smiled again, a better effort this time, and assured them all she was only too happy to have a Caesarean.

'My sister said childbirth's far worse than toothache,' she added naïvely. 'This way it won't hurt a bit until after it's all over, and then only while the scar heals!'

A novel approach to a Caesar, Kelly thought, then wondered about the 'after it's all over' aspect. She turned to Joan.

'What's the procedure after surgery? Will you nurse Alison here?'

'Ask her,' Joan instructed with a smile, nodding towards their patient.

'I was going to go to Rainbow Bay next week to stay with my parents until I was due,' Alison said. Her lower lip trembled. 'I'd still like to go.'

'Then of course you shall,' Kelly assured her, secretly relieved. Her experience in small country hospitals had shown her the strain a neonate and a post-operational mother could put on limited nursing staff. 'And what about your husband? Do you want us to contact him?'

'Not till it's all over,' the young woman murmured. 'I don't want him to think I've made a mess of things!'

'This is a surgical emergency—not a ''mess''—and definitely not your fault,' Kelly said firmly, but she turned away to hide her disapproval of this attitude.

Surely Alison's husband would be happy to have a healthy child and a live wife, however the child was delivered.

'Men!' she muttered to herself, feeling aggrieved on Alison's behalf!

Joan murmured something about preparing a tray and left the room, while Mary and Nancy lifted the humidicrib onto a trolley and opened it.

Watching them work, Kelly realised that they had all been involved in similar situations before and she knew that she had a competent team on hand to assist her.

Joan returned and handed Kelly a syringe with an over-the-needle catheter attached.

'Pre-med,' she said to Kelly as she swabbed Alison's hand. She added the proprietary brand name and amount, and Kelly nodded.

'It will make you sleepy almost immediately,' Joan explained, while Kelly slid the needle into a vein and injected the relaxant. Joan had tape ready to hold the catheter in place for the short time it would be needed. She moved efficiently, attaching a pulse oximeter and monitor leads to the already sleepy woman.

'We have one of your lot—usually Jack or Nick—operate out here every fortnight,' Nancy explained when Kelly joined her by the basin to scrub. 'With general anaesthetics, the doctor gives the medication and Joan does the monitoring while the RFDS sister assists the surgeon. Today I'll do that bit for you, and Mary can take charge of the baby when you deliver it.'

It was the way things worked in the country, Kelly knew. The 'everyone pitch in and help' attitude had helped to settle this inhospitable and sparsely populated land. She pulled on the cap and gown Nancy handed her, tied the strings of her mask loosely round the back of her head, let Nancy help her into gloves then turned back to the patient.

At a nod from her, Joan squeezed the muscle relaxant into Alison's vein. Satisfied that her assistant knew exactly what she was doing, Kelly crossed to the trolley where the surgical tray was laid out. She checked through the instruments and medications and saw the blood components she had brought with her—in case!

'OK,' Joan said quietly.

Kelly took a deep breath and began.

'I'm doing a low transverse section,' she said quietly, talking to herself as much as to her watchers. Through the skin, through the peritoneum, fingers steady. She mentally repeated the steps she'd first learned as a student many years earlier. Nancy passed her retractors and she held the outer layers back, her eyes going to Joan and the monitors—checking silently before she proceeded.

The movements were familiar and, although it was a year since she'd performed the operation, her hands seemed to know exactly what they were doing. She eased the bladder from its position on top of the lower part of the uterus and made a small transverse cut, deepening it until the membranous interior lining was seen.

Nancy took the scalpel from her and, using first one then two fingers, Kelly widened the incision—just enough to allow delivery. The outer surface of the sac was now exposed and, after another check of the monitors and a reassuring nod from Joan, she ruptured these membranes with scissors and reached inside to locate the baby's head. Grasping the obstetric forceps Nancy slapped into her palm, she delivered the head—easing it gently through the abdominal wall.

'Oxytocin?' Joan asked and Kelly nodded, knowing the measured amount of drug would make the uterus contract and should help to prevent excessive bleeding. Joan gave the prepared injection and Kelly waited for a minute before she eased the baby's shoulders through the opening, anxious to keep the mother's tissue damage to a minimum. Once the tiny boy was free, she held him upside down while Mary gently suctioned out his mouth.

The tiny wailing cry brought smiles to all their faces and, with the umbilical cord clamped and cut, Mary took the baby away to clean and wrap him, while Kelly removed the afterbirth and began the job of neatly repairing the incisions she had made.

'You'd make a fine seamstress,' Nancy joked, as the tension eased and she handed dressings to Kelly.

'I enjoy obstetrics,' Kelly admitted, securing the dressings with waterproof tape.

'Do you want to have a look at him?' Mary asked.

She left Joan and Nancy with the patient and stripped off her theatre garb, before crossing the room to check the baby.

'I'll phone and get our ambulance to take you all back to the airport,' Mary said, handing the swaddled bundle to Kelly.

She looked down at the newborn scrap of humanity, marvelling, as she always did, at the miniaturised perfection of eyelashes and fingernails.

Apgar, she reminded herself, thinking of the scores accorded to newborn babies on the basis of Appearance, Pulse, Grimace, Activity, and Respiratory effort. She checked appearance: good, considering he was early, centrally pink—a two; heart beat good—another two; but only one each for grimace and activity, and respiratory effort weak—a one.

She glanced at the numbers Mary had scrawled on a chart attached to the crib. The total of seven was higher than the one-minute assessment. His respiration would be improved by administration of warmed oxygen in the humidicrib, so she settled him onto the chemical mattress and attached the leads that would monitor his progress.

'Shall I wake your boss?' Joan asked, and Kelly nodded. It was time to get their patients back to town.

He was flushed and heavy-eyed when he shambled out of the ward.

'Everything go OK?' he asked. It was a casual question but Kelly sensed an anxiety in the man, as if he felt he had failed in some way.

'Everything's fine,' she hastened to assure him. 'I'm going to use the portable humidicrib to transport the little fellow back to town. That way, he'll be getting some supplementary oxygen during the flight.'

'Good girl,' he said and she was startled by the compliment. 'Two things we must never forget—pressurisation of the cabin, which alters the pressure in splints and infusion bags, and the possible effects of altitude, even with pressurisation, on the people we're transporting.'

Teaching again, she realised, although his head must be throbbing if the way he was massaging his temples was any indication. She considered his warning, and the differences existing in this field of medicine impressed themselves on her mind, while the obvious dedication of the man impressed her in a different way.

'I'll remember that,' she told him, and walked away as Joan called to tell her that Alison was awake.

So much to learn! she thought, feeling an unfamiliar excitement spark to life within her. It was good to be learning again—even better to have new challenges to meet.

'Ambulance is here!' Mary announced.

Excitement turned to trepidation! The first of those challenges was her next plane trip! She wouldn't learn much unless she conquered this stupid fear! She stood by while a burly man helped Nancy lift Alison onto a stretcher, then she walked out beside her patient. Mary followed them, carrying the humidicrib with its tiny occupant.

The ambulance was a huge four-wheel-drive vehicle.

'It's provided by the mining company for the local branch of the State Emergency Service,' Joan explained. 'It's good from our point of view because it has stretchers compatible with the plane's. We can slide yours out and slide this one in its place—a straight swap.'

'I'll sit up front,' Jack announced. 'Here and in the plane. I think I might have the flu, and there's less chance of spreading germs.'

'Thinks he might have the flu!' Joan whispered to Kelly. 'I diagnosed that three days ago!'

Kelly grinned. These people had accepted her so easily although she was only a locum. They had made her feel comfortable, and needed, at a time when she'd been feeling very much alone. Not that she wanted to get involved with them—or the job—but it was nice. . .

She climbed into the back of the vehicle, and seated herself where she could keep an eye on both mother and infant. Looking out through the back window, she saw Mary, Nancy and Joan all smiling as they waved goodbye. It didn't matter what sex, or shape, or colour you were, she realised. If you were the 'flying doctor', you 'belonged'.

CHAPTER THREE

MICHAEL was waiting at the airfield. He helped the ambulance man carry the stretcher across the tarmac, waving Jack away with a stern, 'Keep your germs to yourself! Get on board and up into the cockpit and don't breathe unless you're told to!'

He must be feeling sick to allow himself to be ordered about like that, Kelly thought as the head doctor limped obediently towards the aircraft. Jack Gregory hadn't struck her as a man who took orders easily.

Kelly followed with the humidicrib and Michael, taking it from her when she entered the cabin, fussed over its safe anchorage with exaggerated care.

'I've one of these little fellows due soon,' he explained, demonstrating the technique. 'And, see here!' He crossed to the stretcher and showed her how to check that it was locked into position. 'This bag slides onto one of these hooks,' he added, showing her how to fit the infusion bag to the specially designed rack in the ceiling of the plane. 'And there's oxygen here.'

He pointed out the plane's supply, pulling a mask from a concealed hatch beside the stretcher. Kelly saw the suction outlet nearby then noticed that there were similar fittings on the other side of the plane.

'We can take those seats out and carry two stretchers,' Michael added, reading the question in her eyes.

She shook her head, amazed at the technology available in what was a cross between an aerial ambulance and a mini-hospital.

But when he closed the door no amount of wonder could overcome the numbing panic that surged back to

41

life. Until Alison moaned! An ill-judged movement had brought pain to the tissues now coming out of the numbing effect of the anaesthesia. Kelly put aside her own fears and turned to reassure her patient, talking quietly to her about the baby and explaining the course her convalescence would take.

'I don't much like flying,' Alison confessed as the plane began to accelerate along the tarmac.

'Well, that's OK because I get airsick,' Kelly admitted, thinking that she should warn the girl, but not ready—yet—to admit to her own fears.

Alison looked at her in amazement.

'Then why are you doing this job?' she asked.

Why, indeed? Kelly thought.

'Like most things we do, it seemed like a good idea at the time,' she confessed, slipping into the seat across from the stretcher and fastening her seat belt with fingers that were almost steady.

'That's what I thought when I decided to get pregnant,' Alison confessed. 'I was bored at Wyrangi with Bob away all the time. I thought a baby might be company.'

'And did Bob agree?' Kelly asked, telling her stomach that the plane was still on the ground and there was no cause for alarm—yet. She remembered Alison's remark about his reaction to the Caesar, and wondered about Bob!

'Not exactly!'

The plane did lift now and Kelly, her hands pressed firmly against her rebellious stomach, exerted all her will-power to overcome the waves of nausea. It was fear, not the motion, that made her sick, she realised. Even when her mind was occupied with other things the fear still ate away at her subconscious and found physical form in the churning disorder of her intestines.

Alison was expounding on her erratic relationship

with her husband but Kelly barely heard her. Then
Michael called, 'We're up!' and she undid her seat belt
and clambered shakily to her feet. She made her way
to the seat beside the crib, and reached inside the gloved
opening in the box-like conveyance to feel the
little body.

The baby stirred and Kelly looked around, wondering
if she could anchor the crib closer to Alison so that she
could touch her baby. Not practical at all, she realised.
The interior of the plane was fitted so precisely that
everything had its place.

She examined the little boy, and again noted her
findings on the file attached to the portable incubator.
Pleased with her handling of the situation so far, she
returned to her seat, ignoring the vibrations beneath her
feet—the constant reminders that she was on a plane!

'I'm going to be sick,' Alison announced.

You and me both! Kelly thought, but she reached for
a small dish and eased Alison onto her side so that she
could bring up the small amount of fluid which had
accumulated in her stomach.

The young mother began to cry and Kelly forgot her
own discomfort and tended her patient, wiping her face
and smoothing back her hair, while Alison's pent-up
emotions flowed out in a welter of tears. When the
storm had passed Kelly diverted Alison's attention from
her own perceived 'failure' at having to have a
Caesarean by asking about her family. They chatted for
the remainder of the journey, the conversation broken
only when Kelly stood up to check on the little boy
who, as yet, had no name.

'I kept telling Bob he had to choose something for
a boy,' Alison had complained. 'I chose Laura for a
girl and he was to choose for a boy.'

At the mention of her errant husband Alison's face
crumpled, as if she was about to cry again, so Kelly

quickly diverted the conversation back to Mum and Dad and Alison's assorted siblings.

'Strap in, we're coming down,' Michael called, and Kelly subsided into her seat, delightedly aware that she'd survived the journey without recourse to the paper bags!

But, as the plane touched down, another worry surfaced. She unstrapped her seat belt and made her way cautiously towards the cockpit. As she glimpsed the tarmac racing away beneath them her stomach clenched, but her concern was strong enough to overcome the momentary weakness.

Jack appeared to be sleeping soundly in the copilot's seat. She glanced at him, amazed to see how much younger he looked with the lines of strain wiped away by sleep.

'I didn't do anything about an ambulance to meet the plane,' she whispered to Michael, trusting that he could listen and do things with brakes and control columns at the same time.

He turned quickly towards her and smiled, then swung back to guide the plane around at the end of the runway and steer it back towards the hangar.

'That's my responsibility,' he explained. 'I let the Base or the answering service know what time we'll arrive—our ETA—and they arrange the ambulance. If you look over to the right of our hangar you should see it waiting there.'

Kelly sighed with relief. Imagine getting through two flights and an emergency operation then forgetting something as basic as ambulance transport for the patients.

As Michael opened the door Alison reached out and took Kelly's hand.

'Would you phone my mum for me?' she asked. 'Tell her what's happened. She can phone Bob—although the

Wyrangi grapevine has probably let him know by now.'

Again Kelly felt a twinge of concern for the obvious lack in Alison's marriage of—was it love or simply communication? She wrote the phone number Alison gave her on a slip of paper and tucked it in her pocket. Other people's marriages were no concern of hers.

Definitely no concern of hers! She was only here for two months and would have no time to get involved with patients.

Two ambulance attendants appeared almost as soon as Michael let down the door which provided the steps into the aircraft. They unhooked the fluid bag, unlocked the stretcher and carried their patient away with a minimum of fuss.

'I told the infection zone to stay where he was until we were unloaded,' Michael said, watching Kelly unstrap the humidicrib. 'I'll carry that, you do the housekeeping.'

She looked around the interior of the plane. She had one bag of waste she must carry off, the equipment bag and the cool-box. No other obvious 'housekeeping'. From up front she heard movement, and knew that Jack must be ready to disembark.

She walked down the steps as the ambulance drove away. A curious sense of loss descended on her—as if a friend were leaving, not a comparative stranger. She dropped the paraphernalia on the ground and watched the vehicle go.

'The clerical staff at the office do some follow-up calls to the hospital, but you can always ring yourself and check on a patient.'

She spun around at the sound of the hoarse remark. Jack had come down the steps and was standing behind her. He sounded dreadful but he was still trying to help her understand this novel experience.

Forgetting her so-recent reminder of non-involvement, she said, 'I think I'll probably do just that.'

Then the realisation that she had survived her first flight—two flights, in fact—and functioned well hit her with an overwhelming force, and she flung her arms around him and held him tight, shouting, 'I did it! I did it!'

Sick as he was feeling, the slim softness of her body jolted his hormones into sudden activity. He hadn't felt this way—for how long? Certainly not since he'd come to the Bay. Not since his first love. . .

It had to be the flu that was doing it!

'I'm infectious,' he growled, stepping back so hastily that he nearly fell over the steps.

She recoiled from him, shock darkening her lovely eyes.

'I don't know why I did that,' she muttered, and bent to retrieve the gear she'd been carrying.

He stood and watched her headlong flight towards the hangar, too bemused by his own reaction to her impetuous hug to offer to help.

As she disappeared from sight he gathered his few remaining wits and hurried after her. She was standing in front of the cabinets.

'See, I have been some use on this trip,' he said, dangling the keys from his fingers. He unlocked the first cabinet and reached over to take the equipment case from her.

Their fingers met and he felt hers trembling, as if her nerves were jumping beneath her skin. Glancing quickly at her face, he saw a small scattering of freckles standing out across her nose. The delight she'd shown only minutes earlier had disappeared and, with it, all the colour from her cleanly sculpted face.

It bothered him to think that she was upset, and he searched his flu-racked brain for some explanation.

'Joan Campbell told me she'd never seen a more efficient Caesar.'

'I was only doing my job!'

He tucked the unused equipment into place, guessing—from the brusque way she'd brushed aside his praise—that it wasn't her proficiency that was bothering her. Was it a personal problem?

Hell! He needed a couple of strong cold tablets and about forty-eight hours' straight sleep before he could begin to think straight—so he'd better not start worrying about this stranger's personal life.

'Do I requisition a complete new neonate pack? And should I replace the drugs I used from the obstetrics pack out of the stock cupboard?'

She didn't look at him as she asked the questions, but he could see the colour creeping back into her cheeks and guessed that she had herself back under control.

'Yes, to both,' he replied, trying to act as efficiently as she was, although the way the blood was warming her skin and bringing the translucence back to it was fascinating him so much that he found not staring very difficult. It must be the flu, he repeated to himself, and led her into the small office to show her where the requisition forms were kept.

'I'd better phone Alison's mother before I do any paperwork,' she said, sliding into a chair near the phone.

She looked up at him as she lifted the receiver, and he saw the quick frown that puckered her forehead.

'You'd better sit down before you fall down,' she told him, nodding towards the second chair. 'Should I drive you home then come back and do the requisitions?'

'I can wait,' he told her, but he took her advice and subsided into the chair. His legs were definitely on the wobbly side, now that he thought about them.

He looked out of the window while she dialled and introduced herself, but couldn't help listening to her reassuring conversation with the new grandmother. She was a good doctor, he realised, recognising the inherent interest in her patient that was the hallmark of the best GPs.

'The forms go to Susan when they're completed,' he explained, when she finished on the phone. 'She's in charge of all the stock. We keep similar forms at the Base so if you have a night emergency you don't have to hang around here in the early hours of the morning, filling in forms. Do it next day at the office.'

'And what about the stretcher from the plane? Those ambulance men just whisked it away.'

She was definitely feeling better, he realised, and smiled at the proprietary note in her voice.

'We keep spares here, but Michael will see we get one back. It mightn't be our stretcher, but it will be exactly the same. It often happens, particularly with spinal or neck injury cases where we are trying to mini-mise movement. Susan tells me we have more trouble with the linen—that half the time the stretcher will come back without its sheets.'

He paused for a moment before he sighed and said theatrically, 'Ah, the problems of housekeeping!'

She rewarded his acting with a little smile, and Jack relaxed. Maybe she'd do until Peter came back.

Her head tilted over the desk as she began on the forms, and he watched the shiny hair slide for-ward to hide her face. Would it feel as silky as it looked. . .?

He'd gone to sleep again, she realised when she'd completed the required forms. Did the irregularity of his job make it possible for him to snatch at sleep this way then function efficiently for a short time, although he was obviously feeling wretched?

If it was Strain A of the flu she'd seen, spreading
through the south, then the sooner he was on antibiotics
the better. There were plenty of suitable drugs in those
cabinets, but what was the procedure?

She watched the sleeping man for a moment longer,
her eyes lingering on the strong line of his profile and
slightly aggressive jut of his jaw.

Aggressive?

No, he hadn't struck her as aggressive! She studied
it more closely. Was it a stubborn jut?

He stirred, and she looked quickly away, reminding herself that his jaw was none of her business.
Jack Gregory might be an attractive man but she
was only here for two months—and, attractive as he
was, he was certain to be 'taken'. And why was she
interested, anyway? She was off men at the moment,
wasn't she?

With the silent homily delivered, she tucked the completed forms with a spare blank one into a manilla folder
she found in one of the drawers and stood up, slipping
the folder under one arm. She picked up the bunch of
keys he'd dropped onto the desk, and went quietly back
to the cabinets.

'Pinching drugs?'

She swung to face him, heart hammering in her chest.

'You're like a damn cat!' she swore. 'You're fast
asleep one minute, and the next you're creeping up
behind me to give me heart failure.'

'I just wondered what you were doing,' he said
mildly, but the green eyes, reddened and hazy though
they might be, were assessing her intently.

'I was getting some antibiotics for you, if you must
know,' she told him curtly, feeling as if she'd been
caught in a nefarious act. 'If you don't hit yourself with
something for that flu you'll be laid up for weeks!'
She shrugged. 'I don't know the ethics of prescribing

something from the cabinet, but I decided this was an emergency.'

She glared at him as his continued silence and his strange, half-hypnotic regard twitched along her nerves.

'If you're too stupid to look after yourself then some-one else will have to do it,' she finished lamely.

He stepped forward and smiled, showing even white teeth and the hint of a dimple in the deep crease of his left cheek.

'And what have you decided on?' he asked, reaching out a hand.

She slapped the packet of Augmentin Forte into it, taking care not to touch his skin. Touching his fingers had had a strange effect on her earlier, and she was in no hurry to repeat the experience.

'I was going to take Eryc as well in case you were allergic to penicillin.'

He studied the tablets in his hand, as if wondering what they were or why he was holding them.

'Well?' she demanded.

'These will be fine,' he muttered, then he looked up and she saw the beads of perspiration on his forehead. It must be coming in waves, she realised, remembering a similar infection she'd once had. Hot then cold, OK for a while then weak and nauseous only minutes later!

'Come on, I'll drive you back to your place,' she said. She reached out to take his arm and lead him across to where her car was parked.

'Cabinets locked?' he muttered.

'Of course,' she told him, while telling herself that he was a patient now and touching him should not be affecting her nerves. Especially when, judging by his preoccupation with locking the cabinets, her touch was having no effect on him!

He felt the shivering begin, then her cool hand on

his arm started fires burning so that he was hot and cold at once.

He clutched the packet of antibiotics and allowed her to guide him towards the door. Once he was in bed he'd be OK, and the images of this dark-haired stranger which kept swirling in front of his eyes would go away.

He woke up in bed in his green work shirt and boxer shorts. Someone had removed his shoes. It was dark, but a slim yellow rectangle beneath his *en suite* door told him that the bathroom light was on. He glanced towards the door that led into the living-room and saw a similar rectangle which, as he watched, began to change shape, widening slowly as the door was cautiously opened.

The woman who entered was a stranger, yet she looked both familiar and unfamiliar.

'Awake, are you?' she murmured, in a voice that sent shivers down his spine.

He was about to ask the time, but wanted a better conversational opening with this shadowed stranger.

'Why?' he asked, and heard a voice inside him jeer— oh, that was much better!

'Because I was beginning to wonder if I'd overdosed you,' she replied, mystifying him still more.

'Overdosed?'

'It's Sunday evening,' she explained. 'You've been asleep for thirty hours.'

'Impossible!' he muttered, running a hand across his face and feeling the prickly stubble that confirmed her words.

'Well,' she said judiciously, 'from time to time you did assume a more or less upright position and stagger towards the bathroom, and I woke you a couple of times to force antibiotics and liquid down your throat.'

He remembered a dream where he'd rested his head against the cool firm breast of a dark-haired angel. . .

'Do you want something to eat?' she asked abruptly. 'I've made some soup.'

He shifted into a better sitting position and tried to see her. The final statement lacked the conviction he'd heard in her voice at some other time. Was she afraid he'd reject her kindness? Had he rejected her at some other time?

'I'd love some soup,' he said, injecting what he hoped was the right amount of enthusiasm into his voice. She vanished from the patch of light, and he found himself staring at the place where she had been.

As his brain emerged fitfully from its hibernation he began remembering snatches of things, but could make no cohesive pattern from them. He remembered wanting to strangle someone—surely not a soup-maker—then hurting his foot.

'Here you are. Do you need the light on?'

She sounded nervous and he reached out to turn on the bedside lamp, wanting to see her, to confirm that the dark-haired, blue-eyed beauty he'd dreamt about really did exist. He'd worry about what she was doing in his apartment later!

She was wearing white shorts and a white T-shirt with writing on it. He was puzzled because his angel had been wearing blue—she'd even had blue wings, now that he thought about it!

And his angel had been smiling, not scowling— as this woman was—at the tray she held in her outstretched hands.

'It was a syrupy smile anyway,' he consoled himself, then realised, as she looked up in surprise, that he'd spoken the thought aloud.

She slid the tray onto the table.

'Will you be able to manage?' she asked.

He looked from the woman to the tray, then back to the woman.

'Did Leonie send you?'

He saw her stiffen, drawing herself up a fraction straighter, before she sighed and shook her head.

'First Peter, and now Leonie,' she said with a mocking smile. 'Do all your friends procure women for you?'

'Peter?'

She frowned at him.

'Don't you remember anything at all about yesterday?' she asked, reaching forward to pick up his wrist and press her fingers professionally against his pulse.

'I had a call-out—road accident, people trapped. It took ages to free them but I think they'll be OK.' He paused while he searched through snippets of dream and blurred patches of reality.

She dropped his wrist and stepped back from the bed.

'And someone had a baby—but not at the accident, as I recall.'

The mental effort made him hungry so he reached out for the soup. He was conscious of his visitor's eyes watching him closely.

'Worried I'll spill it?' he joked weakly. He spooned a mouthful of the warm liquid into his mouth, and almost gagged.

'What is it?' he demanded, unable to believe that anything could taste so peculiar.

'Vegetable,' she said hopefully. 'I found vegetables in the refrigerator so I thought. . .'

Her voice faded into silence, but she didn't move away.

He tried another sip—an extremely small and cautious sip!

'No vegetables could taste this awful,' he declared, as his first impressions were confirmed.

She shrugged, and reached out to take the tray.

'When I first made it it tasted bland so I found your spice cupboard and threw in a bit of this and that.'

'This and that?' he queried, still trying to recognise constituents.

'Nutmeg was one,' she offered defensively. 'I can't help it if it doesn't taste too good. I wasn't hired to cook!'

He was about to ask why she was hired when, in a blinding flash of recollection, he remembered an argument with Mrs Katinski and her muttered aside about loose women. This was the woman!

As far as he could remember, she definitely wasn't hired to cook!

He closed his eyes. It had to be a nightmare.

'I could make you tea or coffee,' she offered, dismissing any idea that she might be a figment of his dreams, 'and, now you're awake and I know you're OK, I could go out and get a cooked chicken or a take-away meal of some kind.'

'Is that all you eat? Cooked chickens and take-away meals? You can't cook?'

The fact that here was an adult who couldn't cook diverted him from his other concerns, and he stared at her.

'I've never had time to learn,' she told him, shifting uncomfortably from one foot to the other. 'I will one day,' she assured him airily. 'After all, anyone who can read should be able to cook.'

He turned deliberately to look at the cooling soup, then raised one eyebrow.

'Illiterate, too, are you?' he teased, and saw colour flood into her face.

She leaned forward, picked up the tray and marched

out of the room. So, she had a temper, his angel, he thought, and sank back down among his pillows, suddenly exhausted. He was drifting off to sleep when he heard his front door shut—not quite slamming, but closing with a definite emphasis.

CHAPTER FOUR

KELLY woke at six-thirty, and glanced towards the curtained windows. Perhaps she should try opening them slightly, and looking straight out at the view—not downwards. She crossed the room and parted them about a foot, then stood, entranced, as the glowing, orange-tipped clouds heralded the rising sun.

Elated by the magic of the new dawn, she scanned the bay—from the steep, rocky high headland at the southern end to the cliff-like ramparts guarding the northern approach. And, in between, a stretch of serene water, silver-grey in the early morning light.

It was a beautiful place—as long as she didn't look down!

She turned away, heading for the bathroom off her bedroom. Her first official day as a 'flying doctor'!

An hour later she decided to leave—too restless to wait in the apartment any longer. Jack Gregory was still asleep. She looked in on him but didn't wake him. Sleep would do him more good than pills and potions.

'Another early bird?' Leonie greeted her when she arrived at the old house which served as offices for the Service. 'How's Jack?'

'I heard him up and about during the night. Judging by the depletion of stock in the refrigerator, I'd say he's on the mend. He finished off a litre of orange juice, some yoghurt I bought, and most of that huge bowl of fruit salad you brought over yesterday afternoon.'

Leonie chuckled.

'Sounds as if he's back to normal,' she agreed. 'Come

56

into my office and we'll talk about accommodation.'

A subtle fragrance lingered in the air in the small room, and Kelly looked around, her gaze lighting on a bowl of yellow roses on top of a filing cabinet. She saw Leonie follow her glance and thought she detected a faint colouring in the other woman's cheeks, but when she spoke it was of Kelly's problem.

'I've rung every agent I know.' Something in her voice told Kelly that the initial enquiries had been unsuccessful, and Leonie confirmed this, adding, 'But I'll keep trying. I could get you private board with a friend of mine but—'

'It would be difficult!' Kelly finished for her. 'I do see how inconvenient it would be for the other people in the house to have the phone waking them throughout the night, and someone coming and going at odd hours.'

The phone rang as if on cue and Leonie picked it up, then glanced at Kelly.

'It's a phone consultation. It doesn't sound too complicated—will you take it?'

'Before I've even got a desk?' she joked, reaching across to take the receiver out of Leonie's hand.

'It's Mrs Pearson from ''Willowvale'', a cattle property about an hour's flying time from here,' Leonie murmured, pulling a blue sheet from one of her drawers and pushing it across the desk towards Kelly. 'Here's a list of the drugs they have on hand in the medicine chest.'

Kelly scanned the list as she introduced herself to the caller. She was familiar with the contents of the chests from the time she'd spent in a small country hospital.

'How may I help you?' she asked, after introducing herself to the caller.

'It's a visitor,' Mrs Pearson explained. 'A young Japanese woman here on her honeymoon. We take guests who want to see how a cattle property is run, and we're especially popular with Japanese tourists.'

Kelly remained silent. People had to tell things in their own way.

'She and her husband arrived yesterday morning—flew out from the Bay in our own light plane. In the afternoon a group of the visitors rode out to where the boys are mustering. It was a clear day, warm but not too hot. They had dinner out there around the campfire—a big stew, and damper, and tinned fruit and custard, then rode back in the moonlight. This morning she's vomiting, and very upset, and her husband is making things worse by being panicky and chattering at me in Japanese.'

'Is she running a temperature?'

'No!' Mrs Pearson replied. 'That's the first thing I checked.'

'And is anyone else feeling at all off-colour? Could it have been something they ate which affected her more than it affected, say, the western people in the group?'

'No, I've asked them that. There were eight in the party and they're all Japanese, but everyone else tucked into their breakfast and headed out to watch the boys cut the calves out of the mob in the yards.'

'Have you given her anything to stop the vomiting?' Kelly eyed the anti-emetic drug listed in the medical chest each remote property or settlement kept. It was marked with the asterisk which meant that it should only be given on doctor's advice, but she knew that there were occasions when people doctored themselves or their family.

'No,' Mrs Pearson assured her. 'I checked the chest and knew Number 93 would probably stop the nausea, but rang you first.'

'It could be morning sickness,' Kelly suggested.

'But she's just married! They're on their honeymoon!' Mrs Pearson sounded so astonished that Kelly smiled.

'It does happen,' she said gently, and heard the other woman chuckle.

'I suppose because they're Japanese it didn't occur to me,' Mrs Pearson explained. 'Somehow you don't think of other people behaving like your own young ones. I'll go and ask.'

Kelly waited, smiling to herself as she filled in details on the consultation form Leonie had pushed across the desk towards her.

Mrs Pearson returned with a confirmation of her guess.

'So!' Kelly murmured, satisfaction warming her voice. 'Try to get her to eat something. Small meals, carbohydrates mainly, things like toast or biscuits. She should eat as often as possible, and drink whatever liquids she can keep down.'

She hesitated, trying to picture the young woman 'an hour's flying time' away. 'She won't be able to get patent medicines out there but warn her, gently, about taking over-the-counter medicines, won't you?'

'And if she gets worse?' Mrs Person queried. 'I had dreadful morning sickness with all of my kids.'

'Well, you'll know from your own experience if the vomiting gets out of hand. Normal morning sickness won't affect the foetus, but if it persists to the point where the young woman becomes dehydrated we'd have to bring her back to town.'

'OK,' the cheerful woman said. 'I'll get back on to you if I think there's a problem.' There was a pause, and then she said, 'Oh, and welcome to the Flying Doctors, Dr Jackson.'

Kelly smiled and hung up. She was relishing the warmth of that sentiment when the front door of the building was flung open and Jack Gregory marched in.

'Someone not only unplugged my phone from beside the bed, but also switched off my alarm clock!' he growled, striding into Leonie's office and glaring at both the occupants.

'I unplugged your phone when I called to see how you were yesterday afternoon,' Leonie admitted, with what Kelly considered commendable bravery. The man looked angry enough to eat someone.

'And the alarm clock?' He rounded on Kelly and she knew from the grim expression on his face that he had remembered who she was and why she was here.

'You needed the sleep,' she said in what she hoped was an appeasing manner. Appeasement didn't come easily to her, but she didn't want to jeopardise her chances of staying by arguing with her boss on her first day. As she spoke it occurred to her that she *did* want to stay—in spite of her terrors in the plane and a lack of suitable accommodation.

'I don't need you or anyone else making decisions for me,' he informed them loftily then stalked out of the room, pausing in the doorway to turn and snap, 'Staff meeting in five minutes!'

'Does he sack people in staff meetings?' Kelly asked Leonie, who smiled reassuringly and actually reached out to pat her hand.

'You'll be right,' she said, then frowned as she looked out through the door. 'He's usually the most even-tempered of men. Perhaps the flu has left him a bit grouchy! Come on, I'll show you your desk and introduce you to anyone who's around.'

'A bit grouchy' didn't begin to cover his mood, Kelly thought, following Leonie out of the office.

'This is your desk—although you probably won't be spending much time at it. I've put a roster sheet on it, a staff catalogue—who we all are and what we do—

some information about clinics the Base runs, and the area we cover.'

Leonie waved towards a vacant desk with a neat pile of files resting on it.

'Very well organised!' Kelly said with a smile. She wondered what the staff catalogue would say about Jack Gregory who was at the desk behind hers, head bent behind random piles of files rising like tipsy skyscrapers around the perimeter of the desk's surface.

'And the kitchen-cum-lunchroom is through here. That's Sally, making tea and coffee.' Leonie paused while Kelly shook hands with the fresh-faced teenager. 'Sally's our filing clerk and "gofer". Our other office staff are—' Again Leonie mentioned names and functions. 'And here's the hub of the building. It was originally the radio-room, but now most of our consultations are done by phone. You can see the reference library is along that wall, and maps of the area are here. . .'

Kelly looked around, surprised to see the vast area of northern Australia the Rainbow Bay Service had to cover. Colour-coded pins were dotted across the map and, as Leonie was called away to take a phone call, she moved closer to see what each colour represented.

'Red ones show proper landing strips, green denotes a fortnightly clinic, blue a monthly clinic, orange are rough landing grounds—like straight roads or abandoned Air Force runways—'

Jack must have come in while she was studying it. He reached over her shoulder to point out the main features.

'And the black?' she asked, seeing these pins in small clusters on the map.

'Something I'm trying to work out,' he said abruptly, picking up another two pins and pushing them almost viciously into the map. He turned away from her and

called, 'When you're ready, guys!' in a voice loud
enough to be heard at the front door.

'You'll find we're all guys to Jack,' Sally whispered,
coming alongside with a tray of coffee-cups. 'Take a
seat anywhere at the big table. There are pens and note-
pads on the table if you want something to make you
look busy, and help yourself to coffee.'

Kelly thanked her and seated herself, but she ignored
the coffee. She was bewildered by the strangeness of it
all, and confused by the casual air that seemed to per-
vade the place. Surely an organisation couldn't run
efficiently with such a laid-back approach as she'd
seen so far.

People drifted into the room, one couple—arm
in arm—chatting to Sally and an older woman—
apparently about their holiday.

'Right, let's start with introductions!'

Jack Gregory spoke so briskly that Kelly was forced
to do a quick rethink.

'Kelly here is our new doctor, standing in while Peter
is away, and Jenny is our new nurse, taking
Christa's place.'

Kelly turned to nod at the second 'new girl', then Jack
introduced the others, beginning with an older woman.

'Susan Stone, head flight nurse. Her husband, Eddie,
is our chief pilot. He's on an evac flight at the moment
with Jane, our other nursing sister. Allysha is a pilot,
newly returned from honeymooning with Nick who's
our third doctor—'

Jack, his eyes drawn to Kelly, saw a shudder of reaction cross her face and wondered what he'd said to
cause it. If only he wasn't so weakened by two days in
bed! Surely he normally managed things better than this.

He ploughed on, anxious to finish the meeting and
get on with the work he was doing on the incidence of
motor vehicle accidents.

'Rosters first!' he began.

'These are the pilot rosters,' Allysha said, pushing a sheaf of papers across the table towards him. He took them from her and glanced at them, knowing that Eddie would have worked them out with his usual competence.

'No nursing changes,' Susan told him, pushing her own sheets forward. 'I've slotted Jenny into all Christa's clinics and duty times. The only changes will come when Christa begins work at the hospital at Caltura. Once they have a nursing sister there will we cut down on clinic time at the settlement?'

Jack looked up at her and frowned. He'd been thinking about the pilot rosters when he should have been listening to Susan. He glanced down the table to where the new doctor sat—her black hair gleaming. That hair fascinated him, drawing his eyes like a magnet then directing his attention to the straight profile, the cheeky chin and wide mouth. . . With an effort he removed his attention from her mouth, but his gaze wandered over her slim, slight figure—held very upright.

Too slim? Too slight? He dragged his mind back to work and his frown deepened.

'We won't change the clinic programme at the moment, Susan. Keeping to our old schedule will give everyone time to shake down within a familiar routine,' he said, realising that he would have to reshuffle the medical rosters—again! 'I'll look at all the duty rosters and see what I can work out.'

'But, apart from the Caltura clinic, nothing need change,' Nick argued. 'We put Kelly's name where Peter's was and Jenny's where Christa's was, and keep going.'

'If only!' Jack told him, with a half-smile. 'For a start, I think it's best to have an experienced staff member with each newcomer for at least a month.'

And that's not my only problem, he added silently, but I can't voice the other without fear of sounding sexist. He glanced up and saw the new doctor studying him intently. Could she read his mind? He remembered some of the confused thoughts he'd had about her over the weekend, and hoped not!

Kelly watched him, certain that the juggling of experienced staff wasn't his only problem. Could he be considering not hiring her? Would he contact the Locum Managers and ask for someone else? The thought bothered her, and she forced her attention back to the general conversation.

The talk turned to patients who had been brought to town by the Service in the last fortnight and she realised that, while it might be a totally unstructured meeting, it was covering a lot of ground. She was caught up in the tale of an elderly prospector who hadn't been seen at a clinic for some months when the phone rang.

Sally, who had been seated further back from the table than the others, turned to answer it.

'Taking over Katie's job,' someone murmured, and Nick said, 'Better her than Jack—think what fun we'd have if he took over the radio!'

A chorus of friendly chuckles greeted the remark, but when Sally turned from the desk and said, 'It's an evac, Twin Mountain, one of the Benson twins having difficulty breathing,' the mood changed.

Sally had spoken in a quiet unemotional voice, but as she passed the receiver to Jack the atmosphere in the room was charged with expectancy.

'I'm next on call—let's go, gang,' Allysha said, pushing back her chair and walking out of the room without a second glance to see if her 'gang' was following.

Susan Stone had also risen. She looked enquiringly

at Jack who nodded at her, then she followed Allysha from the room.

Nick paused long enough to collect a note Jack had been scribbling while he listened to the caller. He stopped by Kelly's chair.

'Would you like to come?'

Come now? Today? In another plane?

'N-no, thanks,' she stammered 'I'd only be going along for the ride and I think my time would be better spent reading the information Leonie's left on my desk.'

She knew she sounded unutterably stuffy, but she wasn't ready—yet—to put her nerves to the test in front of other staff.

They were gone before Kelly thought of thanking him for asking. The two clerical staff also left the room, while Sally suggested showing Jenny the store cupboard and whisked her away. Leonie was packing up the papers on the table—signalling that the meeting was over.

Kelly looked at Jack who was talking—low-voiced—on the phone. Maybe he ran a more efficient organisation than it appeared at first glance. Maybe he wasn't the pea-brain she'd accused him of being!

'Come and have a coffee in my office,' Leonie suggested. 'Give you strength to tackle the paperwork!'

She followed Leonie out of the radio-room, waited while she paused to give Sally a message then continued behind her towards the small office off the front entrance hall.

'Jack did the rosters before he realised you were coming in Colin Forbes's place,' she explained, 'so don't take too much notice of the ones I left on your desk. I think he may want to change them again.'

'Why?' Kelly asked, the word coming out more belligerently than she'd intended. 'As Nick said, all he has to do is cross out Colin's name and put mine in its place. Judging by his desk, a little untidiness on a roster won't worry him.'

Colin's name brought back the fitful anger she thought she'd left behind, but she could hardly explain that to the startled woman across the desk.

'It's not quite that simple,' a deep voice said behind her, and she swung around to see Jack Gregory entering the room, followed by Sally with a tray containing three coffee-mugs, milk and sugar.

'I didn't mean that about your desk,' Kelly muttered, embarrassed by her own touchy behaviour. Sally slid the tray on to the desk and departed, Leonie reached out for a mug, and waved to Kelly to help herself. As she leaned forward she glanced at Jack.

He was looking down at her, his fascinating eyes studying her intently.

'No?'

One eyebrow lifted and she quivered beneath the unspoken disbelief.

'It's because of Allysha.' Leonie flung herself into the conversation, obviously hoping to smooth over the antagonism she sensed between them. 'With a female pilot on the staff, there's always the chance of a three-woman flight crew—'

'And would that be a fate worse than death? Is the boss against women in general or just against all-women flight crews?'

Even in her own ears she sounded petty—and unpardonably rude—but she wasn't going to apologise again when he'd greeted her last attempt with such sarcasm. She glanced up at him, wondering if he'd fire her on the spot—which might be a good idea, considering.

He didn't reply immediately, but sat down and spooned sugar into his coffee, concentrating on the task as intently as she concentrated on minor surgery.

'If I had interviewed you instead of Colin Forbes,'

he said at last, 'I would have explained to you that the job requires a certain amount of physical stamina.'

His glance drifted over her, and she was aware of the weight she'd lost in the last few weeks. Beside his tall, solid, athletic body, she must look weak and pale and puny!

'There are occasions when the pilot, nurse and doctor are the only people available to lift a patient into the plane. It's not an easy task at the best of times, but if you have an eighteen-stone man—'

'Surely there are other people at the site—there's the person who called for help, for a start, or the person who drove the ambulance,' she argued.

'The person who called for help on a recent occasion was a ten-year-old boy!' Jack pointed out. 'And there's not always an ambulance.'

'I'm still certain we'd manage,' Kelly insisted. 'Women's strength is often underestimated, but they are capable of anything when they put their minds to it.'

'Like looking at the soles of their feet?'

The words were so softly spoken that she doubted whether Leonie would have heard them. Heat, fired by anger at his mockery, zoomed into her cheeks.

'Exactly!' she countered and met his eyes defiantly.

And why am I arguing so vehemently? she wondered, as the intensity of his green regard made her look away again, strange shivers running through her.

Now she was actually here at Rainbow Bay the idea which had seemed so sensible in far-off Brisbane was nothing short of ridiculous. Let him contact Locum Managers and get someone else, if that's what he wanted!

'I'll grant you women's capabilities,' he said mildly, and she looked at him again, suspicious of this sudden change of mood.

To her surprise, he smiled and she was reminded,

with a totally unexpected—and outrageous—little skipping beat of her heart, that he was a most attractive man.

'I suppose you could have been a weightlifter in a previous incarnation,' he murmured, and she felt his gaze brush over her.

So slender, so fine-boned! he thought—and taut as a bow-string! But as he glanced at her again, seeing the blue veins beneath the pale translucent skin at her temple and throat, she straightened and he sensed the steel beneath the fragile frame.

'I'll still alter the rosters,' he added.

'Then is there something I can do for you?' the newcomer suggested in her cool, unemotional voice.

'Like tidying my desk?' he asked. 'Or perhaps making some soup?'

'*Touché*!'

She raised her hands in supplication and grinned at him, the laughter in her eyes reminding him of the strange dreams he'd had when he was sick. With an effort he forced the unwanted images away, and concentrated on work.

'You'll have enough to do today just getting through the files Leonie has left on your desk,' he told her. 'Especially if she's added copies of all the forms we have to fill in each week before she'll let us go off duty.'

He smiled at Leonie, who was silently watching the byplay.

'She's the real boss of the Base,' he explained, 'and you'll soon learn that she's positively driven by papermania.'

Turning back to Kelly, he saw her looking at Leonie as if reassessing her. She had an exquisite profile, this woman with the shining ebony hair!

The antibiotics must be affecting him to be noticing such things.

He stood up so abruptly that his chair tipped over

and—annoyed at his clumsiness—he bent and retrieved
it, shoving it roughly towards the desk.

'I'll drop the new roster on your desk later,' he said
to Kelly, and hurried out of the room.

He shook his head, trying to clear it of the intrusive,
unexpected, outrageous thoughts. He was far too busy
to worry about women. He had rosters to rewrite—
apart from anything else.

He reached his desk and pulled out new roster forms,
but the clear, sapphire-blue eyes of the new doctor
superimposed themselves on the page.

CHAPTER FIVE

KELLY sat at her desk and read through the information Leonie had provided, but her concentration was affected by the man who sat behind her, coughing occasionally and muttering to himself behind his bulwark of files.

She'd seen similar mountains of folders on a desk in one corner of his living-room, and wondered about his lifestyle if his job required such an excessive amount of paperwork.

Then she wondered why she wondered! She had come to Rainbow Bay for two months partly in response to Colin's pleas, but also because it was an escape. Two months away from Brisbane meant that she could ignore all the excitement and drama of her sister's wedding preparations—and the pitying looks and endless, well-meant queries from friends and family.

'I've put you on the Wooli clinic flight with Susan tomorrow. It's a one-day clinic and leaves from the airport at seven.'

Jack startled her out of her reverie and she looked up at him as he slid a sheet of paper onto her desk. Dark shadows beneath his eyes made the rest of his face look white, as if drained of life.

'You should be at home in bed,' she chided gently, although she couldn't understand the overwhelming sympathy his white face had evoked. 'And I hope you're still taking the antibiotics.'

'I am, and I'm going home to bed right now. I'm sorry I've been such a poor host, but—'

'Don't start apologising now!' she warned him. 'You wouldn't want to ruin your image as the gruff,'tough—'

'Pea-brained boss?'

The smile lit up his tired face and emphasised the golden lights in his eyes. It also started something burning inside Kelly and she sat very still, unable to believe that she could possibly be attracted to this man. Not now! Not when she was supposed to be nursing a broken heart! Surely she couldn't be so fickle!

She frowned at him and the smile faded, leaving him looking even more tired and more sick than he had earlier.

'Here's a key to the apartment,' he said, 'and a card to allow you access to the underground car park.'

The two objects fell onto the neat stack of files. She watched them drop, then reached out to touch them and felt the warmth of his fingers still lingering in the metal.

'I'll keep trying to find somewhere else,' she muttered, studying the key and the slim rectangular card. 'The last thing you need when you're sick is an unwanted lodger.'

'You're more than welcome to stay.'

The statement, delivered in a rasping voice which brought on a spasm of coughing, made her look up at him again. Even with his face masked by a handkerchief, he looked as surprised as she felt. Maybe he was delirious, she decided, watching him as he headed towards the door.

'Wooli files!' Sally distracted her, dumping a concertina case of files on her desk. 'Usually the flight sister takes charge of the files, but Jack thought you might like to go through them. Duplicate files are kept at Wooli, of course, and you'll work from them when you get there.'

Kelly was puzzled. She pulled out a patient file and one glance told her that it was up to date.

'Why duplicate them? Isn't that causing a lot of extra work? No wonder Jack is drowning in a sea of paper.'

'It's handy to have records here for phone consultations,' Leonie explained, appearing from behind Sally. 'We're slowly going over to computers, but some areas have no power so the lap-tops have to operate on batteries and if the batteries run out. . .'

Once again Kelly was struck by the difficulties distance could create, and the sense of challenge returned.

'Actually, the duplication of files has become a habit. Originally, all files were kept at the Base and the flight crew carried whatever they needed, mainly because many of our clinic locations had no permanent building.'

'Consultations on dirt strips in the shade provided by the wings of the plane?' Kelly said, remembering what she'd read of the early days of the Royal Flying Doctor Service.

'Or under the shade of a coolibah tree!' Leonie joked. 'Nowadays most places have a permanent building we use, and where there's a hospital—like Castleford, or Wyrangi, or Wooli—there's actually an office and filing cabinets—the works!'

'So, if there's a hospital at Wooli, why do we run a clinic there?'

'Read the files and see,' Leonie suggested. 'You won't be sitting around doing nothing!'

As the base manager moved away Kelly opened the case and drew out another file, ignoring a nagging reminder that between now and her possible meeting with the person whose name she was reading there would be another night in Jack's eyrie in the sky—and another flight!

Minor surgery, X-rays, blood and urine testing—the flying doctor could be called upon to do anything on these fortnightly visits to small hospitals. The files fascinated her, and images of the people who lived within driving distance of the town called Wooli began to form in her mind.

The phone interrupted her regularly as Sally put through consultation calls, but she remained at her desk until she felt she knew everyone who could possibly visit her clinic.

'You shouldn't be here this late,' Susan Stone told her when everyone else had gone home and she was reading about Wooli in the clinic information folder.

Kelly looked up, surprised to see someone else in the building.

'I came in to get the Wooli files for tomorrow,' Susan explained. 'We got the Benson baby back to town, with Mum and the other twin in tow, then had another evac call immediately. Transfer of a seriously ill man to Brisbane so Nick and I both went.'

'And you've just got back?' Kelly checked her watch. It was seven o'clock and the flight crew had left shortly after nine that morning. 'That's a long day!'

'Actually, we were back at five but I headed home first and put on some dinner for my starving twins. Teenage boys are like bottomless pits!'

Kelly smiled at the mock despair on Susan's face. Once again she was feeling a peculiar sense of acceptance which was rare in most new positions—particularly locum positions.

They chatted for a while then left together, Kelly insisting that she take the files.

'I might have one more read tonight,' she told Susan. 'I promise I won't forget them in the morning.'

'And where have you been?'

Jack hadn't realised that he'd been concerned until the words came out more loudly than he'd intended.

His house-guest propped herself in the doorway, eyes wide with surprise, while the case she was carrying slid to the ground. She was still staring at him when the flimsy catch sprang open and the papers avalanched across the floor.

'Now look what you've done!' she fumed, glaring up at him as she bent to collect the scattered files. 'And it's none of your business where I've been. Who do you think you are? My mother?'

Her anger unsettled him. The words had been—possibly unwise—but they'd been triggered by the relief he'd felt when he heard her key in the lock.

'I was worried. I thought you might be lost,' he said gruffly. He knelt to help her with the files.

'Lost? In Rainbow Bay?' she mocked. 'Do you fuss over all your staff this way?'

Her eyes, now that he could see them more clearly, seemed alight with anger, and again he wondered about this prickly, defensive beauty who had been thrust so unceremoniously into his life.

He handed her the pile of files he'd retrieved and stood up hurriedly, seeking escape from the fascination of those eyes.

'We're a small staff and we work odd hours,' he told her stiffly. 'So we do look out for each other. Is that wrong? Does it bother you to think we might be more like a family than an assortment of colleagues?'

'It might be OK for permanent staff,' she told him crossly, 'but if there's one thing I don't need at the moment it's another family!' She rammed the files clumsily back into the case.

She disappeared into her bedroom.

Jack hesitated for a moment, then headed for the kitchen. He was no gourmet cook, but when he'd woken feeling slightly better from a long sleep he'd decided that the least he could do would be to cook a meal for the woman who'd looked after him over the weekend.

Though why he'd bothered. . .

Kelly dropped the case and mess of files on to her bed. She'd be hours sorting them back into alphabetical order! And that man out there made her skin feel prickly! She didn't know which irritation was worse!

He'd left the curtains drawn and the blind down in the kitchen—she'd noticed that much in between spilling files all over his floor and yelling at him. That showed kindness! And cooking her a meal was another kindly gesture—which she'd as good as flung back in his face.

Mortification made her stomach begin to tremble. What *was* wrong with her? Could it simply be a delayed reaction to Colin's defection?

She washed her face and hands, wishing that she could have a shower but not wanting to appear any ruder than she'd already been.

'I'm sorry if I upset you,' she told him when she re-emerged, 'but I expected you to be in bed, not slaving over a hot meal for an ungracious guest.'

She tried a hopeful smile, but it made no impression on the stony expression on his face. Feeling awkward and uncomfortable, she babbled on.

'After all, I'm only here because there's nowhere else at present. It doesn't mean you have to cook for me.'

'So you'll cook for yourself?' he enquired. 'Or bring your take-aways home and we'll sit at opposite ends of the table and pretend we're strangers?'

Honestly! The man was infuriating. She'd been doing her best to apologise to him and now she felt like yelling at him again.

He waved her towards a chair and waited until she sat down, before disappearing into the kitchen. She heard the oven door open and smelt the succulent aroma of roasting meat. Then a phone rang, and she heard her host curse fluently before silencing the noise with an abrupt, 'Hello!'

He reappeared minutes later.

'Could you help yourself? I've got to go.'

'I thought Nick was on call,' she said, rising from the table. 'If he's not available, let me go. You might be feeling OK now after an afternoon in bed, but you're still not fit.'

He frowned at her for a moment, as if he'd forgotten who she was—again—then he shook his head.

'Nick's coming with me. It's a rare occurrence, but this is a patient who may need manhandling.'

The stony expression vanished and a twinkle of laughter appeared in his eyes.

'As opposed to woman-handling?' she teased, and saw him smile—at last!

'Exactly! It's an old mate from Castleford. He's been on one of his regular benders, and gone a little crazy. If we can get him back to town before he hurts himself or someone else the hospital will dry him out.'

Kelly felt her eyebrows rising. It sounded unbelievable!

'We're like a family,' he repeated softly, whisking his keys off the hall table and heading for the door. 'I should be back in two to three hours, provided we're not asked to divert to somewhere else on the way home.'

'Well, look after yourself!' she muttered, disconcerted by his repetition about the 'family' and by the memory of her own harsh resistance to the concept.

She was asleep before he returned, and she assumed that he was still sleeping when she rose in the morning, helped herself to cereal from his cupboard then headed for the airport. If she was staying any length of time she'd have to speak to him about paying rent, or board. Or should she buy her own food? Be completely independent?

She pictured them sitting, as he'd suggested, like

strangers at either end of the table and chuckled. No!
She'd have to find somewhere else to live. The logistics
of staying on with Jack Gregory were too complicated.

She drove across the airport to the RFDS hangar, and
waved to Michael as she climbed out of the car.

'Do you want to try sitting up the front or will I
shuffle Susan up there so you can be sick in peace?'
he asked.

She gazed dolefully at him.

'So you're assuming it will keep happening?'

'If you suffer from motion sickness it's likely to
happen the first few times,' he said. 'Why don't you
take something for it?'

Kind and understanding he might be, but she couldn't
admit that it was terror, not motion, that made her ill.

'All those preparations make me sleepy,' she said,
which was the truth but not the whole truth! 'Fine job
I'd make of cutting out an ingrown toe-nail when I'm
barely conscious.'

He took the case of files from her and walked with
her towards the hangar.

'I see what you mean,' he said. 'Maybe you should
try some of the new things, like the little buttons that
press on pressure points at your temple or the bands
you can wear around your wrist.'

Kelly smiled at his helpfulness and wondered if she
should confess to fear. But how could she possibly
explain her fear of heights to someone who spent most
of his waking hours steering a fragile craft around
the sky?

Susan appeared and they discussed what had to be
taken. A number of small packages were stacked on
the top shelf in the refrigerated cabinets.

'Replacement supplies for medical chests,' Susan
explained. 'The person responsible for the chest com-
pletes a requisition which goes to Brisbane and we get

a list of what's needed either mailed, phoned or faxed through. Some supplies can be sent on the mail plane but some we take ourselves.'

Kelly nodded. She knew that there were five monitored-dangerous drugs in the chest, and assumed that these would be the ones which had to be delivered. She gestured to the parcels Susan was packing into a cool-box.

'Do people use so much that this replenishment goes on all the time?'

Susan laughed. 'Picturing this entire section of the continent as drug-addicted, are you?' She shook her head. 'Most of the drugs in the chest have an expiry date. We encourage all our chest holders to check the contents every six weeks or so, and destroy out-of-date stock. The five monitored drugs must be returned to us for disposal.'

'Personally collected?'

Again Susan smiled.

'No, they can be returned to the Base by mail in a plain wrapper, but the people responsible often feel it's easier to send us an order then come along to the next clinic and do a straight swap.'

So much to learn!

Kelly took the packed case from Susan, and watched as she dragged out an equipment case similar to the one they'd taken to Wyrangi.

'Did someone show you what's what in these cabinets?'

'Yes and no,' Kelly replied. 'I was told what went where but I think I need half a day out here to go through each cabinet. I hope I get that much time before I'm called to an emergency.'

'If you've no nurse to help you the pilots know where everything is kept,' Susan assured her. She stacked

drugs into another case and, together, they headed for
the plane.

Michael's ploy worked well, and Susan took the
copilot's seat after only a few half-hearted arguments.
Again Kelly concentrated on going through the cases,
seeing what Susan had chosen as necessary and working
out why. She pulled out the files of regular clinic
patients and compared their illnesses or complaints
against the drugs.

Definitely a good idea to take an experienced person
along with each novice, she realised, and silently con-
gratulated the absent Jack for his insistence on this
arrangement.

She was surprised to feel the wheels bump back onto
solid ground! She'd been too engrossed for her fear to
turn to nausea! She'd survived another flight!

'Katrin Schlect was a tourist working her way around
Australia when she first came to Wooli,' Susan
explained as they jolted their way in the back of a filthy
old vehicle from the airfield to the one pub, one store,
five houses and one hospital that called itself a town.
'For some completely inexplicable reason she fell in
love with a place that has absolutely nothing going for
it. She stayed, working first as a barmaid at the pub,
then surprised everyone when the nursing sister left to
get married by announcing that she had the necessary
training and experience and would stay on in charge of
the hospital.'

'Did anyone check the qualifications?' Kelly asked,
picturing the local community's reaction to a barmaid
turned nurse.

'Of course, and they were excellent, but the locals
were a bit wary for a while.'

'Until she did that appendix operation on old Cyril.'
Their driver, who had been silent up to this point,

offered his comment so abruptly that Kelly was shocked.

'Appendix operation?' she repeated weakly.

'That's right!' he told her. 'The silly bloke got sick during the '74 floods when the roads were cut and no planes could land. Sister whipped it out and tidied him up so neat he was getting around good as new a few days later. Never looked back, he didn't, and the folks around here decided Sister was OK!'

Kelly had spent long enough in the country to know the approbation of 'OK' was high praise among the laconic bush folk, and as they stopped outside the tiny hospital she was looking forward to meeting Katrin Schlect.

'This woman's a slave-driver,' she grumbled to Susan when they sat down, after their separate clinics, to share lunch. She gestured towards Katrin, who smiled serenely and continued to list the people she wanted Kelly to see in the afternoon.

'The people who live this far out love to socialise when they can,' Katrin explained. 'And seeing the doctor is a good excuse.'

'But do they need to see the doctor?' Kelly asked, thinking that Katrin could have attended to most of the minor ills she'd seen during the morning.

'Of course they need to see the doctor,' Katrin told her firmly. 'Not because they're sick. I look after the sick ones. But they need a doctor for the excuse to be good, and coming to town—that they need.'

How ridiculous, Kelly thought. Does this happen at all clinics? Wasn't it a waste of precious resources? She shelved the thought and worked through Katrin's list for the afternoon.

'One more,' Katrin called to her when she thought she'd finished. She looked up to see an old man coming through the door. He walked slowly, as if each step was an effort.

'This is Gilbert Grace,' Katrin announced, holding his arm to help him into a chair. 'I've told him he'll have to go back to town with you for tests and I've got a bag packed for him, but he's a stubborn old coot!'

Kelly bit back a smile at the Australianism delivered in what was still a rich Scandinavian accent. As Katrin bustled out she introduced herself to the old man, recalling his name from the staff meeting.

'So, why does Sister think you should come back to town?' she asked.

His face screwed up into an expression of disgust.

'Because she loves poking her nose into other people's business! Wimmin!' he grumbled, but he was shifting uneasily in the chair and Kelly could see red and purple bruising on his arms and legs. Katrin might be right.

'No other reason?' she prompted.

'Well, my stomach's bad and I don't feel like eating much. All I asked her for was a bit of medicine to make my stomach better, and fuss, fuss, fuss, that's all I've got.'

'Would you mind if I examined you?' Kelly asked. 'Just took your blood pressure and pulse, and felt your stomach?'

The old man hesitated while Kelly wondered why his file hadn't been in with the others. If she'd known what had been wrong with him earlier—

'I suppose it can't do any harm, but only my stomach,' he finally agreed, and allowed her to help him up onto the examination couch.

She pulled out a new file-sheet and filled in his name. If he'd rated a mention at the staff meeting his other details must be on record somewhere at the Base.

As well as bruising, there were signs of small sores

not healing well and a quick press of one fingernail suggested anaemia. Talking to him all the time, she conducted as full an examination as he would allow. His pulse was strong and his blood pressure healthily low for a man who looked about a hundred.

She palpated his abdomen, her hands returning several times to the left upper quadrant.

'There's something there,' she told him, as he sat up and buttoned his shirt. 'It could be an enlarged spleen, or a cyst on something else nearby. The only way to tell is through blood tests and scans.'

'They did all that before,' Gilbert informed her. 'Bunged me in that hospital and did tests and tests and more tests. I told them to take the damn thing out, but would they do it? Not on your nelly! Who takes notice of an old itinerant like me?'

'Doctors used to think the spleen was a fairly useless organ and they'd whip it out without a second thought,' Kelly replied. 'Now we realise that it does a bit of good specialists tend to want to keep it in if they can. Maybe they found what was causing the enlargement and thought they could treat the disease instead. Did they tell you anything else? Give you tablets to take?'

'They gave me something with a fancy name, and I took them all,' Gilbert told her, his voice alive with righteousness.

'And did you go back to the doctor for more? Were they something you should be taking all the time?'

While he silently considered this question Kelly regretted the absence of a file on Gilbert. Roll on computerisation, she thought, forgetting that she would only be with the Service for two months.

'They might have been,' he finally admitted, 'but I haven't been where a doctor's been for a while. Hadn't seen any folks for months till I felt bad and thought I'd better call in on Sister here.'

Kelly shook her head, unable to comprehend the life this old man lead—roaming the wild and sparsely populated country of the north.

'Will you come back to town with us?' she asked. 'I do think you need tests to decide what's wrong and specialist attention, for a while at least.'

He looked at her and she thought she saw a flash of fear in his rheumy old eyes.

'Will you visit me in hospital?' he asked, and she recognised immediately that it was a bargaining point. If she said no, so would he!

She bowed her head, and smiled at him.

'I'd be delighted to visit you,' she said, 'provided you promise to tell me about your travels. What do you do, wandering alone in the outback?'

'I'm a prospector,' he said simply. 'I look for lots of things, but mostly gold.'

His reply plunged Kelly into further disbelief. As far as she knew, prospecting these days meant teams of geologists and drilling equipment and helicopters, not old men wandering at will across the continent!

Susan poked her head through the door to see if she was finished.

'Gilbert's coming back to town with us,' Kelly told her, and saw the surprise on Susan's face.

'Katrin and I had both tried to talk him into a trip to the Bay,' Susan whispered to her as they walked out to the car that would take them back to the plane. 'He was dead set against it!'

'If you'd already seen him why send him into me?' Kelly demanded. 'I didn't have a file, and it was sheer luck I picked up the enlarged spleen.'

'No way it was luck. Joan told me what a great Caesar you did, so I knew you'd find his problem. He's a cantankerous old bugger and Katrin and I decided that a newcomer might impress him more than us old hands.'

She turned to Kelly. 'And it worked!' she added with a triumphant smile.

Kelly followed her into the car. She was tired, but pleased with the way she'd handled the day. They bounced their way out of town until the plane came in to view, gleaming in the rays of the setting sun. Would flying in darkness be easier? she wondered. She'd drawn back her bedroom curtains a little more this morning, and looked out over the bay before sunrise. The fear had been slightly less—but she still hadn't looked down!

'I don't like these flying machines,' Gilbert grumbled as Michael helped him up the steps.

'Nor does Dr Jackson,' Michael whispered to the old man, 'but it's our secret. We're not telling anyone else.'

Gilbert turned and winked at her, and Kelly realised that Michael's words had comforted their patient. Was sharing a fear a way of helping overcome it?

Psychologists thought so, she remembered, thinking of the support groups which abounded for people with various phobias, but did it also work on a personal level?

She was still mulling it over when they lifted into the air, but not for long. Her next thought was that they must have hit an air pocket. She jolted upright and saw, through the windows, the bright lights of the Rainbow Bay airport.

'Great help you were—you slept all the way,' Gilbert growled.

'I can't believe it!' Kelly muttered, thinking of the previous, muscle-tensed, stomach-churning flights she'd undertaken.

'Well, don't go to sleep on my hospital visits,' he warned her. 'A deal's a deal!'

Susan came through from the cockpit and unlocked the door.

Something else I'll have to learn to do, Kelly thought,

then realised, that she was beginning to take this erratic life for granted.

She helped Gilbert out of his seat and picked up the small bag Katrin had packed for him, steadying him down the steps and across to the ambulance. Peeling off one sheet of the file she'd completed, she handed it to the attendant and watched as the old man was whisked away.

Susan was heading for the hangar with the equipment bags banging against her legs, so Kelly followed her.

'Get off home,' Susan ordered. 'I'll put this stuff away and I completed the requisitions on the flight. You're on duty tomorrow and on call, if I remember the roster rightly, from six tomorrow evening. Get what sleep you can tonight.'

Kelly thanked her and walked away, but returning to Jack's flat wasn't exactly going home. In fact, it was a very dubious prospect. Would he fix her a meal after her rudeness last night or should she pick up something to eat?

Her brain felt disorientated after the brief sleep, too disoriented to be making even the most basic of decisions. But was it the effects of the sleep or the growing uneasiness about seeing Jack again that was confusing her?

She thrust aside the irritating question. Why should she feel uneasy over the man? Ignore him! Let him do what he liked! Let him cook if he wanted to! Anyway, if he hadn't cooked anything for her she could always have a bowl of cereal.

CHAPTER SIX

'IT's simple and nutritious and I've been eating it for dinner for years,' Kelly snapped at Jack when he walked into the apartment an hour later and raised that infuriating eyebrow at her 'dinner'.

She'd had a shower and washed the dust from her hair as soon as she arrived 'home' to the empty apartment. Feeling tired after the shower and deciding to make it an early night, she'd twisted her wet hair up in a towel on top of her head and pulled on her favourite cotton bathrobe.

And now she felt uncomfortable, being caught like this, and had taken her embarrassment out on him— again!

He nodded acknowledgement of her words and proceeded to unwrap a pizza, fat and succulent, heaped with olives and anchovies, and runny with cheese— exactly how she liked it!

'Guess I'll have to eat all this on my own!'

She wanted to hit him! Teasing her like this! She swallowed the saliva running into her mouth. Would he offer her some?

She waited, studiously ignoring the strong, tanned hand that was arranging a number of the slices on a single plate.

He didn't so much as glance her way! Infuriating man!

Physical violence suggested itself again, but she knew that it would be futile. Perhaps she could try for a light-hearted approach?

Pushing her bowl across the bench towards him, she

smiled and said, 'Swap a bit of cereal for just one slice?'

He made a rumbling noise she took to be a laugh, and turned to her, his magnificent eyes twinkling into hers.

'I thought you'd never ask,' he murmured, and Kelly felt her bones begin to quiver, and gripped the bench to stop her body falling off the stool.

I can't be reacting to him as a man! she told herself, eyeing him with extreme caution as he placed an equal number of slices on a second plate and pushed it along the bench towards her. I hardly know him, for one thing, and I'm not sure I like what I do know of him, for another. Too authoritarian, too immersed in his work. Such single-minded men made rotten husbands.

Again she gripped the bench. Husbands? And since when had she been considering the men she met in her work as husband material?

'So, how was your day?' he asked, when he'd settled himself on another stool across the bench from her.

She eyed him cautiously, trying to decide if there was anything other than polite interest behind the question, but he was studying his pizza and she couldn't see his expression. With great deliberation, he chose a slice and began to eat.

'It was great,' she began slowly, thinking back to her arrival at Wooli. 'I froze off a few sun-spots, prescribed some antibiotics for a sore throat, checked sugar levels on a diabetic patient, did about forty blood pressures, numerous pulses, looked at old wounds, stitched up a couple of new ones, took out a splinter. . .'

'And?'

He had glanced up, and she knew that he was watching her intently as he waited for a verdict.

'I felt I was wasting my time,' she confessed. 'Not all my time,' she continued, wanting to discuss the situation—not antagonise him. 'The old man you'd mentioned—Gilbert Grace—came in and we brought him back to town, and some of the things I treated Sister Schlect might not have diagnosed. . .'

Again her voice trailed away as she tried to find words to describe an unidentified concern.

'Did you see Marion Wakeley? And old Biddy Rush? Did Rob Bartlett call? And Hugo Watson?'

Kelly didn't reply for a moment, her mind busy putting names to faces and her lips busy with the pizza.

'Yes,' she said, after she'd finished her first slice, 'I saw all of them.' She was puzzled. 'Do they always come? Would you consider them hypochondriacs?'

He smiled at her and shook his head.

'You'd have seen more minor injuries and illnesses today because word gets around when a new doctor is visiting. Many of them came to have a look at you, to check you out!'

'Well, I hope they were satisfied!' she retorted, annoyed to think that she'd been under scrutiny without realising it. She picked up another delicious slice.

'If you could persuade old Gilbert to come back to town with you I'm sure you charmed the pants off the lot of them,' he told her, and she stared at him across the half-raised food, stunned by what seemed like a compliment.

He looked away, back to his plate, and he, too, began to eat again. There was something happening between them that she couldn't understand, something that made finding a place of her own more and more urgent.

'What about the people you mentioned? Are they the local gossips who will spread the word about my abilities?' she asked when the silence became uncomfortable.

He faced her again, his expression serious now.

'No,' he said, 'they're people who have had a bit of trouble coping in the past.'

Knowing this man's casual speech patterns, a 'bit of

trouble coping' could mean anything! She wished that she had a mobile eyebrow she could lift at him.

'Marion was a city girl. She was fine while her children were young and she was kept busy from dawn to dusk, but the kids grew up and didn't need her any more and the isolation got to her. We didn't realise anything was wrong until she took an overdose one day and we had to pump her stomach out and fly her back to the Bay.'

Kelly thought of the plump, jolly woman, and shivered at the depths her despair must have reached.

'Overdose of what?' she asked, to hide the quick lurch of sympathy. If this man, who obviously knew the woman well, could be so clinical about such a desperate action then so could she!

'A cocktail of everything she could mix up in the drug chest. Fortunately, she took enough nasties to make her vomit, and her husband, assuming that she had a bug of some kind, took her to town when the vomiting continued and we flew her out.'

'But she came in to show me a brown age-spot on her hand. I didn't prescribe anti-depressants to her. Should I have?'

She frowned, certain that she couldn't remember seeing any regular prescriptions in the file notes.

Jack chuckled again.

'Coming to town once a fortnight is better than all the anti-depressants in the world,' he told her. 'We decided to put her in charge of the fortnightly women's meetings in the lounge at the hotel. Everyone brings a plate, and the women get together. Rob had a similar problem, and he now organises a local Progress Association. He spends all his spare time writing letters to the government. He gets the men together in the pub and they tell him what they believe needs doing, and off goes another letter.'

Kelly nodded, understanding that the get-togethers were a far better long-term solution than drugs.

'And what of Biddy? And the other man?'

He must have recognised her interest for he pushed his plate aside and leaned a little closer, his hands loosely linked on the bench-top.

'With Biddy it was alcohol—Hugo also. Again, they became redundant—not sacked from their jobs like a city redundancy but unable to work any longer because of their age. With nothing to do, they turned to drink. Katrin took the law into her own hands and forced the publican to limit the amount of alcohol he sold them—'

'How?' Kelly interjected, wondering about the legality of such a move.

Jack's smile lit up his face.

'By telling him that the entire district would know he murdered them if he let them go on at the rate they were going. We helped out by arranging for Hugo to take over our fuel store at the airfield and putting him in charge of getting patients from outlying areas in to town to attend the clinic, so that at least one day a fortnight he had to be sober!'

'And, if there aren't enough patients for him to collect, no doubt Katrin bullies a few extra into coming!' Kelly suggested, catching on to the system.

'Well, sometimes!' he admitted. 'Biddy comes to the clinics to mind the kids while their mothers are seeing the doctor or socialising at the hotel. More often than not, there's a woman who's not feeling well and Biddy goes home with her to give her a hand until the next clinic.'

Kelly looked at Jack Gregory and shook her head. She wasn't certain which was foremost in her thoughts—a mounting respect or utter astonishment.

'You sit here hundreds of miles away from these people, and manipulate their lives!'

'Manipulate's an ugly word,' he argued soberly. 'Like all medical people, we try to understand the underlying problems. It could be compared to Gilbert's enlarged spleen. Specialists will try to find something that is causing the enlargement, and treat the disease rather than remove the spleen.'

She knew what he was saying, and felt admiration for his concern and involvement swell in her heart.

'So you're the outback specialists?' she teased.

'We try to be,' he said soberly, 'but don't think we're miracle workers. It's not always as easy as I've made it sound with those Wooli patients. There are plenty of ills we can't cure out there.'

He sounded depressed by this knowledge and she had to fight an urge to reach out and cover his hands with hers.

Shock at such a thought made her turn back to her pizza, and they finished eating in silence.

'I'll wash the pla-'

'There's a dance at the hospital on Fri-'

They spoke together, drowning out each other's sentences. It made Kelly feel even more fidgety, and she slipped off the stool and carried the plates across to the sink.

'This dance,' Jack continued. 'It's a yearly affair which all the medical people in town try to attend. Gives us a chance to see each other socially and remember what people look like in the flesh, as most of our communication with hospital staff and specialists is by phone.'

He had followed her and was hovering behind with a tea-towel masking one hand.

'I'm only here to fill in. I don't need to meet these people socially,' Kelly told him. 'Please don't feel obliged to include me in festivities.'

He couldn't know that she'd seen this job as a chance

to be on her own—a chance to sort out her thoughts and feelings about the wedding, and to rise above the disappointment of Colin.

'I don't feel obliged to do anything,' he said crossly, then he paused and flapped the tea-towel against his leg for a moment. A strange uncertainty in this man who seemed so in charge of his life communicated itself to Kelly. She took the tea-towel from him and dried the plates.

'I was actually asking if you'd mind going with me,' he muttered. 'As a favour to me. . .!'

The effort of explaining overcame him at this stage and the words dried up.

She turned, frowning, towards him and saw embarrassment and the hint of something else in his eyes. She studied him consideringly. He was a good-looking man in a dark, solidly dependable kind of way—he should have every single woman in the district chasing him. Or was that the problem?

'You're asking me because you need a partner—and preferably one who won't see a single invitation as a life-long commitment.'

She voiced her assumption, but didn't laugh because she knew that would upset him. Besides, something about the situation made her feel more sorrow than mirth.

'I assume there'll be someone at the dance who needs to see you with another woman, or someone to whom you need to prove you have a partner?'

He smiled now, and the tensions seemed to flow out of his body.

'The latter,' he admitted. 'I've just heard that my ex-wife's doing a three-month posting at the hospital up here and, stupid and childish though it might be, I found myself regretting that I didn't have anyone I could take along. Showing off, isn't it? Or is it false pride?'

He held out his hands in supplication, then rushed on.

'Whatever! It was unpardonably rude of me to ask you for such a petty reason. But come anyway? We can go with all the staff—in a group—not on our own. It's usually a good night!'

His eyes begged for her understanding, and she wondered about a woman who could have left a man like Jack Gregory—and left in such a way that he wanted a shield against her. Yet, at the same time, she understood exactly how he felt. She knew she'd get through her sister's wedding in two months time with more pride intact if she had a handsome man by her side. A handsome man by her side?

'Hey,' she said, smiling as casually as she could, considering the sudden surge of excitement she was feeling, 'I know exactly how you feel. How about we make a deal? I'll go to the dance with you if you come to a wedding with me.'

He grinned at her, his expressive eyes dancing with delight.

'Done!' he said, and reached out to clasp her hands.

His touch sent tingling shocks through her system, and she pulled away as he asked, 'Whose wedding?'

'It's my sister's—it's in two months time,' she muttered, and hurried towards her bedroom. But at the door she turned, and looked back at the man who was causing such havoc within her.

'She's marrying Colin Forbes,' she told him, then disappeared into the room.

Why had she told him that? she wondered. Had she hoped that evoking Colin's name might nullify the physical effect Jack had on her? She slumped down on the bed and buried her head in the pillows.

Jack watched her go, puzzled by that last remark. He'd decided—thinking far too much and far too often about his newest staff member—that Colin Forbes had

something to do with Kelly Jackson's defensive attitude—something to do with whatever pain she held
inside her when her body went taut and the lovely eyes
shut out the world around her.

And why had he seized on her suggestion that he had
an ulterior motive in asking her out? Why had he made
Anne an excuse? True, it was always good to have a
buffer between himself and Anne, but he'd asked Kelly
Jackson to accompany him because he. . .

Was attracted to her?

The thought made his brain stop working. He barely
knew the woman! Of course he couldn't be attracted to
her—and yet he hadn't felt so. . . His mind searched
for the word. It was more baffling than confusion,
uneasier than restive. The only thing he did know was
that he hadn't felt like this for years! Certainly not with
any of the women he'd courted sporadically since he'd
moved to the Bay.

He sighed as he turned towards his desk. He had no
time to worry about such things—for a start, there was
the collation of figures for the Australian Council of
the RFDS meeting, then he wanted to get back on to
his survey of MVA's in the area. Motor vehicle accidents were providing more and more work—with more
and more fatalities and serious casualties—and he was
certain that a pattern was emerging within this area. For
a moment he regretted not taking the computer course
he'd been offered last year.

He reached the desk as the mobile phone rang. Pulling
it out of his pocket, he answered then listened to the
clicks as he was switched through to the caller.

'I'm sorry to bother you at home,' Lynne Pearson
apologised, 'but I spoke to your new doctor on Monday
about a Japanese guest who was nauseous and
vomiting.'

Jack glanced up to see Kelly walk hesitantly out of

her bedroom, crossing towards him as if drawn against her will.

'We established she's pregnant, and decided that it was morning sickness. Since then I've been giving her small meals, and plenty of fluids, but she's having trouble retaining food and her husband's becoming hysterical.'

'Is she retaining liquids?' Jack asked, and nodded when Lynne assured him that she was.

'Is she strong enough to get up and walk around? Is she feeling OK in between the bouts of nausea?'

'I don't know,' Lynne replied. Kelly finally reached his desk and stood, like a silent shadow, across from him. He dragged his eyes away from the deep-V opening of her bathrobe, and concentrated on Lynne's voice.

'She's refused to get out of bed since this started. This morning I suggested we fly her back to the Bay to see a doctor, but her husband said she was too sick to travel. Now he's convinced she's dying!'

'He obviously wanted a housecall!' Jack said lightly. He was trying to think through the situation. Was it a severe case of morning sickness or a warning of something else?

'Is she complaining of any pain?' he asked.

'No, I asked him that and he said only sickness, that's all!'

Instinct told him to go, although he knew that it could be a wasted journey.

'We'll come out,' he said quietly. 'Leave her in bed. I'll examine her there first, then we'll fly them both back if it's necessary.'

'For her health or my sanity?' Lynne asked, and Jack smiled as he said good-bye, then asked the after-hours operator to notify the pilot on call that they were off to 'Willowvale'. 'Tell him I'll be at the hangar in half an hour.'

'Was it the Japanese tourist?' Kelly asked.

He nodded.

'Should I have suggested she return to town when I spoke to Mrs Pearson on Monday?'

She looked so concerned—so uncertain for someone he had assumed was full of confidence—that he hastened to reassure her.

'It probably is morning sickness, but we've a communication problem as well as a medical one. If we bring her back to town there are Japanese speaking doctors at the hospital who can sort things out.'

He closed the file on his desk, knowing that he should be on his way but reluctant to leave.

'Can't a nurse do a simple evacuation like this?' Kelly suggested, and, for a foolish moment he wondered if she felt equally reluctant about his departure. 'You're still not well, and being up half the night won't help your recovery,' she added, dispelling any idea that it might be his company she wanted!

'A nurse could go, but. . .'

He hesitated, fidgeting with the edge of the filefolder, unable to explain the part some inner voice played in many of his decisions. She'd think him fanciful!

Looking up, he found her eyes studying him intently then she gave a little nod and finished for him, 'But you think you should.'

She continued to scan his face, as if trying to see beyond it—into his mind. 'Is it because you find it difficult to delegate tasks or an instinctive belief that, this time, you'll be needed?'

He grinned.

'Tonight it's the latter,' he assured her, then he waved his hand towards the piles of paperwork on the desk, 'but you're not far wrong about delegation. I tend to find it easier to do some things myself, rather than take the time to explain what I want done to someone else.'

She walked around the desk and stood beside him—too close, he realised as his gaze slid downwards and he glimpsed the shadowy swell of one full breast where the robe gaped slightly open.

'What are you doing here?' she wanted to know, opening the folder and running a finger down his columns of figures.

'The Australian Council wants a comparison of flying hours with patient consultation hours, and clinic time against evac time. It's all in that letter.'

Unwilling to move, he watched her read through the letter.

'Your computer records could provide this for you,' she told him, lifting the computer print-outs from the file. 'It's a matter of telling the computer what you want it to compare.'

He sighed and waved his hand towards the computer terminal, banished to the floor in the far corner of the room.

'I had a staff member who knew how to tell a computer to do things but, unfortunately, she's now in France. Most of the others are computer-literate but they're not programmers. They are also busy with their regular work so I don't like asking them to fiddle around with an extra project like this. I can do it in my head,' he added with a smile he hoped might stop her thinking that he was a complete idiot. 'It just takes longer!'

He glanced down at his watch, knowing that he should be on his way, but finding it difficult to make the move.

'Do you mind if I have a go at it?' she asked, turning towards him with that challenging gleam in her eyes and a smile twitching at her lips.

She was laughing at him! She *did* think he was an idiot!

'I suppose it can't hurt,' he said gloomily, and turned

away, pausing at the door to add, 'But don't stay up too late. It could be you going out tomorrow night.'

It was an attempt to regather some control over the situation, but when she waved him absent-mindedly away he knew that it hadn't worked.

Damn the woman! he thought as he travelled down in the lift. As well as being distractingly beautiful and—from all reports—a good doctor, she was now going to prove herself a computer-brain! Feelings of inadequacy he hadn't experienced since he was fourteen surfaced. Feelings of inadequacy mixed with the even more disruptive stirrings of desire.

Kelly was pleased when he finally disappeared through the door. It was hard to set her mind to even the simplest of tasks when he was around. Before the phone call had brought her out of her bedroom she'd been trying to read some old Base reports, but had found it difficult to concentrate, knowing that Jack was in the apartment.

She had steadfastly refused to consider why this was so, assuming that her reaction to him was probably a transferred reaction from the recent turbulent events in her life. A psychologist would be able to explain it beautifully!

Now freed from the constraints of his presence, she lifted one of his paper mountains to the floor, then put the computer in its place. If the Base kept halfway decent records she should have these figures for him in a couple of hours. Would he be back in a couple of hours? she wondered, and sensed a wistful longing in the thought.

'You should be in bed,' he greeted her, but he didn't sound as if he meant it! In fact, he was smiling so broadly that she could almost imagine he was pleased to see her.

'Instinct proved correct?' she asked, returning his smile with one of her own.

He nodded, and she sensed the elation of a successful diagnosis.

'She was dehydrated, and the vomiting had become quite severe. I'd vaguely considered a gut obstruction, but felt there should have been pain and more distension.'

'There's less pain and less distension in a higher obstruction,' Kelly pointed out, then considered how she would have reacted. 'But less reason to suspect such an obstruction—especially in a young woman who's unlikely to have had an earlier operation which could have caused adhesions.'

He nodded his agreement.

'I was thinking all of that until I examined her. There was the tiniest mark on her abdomen that could have been from an excised mole. I asked about it, and it turned out she had had her appendix removed when she was only a week old.'

'Appendix adhesions would usually affect the bowel, not the small intestine,' Kelly argued, caught up in the diagnostic game.

'I was content to go with the possibility of bowel obstruction and began massive fluid resuscitation. I knew an emergency operation back at the Bay was a possibility, and the surgeon would want her fluid balance close to normal before he'd operate.'

'And what about the flight?' Kelly asked. 'Wouldn't there be a danger with cabin pressure for a patient with a gut obstruction?'

He looked surprised that she should know this, and she chuckled.

'I didn't have long to prepare, but I did do some homework before heading north,' she told him.

He shook his head.

'I'm beginning to realise that!' he admitted. 'We can adjust the pressure in the cabin. I did suction out her stomach as soon as we were on board, and Eddie flew us back at a lower altitude than normal to minimise any danger.'

Kelly looked up at him, and read the satisfaction that seemed to glow in his eyes and shine in his skin.

'So how do you know you guessed correctly?' she prompted, knowing that there must be more to the story.

'I went up to the hospital and waited while they did the X-rays. It was immediately obvious, with air and fluid pockets showing and that ladder-like pattern of dilated bowel.'

'Had it blocked completely? Was it strangulated?' Kelly asked, picturing the X-rays in her mind.

'No! She was lucky, I guess, that Lynne decided to phone us. I wouldn't have liked her chances if it had gone unchecked much longer.'

He stepped backwards and was about to turn away, and Kelly, wanting to continue this strange interlude of sharing, asked quickly, 'And why were the adhesions so high? Did your clever brain work that out as well?'

His smile broadened, and he shook his head.

'Work it out for yourself,' he told her. 'You're a doctor.'

He walked through to the kitchen and she heard him fill the kettle. She stood up, stretched, picked up the completed sheet of figures she'd copied from the computer screen and followed him.

'Small abdominal space at the time of surgery. I suppose scar tissue could have formed anywhere within it, and the first swelling of her uterus with pregnancy tightened the bands of adhesions and caused the partial obstruction.'

He turned and bowed.

'Smart girl, aren't you?'

'Smarter than you think,' she retorted, and handed him the piece of paper. 'Your figures, sir! They'll be neater when I print them out at the office tomorrow, but at least they're done.'

He gazed at the sheet of paper in astonishment. He'd been working on the damn thing for weeks and she'd produced them in three hours!

He looked up and caught her watching him, and again he sensed an uncertainty beneath the beautiful façade.

'Thank you,' he said, and saw her head dip in acknowledgement, then she lifted it and the blue eyes challenged him.

'I could teach you all you need to know about computer programming to make them work out comparisons for you,' she suggested. 'And in return. . .'

She paused, and he saw the laughter she held within light up her face.

'. . .you could teach me to cook.'

'Deal!' he said, and reached out his hand, but when she took it and her cool, slim fingers pressed against his palm he wondered if it was such a good idea.

CHAPTER SEVEN

KELLY woke and pushed her curtains a little further apart, repeating what was becoming a ritual. Looking out at the cloud-dappled sea, she wondered if she would ever tire of its changing beauty.

You won't have time to tire of it, a voice inside her head informed her. You'll be gone from here in two months.

The thought depressed her—or was it Jack's presence she missed? She'd heard him leave the apartment earlier and knew that he hadn't returned.

She dressed, although it was too early to go to work. Checking that she had the mobile phone in her bag, she let herself out of the apartment. She would walk along the Esplanade and find somewhere to have breakfast.

He was sitting at a table on the pavement, staring out towards the water, and she saw him too late to back away. The movement of the waitress, waving her to another table, made him turn his head and he half smiled, then beckoned her to join him.

'I'm not following you,' she said, unnerved by the unexpected encounter. 'And I'd be quite happy to sit at another table if you'd prefer to be alone.'

The smile widened, but his eyes were serious when he said, 'It's a beautiful morning. Why shouldn't we share it?'

He saw the wariness in her eyes and remembered her precipitous retreat early the previous evening—after. . .

'What did Colin Forbes mean to you?'

The question was out before he realised that he meant to ask it and, judging by the expression of shock in her eyes, it was the last thing she wanted to discuss.

Yet, as he watched a faint trace of colour fluctuate beneath her fine skin, he sensed that she would answer him honestly.

'He is—was, perhaps—my best friend.'

The blue eyes told him quite plainly that the conversation was closed, but his perplexing reactions to this woman prompted him to ignore the warning.

'No more than that?'

He saw her stiffen, then her head tilted towards him.

'Yes, he was more than that, if you must know,' she said succinctly. 'He was the man I always thought I'd marry—one day!'

His stomach tightened with an inexplicable anger and he wanted to belt this man who had brought shadows into those beautiful eyes.

'One day? When he felt like it, I suppose? He kept you dangling on a string until you were what? Thirty-one? Thirty-two? Then calmly turned around and decided to marry your sister! Some hero!'

She had looked quite startled when he'd begun his tirade but, glancing at her now, he suspected that she was laughing at him. The anger escalated into the rage she seemed to provoke so easily.

'And what's so funny?' he enquired through clenched teeth.

'Your image of Colin!' she said, chuckling quite openly now. 'He's not like that at all. It wasn't him, you know, who didn't want to marry earlier. That was my fault.'

She looked at him and the merriment died out of her eyes.

'He wanted us to get married while we were students, but I felt we should go out with other people first, and finish our studies, travel a bit—do some of the things we talked about doing before we settled down.'

'And he went along with this?' Jack growled.

She looked surprised that he should ask the question. 'Of course he did,' she told him. 'He loved me!'

'If he'd really loved you he would have shaken such nonsense out of you, or kissed you so hard that the mere thought of another man would have vanished from your beautiful head.'

She blinked at him and faint colour shaded her cheeks again. He struggled against an urge to lean forward and demonstrate his theory.

'That's ridiculous!' she retorted, but her voice was lacking its earlier conviction. 'Colin agreed with me. He took out other women.'

'Who must have loved it when his "best friend" was introduced.'

Her colour deepened—with anger this time, not embarrassment, he suspected—but the waitress chose that moment to return with Kelly's coffee and toast.

'I don't know why I'm bothering to talk to you!' she snarled at him as the waitress walked away. 'You wouldn't understand!' She glared her defiance, added, 'I loved Colin!' then picked up her coffee-cup and turned to look out across the park, where twisted bread-fruit trees framed the calm water of the bay.

Well, at least she was talking of love in the past tense, he thought gloomily, and ordered another cup of coffee.

Kelly felt a shiver run through her when she heard him speaking to the waitress. She had walked along the front, seeking an interval of peace, and found Jack instead. Every encounter with Jack Gregory was proving disruptive—a sparring match. If she wanted to keep this job—and she knew, in spite of her fears, that she did—she would have to learn to control her reactions to him.

'Did you have a busy night?' she asked, and caught

the look of surprise that flashed into his eyes. 'It's normal conversation,' she teasingly explained. 'The kind of thing most colleagues would have over breakfast!'

He smiled, and the shiver his voice had caused became a shudder.

'Not too busy,' he replied, his lips still twitching with mirth. 'Only one phone consultation after you went to bed. I hope your on-call is as quiet tonight!'

The tension eased and Kelly knew that they would go off to work pretending that they were nothing more than colleagues—which they were, weren't they?

Hope it's as quiet tonight! She remembered Jack's words fifteen hours later as the plane battled through vicious turbulence towards a twelve-year-old boy with a broken leg.

Bill, a pilot she hadn't previously met, had warned her that the trip would be rough and had told her to stay strapped in her seat. She didn't point out that her nervous disposition and unreliable stomach made movement more impossible than unlikely!

The flight was every bit as bad as she'd feared, and by the time the welcome bump of wheels on solid earth told her that they had landed she was drained and exhausted. Again she wondered if she should admit to this weakness and resign. How could she care for a patient when she herself was being sick every ten minutes? Depression dogged her as she pulled the equipment bag out from under the seat and prepared to leave the plane.

'The weather's worsening,' Bill said cheerfully. They had halted near a cluster of lights at the isolated farm airstrip and were disembarking to greet the anxious family, huddled in their truck on the edge of the runway. 'I contacted the family and asked them to bring the boy to us. Let's get him on board, make him comfortable and then get the hell out of here.'

He seemed more concerned about the weather than the patient, Kelly realised, but she had no time to consider the implications of that unwelcome thought. Instead, she greeted the Fletcher family and was introduced to her patient, Barry. She gestured to the father to carry the child into the cabin where she could use a strong battery light to examine his leg.

'How did it happen?' she asked the white-faced boy as she strapped him on the stretcher.

'Fell off the pony and my foot got stuck in the stirrup,' he told her, and she guessed, from the casual way he spoke, that he was trying to make light of it—trying to be a man! Her heart filled with sympathy for him, and she tried to be as gentle as possible while she examined him.

His respiration was good, and there were no signs of shock. On Kelly's advice, his father had administered morphine from the medicine chest—she checked her watch—two hours ago. At least he would still have been in a euphoric haze when they moved him.

'Did your leg twist in the stirrup?' she asked, feeling the heat and swelling around his knee.

'Must have,' he replied, 'because I ended up on my face.'

He pointed to the antiseptic-painted grazes down one cheek.

Bill had settled Barry's mother into a seat, and strapped her luggage into place behind a light protective net.

'We've got to go,' he murmured to Kelly as he squeezed past to reach the cockpit. 'You'll have a few more minutes while I gather speed, but once we're up you're to stay strapped in and do anything you need to do from your seat—understand?'

She nodded. How could she tell him that she'd been so paralysed by sickness on the way out that movement had been the last thing on her mind? And if the trip home promised to be worse. . .

'It's likely to be a spiral fracture,' she told the boy, projecting all her mental efforts towards her patient. 'The bones broke under pressure when your leg twisted. Your knee could be dislocated as well, but all I can do for the moment is splint it to keep it immobile. The doctors at Rainbow Bay will X-ray it, then set it for you. Looks like crutches for you for the next few weeks.'

Knowing how kids loved being on crutches, she smiled at him and an answering smile lit up the pale, freckled face.

The plane was accelerating along the strip, and she stood, feet apart to steady herself, and slid a long metal splint under the injured leg, then padded the leg to prevent pressure points forming. Bill called to her to strap in, and she felt the lurch as they lifted off the ground. She slid the first of the bandages that would hold the splint in place beneath it, and sat down, her fingers fumbling with her seat belt.

The destabilising effect of the wind was immediately noticeable, but Kelly leaned across the narrow aisle and continued to work, her mind totally focussed on her patient.

Once she was satisfied with the splint she tested Barry's peripheral pulses on both sides, feeling for any change in rate or rhythm—particularly in the one beyond the injury. She jotted notes on the new file, then pinched his toes.

'Feel that?' she called to the boy over the noise of the engines.

He nodded, and muttered an obligatory, 'Ouch!'

'Any numbness or tingling in your toes? Pins and needles?' she asked, and watched him shake his head in response. Another lurch, another note on the file. Then back to her patient, checking skin colour this time—pallor or redness in the extremity of the injured leg that might indicate the onset of complications.

'How's the pain?' she asked, and saw him grimace, then shake his head.

'Can't feel a thing,' he joked, but she knew that the alleviating effect of the drug would be lessening. Still, if there was internal swelling, causing problems in the leg compartments and compromising blood vessels or nerves, he'd be in too much pain to be joking with her.

She made a final note, then began her assessment again, knowing that the situation could change very quickly. Repeated assessments were the only way to pick up early warnings of complications.

The difficulties of conducting a proper examination from a seated position with an aisle between herself and her patient came home to her when she moved unwarily and winced at a sudden pain in her side. The pressure of her body, straining against the seat belt, must have caused a bruise, and the arm of the seat had pressed on the tender spot.

'My professors at medical school would be horrified if they could see me doing this,' she told Barry, leaning over to pinch his toes again. 'They had very definite ideas on where and how one should stand to conduct a patient assessment.'

He smiled at her, but she could see that the effectiveness of the drug was wearing off. She checked the time, trying to remember how long the flight out had taken. She was loath to attempt to give even a subcutaneous injection in a plane that was lurching and bumping as badly as this one. Also, there was the consideration of surgery to reduce the fracture. The anaesthetist would have to take into account the presence of a recently administered painkiller.

'We should be nearly back to the Bay,' she told him, praying that she was correct. 'Think you can you hang in without more pain relief?'

She went on to explain why, and he seemed to understand.

'I'll be OK,' he assured her, then he nodded towards the rear of the plane, 'but Mum might need an ambulance as well.'

Kelly had been so concerned with the boy that she hadn't given his mother a thought. Mrs Fletcher had chosen a seat at the rear of the cabin, and Kelly turned towards her.

She's as sick as I was on the flight out there, she realised, as the woman bent forward, her head in her hands, and moaned pitiably.

As I *was*! The words repeated themselves in her head, and she realised, with a surge of utter delight, that her stomach hadn't rebelled once on the trip back. Wheels hit the tarmac and screamed their protest as Bill applied the brakes, but confidence that she could do her job under difficult circumstances was sending the blood rushing through her veins.

Wait till I tell Jack, she thought excitedly, then remembered that he didn't know of her fears or her weak stomach. What's more, he would expect her to do her job so would see nothing miraculous in it!

Her elation disappeared, but she smiled and joked with Barry as they taxied to a standstill. When she heard Bill's 'OK' which meant that they could unbuckle she went back to see Mrs Fletcher, offering her damp tissues for her face.

When Bill opened the door she saw the rain lashing against the plane, and the red tail-lights of the ambulance backing up as close as possible to the bottom of the steps.

'Grab one of these big umbrellas,' Bill suggested,

handing one to her and one to Mrs Fletcher. 'Let the ambulance guys manage the stretcher, and you hold the umbrellas over the lad. Just be careful you don't blow away once you get outside the door.'

They battled their way across to the waiting vehicle. Barry forgetting his pain in the drama of the wet and windy transfer.

'We don't fly in rougher weather than that,' Bill told Kelly after the ambulance had departed and she was tidying the cabin.

'You don't fly!' she echoed incredulously. 'I hadn't thought about weather restrictions. What happens if there's an emergency?'

'Sometimes one of the other bases can cover for us. We can be grounded by the weather here on the coast when conditions beyond the ranges are quite placid. During the cyclone season the entire north can be affected, but the cyclonic winds usually abate quite quickly. We do whatever we can, but in bad weather we have to tell ourselves that the people out there are no worse off when we can't fly than they would be if we didn't exist.'

It seemed a strange philosophy, but Kelly could understand the frustration the staff must feel if they were grounded by the weather when an emergency occurred within their area.

She carried plastic waste bags, laundry and the equipment case back to the hangar, feeling the rain soaking into her skirt in spite of the umbrella Bill held low over her head.

'I thought summer was the wet season up here,' she complained, shaking the water from her legs.

Bill smiled at her.

'That's when you see real rain,' he told her. 'Not just weak, annoying stuff like this. Rain's OK for flying, although the clouds cause turbulence. It's the wind that keeps us on the ground, and this one's picking up.'

He'd been correct, Kelly realised next morning when she left her rain-washed view and walked through to the kitchen to find Jack, peering morosely through the window. She approached uncertainly, the conversation about Colin still lingering in her mind.

'We're grounded,' he grumbled before she had time to ask why he wasn't on his clinic flight. 'Nick can't get back from Wyrangi, although, I suppose, if the weather's all right further north he could go straight to Coorawalla from there and do my clinic.'

He brightened perceptibly, and Kelly realised that he was totally focussed on work. She smiled with relief— their 'colleague' relationship was obviously intact— then watched as he punched some numbers into the mobile phone that was never far from his hand.

'Eddie? It's Jack.'

How unnecessary, Kelly thought, knowing that she would recognise his voice immediately. She poured cereal into a bowl and listened to one side of the conversation, which had begun with a request for a weather report.

'So, if it's clear at Coorawalla you could take Nick and Jane across there when they finish.'

There was silence as Eddie responded, then Jack explained, 'Well, usually he'd be finished by lunchtime. You might ask him what he's got scheduled and get back to me. By tomorrow afternoon the wind should have cleared here, and you can fly straight home.'

Another pause followed, then Jack laughed.

'I'd be delighted to take Susan, but I'll get the Air Traffic Authority to fax me through a weather report at midday and if you're using bad weather as an excuse to dodge the dance I'll tell her!'

'Eddie not a dancing man?' Kelly queried when he turned, still smiling, towards her.

'He loves a party as long as no one asks him to get up and move about,' Jack replied. His smile faded as he walked back towards the window.

Kelly, following his movement, realised that the blind was up, and had been since she had walked into the kitchen. Glancing towards the living-room, she saw the curtains still closed, but she knew that her fear must be diminishing because the windows hadn't immediately drawn her attention.

'But, by the look of things, he won't be making excuses,' Jack remarked. 'It seems set in. If you look at the way the palm trees are swaying the wind's getting stronger not lighter.' He turned towards her. 'You'd better come to work with me. The fewer cars on the road the less risk of accidents.'

She accepted the offer of a lift quite gratefully, but declined to look down at the palm trees. One step at a time was enough in her battle against her acrophobia.

Instead she looked at Jack, professionally this time, but when he turned and caught her speculative gaze embarrassment surged through her.

'A few days of inactivity might do you good,' she said unsteadily, her head held high in an effort to hold her ground.

'Inactivity? Let's get to work, woman, so you can see the kind of ''inactivity'' grounding the planes produces.'

By mid-morning she knew what he was talking about, and by six o'clock that evening she was exhausted. The phone had rung constantly, and she had coped with consultations and evac calls while Jack had spent the entire day on the phone, arranging alternative transport for urgent cases.

She had heard his voice in the background, cajoling

commercial airlines into taking patients south to the city, soothing the nursing sisters at small bush hospitals who would have to keep their Priority Two and Three patients a little longer and swapping favours with other Bases when an emergency meant that a plane must be despatched from elsewhere and a patient air-lifted to care.

'Sally will drive you home,' he told her when he stopped by her desk with what must have been his tenth cup of coffee for the day.

'You're staying on?' she asked, and saw his decisive nod.

'But what can you do here that you can't do from your home?' she demanded, worried by the strain that had reappeared on his face.

'I can keep in better contact,' he pointed out. 'This weather is extending up and down the coast and about a hundred kilometres out to sea. We have people scattered along that coastal strip whose only contact is by radio, and many of the prawning and fishing boats rely on radio. They could be riding out the storm in a sheltered bay, but in bad weather anything can happen.'

She wanted to argue that there were other listening posts who could alert them but she sensed his need to be involved, and hesitated.

'I could stay with you,' she suggested, but he shook his head.

'One of our former radio operators is coming in to push the buttons and twiddle the knobs for me,' he said, and the quirky smile on his face made her heartbeat flutter.

'What about food? You'll need to eat.' She didn't know why she was persisting, but she felt uncomfortable about leaving him. Or uncomfortable about going back to his apartment while he remained at work?

'Are you offering to cook?'

His smile broadened and the fluttering became a drumming that coursed through her blood.

'I've already ordered a pizza,' he added. 'Now, if you've no further arguments, you're keeping Sally waiting.'

A smile stretched his lips and warmed his whole face. It sent sparkles of delight tap-dancing their way down her spine and she stared at him in horror, unable to believe the effect this virtual stranger was having on her.

'Pity if the weather stays like this for the Hospital Ball,' Sally remarked as they drove through the wind- and rain-swept streets.

'Hospital Ball? Jack said it was a dance—he made it sound like a casual country hop.'

Sally took her eyes off the road long enough to roll them upwards in mock horror.

'Men!' she muttered in a worldly way. 'Did he happen to mention it's black tie?'

Mentally Kelly discarded the white cotton frock she'd decided to wear, pleased that she'd found out now and not when she walked into the affair. Black tie meant formal, and a formal gown had been the last thing on her mind when she'd packed and headed north.

'With any luck, the weather will break and I'll be called out on an evac flight.' Nick was actually on duty, but if he'd done a double clinic trip she could offer to swap!

'Oh, you should come—it'll be great fun,' Sally told her, pulling up in front of the apartment building. She turned and studied Kelly for a moment. 'If you need something to wear, my sister's about your size,' she said. 'She's got a few ball dresses, and I know she'd be happy for you to try them and wear whichever one you fancy. I'll bring them to work tomorrow.'

Satisfied with this arrangement, she nodded for Kelly

to get out and, amused by the management skills of the teenager, Kelly obeyed.

By the next evening the rain had lessened but the winds kept all but the big commercial planes on the ground. Kelly had left work late again, and now stood in her bedroom, surveying herself in the first of Sally's sister's evening gowns.

It was black, a colour she favoured for evening wear, but Sally's sister was either a smaller build or an exhibitionist for the fitted bodice pushed Kelly's breasts into such prominence that she blushed at her own reflection.

Unzipping the second gown from its cover, she shook her head. Exhibitionist! she decided, as she pictured herself in the tiny red satin mini with an absurd train trailing from the back of the waistline.

'How are you going in there?' Jack called. 'Do any of them fit? I rather liked the red one.'

The entire staff had been treated to a showing of the gowns—fortunately on their hangers—earlier in the day.

'I daren't try it on,' she called back. 'I know it would confirm Mrs K's original impression of me. I'm up to the purple.'

She heard him chuckle and her heart hummed to itself. She ignored the inner music, having decided that these reactions to Jack must definitely be a reflexive hangover from Colin's defection.

She pulled on the third gown, knowing that it would have to do. Susan would be wondering if they'd forgotten her.

It was a dark shot taffeta, with little puffs of off-the-shoulder sleeves and a neckline that seemed modest in comparison to the black creation. At least her nipples were decently covered and stiff petals flared up from beneath the bustline to mask the bare skin above nipple-level. She studied her reflection, and nodded. Glancing downwards, the swell of visible breast made her feel uncomfortable, but from front-on she appeared well-covered and quite demure.

The skirt flounced out and bunched in places, and she patted it down. It wasn't a style she'd have chosen herself but it looked all right. She grabbed her handbag and hurried out, but a long, slow whistle from Jack brought her to an abrupt halt.

She tugged at the petals, then realised that he was looking at her legs. Following his riveted gaze, she realised that the material was not casually but strategically bunched, and yards of black-stockinged leg were visible on each side.

'Oh, it's impossible!' she grumbled. 'I'm sorry, but I can't possibly go to this affair. When I said yes I thought it was a casual get-together type of thing.'

She didn't add that the sight of her 'partner', resplendent in his dinner-suit and snowy white shirt, had confused her so much that her legs were shaking.

'A deal's a deal,' he said implacably, then he stepped forward and took her hand. 'I'm sorry about the whistle, but you look great.'

'And half-naked,' she mumbled. 'I was more worried about the top half, and didn't notice how short the skirt was in places.'

She twisted her torso, trying to see if her legs looked as visible as she thought they did.

'I wouldn't worry about the top half either,' he murmured, his voice deeper than usual.

Looking up again, she saw him studying her and realised, belatedly, that if she could glance down and see acres of bare flash so could he.

'Come on!' he said, a warning note in his voice. 'You can't back out now.'

She turned back towards her bedroom and, in the

mirror, caught a glimpse of a stranger in a dark taffeta gown. Something snapped inside her and she straightened slowly, taking on the character of the person in the mirror.

'Back out? Me?' she teased, and she reached out to take his arm. 'Never!'

Jack glanced down at her and saw the deep blue eyes sparkling with challenge.

This was a mistake! The realisation thudded into his brain at the precise moment that desire began to stir, and dormant urges came thrilling back to vibrant and demanding life.

He dragged his attention away from her eyes, then found himself looking at the soft swell of creamy-white breasts.

'We'd better leave *now*,' he said, emphasising the last word so strongly that her forehead creased slightly.

'Well, I'm not holding you up,' she told him and, tucking a small black handbag under her arm, she led the way towards the door.

He'd seen more of her legs when she'd ambled around the apartment in shorts after work, he told himself as he forced his gaze from the flash of black stocking. He followed, but reluctantly, every instinct warning him of trouble.

CHAPTER EIGHT

KELLY'S new persona flirted shamelessly, chattering to the hospital staff Jack introduced and fluttering her eyelashes at the outrageous compliments the younger, more exuberant personnel were paying her. She was aware of his hovering presence at all times, and decided that he must be staying close to her so that his ex-wife—when and if she arrived—would realise they were together.

From time to time she turned to him, laughing up into his face at a joke someone had told or touching his arm when he spoke. The woman could be any-where—could be watching right now—and Kelly knew that she had a part to play—a part she was enjoying playing!

Someone pushed into the circle of people, and she stepped back a little, missed her footing and stumbled against Jack. He put an arm around her waist to steady her, and she felt the heat of his hand burning through the thin fabric of her gown

'Don't overdo it!' he growled into her ear, but he didn't release her and she nestled closer, a peculiar sense of security easing into her mind.

'So, Jack, how are you?'

The voice was beautifully modulated, clear as a flute, and it brought the chattering group to immediate silence.

Kelly felt Jack's fingers clench, and his arm stiffened so that she was held more tightly.

'I'm fine, Anne,' he murmured. 'Yourself?'

Bravo, Kelly thought. That showed just the right amount of polite disinterest.

118

'Extremely well,' the tall blonde replied, her eyes assessing Kelly before returning to focus on Jack. She smiled, revealing exquisite white teeth, and added, 'Although I don't think much of your weather. People come north in winter for sunshine.'

Kelly felt the tension in the skin and bone and muscle beneath his civilised suit, and anger flared.

'Oh, dear, Jack, you really should have organised the weather better,' she murmured, looking up at him and batting her eyelashes in mock disapproval.

The tension eased, and she thought she felt his chest move, as if he might be laughing silently. He grinned down at her, then turned back to the newcomer.

'Kelly, this is Anne Harrison. Anne, Kelly Jackson.'

Anne Harrison nodded regally at Kelly, who was busy concealing her delight that the other woman was called Harrison, not Gregory. She must have remarried.

The band, which had been enjoying a break, began to play a slow tune. Ned Cummings, an eye specialist who had joined their group, turned to Anne and asked her to dance. Kelly watched incredulously as the woman shook her head, then held out her hand towards Jack.

'I'm sorry, Ned, but this tune has sentimental attachment for Jack and me. Doesn't it, darling?'

The deliberately provocative voice twisted like a knife in Kelly's stomach, and the 'darling' increased her fury. She stiffened, then slid her arm around Jack's broad back and smiled sweetly at the other woman.

'Oh, what a shame,' she said in a syrupy tone she didn't recognise as her own. 'You might have to miss out this time. He's promised faithfully to have every slow dance with me.'

She looked up into Jack's face with what she hoped was the correct amount of blind adoration, and added, 'We move so well together—in every possible way!'

Jack made a noise that could have been a smothered

growl or gurgle of laughter but Kelly was busy, trying
to push his body towards the dance-floor, and couldn't
stop to analyse it.

It had been a growl! She knew immediately they were
safely away from 'that woman' and she had insinuated
herself sufficiently close to him to make it look as if
they were dancing. Looking up into his face, she saw
that his eyes were stern, the golden lights that danced
when he was happy completely blotted out by the green.

'Every slow dance—you promised!' she whispered,
her lips twitching into what she hoped was an
engaging grin.

'How come no one's strangled you before this?' he
asked grimly, but his hands had gentled on her back
and they *were* moving together very successfully.

For a few moments she let the music carry her into
a fantasy of—

'Why Anne Harrison? Has she remarried?' Speaking
of his ex-wife should keep all unwanted thoughts at bay.

His feet faltered for a moment, but he responded
calmly. 'She always used her maiden name—for professional reasons, she said.'

His voice revealed neither disappointment or pain—
yet the woman must have left some lasting impression
on him for him to have asked Kelly to accompany him!
She puzzled over it for a while.

'Was that OK with you?' She couldn't help probing,
although every instinct told her to drop the subject.

'Whatever she wanted was OK by me at that time.'

The flat statement told her far more than she wanted
to know—told her he must have loved Anne very
deeply when he married her. Why else would he have
not cared whether she took his name or not? She glanced
up into his face, searching for remnants of the pain he
must have suffered, and pressed a comforting kiss
against his neck.

'You are tempting fate, lovely doctor,' he muttered, his hands tightening against her skin.

She let her eyelids drift downwards, shutting out the repetition of the warning in his eyes, and gave herself up to the rhythm of the music and the feel of his solidity and warmth against her body.

'The tempo has changed,' he said firmly what seemed like an age later. Snatched from a dream of strange fulfilment, she shifted so that she could look up at him, and tried to blink away the fantasy. But the golden flecks were back in his eyes and silent messages, too old for words, seemed to be passing between their bodies.

Shocked by the implications, she pulled away hurriedly, then realised that she didn't want to go back to the others—didn't want to be part of a crowd, or face Anne Harrison again. She began to sway and swing to the up-beat number.

'Come on,' she tempted, 'show Sally and the other youngsters what a couple of oldies can do.'

'I knew you were a troublemaker the moment I set eyes on you,' he grouched, but his feet picked up the rhythm and she was soon mirroring his movements as he took the lead.

The music swirled around her, faster and faster, until—her feet flying in a final flourish—she was ready to collapse. The beat slowed then stopped, and she slumped against him and felt his arms tighten around her body. Beneath her ear his heart drummed, fast but steady—nothing like the mad cavorting of her own unreliable mechanism.

She reminded herself why he'd asked her—it certainly wasn't because he was attracted to her in any way! But she did have a part to play!

She eased herself out of his embrace.

'I need fluid replacement, and fast,' she told him, then, aware of Anne watching from the sidelines, she stretched up and kissed him quickly on the lips. 'Prefer-ably non-alcoholic, if this medical gathering can supply such a thing.'

She added the qualification to cover the shock she'd felt when her lips had brushed across his. It had sparked like a flash-fire, and still tingled on her skin.

He kept one hand tucked into the small of her back and steered her off the floor, but his silence was omin-ous and she knew that she'd probably overplayed her part.

Sally distracted them both by asking Jack if Kelly didn't look filthy in the taffeta dress.

'If ''filthy'' in your dreadful teenage slang means exceptionally attractive, then, yes,' he told Sally before allowing her to cajole him back onto the dance-floor, first checking to see that there was a jug of mineral water on the table and finding a clean glass for Kelly.

She sat back with her cool drink, thankful that the rest of the RFDS staff were up dancing. She really had to sort out these reactions to Jack—had to think them through and find some rational reasoning behind them before the situation erupted out of all control.

'So, how long have you and Jack known each other?' Anne Harrison slipped into the chair beside her.

Don't overdo it, Kelly warned herself, before reply-ing casually, 'Oh, I don't know. It seems like for ever.'

Anger flickered in the woman's cool grey eyes.

'And do you consider he's finally over the grief of Carrie's death?'

Had Carrie been their child? Shock held Kelly riveted to her chair.

'I think so,' she said carefully, fighting off images of Jack's despair. Was the death of a child something you ever got over? Surely not! Yet she knew Jack had been in Rainbow Bay for seven years—alone, as far as she could gather—so it must have been that long ago.

'Well, you'd know,' the other woman was saying caustically when Kelly dragged her mind back to the conversation. 'When we were married he couldn't say a sentence without mentioning her name.'

Maybe not a child!

'I thought the best thing I could do was to let him get away—to a place like this where there were no reminders of her. I told him at the time it was the only way, although he was devastated at having to leave me as well.'

Kelly battled to make sense of the words. Somehow, they didn't equate with her instinctive knowledge of Jack Gregory. True, he was a sensitive man who would mourn the death of a loved one deeply and sincerely, but she couldn't imagine 'her' Jack dancing to any woman's tune!

Unless it suited him!

She nearly laughed out loud as relief began to edge away her uncertainty. Was the dedicated, hard-working, totally focussed boss of the Base manipulative enough to have let Anne think the move north was her idea?

'Of course, I'd have followed sooner only I had my specialty work to complete. . .'

If she'd really loved him, would the desire to pursue a career have stopped her following him? Kelly wondered.

She considered what she would have done herself, while Anne sent one poisonous conversational barb after another—'Jack would whisper. . . Jack used to say. . . When we made love. . .'—into her skin, and Kelly found herself praying that the choice had been his. Even devastated by grief, he must have been able to see this woman for what she was, and learnt some manipulative skills from her.

The music stopped and the RFDS staff made their way back to the table. Kelly watched Jack and Sally approaching. His head was bent to catch Sally's conversation, then he straightened up and his laugh rang out.

Something inside Kelly shivered to life and she looked at him again as an idea so momentous—so ridiculous—formed inside her head.

She knew that Anne had risen at his approach, but she couldn't move, paralysed by the realisation that she'd never looked at Colin and felt such an overwhelming surge of emotion. But she'd loved Colin, and assumed that one day they'd. . .

'My dance, darling!' she heard Anne murmur. There was a deep-toned rumble which she took to be Jack's reply. He'd have to rescue himself this time. If he wanted to be rescued! she thought, noticing the way Anne was batting her eyelashes at him.

'Are you going to let her get away with that?'

Sally's abrupt demand brought her out of her miserable reflections on love and lust and unlikely attractions. She glanced towards the dance-floor and saw Anne draped full-length along Jack's body.

'No, I'm not!' she muttered, springing out of her chair and marching around the table towards Bill, who was on his own because his wife had gone south to visit a sick parent.

'This is a rescue mission,' she told him as she dragged him to his feet. 'I'm supposed to be protecting Jack from "that woman" and I've let him down. Now, dance me over close, let him introduce you to her then cut in.'

Bill looked confused but he seemed to have grasped the important bits so she let him lead her onto the dance-floor.

'And don't take no for an answer,' she warned him as they approached the pair.

Jack's good manners did the rest. As Kelly had predicted, he stopped dancing and introduced his ex-wife to Bill then politely handed her over when Bill asked her to dance.

Kelly saw Anne's anger in the rigid way she moved, but Jack's eyes were dancing as he took her in his arms and murmured, 'Your doing, I take it?'

She nodded, too full of emotion to speak, then remembered that she was supposed to be playing a part. Could her act conceal the unfamiliar turmoil within her body?

'I relaxed my guard there for a few minutes,' she responded, looking up into his face with a repentant smile. 'But I came good in the end, didn't I?'

He stared at her for a moment, then frowned and shook his head as if to clear it.

'You did want rescuing, didn't you?' she asked as panic jolted her heartbeat.

'From Anne?' he asked, still regarding Kelly with a puzzled frown.

'No, from the Abominable Snowman!' she growled, unsettled by the sudden change in his behaviour. 'Of course from Anne! Isn't that why you brought me along tonight? Wasn't that the whole idea?'

He shook his head again, but she didn't think that he was replying to her questions.

'Let's just dance, shall we?' he muttered, and drew her closer until she could feel his body beneath the soft black wool of his suit. In her mind the dance became a prelude to love. Jack's hand held her against him in an erotic *pavane* as their feet barely moved on the polished floor and their bodies swayed together to the slow beat.

Cautionary voices inside her head were drowned out by the incandescent joy she was experiencing. She gave herself up to the music and to the sensations intensified by it as Jack held her in his arms. It was Bill who had given Jack back to her, and he who broke through the brittle shell of her enchantment.

'The answering service just paged me. MVA involving two cars on the old surveyors' road. I phoned the weather bureau and they've given us clearance—the wind's dropped enough for safety. We can land on the road, but we'll need two planes—they're talking up to ten injured, some of them seriously.'

They walked back towards their table while Bill was speaking, and Kelly saw Susan on her feet and knew that she had guessed what was happening.

'You get out to the airport,' Jack said to Bill. 'Call Michael to take the second plane.' He picked up his mobile from the table and prodded a memory button, then identified himself and listened quietly. Susan joined them, a dark silk cape around her shoulders, ready to go as soon as Jack gave the signal.

Word must have filtered through the dancers for Leonie also appeared, and rested her hand on Jack's arm. She waited until he folded up the mobile, then said, 'We're short of nurses. Jane's in Coorawalla and Jenny's off duty. Do you want me to come?'

Kelly was surprised by the offer, then realised that Leonie must have had medical experience before she became Base Manager.

'No, if it's as bad as it sounds we'll need a doctor on each flight. Susan can go with Kelly and Michael, and I'll fly out with Bill.'

Kelly was pleased he hadn't suggested that they all go in one plane—the wind had dropped, not disappeared! It didn't occur to her that it might be policy until Susan explained as they drove, in their finery, towards the airport.

'If something happens to one plane, and it has to turn back, you have a second medical team on the way in the other.'

Kelly was still considering the implications of 'some-thing happens' when Jack began to list the equipment they would need to load.

'A Thomas pack on each plane, fluid and blood prod-ucts, extra spinal stretchers, cervical collars and splints, extra large-bore needles—'

'We'll cover the needles and drugs if we take two emergency packs on each plane,' Susan pointed out, and Kelly felt the tingling of anticipation.

This drive through the darkened streets was the open-ing scene in an emergency dash that might save any number of lives. The extraordinary challenge of the Flying Doctor Service struck home and she realised that she could grow to love this job with as much passion as Jack had for it. If she ever conquered her fear and the air-sickness!

They ferried equipment out to the planes while Bill and Michael conducted their pre-flight checks.

'I don't know what Sally's sister will think if I wreck her ball-gown,' Kelly muttered to Susan when they finally boarded for the flight.

'There are overalls back there. We'll change on the flight,' she told Kelly, dropping into a seat and strapping herself in.

'Aren't you going to sit up front?' Kelly asked. She wouldn't be able to hide her weakness from Susan if they were sharing the cabin.

'No, Michael will want to tell me all the latest details of his wife Melissa's pregnancy, and I'd rather sleep. Wake me when he gives a ten minutes to landing call and I'll get changed then.'

She closed her eyes and, to Kelly's astonishment, her shoulders were soon rising in the unmistakable rhythm of sleep.

They lifted into the air and she forgot Susan, feeling only gratitude—as her stomach rebelled with its customary violence—that they had left the ball before supper was served.

She was weak but in control by the time Michael warned them that they were coming down. The turbulence had stopped once they crossed the mountains, and she'd had time to seal her tell-tale paper-bags in a plastic waste container before she woke Susan.

Seemingly unhampered by the restricted space, Susan made her way to the rear of the cabin and returned with two blue sets of overalls.

'They only come in medium and large,' she apologised to Kelly. 'You'll have to roll up the legs and arms, but they're more practical than shot taffeta when road accident victims are bleeding all over you.'

Kelly accepted the proffered garment and stood up unsteadily to strip off her gown and clamber into the heavy cotton suit. She realised from Susan's detachment when she spoke of their potential patients that she was preparing herself for the likely horrors ahead. All medical people who dealt with road accident victims had their own defence against the horrific injuries they had to witness.

They strapped in again while the plane touched down then piled equipment by the door, ready to go into action the moment it was opened.

An ambulance was already at the scene, and Kelly was surprised until Susan explained that it was from a nearby mining camp.

'The camp's in rugged country, so the mining company put in a good road and a fully equipped ambulance. Having it means any injured employee can be rushed to the nearest landing ground for an emergency airlift to town.'

Grabbing the equipment cases, she and Susan hurried towards the side of the road where lights running off motor vehicle engines lit up the tangled wreckage.

Michael followed them with the big Thomas pack which contained enough equipment to stabilise a life. He dumped it on the ground within the circle of light, then returned to the plane for stretchers.

'Airways, breathing, circulation,' Susan was muttering to herself, and Kelly knew that they were the first priorities in any accident.

'I've got oxygen on the worst of them but I only carry three kits,' the ambulance man said as Kelly drew closer to where a number of the wounded were lying some distance from the wreckage. 'There are three or four still in the cars, but I thought I was better tending to this lot.'

Kelly nodded. Susan had headed for the group who were working to extricate the others from the tangled metal, and Kelly signalled for her to stay there. If the trapped people were still alive they would probably need fluid and painkillers to keep shock at bay until they could be freed.

She knelt beside the first victim, and began to work. There was no time for files—these people would be tagged with bright cards which detailed what had been done for them and passed on to have their full assessments done in hospital.

'Do we try to take them all back at once or can we begin to ferry them out?' she asked Jack when he appeared by her side a little later. 'I've two suspected internal bleeding I'd like out of here ASAP.'

He nodded and said, 'Start ferrying. I'll send Michael over. You right to travel with them?' he added as an afterthought, and she ignored the protesting lurch of her stomach and agreed that she was 'right'.

'Have you any walking wounded?' Michael asked as he joined her, and bent to help the ambulance driver lift a patient onto a stretcher.

'One suspected fractured collar-bone. He was thrown

out and seems to have landed on a remarkably hard head. No sign of concussion, but I'd be pleased to see him in hospital for observation and the collar-bone is an ideal excuse.'

'We'll take him as well, then,' Michael told her, as she handed a fluid bag to one of the many helpers who had materialised out of the darkness. She showed the man how to hold it above the patient while they transferred him to the plane, then crossed to where a young man was kneeling anxiously above her second urgent case.

'Is she a special friend?' she asked, and saw the moisture in his eyes when he nodded.

'Well, how about you go with her to the hospital?' she suggested, explaining that the plane was leaving almost immediately then flying back to help evacuate the others.

When Michael returned with the second stretcher, she helped to transfer the young woman onto it and handed the fluid bag to her friend.

'Keep it high,' she warned him, before turning to the other patients they would leave for the next trip.

Two had suspected spinal injuries. She had checked the cervical collars the ambulance man had fitted and supervised the sliding of spinal stretchers under them. They were warm, breathing oxygen and immobilised, with fluid and pain-killers dripping into their veins. They would be classified as 'delayed' on a triage system—while the two she was taking first were in the 'immediate' class, where life-threatening injury was correctable if treated within one to two hours.

She left the ambulance man in charge and ran back to the plane.

'Strap in for landing,' Michael called, and Kelly jerked her head up and peered out of the window, unable to believe that they could be back at the Bay already. She saw the runway lights and realised, without a flutter of concern, that she was looking downwards from what was still a great height.

It's mind over matter, she marvelled, strapping in but leaning forward to keep one hand on the thready carotid pulse of the less stable patient.

'Hang in there,' she whispered to him, willing him to live, as urgently as she had throughout their journey.

She saw the flashing lights of the ambulance as they taxied towards the hangar, and men appeared in the doorway as soon as it opened. The paramedics accompanying the ambulance took one look at the red tags and their movements quickened, so that the two patients were gone before Kelly fully realised it.

She helped the young man down the steps and across to the ambulance, while the bearers slid the vehicle stretchers into place on the plane.

'Check the stretcher locks,' Michael told her when she came back on board. He closed the door, pushed past her to the cockpit and she felt the wheels roll beneath them before she'd had time to test the first stretcher.

They touched down on the familiar roadway. Most of the onlookers had departed, and the scene was less brightly lit than before. Jack came to meet her.

'I've sent the "query spinals" and two other minor injuries back with Bill and Susan, but we've a major problem.'

His face was tight with concern and she was about to reach out and touch his arm when he did exactly that to her.

'We've one fellow still trapped. We've cut away what we can and we've jacked up the weight that's been holding him in and propped it so it's safe, but one foot is caught in tangled metal that must be part of the engine mountings. We haven't a tool that will cut it and can't use an oxy without the risk of burning him or setting fire to petrol. . .'

'You'll have to amputate?' she asked, knowing that it was the final option in these situations.

He turned her towards him and looked down into her face, so gravely concerned that she wanted to reach up and wipe the lines of strain from his face.

'I've tried,' he told her with a savage edge to his voice, 'but I can't get in there. I'm too damn big!'

'I can do it,' she faltered, keeping her eyes steadily on his—although her pulse was racing at the thought. 'Is he stable enough to withstand the shock? Can we get at his upper leg and wrap it to reduce bleeding? A tourniquet above his ankle won't do much good. . .'

She was thinking aloud, already planning what would have to be done, so the quick hug, and the husky, 'Well done,' he muttered in her ear confused her.

She backed away from the distraction of his presence.

'I'd like to have a look or feel around in there first,' she told him, and he led her to where the remaining spotlight illuminated the mangled metal remnants of two vehicles.

The man was unconscious, slumped in what remained of the front passenger seat after the rescuers had cut most of the car frame away from him. One leg was bent at an unnatural angle away from him, and the other disappeared under what had been the heavy engine of the four-wheel-drive his driver had slammed into.

There must be another car engine there somewhere, Kelly thought as she eyed the props installed to keep the weight from dropping down on her. She took a deep breath and slid her torso forward into the narrow aperture, one hand running down the man's leg so that she could find where the obstruction was.

'He's barefoot, which is one blessing, and the

obstruction's high up on his foot just beneath his toes,'
she reported as she backed out.

Surveying the instruments Jack had assembled for
her, she ignored the tremor of despair they caused and
added, 'The light's no use as I can't see anything anyway. I'll have to do it all by feel. The metal's so tightly
embedded in his skin that the blood supply would have
been cut off to his toes after the accident occurred—'

'So he'd have lost them anyway,' Jack assured her,
seeing the pain beneath the valiant exterior she was
showing to the men gathered around the scene.

He watched her grasp the sharp-toothed blade, and
knelt beside the opening with clean dressings in his
hand. He touched her arm and she looked up at him,
her eyes huge in her pale face and the tiny freckles on
her nose accenting her concern and compassion.

'Say when and I'll get the men to lift him immediately. I'll dress the wound when we get him free,' he
told her, pretending to a calm he was no longer feeling.
He'd have given his own right toes, and possibly a few
fingers as well, to spare her this.

Then she grinned at him and raised a thumb, before
dropping to the ground and wriggling her way into the
space. He tried to picture the operation so that he could
time it and be prepared; tried to imagine her lying full-
length on the ground, her arms stretched beyond her
head and aching as she manipulated the saw-toothed
knife. But images of her face were all he could conjure
to the screen of his mind—images of her quick smile,
her blue eyes and the way her skin wrinkled on her
forehead when she puzzled over something.

'We've got him, boss!'

Had he heard her call? He slapped the dressings on
the wound, and held them there while the men placed
the injured man on the waiting stretcher.

He saw Michael bend to help Kelly to her feet, but

he couldn't go to her as he was too intent on flushing the bloody foot, then padding it, binding it and checking his patient for signs of deepening shock. He worked steadily, even while the man was carried to the plane. But when Michael came on board, one arm steadying Kelly's wavering footsteps, he paused to glance at her—taking in the blood that stained her overalls and the sheet-whiteness of her face.

'Take her up front, Michael,' he ordered harshly. 'She's done enough for one night.'

CHAPTER NINE

KELLY couldn't remember the journey home, but woke in her own bed next morning, heavy-headed and dis-orientated. Memories of the accident flashed through her mind, but they were diminished in importance by recollections of being held in Jack's arms.

Was she remembering the vivid sense of belonging she'd experienced when they'd danced together or had he lain with her and kissed her, talking soothingly until she had fallen asleep in his arms?

She brushed her fingers across her lips. They tingled slightly but that told her nothing. Recently thoughts of Jack set up tingly responses all through her body.

And where did Colin fit into all this? Why was his name recurring so vaguely?

She tugged at her hair, hoping that pain might jolt her brain cells back to life, then concentrated fiercely—trying to piece together words and images.

'I'll stay with you,' she seemed to remember him saying. 'I'll hold you and kiss you, and comfort you, but I'm not Colin, Kelly—I'm not a substitute for some-one you imagined you loved.'

Had she dreamt it? Dreamt her lips stumbling over the word 'substitute' as she tried to deny his assumption?

She sat up, shocked by the next images flashing in her mind.

Surely she hadn't turned to him and offered her body—hadn't asked him to love her instead of comforting her?

'Not tonight, my lovely one,' her dream lover had said. 'Not when you don't know what you're doing.'

135

She remembered being held a little away from his body, then his hands turning her so that she was curled against his stomach.

'Don't think I don't want you,' the deep voice had murmured in her ear, so clearly that the words were repeating themselves in her head. 'But I want you wanting me as a person, Kelly,' he'd said. 'I want you coming to me—Jack Gregory—willing to give yourself, one hundred per cent, because it's me you want, not an escape from the past or a small adventure to lead you into the future.'

It must be a dream, she told herself, but she was reluctant to leave the safety of her bed—reluctant to face the man who had featured so realistically in that dream.

The apartment was uncannily silent when she finally emerged from the bedroom.

A note from Jack explained that he'd given her a sedative on their return from the accident, and he was sorry he'd had to leave her but he had a business appointment.

She felt depressed, and knew that it was probably a reaction to the sedative—as were the dreams! She showered and dressed, then pushed the curtains a little wider apart. She would open the living-room curtains as well, she decided, as the sparkling water eased the anxiety enough for her to risk a downward glance.

Her stomach still swooped with fear, but she knew that her reaction was less extreme. Besides, Jack had put up with her eccentricity for a week without complaint. That was long enough!

As she contemplated the same view from the living-room the sunshine beckoned to her, and she hurried back to her bedroom, thrust the mobile she must carry as second on call this weekend into her handbag, picked up the keys and left the apartment.

A brisk walk along the foreshore convinced her that she'd imagined the conversations and cuddles with Jack. Delayed shock and the sedative had combined to play tricks on her mind.

Yet, as she gazed out at the beauty of the sunlit bay, she wished that he was there to share it with her—and wished that the dreams had been true!

I must need food, she told herself. Why else would I be thinking of him that way? She crossed the road, making for the line of pavement cafés that offered coffee and light snacks throughout the day.

She paused at the first place, where she and Jack had shared breakfast, but it was too crowded, so she moved to the next, where potted plants separated the tables into little oases of green.

Perhaps here, she thought, then her heart skidded to a halt.

Jack Gregory sat at one of the inside tables, his head bent confidingly close to a blonde who looked, from this distance and half-hidden by greenery, remarkably like his ex-wife.

So that was his 'business', Kelly thought bleakly, hurrying along the road with little concern for fellow pedestrians. She found a vacant table some distance away and slumped into a chair.

The strange, exciting memories she'd woken with had been snatched away from her. If she'd needed proof that she'd imagined the entire episode then surely his head bent towards his ex-wife was enough.

She gazed blankly at the menu, knowing that any amount of coffee and any number of cakes wouldn't cure the silly ache around her heart.

Kelly avoided Jack as much as possible after that—not difficult when their clinic flights kept them apart the following week. On the days she was at the Bay she would go straight to the hospital after work and sit with Gilbert for an hour, then eat in the cheerful anonymity of the big staff canteen, while her lunch hours were spent searching for somewhere else to live.

The search was unsuccessful, so she was pleased when she heard that he was flying south to a conference on Friday evening.

'Nick's on call tonight, and you're on Saturday night and Sunday. I'll be back before six on Sunday to take over from you.'

He stood in the apartment doorway, his suitcase in his hand, and frowned at her.

'I think I can manage to remember a two-day roster without your help,' she told him waspishly. She was battling an almost overwhelming desire to pretend they 'belonged'—to lean forward and kiss him goodbye!

'Yes, well. . .'

His hesitancy was strange in such a controlled man, but she couldn't stop to analyse it. The dreams she'd had after the accident kept recurring in her mind—so vividly that she could feel his skin on hers!

She glared at him, wanting him out of here—now! Before she weakened!

'Get going,' she urged. 'Your precious Service must have survived your absence before. It can't possibly fall apart in two days.'

'I wasn't thinking of the Service,' he retorted, still frowning, but he didn't tell her what was in his thoughts.

'Any messages for your family?'

It was her turn to frown.

'You are from Brisbane, aren't you?' he persisted. 'I'll have spare time, and could give your folks a call.'

'Why?' she asked bluntly—too shocked by this sudden interest to consider politeness.

He shrugged.

'You're new up here. I thought I'd offer, nothing more.'

She studied his face and sensed an uneasiness in the eyes that didn't quite meet hers. It communicated itself to her, filtering through her skin. More memories of the strange dreams rose in her mind, exciting her unreliable body.

'It was a kind thought,' she muttered, 'but I'm not exactly at the end of the earth. I can phone home whenever I like.'

'Yes, well. . .'

'Go!' she ordered, as the tension between them reached snapping point.

'I'm going,' he grumbled, without moving. 'Kelly, I. . .'

He looked at her, his eyes no longer avoiding hers but seeming to see right into her soul. She was held motionless beneath that steady regard, but the silent communication of those eyes could not be right. They barely knew each other!

'We'll have a bit more time together next week,' he said at last, then he turned and walked away.

'It's a sick child on a property west of Castleford,' an anonymous voice told her. 'I've paged the pilot and will switch you through to the caller.'

The woman sounded calm as she reported her son's symptoms of lethargy and a sick stomach, but Kelly realised that she could be holding her fear at bay until help arrived.

Then she began to cough, and Kelly waited until the spasm had finished before saying, 'Are you OK yourself? That cough sounds painful.'

One sympathetic word and the calmness disappeared.

'I'm feeling dreadful,' the woman wailed. 'I've been sick all week, and the baby's coughing as well. Now

Toby looks as if he's fading away and won't eat or play or do anything, and my husband's taken cattle to the market.'

'Is there someone on the property you can leave in charge if we fly you all back to town?' Kelly asked.

The crying became an occasional snuffle.

'I can get my dad to come over,' she said. 'He lives next door, but my brother runs the place now. Dad would be glad of something to do.'

'Well, you organise him and pack up what you'll need for all three of you,' Kelly told her. 'We're on our way.' She used the phrase that had eased the fears of so many people over the years since the Service had begun.

It was three o'clock on Sunday afternoon and her third evac call since she'd begun duty at six the previous evening. She thought for a moment then dialled the nurse's mobile number, reaching Susan.

'I think I might need a hand,' she said and explained the situation.

'Poor woman! I'd be glad to come along,' Susan said. 'See you at the airport.'

As Kelly drove along the now-familiar roads she wondered about the reserves of stamina it was possible to find when duty called. In spite of her fears, she felt a rush of adrenalin every time she headed for the airport, and her mind seemed to sharpen as she anticipated the challenge that lay ahead.

She arrived at the airport to find Allysha and Susan already there.

'So Jack's worst fears are about to be realised,' she said in greeting. 'An all-woman flight crew.'

The other two laughed, then Susan explained that Michael had been on duty but Melissa had finally gone into labour and he was at the hospital.

'So, let's show them what the women can do,'

Allysha said cheerfully as she made her way up to the cockpit! 'It's still windy so stay strapped in,' she reminded them before disappearing from view.

'I get airsick,' Kelly admitted, before she humiliated herself in front of Susan.

'So did I for the first year,' Susan consoled her. 'Cleared up after I had the kids, strangely enough.'

They talked about her teenage twins and Kelly's youngest brother who was the same age, and once Kelly was over her initial bout of sickness the flight passed quickly.

Allysha touched down on the dirt strip, built within walking distance of the property's main buildings. Susan let down the door and led the way out, with Kelly following.

A woman waved to them from the wide verandah of the house, but as Kelly approached she could see a tired slump to the thin shoulders and a pallor in the pretty face. The house had a patchy garden, but beyond it stretched miles of treeless plain without a sign of human habitation.

'Next door' could be twenty miles away, Kelly realised, and looked again at the woman who had made this her life.

'I'm Linda French, and I don't usually weep on the phone,' she assured them, then turned aside to cough again. 'It's this cough—it keeps me awake at night, and Toby being so. . .'

She frowned and hurried them inside to where a small boy sat at a table, gazing blankly at a bowl of jelly that was melting as he watched it.

'We've all had this cold,' his mother explained, 'but it's hung on longest with him, and he's lost weight.'

A baby started crying, and Susan followed Linda from the room while Kelly knelt to examine Toby. His skin was hot and dry, his cheeks flushed, and, although he responded to her voice, he didn't seem able to concentrate for long.

She examined him carefully but his breath had given her a clue. She pulled a bottle of glucose test strips from her bag.

'I need some of your blood,' she explained to Toby. 'A little prick on your finger.'

She swabbed the pad on his forefinger but nothing, not even the emerging bead of blood, interested him. Pressing a drop onto each coloured segment, she timed the reaction before blotting it, then timed it again for a visual reading.

Acidosis was present, but was it life-threatening? Physical signs showed dehydration, but glucose balance was the most urgent consideration. She called to Linda.

Lead in gently, she warned herself, remembering that Linda was far from well.

'Can you tell me a bit about your family's medical history?' she asked, her hands continuing their search for other clues. 'Anything running through your family, or your husband's family, that we should consider?'

Linda thought for a moment.

'Pete's dad's a diabetic,' she said, 'and my mum died of a heart complaint. Are those the kind of things you need to know?'

Kelly nodded.

'Hereditary heart disease is something the family should be aware of, but it's not the problem now. Has Toby been tested for diabetes?'

The woman grew even paler, and Kelly rose to stand beside her.

'It's something that can be regulated quite easily these days,' she assured her. 'If that is the problem then you and Toby will be taught how to test his blood and how to treat any imbalance, but the most important thing now is to get him to town where he can be stabilised and a programme worked out to suit his needs. Now, is he on any regular medication?'

Her mind scouted through the things that reacted with insulin, then Linda shook her head.

Susan returned, holding the baby on one hip.

'Will you begin treating him here or on the plane?' she asked, and Kelly thought for a moment.

'On the plane,' she decided. 'I'll carry him across while you help Linda do whatever she has to do before we leave. I'll send Allysha to give you a hand with the bags.'

'Allysha's here already,' a cheerful voice called, and they turned to see the pilot in the doorway.

'We're taking you to town on the Flying Doctor plane,' Kelly said to Toby, who showed no sign of interest or objection when she picked him up. 'Your mum's coming too, and the baby. Won't that be fun?'

Who are you kidding? his look seemed to say, so she set off with him perched on one arm and her equipment case in her hand.

Once on board she settled him on the stretcher, explaining about the straps to hold him in place and the equipment hanging above him.

'First, I put this little mask on your face to help you breathe.' She fitted a child's mask to the oxygen outlet, and gently manoeuvred it onto his face.

'Next, I'm going to put a needle in your arm so we can put some medicine into your blood. It will hurt a little when I prick you, but I'm sure you're a brave boy and it's better than having to drink it.'

There was not a flicker of response, and barely a flinch as she found a vein and inserted a wide-bore catheter. With his blood pressure and pulse out of the normal range she had to assume dehydration of up to twenty per cent. Estimating his weight, she worked out an initial dose of insulin and administered it as an intravenous bolus, then piggybacked the insulin to the isotonic fluid line and adjusted it to give a constant concentration once the initial dose had acted.

She had finished by the time the others came on board, and helped Susan settle into a seat with the baby in her arms.

'Once we're in the air I want to listen to your chest and check your blood pressure,' she told Linda. 'You sound as if your need for medical treatment is equal to Toby's.'

Linda smiled wanly, settling into a seat across from her little boy and reaching out to take his hand.

'He'll be fine,' Kelly assured her, and saw the pale face light into a grateful smile.

When Allysha called that they could move Kelly examined Linda, confirming that she was healthy in spite of her cough. She checked on Toby, testing his glucose levels for the second time and seeing a slight drop in the intensity of the colour on the test strip.

A faint change in the rhythm of the engines' beat made her look towards the cockpit and, at that moment, Allysha turned her head.

'Could you come through here, Kelly?' the young woman asked, and Kelly, instinctively aware of a problem, dragged her feet reluctantly towards the cabin.

'See that light,' Allysha said, pointing to a light blinking in the midst of a mind-boggling array of dials and knobs. 'It's a warning of a low oil pressure mix in one engine.'

So here I am, with my fear of heights, about to fall out of the sky! The thought flashed through Kelly's mind in a microsecond, so she still caught Allysha's next words.

'I'll have to close the engine down before the problem causes enough damage to shut off power completely. Do you need any electrical equipment?'

Kelly shook her head, and Allysha continued, 'Good, because once the engine's shut down I'd like to switch off the electrical circuit which includes the cabin lights and electrical outlets to preserve power in the battery while we descend.'

She was speaking so calmly that Kelly found it hard to believe that it could be a real emergency.

'The plane will stay up on one engine,' Allysha assured her, 'but it takes a bit to hold it in asymmetric flight, and we could have a problem once we begin to descend.'

'Do tell me!' Kelly muttered through parched lips. She watched Allysha pull the power lever towards her.

'I'm feathering it now,' she said. 'I'll explain about landing shortly. Do you want to tell the others?'

Kelly thought for a moment.

'Susan has flown so much that she will probably know there's something wrong. And if you turn off the cabin lights Linda will presumably guess there's a reason. You promise me we'll come down safely and I'll go tell them.'

Allysha chuckled.

'I'm not promising anything, apart from the fact that I'll do my best.'

Kelly was leaving the cockpit when she added, 'And, if Susan can manage back there, I'd appreciate your company up here.'

Great! Now I'm going to watch us crash! Kelly thought, but a fatalistic calm had spread through her and her voice was steady as she squatted down in the aisle beside Linda and Susan and explained what was happening.

'We can land quite safely on one engine,' Susan announced in her firmest 'pilot's wife' voice. 'Linda, you take the baby, and I'll get some pillows to hold when we brace on landing. Toby will be safest of us all because he's strapped down.'

She patted Kelly on the arm.

'I'll manage here, but I'm sure Allysha could use some moral support.'

Kelly found herself moving back towards the cockpit, the situation taking on the unreality of a dream.

Allysha was speaking calmly into the radio, notifying Rainbow Bay control tower of the problem.

'There's a private strip ten minutes from your present position if you need to make a forced landing, but we'd prefer you to come in here where we can have emergency equipment standing by.'

'Wouldn't we be better getting down onto the ground as quickly as possible?' Kelly asked, when the technical part of the conversation had concluded.

'Not really,' Allysha told her. 'If we can limp to the Bay they will clear the runways for us, and keep other traffic in holding patterns until we touch down. The problem with private strips is that once we start our descent we haven't the power to climb again.'

'So if there's anything on the strip we hit it?'

'Exactly!' Allysha said, and to Kelly's amazement she actually smiled.

'There's also the fact that it's hard to hold the plane steady. Every time I lower the power on our approach, or when I put down the flaps or landing gear, it changes the dynamics. If I can't hold her steady and a wing clips the ground I'd rather have the airport fire engines standing by than the odd kangaroo or emu we're likely to find on the private strip.'

'You've another alternative strip at. . .'

Kelly heard the radio give bearings, and realised that they must have passed the first possible emergency landing place. The officer guiding them in from the control tower was offering new alternatives all the way.

The thought cheered her and she actually peered downwards and saw the tops of the mountain range, the Great Divide, that stretched down the eastern coast of Australia.

'We'll soon be over the cane fields,' Allysha told her. 'Nice flat ground and tall waving cane to cushion the impact.'

Kelly hoped she was joking, and left her seat to go back and check on Susan and their passengers. The baby was back on Susan's lap and Toby was sleeping and, as far as she could tell in the uneven light, his skin looked less shrunken. She took his pulse and blood pressure, pretending that this was a normal day and a normal flight. She wrote on his file, checked the flow of the fluid and insulin then returned to the cockpit.

'Ten minutes, then we'll start to descend,' Allysha warned her. 'Has Susan explained to Linda how to brace herself?'

'They're both practising in there,' Kelly replied, 'complete with pillows packed around the baby. Susan has shifted to an aft-facing seat so she can stay upright and hold him, and monitor Toby and Linda at the same time.'

Kelly was surprised that her voice sounded so calm, but she was even more surprised to find that she could look out of the window without a hint of the fear which had dogged her all her life.

'Could you shut down the oxygen?' Allysha asked, and Kelly heard the first evidence of strain in her voice.

'Hey, we'll make it,' she said lightly. 'I haven't been miraculously cured of my fear of heights and flying for nothing. Fate must have an airborne life in store for me.'

She saw Allysha smile, and moved back to switch off the oxygen and remove Toby's face mask. She watched him for a moment, then hurried to the rear storage area and found more pillows. Using these, she padded the straps that held him on the stretcher, then she checked the cabin for any loose equipment that might be flung around.

'I've secured everything,' Susan said calmly and Kelly grinned at her, thankful for her competence.

'I think I'll disconnect the drip,' Kelly said as Allysha called that they were beginning the descent. 'If we hit roughly the tube could tear from his arm.'

Susan nodded, and Kelly removed the IV line and the catheter. She could restart the infusion in the other arm once they were on the ground.

She could feel the roar of the labouring engine drumming beneath her feet, and heard Susan order her into a seat.

'I'll go back up with Allysha,' she heard her own voice say and, after checking that Linda was bent over with her head braced against her cushioned knees, she walked forward and strapped herself into the copilot's seat.

'Are you really afraid of flying?' Allysha asked, and Kelly realised that she needed some sense of normality even though her entire being was concentrated on keeping the plane balanced.

'Petrified,' she said and felt her stomach lurch as they turned, dipped for an instant, swayed and then settled again at a lower altitude. 'Coming up here even for two months must rank as one of the most masochistic acts in the history of womankind!'

She continued to talk, her gaze fixed on the movements of Allysha's hands. She chattered on about her life, about the embarrassment of having the man she'd always thought she'd marry—one day—deciding to marry her much younger sister instead, and the need to escape the awkward silences and embarrassed remarks of her friends and family.

She hadn't meant to tell anyone up here about her

private life—her past—but if Allysha wanted conversation while she tried to save their lives then the least
Kelly could do was provide it!

'Brace now!' Allysha called, and the runway came
up to meet them.

Kelly watched, fascinated by her own perverse reactions to this drama. The wheels bumped, then steadied
and she saw the tears stream down Allysha's face.

'You were wonderful,' she said, patting the pilot's
arm in reassurance. 'Now all you have to do is stop
the thing!'

She glanced outside and saw the fire truck, keeping
pace with them, then the familiar curve of the RFDS
hangar came into view and she felt a sense of homecoming sweep through her body.

They slowed and crept towards their apron. The
ambulance was there, so some time during all the drama
Allysha had called the Base.

They stopped and Allysha slumped forward, her head
resting on her arms. The door must have been opened
from outside for suddenly Nick was there, lifting his
wife's head and hugging her to him.

Kelly squeezed past him, and began to unstrap her
patient. Susan was herding a shaky Linda out of the
plane, and willing arms were reaching out to support
both women. The ambulance men came in.

'I'll carry him out,' the first of them told Kelly. 'Is
he ready to go?'

She nodded, and picked up the fluid bags. 'I'll start
another drip before you head off,' she said and followed
the man to the waiting vehicle. It was dusk, she realised,
and wondered if their landing would have been more
difficult in the dark. One day she'd ask Allysha.

She fitted another catheter and started the drip, wrote
up the medication on the child's file, checked that Linda
was OK and had somewhere to stay if she wanted to

leave the hospital, then she climbed wearily out of the ambulance and headed back towards the plane.

'Everyone else is getting a hug,' a deep voice murmured, and she turned to see Jack, standing in the deep shadow beneath a wing. 'Would you like one?'

He waved his hand towards the hangar where Susan was locked in Eddie's arms, then towards the rear of the plane where Nick held Allysha tightly while she spoke to Jeff, their mechanic, and some official-looking men in uniform.

He opened his arms and she moved into them, feeling the solidity of his body and the warmth that emanated from it. He even smelled comforting! It was her last conscious thought.

CHAPTER TEN

'SHE gets airsick every time she flies?' Jack asked incredulously. 'And why did no one on the staff think fit to mention this to me?'

Kelly's sudden collapse had filled him with terror, although he kept telling himself that it was only a faint—and understandable considering what she'd been through. He'd caught her before she fell and managed to lift her in his arms, but his mind had gone blank. Fortunately Allysha had hurried over and suggested he put her on the stretcher in the plane for a few minutes.

'Well, Michael said she was always OK on the flight home—that she was never sick when tending a patient,' Allysha explained, snapping on the battery-operated lights while he lowered his white-faced burden very gently onto the stretcher.

'She's terrified of heights, I knew that,' he muttered, 'and I was too stupid to connect the two.' He sighed, then turned back to the pilot.

'I'll take care of her,' he said. 'You finish up with the officials then get off home. Jeff can put the plane away. Tell Susan to go as well.'

Allysha hesitated, looking down at Kelly.

'She talked to me all the time,' she whispered. 'Sounding so calm and unconcerned, although she must have been terrified.'

Jack nodded, and rubbed at Kelly's cold hands while Allysha hurried back outside.

Her dark eyelashes fluttered like tiny fans against her cheeks, then her eyes opened slowly. Relief coursed through him and, with it, the irrational anger that the easing of unbearable tension brings.

'Why on earth did you take on a job like this?' he demanded, reaching forward and gripping her shoulders, but resisting—just—the urge to shake her. 'Normal people who are afraid of flying don't become air hostesses or pilots or flying doctors.'

The blue eyes regarded him with such astonishment that his fingers relaxed, and he slumped down onto the edge of the stretcher and drew her up into his arms.

'Oh, Kelly!' he whispered, running his hands over her back, needing to feel the substance of her.

She absorbed the comfort of being held close against him, comfort and a sense of belonging—which she knew was ridiculous, but she'd worry about that later.

They got a message to me on my flight north,' he muttered. 'I was so worried—and there wasn't a damn thing I could do. I thought I'd go mad—just thinking about the danger you were in.'

It was a plural 'you', she knew that, but for the moment she wanted to take it as singular—wanted desperately to know that someone cared about her.

She lifted her head and rubbed her cheek against his chin. Their lips brushed, felt the special sensitivity of skin and returned to touch again—to cling, then press, demanding knowledge and communion. As the kiss deepened Kelly twisted in his arms, her body folding into his with a pliant meshing of flesh and bone.

An almost soundless whimper of delight sneaked from her throat, and her blood tingled at the deep, rumbling growl of reply. Her hands moved against his chest, while his found the fullness of her breasts and sent them into an anticipatory frenzy with feathery touches and tender pressure.

Excitement she had never experienced sprang to life in every cell, and warmth stole over her as she relished this new awakening. Her body felt as if it were unfolding, unfurling itself for the very first time and filling to overflowing with the uncharted sensations his kiss was arousing.

He would be a wonderful lover, she realised as her body responded so slavishly to his.

Lover? her mind echoed. A man you barely know? And what about Anne? But her body ignored the silly queries and softened in his arms as her receptiveness intensified to an almost painful need.

Voices intruded into the fantasy, and she was slammed back to reality. She pushed herself awkwardly away, and patted ineffectually at her clothes while her mind searched frantically for a way to handle this situation.

Keep it light! her head warned. You have to work— and live—with him.

'So, do you seduce all your staff on this stretcher, or just the ones who faint in your arms?'

His fingers bit into her shoulders, but she accepted the pain as a sign that he was gathering himself together again.

'It's more than a simple seduction, and I think you know it,' he said, his voice deepened by the power of the emotion that had erupted between them.

She shook her head, suddenly exhausted and so confused that she couldn't think at all!

'I don't know anything,' she muttered, and pushed away the large hand he extended to help her to her feet.

He growled again, a different kind of growl, and she was glad that she couldn't make out the words. But, when she did stand, she was grateful he'd kept an arm around her, for her knees wobbled stupidly and her bones had turned to cotton wool.

He helped her across the tarmac and into his big silver Range Rover, ignoring her protests about being able to drive. She sank back in the warm leather seat and closed her eyes, her mind replaying—not the drama of their landing—his kiss.

'Do you want an early night or would you like to go out to dinner?' he asked, pulling up outside the apartment.

'You're on call, you don't want to go out to dinner. It's a waste of money if you have to go before you've eaten.' She knew she sounded belligerent, but she was becoming increasingly uneasy in his presence—uneasy because of the awareness that tugged at her skin and etched itself like acid along her nerves.

'Well, thank you for pointing that out,' he snorted, then he pushed himself out of his seat, slammed the door and strode around to open the door on her side.

She could feel the waves of anger flowing from him. Anger and desire—a potent mix that strained her resistance to snapping point.

'Look,' she told him when they were being whisked upward in the lift, 'I came up here to escape, to get away from someone I thought I loved—someone I thought loved me.'

She heard him mutter under his breath and reached out to touch his arm, wanting his attention, his understanding. She looked into his eyes, darkly green this evening, and knew that her own would reflect her pleas.

'If I fall into bed with you I won't know why. I won't know if it's just a rebound thing, something I'm doing to soothe my pride or boost my battered ego, or if it's a real attraction to you. Can you understand that?'

He looked down into those mesmeric eyes and tightened his lips.

Does the why matter? he wanted to ask, but he knew that it did. She was repeating the very thing he'd said himself—when she'd turned to him after the road accident, wanting a physical release from the horror of her memories.

And he'd fallen into bed that way himself once—seeking relief from grief and pain. It had been the greatest mistake of his life, and the scars had taken a long time to heal—mainly because he'd hurt another person. Badly!

'Jack?'

He looked down into her face as she prompted his answer. It was still pale from strain, the scatter of freckles so clear he wanted to touch—to count—them.

His mind cleared and he knew, without doubt, that her answer to the 'why' mattered to him as well; knew he wanted this woman in a way he'd never wanted a woman before—but he didn't want her uncertainty.

And he certainly didn't want her if all he meant to her was a substitute for Colin Bloody Forbes.

'I suppose I can,' he agreed angrily as the lift doors opened on his floor. 'Although, in my opinion, you can't have been too heart-broken over this other chap if you're reacting to me the way you are!'

'Well, thank you, Dr Fix-it!' She flung herself out of the lift and strode down the passage towards his door. She had her keys out and the door open before he caught up. 'I'm going to have a shower,' she announced in lofty tones, 'then. . .' she paused and swung around to glare defiance at him '. . .I'm going to have a bowl of cereal and go to bed.'

'And he can't have been too good a lover either,' he thundered, infuriated by her attitude and his own frustration, 'or you wouldn't have responded to my kiss like a starving man falling on food!'

She spun around, and her eyes flashed sparks.

'Colin and I were never lovers!' She spat the words at him. 'We were best friends and we loved each other. We always knew we'd end up together one day.'

He was confused at first, then felt an overwhelming joy as the words sank in. He smiled, sensing victory.

Once she'd realised that the wretched man had only been a good friend she could begin to consider her own feelings again.

'Oh, we did, did we?' he murmured, emphasising the 'we' just enough to turn her anger towards Colin this time.

But the ploy backfired. She looked at him blankly for a moment, then an expression so bleak that it cut through him like a knife filled her eyes and her shoulders slumped as she turned away and walked through into her bedroom.

So the bastard had hurt her that badly! His fingers clenched into fists as he thought of the physical damage he'd like to do to Colin Forbes.

Kelly removed her clothes with fingers shaking from the strain of the emotion-charged day.

Of course she'd loved Colin! Still loved him, in fact. They had both gone out with different people over the years—even fancied themselves in love from time to time—but their friendship had survived all competition and grown into a deeper bond than shared sexual pleasures.

Until Libby had returned from overseas—all grown up. . .

She shook away the thought, trying to rationalise the present—not the past.

Her response to Jack Gregory had been purely the result of the tension she'd been under—tension she'd hidden from Allysha, Susan and Linda.

She looked out through the gap in the curtains to where the moon was rising, lighting a silver path across the water. Forgetting Jack and her doubts and torments, she walked slowly across to the wall of glass, steadied herself against it with one hand and peered experimentally downwards.

Her stomach heaved and she shrank back—not quite

cured, after all! Not cured of her fear, not cured of her love! She sighed and blinked away the sudden moisture in her eyes, knowing that tears would be of self-pity—nothing more!

She hurried into the bathroom and ran the shower as hot as she could bear, then stood under it until the tension in her muscles had given way to lethargy. Drying herself sketchily, she pulled on her bathrobe. She'd have something to eat then go straight to bed.

'I've stir-fried some chicken strips and vegetables. I thought you might need more nourishment than cereal.'

She looked at this man who had made her so angry, and saw the anxiety in his eyes and the uncertainty in his tentative smile.

'It smells delicious,' she murmured, and slid onto a stool at the kitchen bench, returning the smile with a trembly effort of her own. He turned away—abruptly, she thought—and served up their meals, but by the time he joined her on a stool across the bench he was his cool composed self again.

'I can't employ you and not have you fly,' he said. 'We need the three doctors to remain effectively operational.'

So, he'd been anxious about her ability to continue working, she realised, and disappointment scrunched its way into her heart.

'I have no intention of not flying,' she retorted, straightening up as she sensed another battle.

'But you can't keep going if you're sick every time,' he told her, lifting one hand and running it through his hair. 'I should have put two and two together when you admitted you were afraid of heights.'

'I'll get over it!' she argued stubbornly. 'And I've proved I can still do my work. I'm never sick when I have a patient to tend.'

He frowned at her and, unable to bear the intensity of his scrutiny, she ducked her head and concentrated on her food.

'But why, Kelly?' he demanded. 'Why put yourself through this torture? Weren't there other locum positions you could have taken that would have got you away from that. . .fellow? Why choose something you knew would be sheer torture for yourself?'

She glanced up and saw that he was genuinely interested. Something inside her gave way and she knew that it was time to talk about it.

'It was like starting again,' she explained. 'I decided that if I'd been wrong about Colin I might have been wrong about other things.'

She grinned at him in another mercurial change of mood, then shrugged.

'That was the first great revelation because I'd always believed that I knew everything and I'd rarely considered that I could be wrong.'

He watched the self-mockery dance in her eyes and knew that he loved her. But he'd rejected her once—although he wasn't certain that she remembered it—and frightened her with his passion earlier this evening. He must let her come to him next time, free of the past and the doubts that haunted her.

'Coming here meant having to deal with something else, apart from getting over my. . . Apart from getting over Colin.'

Again he was struck by the valour of this woman he'd only recently met.

'You'd be so terrified about flying you wouldn't have time to think about him. Was that the scenario?'

'Something like that,' she admitted, smiling across at him. 'Stupid, wasn't it?'

'Pretty stupid,' he agreed, fighting an almost overwhelming urge to walk around the bench and gather

her into his arms. 'I'm no psychologist but I'm not entirely certain that the way to tackle fear is by head-butting it.'

'Well, it's my way!' she told him cheerfully, and tucked into the rest of her dinner.

Her way, too, to stand alone now. He could understand that desire because for so long she'd had Colin—she'd known him for ever, he remembered her saying—and he'd let her down. Even her family, happily preparing for the wedding she'd thought would be hers, had—in their way—betrayed her.

He began to talk about the schedule for the following week, and watched her relax as she questioned him about the places she would be visiting on the clinic flight and become more and more engrossed in his stories of the work he loved.

'Will you be able to keep to the rosters with that plane out of action while they fix whatever's wrong with it?' she asked, and he was pleased by the steady timbre of her voice.

'They can drop the engine and put a new one in in a matter of half a day,' he replied, 'but I guess it will need a major service after that so the mechanic can check the shut-down didn't cause damage to anything else.'

An evac call interrupted them, and he touched her lightly on the top of her head and said, 'Have an early night,' before hurrying back to the airport.

Kelly took herself willingly to bed, and made herself think about the future, not the past, as she drifted off to sleep. She was scheduled for a day in the office tomorrow, then off to Castleford the following morning. Another new experience!

'Right, computer lesson number one this evening,' Jack announced when he appeared in the office late next afternoon. 'I'll take home the work I've been doing on the MVAs and we might use it as an example.'

Kelly spun slowly around. Her heart had lurched in a most unfamiliar fashion when she'd heard his voice, greeting Sally in the radio-room, but she'd had it back under control until he walked past her desk and smiled at her.

'I'm going up to the hospital to see Gilbert after work,' she told him, trying to ignore the messages his gleaming green eyes were transmitting.

'Then I'll go home and have dinner waiting when you return from your mission of mercy.' He sighed theatrically. 'How pleasantly domestic it all is!'

'Don't kid yourself,' Kelly retorted, but her lips had twitched into a smile and a warm glow had replaced the lurching sensation in her chest.

She turned back to the Castleford files, but her mind was more on the shuffling movements from the desk behind her and the muttered conversation he seemed to be having with himself. Something about 'preferring the company of an old reprobate like Gilbert to that of a fine upstanding man like himself'.

Biting back a gurgle of laughter, she found herself realising how easy it was to laugh in Jack's company. Had she and Colin laughed together much? She thought back. . .

'Something worrying you in that file?'

Jack's voice brought her out of the past, and she looked up to find him standing by her desk, peering anxiously down at her.

'Why?' she asked, while her mind shifted gear, and her fingers resisted the temptation to reach out and touch the hand that rested on her desk.

'Because you're frowning,' he pointed out. 'If you're worried about something maybe I can help.'

He spoke patiently and she knew that he was thinking

only of work, although her mind had picked up another meaning in the words.

'It's not the files, and I think you make things worse,' she said bluntly, upset to find that her memories of times with Colin were becoming unreliable. Surely they must have laughed together some time!

The man still hovered by her desk, and the message arcing between their bodies wasn't doing much for her concentration.

'Go home and cook the dinner,' she told him, waving him away. 'I'll be back from the hospital by seven, which should give us a few solid hours at the computer before it's time for bed.'

He moved away, still muttering, and she was certain that she heard him repeating 'time for bed' in an unnecessarily husky undertone.

'They're going to cut me open tomorrow,' Gilbert announced when she arrived to visit him.

Kelly studied him for a moment, trying to tell if he was upset by this decision.

'It's all right, girl,' he said, and she smiled to think that he was worrying about her reaction. 'It's time I was thinking of settling down.'

'Settling down? I can't believe it.'

She picked up his file and read it, while he explained that he had a little place on the beach a few miles south of town and a sister who lived next door.

'Bit of heaven it is, though I might go there instead. One way or the other, it'll be good!'

She glanced up at him, wondering if he'd had some pre-medication already and his mind was wandering. His voice sounded strong and he was smiling, so she smiled back then returned to the notes.

The doctors had decided that a splenectomy was the only option because blood tests showed that Gilbert's spleen was destroying white cells and platelets, as well as the older red blood cells which it was supposed to destroy. Further tests had shown that it was no longer producing antibodies or performing its blood cleansing functions, and the operation was indicated.

She hid the shiver of apprehension the logical outline caused, and concentrated on recalling his conversation.

'You've got a sister at Rainbow Bay? How come I've never met her? Doesn't she visit you?'

'Didn't tell her I was here,' Gilbert admitted. 'Didn't want her fussing! Or worrying over me.'

'But surely the hospital would have contacted her. They always ask for a next of kin on their forms.'

'Didn't tell them about her,' he said.

Kelly looked up. Gilbert was fumbling in his wallet. He pulled out a creased slip of paper, and handed it to Kelly. She read the faded writing.

'Do you want me to contact her and tell her about the operation?' she asked. 'I'd have to do it tonight, because I've got a clinic flight tomorrow and I'll be out of town.'

'Tell her after it's over and I'm OK,' he suggested, then shut his eyes in a signal to Kelly that he had done all the talking he wanted to do for one afternoon.

She turned away, and he called after her, 'Tell her tomorrow night. Don't let anyone else tell her. And tell her I'm not sorry it happened like this!'

She repeated the words in her head as she walked back to the nurses' station. Not sorry it happened like this?

'What time is Gilbert's operation scheduled?'

The sister on duty consulted her list.

'He's halfway through the list so it will be midday if they're going well, and later if there are any hitches.'

'I'll be at Castleford, but I can phone from there when I stop for lunch,' Kelly promised.

She detoured through to the maternity ward to meet Michael's new son and say hello to Melissa, then headed back to Jack's apartment. She was unsettled by her visit to Gilbert, but a delicious meal and a shared bottle of wine—a treat since they were both off duty—relaxed her enough to be teasing Jack by the time they settled in front of the computer.

Too close!

It was her first thought as he pulled his chair up against hers and she felt his warmth.

It isn't worrying him, she told herself, watching him open the file and show her the facts and figures he'd been collecting.

'I'm working out distances from towns,' he pointed out. 'It's a two-tiered survey, taking into account drivers who've been drinking and drivers who've stopped in town for a meal.'

'Drivers who've been drinking could crash any-where,' she said, drawn into his figures in spite of his closeness.

'I know they could,' Jack agreed, 'but preliminary figures show they don't. Look at this.'

He produced a map, and indicated where the accidents had occurred.

'It's usually two hours' driving time from town. At first I thought it might be road conditions, but five of these accidents were on straight roads and the driver simply lost control of the car.'

'Speeding or falling asleep?'

'I think falling asleep, but I'm guessing. I've got some other figures from the university, where they tested students responses to alcohol.'

He pulled another page out of the folder and pushed it across in front of her, his fingers brushing against hers as she picked it up.

'Kelly!' he muttered hoarsely, and she turned to him,

suddenly aware that the shafts of sexual yearning she'd been experiencing were not one-sided.

Their lips met, then their hands drew each other's bodies closer. Kelly's mind expanded to a white heat of desire which blotted out all conscious thought.

'Come to bed with me?' he murmured a little later as their fingers tangled in a scramble to push clothes aside and feel the texture of heated skin.

Anne's image rose in her mind—Anne and he together! Business! It was like a red light flashing a warning again and again, but her body still hungered for him.

'It would only be sex,' she whispered against his lips. 'An easing of frustration—mutual pleasure—a kind of exercise.'

The thought excited her unbearably, although she'd always believed that sex was part of a commitment, not a sport. And could there be commitment with the past unresolved?

'That's all?' The words grated into her ears and she knew that she'd spoilt the moment.

'Well, it could hardly be love,' she said tartly, pushing him away and adjusting her clothes. 'We've known each other less than a fortnight.'

'So is there a time rule for falling in love? Must it take a month—a year? Or is time your excuse because you're determined to believe you still love Colin Forbes—determined not to get involved with people while you endure your self-imposed mourning for something that never existed?'

'And what about you? What about your past? Don't you realise Anne has come up here to patch up your marriage?' she argued vehemently, searching for stability in a world that was spinning out of orbit.

He drew back and looked at her, his eyes wide with surprise.

'Anne came up here to do a locum. Our marriage is deader than the unicorn and dodo and—'

'Does Anne know that?' she interrupted, unable to believe such transparent astonishment.

'Of course she does,' he said gruffly. 'And you're using her as another excuse.'

'I don't need excuses,' she fumed—disbelieving, uncertain, hesitant to commit to something so physically overwhelming—then she remembered his earlier words, and found another argument to use against the sorcery of his appeal. 'And I did love Colin!'

'Like this, Kelly?' he asked, and turned her head so that his lips met hers, and the fire he could fan to life so easily flared through her body to burn between her thighs.

The kiss drained her resolve and stole her breath. Her body relaxed against his and the fever began to build again, but before it could peak his hands settled on her shoulders and, with a quiet deliberation, he pushed her away.

'I won't compete with him, Kelly. Not in your mind or in your heart. Other men might have managed that for a short time, but I would want to know you are mine, all mine, and only mine.'

He turned back to his files.

'What do you mean, "other men"?' she demanded, her nerves jumping with tension.

'You told me you both went out with other people,' he told her, without raising his head.

' "Going out with" doesn't equal "slept with"!' she retorted.

'You're telling me you're a virgin?' he muttered with such obvious disbelief that she wanted to hit him.

'I *am* not!'

The retort took her back to childhood arguments. . . You are *too*! I *am* not! Then she glanced towards his face and saw that wretched eyebrow lifted. She paused as heat zoomed through her body, then she glared defiantly at him as she gabbled out an explanation not even Colin knew.

'It's none of your business and I don't know why I'm telling you but I had a boyfriend once—at school—before I met Colin. I was stupid—thought I was in love. . .'

She hesitated, realising that she didn't want the long-forgotten memories to surface, but it seemed that he sensed the pain and shame curdling in her stomach for he reached out and drew her close so that her head rested on his shoulder.

'He was. . .' She found she couldn't say the words to describe the rough demands of that strong young male, forcing acquiescence with emotional pleas and blackmailing threats.

'I didn't enjoy it!' she finished bluntly and pulled away from him, concentrating fiercely on the computer screen to wipe out the images she'd kept hidden for so long.

'So Colin was a convenient excuse for non-involvement,' Jack said quietly, and, ignoring her protests, he pulled her back into her arms and kissed her very tenderly on the lips.

'That's nonsense!' she muttered, turning away from him. She scanned the computer feverishly, seeking distraction in the figures he had accumulated but didn't know how to collate.

CHAPTER ELEVEN

HAD the heightened sensitivity of their nerves triggered extra power in their brain cells? Kelly pondered the question as she drove towards the airport next morning.

She and Jack had certainly achieved a great deal of work once they'd realised that they had to keep their hands off each other in order to concentrate. They had identified places where road signs could warn drivers of fatigue, and had drafted a letter to the publicans within their area, pointing out the accident rate among drink-drivers and asking if they could provide basic accommodation for people they knew to be affected by alcohol.

By midnight they'd been satisfied with what they had found, and had said courteous goodnights to each other before disappearing into their separate rooms.

But not to sleep—or not in Kelly's case. She'd lain awake and wanted Jack's arms around her.

'Ready to get back on the horse?' Susan joked when they met outside the hangar next morning. She nodded towards the plane.

'I hadn't given Sunday's flight another thought,' Kelly stammered, utterly amazed that she'd not been tortured by the memory.

'Well, that's a good sign you're getting used to our life,' Susan said with a warm chuckle.

'I don't want to get used to it,' Kelly told her firmly. 'I'm not here for ever, you know!'

'Jack Gregory said that when he first arrived,' Susan told her. 'And now you couldn't shift him with dynamite.'

They walked companionably into the hangar, selected the equipment they would need and headed for the plane. Susan was chattering on, talking about Castleford, suggesting that Kelly have dinner at her place later in the week. . .

Kelly hoped that she was making appropriate responses, but her mind was on Jack Gregory and this revelation that he, too, had come as a locum.

'Did you realise you're down for three minor procedures this morning?' Susan asked, turning from the patient list she'd been making out while the plane took off.

'Three? I know there's a man with a basal cell carcinoma and a child with a couple of stubborn warts. . .'

'And a tooth extraction!' Susan announced, then chuckled as Kelly's face showed her protest.

'Helen Jensen, the nursing sister at Castleford, used to do extractions, but she says she's getting too old and feeble for the tough teeth and has assigned today's patient to you.'

'I can't pull teeth,' Kelly cried.

'Of course you can,' Susan told her. 'Helen will stand behind you and tell you exactly what to do.'

'Well, if Helen's dictating the steps then you could do it.'

Susan smiled smugly.

'I'm far too busy with the clinic,' she said. 'There are more pregnant women per head of population in that area than in the rest of Australia.'

'Is that a fact or a generalisation?' Kelly asked, and, diverted by the statement, she forgot about the tooth until the patient was actually shown in by Helen some hours later.

He was guided to a chair which Helen had pulled out of the storeroom. It was used by the dentist the

RFDS flew out to Castleford twice a year, she'd explained.

'Know what you're doing, do you?' the grizzled old farmer demanded, sitting down in the chair and resting his head back against the head-rest.

'Naturally!' Kelly assured him, remembering Rule One—always show confidence in front of your patient!

'Are you allergic to anything you know of?' she asked, reading the label on the anaesthetic Helen had handed her.

'Nothing!' the fellow told her, 'except pain!'

'Well, the needle will hurt a bit,' she told him while her mind dredged up the pattern of the facial nerves that would reach into his jaw and be numbed by the anaesthesia.

'It's the last molar on the lower left,' Helen explained, peering over Kelly's shoulder into the man's mouth. 'I looked at it the other day.'

She nodded as Kelly tapped the offending tooth with a probe and the man groaned.

Helen drew up the anaesthetic and handed Kelly the needle and syringe. 'Use half on the outer side of his gum and the other half on the inner,' she prompted.

Steeling herself, Kelly forced the needle into the man's gum, twisting around so that she could see what she was doing.

'All the dentists I've seen have natty little mirrors on sticks that help with this kind of thing,' she grumbled, easing the fluid into his gum.

'You don't need mirrors, girl!' the man told her. 'Just yank the damned thing out.'

'It's not quite that simple,' Helen whispered.

'I'd already figured that out,' Kelly whispered back as she stared in dismay at the instruments Helen had assembled.

'We'll leave you for a few minutes while that takes

effect,' she told her patient then she picked up the tray and walked across the room, Helen following.

'The dental forceps help cut the membranous tissue from around the tooth,' Helen explained. 'As you slide them down they expand the socket so you can pull the tooth out.'

'And this little number that looks as if it's straight out of the Spanish Inquisition?' Kelly hissed, pointing at a corkscrew-like implement.

'It's a dental elevator,' Helen replied. 'Once you get down to where the roots branch out, you slide it in between the roots and rotate it. The theory is that it pushes the tooth upward and outward and you don't leave the roots behind, which can happen if you tug and the tooth breaks.'

Kelly felt ill at the thought, but she headed back towards her patient and prodded his gums to assess the numbness.

'Sure you wouldn't rather go to town and have a real dentist do this?' she asked. 'We could take you back this afternoon.'

'Take it out, girl,' the man ordered with a lopsided smile. 'I'd far rather sit here and watch your pretty face than any of the old fellows who'd be hurting me in town.'

She took a deep breath and began, surprised to find how tough the tissue was. She had the tooth loose in its socket before she turned to the elevator. Common sense dictated how to use it, and she persevered with the rotation until she felt the upward movement and heard the sucking noise as the stubborn molar tore from its moorings.

Helen passed the man water, then held a bowl for him to rinse his mouth.

'Be careful prodding it with your tongue,' she told him. 'And protect that side of your mouth when you eat or drink. No alcohol for twenty-four hours because it could make you bleed more, and come back to me if it keeps bleeding or becomes especially painful.'

Listening to Helen's list of instructions, Kelly realised that she'd done it often enough to know the warnings by heart.

The patient thanked her and left, mopping at his face with a huge red bandana.

'You ready to go home?' Susan asked, poking her head around the door of the consulting-room.

'Go home? It's not lunch time yet!'

Susan and Helen both laughed.

'It's four o'clock and your pilot will be champing at the bit,' Helen told her.

'They like to be on time to keep in sweet with the control tower,' Susan explained, helping her load the files back into their case then leading the way to the car. 'That way, when an emergency does arise, the control tower treats us kindly instead of muttering dire threats about people who are always late.'

It wasn't until they were in the air on the way back to the Bay that Kelly remembered that she hadn't rung to enquire about Gilbert. She considered phoning the hospital from the plane, but a reluctance to face Jack again made her decide to drive up and visit her old friend straight from the airport.

'I'm sorry, we phoned the Base and let them know. He died before the operation—in the early hours of the morning.'

The nursing sister was studying her intently and Kelly wondered if she looked as devastated as she felt.

'Did someone tell his sister?' she asked, and the woman shook her head.

'We've no next of kin on record. We phoned your Base because he was initially your patient.'

He couldn't have known that he was going to die,

her mind argued as she made her way out of the ward and waited for the lift to take her back to the foyer.

She searched through her handbag for the piece of paper, then remembered leaving it on her dressing-table at the apartment. With a heavy heart she headed homewards, chiding herself all the way.

It's what comes of getting involved, she reminded herself. And that's the one thing you weren't going to do while you were here! She let anger swamp her sorrow, anger with Gilbert that he hadn't sought medical help sooner and anger with herself for caring!

'Someone upset you?' Jack enquired when she stormed through the door, still railing at herself. He was standing in the living-room, and she had to fight the urge to fling herself into his arms and howl like a hurt child.

'Only my own stupidity!' she sniped at him, flinging herself towards her room instead—to get the address she needed.

'I think she wants to be left alone,' a soft voice pointed out, and Kelly swung around to see Anne Harrison, settled comfortably behind the computer—with a second chair, probably warm from Jack's body, drawn up close beside her.

Her teeth clenched together and only a tremendous effort of will prevented her from grinding them.

'You've heard about Gilbert,' Jack said quietly

She spun to face him, praying that he couldn't see the tears in her eyes. The look of concern on his face was her undoing, and she felt the rage flow out of her body. She nodded, breathing deeply as she battled to regather some control.

'I told him I'd tell his sister,' she said as calmly as her fragile composure would allow. 'I'm going there now.'

He nodded, as if he'd expect that of her, and said quietly, 'I'll drive you. Do you want to go right now or would you like something to eat first?'

'You've got a visitor,' she pointed out. 'And I'm perfectly capable of driving myself.'

'So I see,' he said, glancing down at her hands which were trembling with the confused emotions coursing through her.

'I'm hardly a visitor!' Anne remarked, and Kelly realised that she must be following every word they had said.

'Anne called in to use the computer,' Jack explained. 'Her furniture, including her computer, hasn't arrived yet. She can finish what she's doing and let herself out.'

Kelly stared at him for a moment, seeing the message in his eyes that told her that Anne meant nothing to him.

She wanted, desperately, to believe it, but disbelief was part of her own uncertainty.

'I want to go now,' she said belligerently, needing to test that message.

He picked up his car keys and mobile phone and ushered her towards the door.

'You've got the address?'

How stupid! She wheeled back around and dashed into her bedroom to find the slip of paper. She could hear Jack's voice, low-pitched as he murmured something to Anne, and her more strident tones as she argued.

She returned to the hall and handed him the folded piece of paper.

With Anne's protests still hanging in his ears, Jack caught and held the fingers that trembled against his. What could he say to Kelly to ease her pain? Most of his conversational gambits led to an argument. He relaxed, and chuckled inwardly as he opened the door. Maybe that was the way!

'It's OK to be upset when a patient dies,' he said, summoning a lift. 'I've cried myself often enough.'

The blue eyes, awash with unshed tears, looked up into his face.

'I didn't want to get involved. It's one of the reasons I took the locum here. No regular patients, no involvement!'

'Oh, I noticed the "no involvement" when you spent three lunch hours searching for the perfect gift for Alison's son, and who knows how many hours talking to her on the phone when she wanted to complain about her husband,' he said blandly, and heard her gasp of astonishment before she rounded on him.

'How did you know that?'

'Good detective work!' He grinned at her because he loved the way her moods shifted and he was pleased that he'd banished her tears, for a moment, at least. 'Actually, I knew about the counselling sessions because her husband phoned me to say that things were much better between them since she'd spoken to you. And asking people about baby shops was a dead give-away. I didn't think you'd be taking rattles and bibs to Gilbert.'

They reached the basement and he led her towards his car.

'Colin always said I became too involved,' she admitted as he opened the car door for her and waited for her to climb in. 'He said I was always too involved with other people, or with my patients, to take him or any other man seriously.'

Jack shut the car door, and looked upwards until the names he'd like to call Colin Forbes had been mouthed in silence.

'He said other doctors can do their jobs quite success-fully without becoming caught up in the patients' private lives, and that all I was doing was cluttering up my life with unnecessary emotional ties,' she added dolefully when he took his seat behind the wheel.

He turned to stare at her, and shook his head.

'And this is the guy you're so hung up over?' he demanded. 'This is the fellow you claim you love?

'Loved!' she said sadly, meeting his gaze with a forlorn stare. 'I realise I couldn't have still loved him when he asked if he could take my sister out and I said yes.'

'Well, if you realised that then, why are you skulking up here pretending to nurse a broken heart?'

Her eyes sparkled dangerously.

'I didn't realise it then, I just know now that I must have subconsciously known it back then to have done something so stupid.'

He groaned.

'And I talk about your head-butting your problems? Conversations with you are one long head-butt.'

She ignored his comment, and added, 'Not that it was entirely stupid because they really are well suited to each other. She'll devote herself to him, and never let him down because of her involvement with someone else's problems—and she can cook!'

He chuckled and started the engine.

Kelly was OK again if she could make jokes against herself. He glanced at her and saw the smile which confirmed his thoughts. It was something else he loved about her, this habit of judging herself with the same ruthless honesty she used to judge others.

They drove through the lamp-lit streets, then down the highway to the south.

'Do you know the place?' she asked, and he nodded, content just to be with her.

'We turn off in about ten minutes,' he told her.

There were about a dozen houses at Devil's Cove, and it looked much as it must have looked since the area was settled.

'There's no number,' she said, reading the address

he handed back to her. 'It says Mrs G. Robinson, The Pink House, Devil's Cove.'

'Well, let's take it literally, and hope she hasn't painted it since Gilbert last visited.'

He drove down the narrow road, following the curve of the beach. Ahead he could see the jutting, three-pronged headland that gave the Cove its name.

'A pink house,' Kelly said and he slowed, turned the car and stopped outside it.

They climbed out and made their way up the path, Jack going on ahead to knock.

But there was no response.

Kelly began to shiver, and he hurried her back to the car.

'Sit there,' he told her. 'I'll see if the neighbours know where we can contact her.'

She watched him walk away and wondered, for some obscure reason, about Carrie who had died. A door opened and she saw his dark head bend courteously towards the woman in the shaft of light. The silhouette of his profile was so clear that it could have been cut from black cardboard. She imagined her fingers running across it and shivered as the arousal his touch had triggered the previous evening flared back to life.

He walked back towards her, and she tried to still her leaping pulse. How could she feel this way with Gilbert dead, and her promise to tell his sister still unfulfilled? Not to mention Anne, sitting back there in his apartment!

But when he climbed into the car and reached out to draw her close she knew that the magic had come alive in him as well. He kissed her deeply, his hands slipping under the weight of her hair and moulding themselves against her skull.

'His sister's on a cruise—her first holiday in years—the neighbour said,' he murmured when they paused for breath. 'I have the name of the cruise line but I wonder if—'

'Yes, let's tell her when she comes back,' Kelly agreed, then realised that he hadn't said that.

She looked up into his eyes, shadowed in the dim light in the car, and he nodded, his lips twitching into a smile.

'Yes, you did read my mind,' he confirmed, and kissed her again.

They were different kisses this time, still full of passion but deeper and somehow calmer, as if their bodies knew that time was on their side.

Kisses of commitment, Kelly thought, then wondered why such a thing would have popped into her mind.

'Who was Carrie?' she asked, when the hunger had diminished and they sat, their arms around each other, and looked out across the darkness of the sea.

She felt his chest fill with air as he inhaled slowly.

'She was my first love, Kelly,' he said quietly. 'We met in med school, and soon became inseparable. Anne was her best friend and we formed a threesome. She was twenty-two—we were all in fourth year—when she started feeling tired all the time.'

She felt his fingers bite into her arms and her hand tightened on his shoulder.

'We were at the age when we assumed we'd live for ever. We were almost doctors and were certain we knew everything, so we didn't consider there might be something seriously wrong.'

'Leukaemia?' Kelly whispered, thinking of the age group that was vulnerable to rapid onset of the acute form of the cancer.

'Leukaemia,' he confirmed. 'She died six months later.'

Kelly heard regret and a hint of self-blame in the single word and hurried to argue.

'But if it had been diagnosed earlier would it have made much difference?'

'Not much,' he agreed. 'She might have had time to undergo more chemotherapy, had a few more months' remission.'

'Would she have wanted that?' Kelly asked quietly. 'In cases where long-term remission is possible I'd go for all the treatment I could get, but with a medical inevitability I don't know whether I would choose to prolong things.'

She was trying desperately to sound clinical, to jolt him out of the past with a technical discussion, but her throat was thick with tears and the words came out as a husky whisper.

He wrapped his arms around her and held her close.

'She chose not to undergo the second course of chemo they offered,' he admitted. 'I argued, but she refused. I was devastated, Kelly, but that's no excuse for what happened next.'

Kelly frowned into the darkness.

No excuse for what happened next?

She waited.

'I married Anne six months later. We'd been through so much together while Carrie was ill. She'd been so good to me, such a support and comfort—such a fine friend.'

A fine friend, that's what Colin had been—still could be, possibly, Kelly realised.

'It didn't work?' she asked into the lengthening silence.

He moved and she sensed that his sadness was easing.

'Friendship wasn't enough. Oh, we were compatible enough, and she was willing to give me as much time as I needed to get over Carrie, but. . .'

He pressed his lips against her hair, and she felt tremors starting in her body.

'But?' she persisted, wanting to hear it all.

'But it was a mistake, Kelly. Right from the beginning, it was a huge, unmendable mistake. And I made things worse by refusing to admit it—by refusing to face up to the fact that I, the all-knowing Jack Gregory, might have been wrong. We battled on—unhappily on my side, Anne says, contentedly on hers—until I knew I had to do something about it.'

'And what did you do?' She was shivering with tension, but she had to know—had to match his thoughts with hers.

'I ran away,' he said simply.

As I did, Kelly thought.

'There was a locum position offered up here, and I took it.'

He paused but didn't point out the obvious comparison.

'I talked to Anne first. I finally admitted the mistake, and tried to explain—to apologise for disrupting her life the way I had. She couldn't see it, said I needed more time to get over Carrie—tried to excuse me in so many ways, but there was no excuse, Kelly. I'd made a mistake and, in doing so, had hurt the one person I should never have hurt.'

He slumped forward over the wheel for a moment, then the engine roared as he brought it back to life.

They drove home in silence, stopping on the way at a fast-food outlet for a hamburger. Anne was still working at the computer when they returned, and Kelly said goodnight and fled to the sanctuary of her room.

Where did Jack's story leave her?

And where did his lingering compassion for Anne leave him? Too many questions and no answers because he had left for a three-day clinic flight before she was out of bed next morning. She had dinner at the Stones' that night, laughing with the twins as easily as she did with her own younger siblings. Returning to the apartment, she phoned home and found that she could enjoy her mother's excitement over the wedding arrangements. The uncomfortable bitterness she'd felt had vanished so completely that she wondered why it had ever existed.

She missed Jack more than she had thought possible, although her own clinic flight and two nights on call kept her busy.

'Where are you? I thought you'd be waiting at the apartment with a roast in the oven,' he teased. It was Friday evening and his voice, coming so clearly over the airwaves to the little mobile phone, sent her pulse into riot mode.

Nothing's settled between us, she cautioned herself in an attempt to curb her inner agitation. We've talked, that's all.

'Last time I came home you had another home-maker there,' she reminded him.

'Not tonight, or any other night,' he told her. 'Seems she lost interest in domestic duties when I told her I'd found something special.'

Found something special?

She wanted to ask him what he'd found but her patient stirred, reminding her this was hardly the time or the place. . .

'I'm on a straightforward transfer to Brisbane,' she said quickly. 'I should be home by midnight.'

But she wasn't—because they diverted on their way home to collect a stockman injured when he was crushed against a fence by a distraught cow. She arrived back at the airport at four in the morning and crept home to bed. By the time she was awake again Jack had gone.

CHAPTER TWELVE

IT WASN'T a loud, disruptive noise or the thin line of light shining beneath her door that woke Kelly, but suddenly she was awake and aware that Jack must have returned. She lay in bed and listened, imagining that she could hear him moving. The glass doors slid open and a chair scraped on the balcony that faced outwards over the bay.

Because of the shape of the apartment, she could see his silhouette through the gap she now left in her curtains. He was hunched forward in the chair, his head in his hands.

He needs some fresh air. He'll go to bed soon, she told herself, and turned over to go back to sleep. But sleep wouldn't come—not when she sensed pain in the man who sat and stared out at the sea.

Sliding out of bed, she dragged her bathrobe over her skimpy nightshirt. She opened her door without trying to be silent, wanting to warn him of her approach so that she wouldn't startle him.

'Jack?' she called as she drew closer to the windows.

The chair scraped again and he turned his head towards her. The moonlight seemed to accentuate the lines of agony in his face, and she forgot her fears and rushed forward to draw him against her body and hold him tightly.

'What is it? What's happened?'

He moved his face against the soft fabric of her gown, and she felt a shudder rip through him.

'The call was from a small township a half-hour north of here. White-water rafting has become popular in the

181

mountains behind the town and a group of high school kids had hired equipment and spent the weekend riding the rapids.'

'And one was killed?' She knew it must be bad for him to be so shattered.

He shook his head, and she felt his despair through her clothes and skin.

'He's in a coma. The raft tipped and he was thrown against a rock as he tried to hold onto one of the girls. Heaven knows how, but the others got him out and one of the boys went for help. By the time State Emergency Services transported them to the plane they were all suffering mild hypothermia but, apart from Lachlan, they were all OK.'

'Lachlan?' she echoed hoarsely, dread gathering in her heart.

He raised his head and looked up into her eyes.

'It's Lachlan Stone, Kelly, one of Susan's and Eddie's twins. He and Stewart, with Leonie's son, Mitchell, organised the outing. Stewart and Mitchell are both blaming themselves. They're refusing to leave the hospital, determined to keep talking to him because they've heard it helps reverse the effects of coma. Eddie and Susan are there too, of course. They're both in shock, and Leonie's trying to take care of them, as well as comfort Mitchell.'

Kelly remembered herself saying that she didn't want to be part of this RFDS family, but she also remembered Susan talking about the boys with such pride and the fun she'd shared with them on Wednesday evening.

She felt her heart tighten in pain and knew that she was part of the 'family' whether she liked it or not and, right now, she had one member who was her sole responsibility.

'There's nothing to be gained by sitting and brooding over it,' she told him briskly. 'You'll be needing all your marbles when you have to start juggling the rosters again to fill Eddie's and Susan's places, and for that you need some sleep.'

She glanced at her watch and was surprised to see that it was after two. He'd been gone since mid-afternoon! She thought about it and realised that he must have waited at the hospital while the scans and X-rays were done. Knowing Jack, he'd have stayed until he was certain there was nothing else he could do.

'How bad was the injury?' She massaged the knotted muscles in his shoulders while waiting for his reply, and was pleased to feel the tension easing slightly.

'He was wearing a helmet and there's no sign of a skull fracture, but the deceleration as his head hit the rock must have caused diffused injury to the brain to account for the prolonged concussion. They've scanned him for haematoma and that's clear, but there must be injury to the fibres in the brain stem to account for the coma. It's too early to tell if there's likely to be perma-nent damage—'

'And it's the not knowing that's worst of all for his family and friends,' she finished quietly, her fingers still kneading at his shoulders and neck.

'Knowing and not knowing,' Jack agreed. 'Susan's seen too many people left permanently disabled as a result of brain damage to not know the possible outcome.'

He groaned and shifted away from her, lifting his hands to rub them over his face—as if the physical action could erase his dread.

'You should go to bed,' she repeated. 'Would you like a cup of tea first? My culinary ability stretches that far.'

He shook his head and straightened up, shrugging off her soothing hands.

'You're right about getting some sleep,' he said, his voice hoarse with emotion.

She watched him hoist himself to his feet, then he reached out and touched her shoulder.

'Thanks,' he said quietly. 'I'll be OK now.'

She waited while he made his way back to his bedroom, then returned to her own bed. But sleep was gone. Images of the teenagers' terror when their raft spun out of control and flung them into the water danced in front of her eyes. She tried to shut them out, but they wouldn't disappear.

Sleep wasn't the answer, she decided, and made her way quietly towards Jack's bedroom. A light was on and—pushing open the door—she saw him propped against the pillows, frowning at the book he held in his hands.

'I don't want to be alone!' she whispered, taking tentative steps into the room.

He didn't move, except to lift his head so that he could watch her progress towards him.

Jack saw the uncertainty in every step, and he had to force himself to remain immobile when every cell in his body yelled for him to get up and take her in his arms.

'Will you hold me?' she said when she'd finally made it to the bed.

'For comfort or for love?' he asked bluntly, watching her face intently to detect any hint of prevarication.

She shrugged.

'Comfort, I suppose,' she admitted and, although his stomach plummeted with disappointment, he admired her honesty.

Then her lips trembled into an uncertain smile, and her lovely eyes looked into his.

'But I could do with some love as well,' she added.

'*My* love?' he demanded, clenching his hands into

fists in an effort to stop them moving towards her.

'Your love,' she responded huskily, her smile widening now.

His heart nearly burst with the love he felt for her, but there was one last hurdle to be leapt.

'And Colin Forbes?'

She looked at him for a moment, then her eyes began to twinkle.

'Colin who?'

He reached out and drew her towards him. The ripe softness of her body inflamed him, but he reminded himself that his brash, cheeky Kelly was all show and that the young woman he loved so deeply was both sexually inexperienced and carrying scars from her previous physical relationship.

Drawing her down onto the bed, he touched her face, her eyelids, and slid his fingers through the silky hair. He kissed her, teasing at her mouth, then deepened the fervour until her lips parted willingly and her tongue slipped out to greet his.

He ran his hands across her back, lifting the flimsy nightdress to feel her skin, to warm and comfort her so that she would relax. He fought against his own excitement, aware that one wrong move could bring back memories which would cool her growing pleasure and kill this opportunity to express their feelings for each other.

Kelly felt the apprehension thudding in her heart, but Jack's lips were generating such excitement in other parts of her body that she ignored it. His fingers traced the contours of her arm and shoulder, their tips lingering in the sensitive hollows of her neck and trailing across her chest with fire following in their wake.

And all the time he talked to her, murmuring of love—calming the panic that lay beneath the surface of her wonderment and adding another dimension to the delight his lips and hands were providing.

His fingers skimmed across her breasts, brushed against her thighs, and the past was burned from her memory as her body responded, twisting to press against his—a participant now in this slow dance of delight.

Heat suffused her skin and thundered in her blood, and an aching hunger grew and grew, fuelled by his lips and hands, the satiny texture of his skin, the solidity of flesh and bone and, most enticing of all, the need she felt within him—a need she was certain matched her own.

'Please, Jack,' she whispered when the agony of wanting him became too much to bear.

He lifted his head and looked down into her face, his eyes shadowed. She sensed the hesitation in him, and knew it was for her.

'Please, Jack,' she repeated and drew him down on top of her, moving beneath his solidity and warmth— feeling the easing of the tension as their bodies found each other and then the building and rebuilding of it as the movements of the dance of love began.

She was consumed by it, carried into a place where nothing but pleasure existed, but the glimpses she felt weren't enough and she struggled, fighting for something she barely understood but knew was there, just beyond her reach.

With hands and voice he soothed her, calming the desperation of her need—touching her, lips against her breast, encouraging and inciting all the fiery hunger until the magic built again, higher and higher, then broke against a fabled shore and left her spent and shaking in his arms.

She buried her face in the angle of his neck and shoulder, unable to explain the turbulence of her feelings or the might of the experience. His arms wrapped around her, protective and understanding, and his lips murmured gruff tendernesses against her hair.

The phone woke them as dawn crept into the room. Jack let go of her to answer it, and Kelly turned and snuggled against his back.

'That's great news, Leonie,' he said, and she felt a spurt of sheer joy, so sweet and piercing that she couldn't stay in bed but rose, pulled on her discarded nightshirt and headed towards the windows.

The waters of the bay were ruffled by a light wind so the reflection of the sunrise tipped the crests of the waves to a rosy glow. Every dawn a rebirth, she thought as she watched the sun push up over the horizon. New life and new hope, new beginnings.

She felt Jack's arm touch her shoulder, then his body fitted against her back as he shared the splendour of the sunrise with her. When the gleaming, orange orb hung suspended above the water he turned her in his arms and kissed her deeply.

She felt her bones weaken in response, then remembered the call.

'Lachlan's OK?' she asked, looking up into his beautiful eyes.

'He will be,' he told her. 'Seems he remembers everything that happened, which is an excellent sign.'

He was quiet for a moment, then he said, 'And you? Are you OK? Can you remember everything that happened?'

She felt heat flaring into her cheeks and nodded, then lifted her lips to meet his gentle kiss.

'I love you, Kelly Jackson,' he murmured against her skin.

'I love you, Jack Gregory,' she pledged.

MILLS & BOON®

Medical Romance™

Catch a *Rising Star*
for magical stories that reach deep into your heart

September 1997 is a special month as we introduce authors you will find memorable— they're all names to watch for in the future.

JENNY BRYANT ☆ A Remedy for Heartache
LUCY CLARK ☆ Delectable Diagnosis
JESSICA MATTHEWS ☆ For a Child's Sake
HELEN SHELTON ☆ Poppy's Passion

Each one is a

Bureau de Change

How would you like to win a year's supply of
Mills & Boon® books? Well you can and they're FREE!
Simply complete the competition below and send it to
us by 28th February 1998. The first five correct
entries picked after the closing date will each win a
year's subscription to the Mills & Boon series of their
choice. What could be easier?

1.	Lira	Sweden	___
2.	Franc	U.S.A.	___
3.	Krona	Sth. Africa	___
4.	Escudo	Spain	___
5.	Deutschmark	Austria	___
6.	Schilling	Greece	___
7.	Drachma	Japan	___
8.	Dollar	India	___
9.	Rand	Portugal	4
10.	Peseta	Germany	___
11.	Yen	France	___
12.	Rupee	Italy	___

C7H

Please turn over for details of how to enter...

How to enter...

It's that time of year again when most people like to pack their suitcases and head off on holiday to relax. That usually means a visit to the Bureau de Change... Overleaf there are twelve foreign countries and twelve currencies which belong to them but unfortunately they're all in a muddle! All you have to do is match each currency to its country by putting the number of the currency on the line beside the correct country. One of them is done for you! Don't forget to fill in your name and address in the space provided below and pop this page in a envelope (you don't even need a stamp) and post it today. Hurry competition ends 28th February 1998.

Mills & Boon Bureau de Change Competition
FREEPOST, Croydon, Surrey, CR9 3WZ
EIRE readers send competition to PO Box 4546, Dublin 24.

Please tick the series you would like to receive if you are a winner

Presents™ ❏ Enchanted™ ❏ Temptation® ❏
Medical Romance™ ❏ Historical Romance™ ❏

Are you a Reader Service™ Subscriber?　　Yes ❏　No ❏

Ms/Mrs/Miss/Mr_____
　　　　　　　　　　　　　　　　　　　(BLOCK CAPS PLEASE)

Address_____

_____

_____ Postcode_____
(I am over 18 years of age)

One application per household. Competition open to residents of the UK and Ireland only. You may be mailed with offers from other reputable companies as a result of this application. If you would prefer not to receive such offers, please tick box. ❏　C7H

Mills & Boon® is a registered trademark of
Harlequin Mills & Boon Limited.

DISCOVER
THE SECRETS WITHIN

*Riveting and unforgettable -
the Australian saga of the decade!*

*For Tamara Vandelier, the final reckoning with
her mother is long overdue. Now she has
returned to the family's vineyard estate and
embarked on a destructive course that, in a
final, fatal clash, will reveal the secrets within....*

50ᵖ OFF COUPON
VALID UNTIL 30/11/1997
EMMA DARCY'S *THE SECRETS WITHIN*

9 904170 180504

0472 00166